LAWLESS LOVE

Soon the desperadoes arrived back in the clearing, faces aglow with victory. Jessica strode forward to face them with hands balled on her hips. "It's shameful the delight you men take in your sinful doings."

Cole swung down to grin at her. "Sin is always fun, sugar. How 'bout a victory kiss?"

Before Jessica could protest, Cole hauled her close and soundly smacked her lips, while his brothers hooted catcalls.

Her face was flaming. "You thief."

Cole grinned unabashedly. "I'm a bandit, sugar, and I take what I want."

"Hey, no fair!" protested Gabe. "How come we don't git no victory kisses from the lady?"

"Yeah, how come?" asked Billy.

Cole swung around. "Because if we don't hightail it, someone's bound to come along and discover us. Let's ride, boys. We can fight over the lady later."

Other *Love Spell* books by Eugenia Riley:
A TRYST IN TIME
TEMPEST IN TIME

BUSHWHACKED BRIDE

EUGENIA RILEY

LOVE SPELL BOOKS NEW YORK CITY

LOVE SPELL®

June 1999

Published by

Dorchester Publishing Co., Inc.
276 Fifth Avenue
New York, NY 10001

ISBN 0-505-52320-5

The name "Love Spell" and its logo are trademarks of Dorchester Publishing Co., Inc.

Printed in the United States of America.

*This book is dedicated, with love,
to my hero and husband,
Sterling,
in celebration of thirty
happy years of marriage—
and here's to thirty more!*

BUSHWHACKED BRIDE

Prologue

Of all the "true life" Old West adventures Jessica Garrett had endured for the sake of her dissertation, this was by far the nuttiest. Though the year was 1999, she found herself plunged back so far into the "Wild West" that she half expected to watch an outlaw on horseback materialize over the next rise.

Never in her wildest dreams had Jessica envisioned herself as a guest at the Broken Buck Dude Ranch, which she'd already renamed "The Dude Ranch From Hell." But here she was, a passenger in an antique, nutmeg-yellow stagecoach that bounced and slammed its way down an old mining trail through the mountains west of Colorado Springs, the rough ride jarring the very bones of Jessica and the other three occupants. On the door of the old conveyance was emblazoned in flowing red Victorian script the monogram "LL." Jessica could hear the stage's springs groaning, and the rattling of

11

Eugenia Riley

glass panes in two unlit lanterns attached to the coach's exterior.

Glancing out her window, she caught a view of steep mountains, lined with fir, pines, and aspen, the landscape jutting up sharply toward the misty heavens. Overhead, her demented host, Woody Lynch, clucked to the team of horses, who snorted and plodded along while fertilizing the trail. The summer day was dry and dusty, and a distinct aroma of *eau de manure* rose from the wagon wheels to assault Jessica's nostrils.

From somewhere within the faded burgundy velvet interior of the stage came the canned strains of Gene Autry's "Back in the Saddle Again." Her host had an eccentric fondness for cowboy music, which he piped in everywhere at the ranch.

The inside of the stage was far smaller than Jessica had envisioned, and she disliked being crammed in with three male colleagues from the history department at Pawnee College in Greeley. All four were "guests" at the Broken Buck—though "inmates" might be a more apt term. For the Broken Buck specialized in a "re-enactment" atmosphere in order to provide "authentic Old West adventures."

Today's misadventure was entitled "A Picnic at Mariposa," Mariposa being a ghost town somewhere in the hills west of the ranch. In keeping with the ordeal, all four participants had been required to wear genuine Old West costumes. Jessica was ensconced in a long, cinnamon-brown calico dress, a huge slat-bonnet, and granny shoes.

As for her companions, next to her, elderly Professor Harold Billingsly, in fringed buckskins and felt frontier hat, held a close resemblance to Buffalo Bill Cody. Across from her, fair-haired, mid-thirtyish Professor Stan Wilkins looked ready to wrestle a few calves in his boots, jeans, western shirt, and Stetson. And their illustrious leader, Professor Walter Lummety, appeared the typical pot-bellied sheriff as he lounged with his head lolling on his chest, his double chin partially obscuring his tin law-

12

man's badge.

Jessica mused ruefully that the four of them looked like escapees from a Wild West show—or a mental institution. When the stage arrived at "Mariposa," they'd doubtless be treated to a "picnic" of greasy corn dodgers and cold, slimy beans.

Wincing as the coach hit a pothole and her bottom came down hard on the thinly padded seat, Jessica asked herself how on earth she'd managed to get into this predicament. Never in her twenty-seven years had she felt so foolish. Of course it was all Walter Lummety's fault. As history department chair, Walter had organized the faculty summer field trip, and since the theme had been "Life in the Old West," Jessica had cheerfully signed on. After all, the subject of her dissertation was "Frontier Living: Women's Issues." So the tour seemed tailor-made for her. In the month they'd been on the road, they'd visited Yuma Territorial Prison, Indian ruins in New Mexico, a living farm in the Texas hill country, and numerous western history collections.

They were now on the last leg of their journey, which had been palatable—up until now! Unfortunately, Walter had one fatal flaw—a cousin who owned a primitive dude ranch that should have been dubbed "Outhouse of the Nation."

Woody Lynch was, mildly put, a lunatic. He took his role as dude ranch host so seriously that he perpetually dressed and behaved as if he were actually living in the Old West; already, Jessica was sick of his nasal twang and crusty speech. And conditions at Woody's ranch were appalling—no electricity, outdoor plumbing, crude lodgings. Of course, she *had* wanted to experience authentic frontier living, but she was learning far more about the travails of pioneer life than she'd ever wanted to know!

The strains of Gene Autry's voice faded away, and above them, Woody picked up a microphone—a *microphone*, for a man Jessica had spied washing up at the horse trough this morning!—and began to huff away in his cowboy jargon. Across from Jessica, Walter Lummety jerked awake with a loud snort.

"Well, hello there, little cowboys and cowgirls," Woody drawled. "Hope old Gene put y'all in an Old West state of mind. Now, maybe you little guys and gals been wonderin' 'bout this here stage we're ridin' in. Why, this here's a *genu-wine* antique, I'll have you know. The wife and me bought it at an auction three years ago, and restored it to its former glory. Figured our dude ranch guests deserved to ride in style."

They hit another bump, and Jessica winced.

"Now, let me tell you all about the history of this fine old chariot. Ya see, folks, over a hundred years ago, the most famous parlor house madame in these parts, Lila Lullaby, bought this here coach from the Singletree Line, after them boys went under and pulled out of old Colorado City. Then Lila started up a delivery service of her own. She had this here coach painted yeller, then she and a few of her line gals use 'ta take it out to the mines and back. If you'll pardon my frankness, folks, old Lila's specialty was service with a smile. She and her gals use 'ta deliver up a lot more than passengers and mail, if you know what I mean. Caused a pure-dee scandal in these parts. Hear tell the old Cumberland circuit rider use 'ta make his rounds, beating his Bible and warning them miners all about the perils of perdition. Then, old Lila and her gals would come along and teach them menfolks the true meaning of sin."

As Woody guffawed, Jessica noted that Stan was smiling sheepishly, Walter appeared embarrassed, and Harold, amused.

Woody loudly cleared his throat. "Hear tell after a few years, the sheriff chased off old Lila and her gals, and they set up shop near Trinidad. A pure-dee shame, weren't it?"

As Woody paused, Jessica muttered sarcastically, "Well, thank goodness. I've heard all that I ever want to hear about Lila Lullaby."

Walter Lummety flashed her a sheepish look.

Gruffly, Woody continued. "Now, folks, if'n you'll just look to the east, you'll spy a natural-like stone dike known as Reklaw Ridge. And this here valley is called Reklaw Gorge."

Her attention at last piqued, Jessica glanced out her window at the stone ledge zigzagging its way up the spine of the mountain. Reklaw Ridge. A picturesque-sounding name. The dikes of Colorado, a natural phenomenon caused by volcanic activity deep in the earth, never failed to fascinate her.

"Behind them there dikes is where the old Reklaw Gang use'ta hide out to ambush the stages coming out from old Colorado City," Woody went on. "You best lay low, folks, cause Reklaw Gorge is known to be haunted. That's right, *genu-wine* ghosts. I hear tell some folks can still hear them outlaw bullets whizzing by. Wouldn't want for none of them ghost riders to ambush you. Nossir. Why, them old Reklaw boys might even rob this here stage. Sheriff Lummety, you'd best keep your eyes peeled, partner."

Across from Jessica, Walter grinned. Jessica groaned. Would Walter's idiot cousin never shut up?

As if he'd read her mind, Woody remarked, "Well, folks, since I know you been missing the old mood music to accompany our little joy ride, you'll be right pleased to know our next selection is Roy Rogers and his Sons of the Pioneers. Lay back and enjoy the view as we hear 'Tumbling Tumbleweeds.' I reckon I'll be talkin' at you again in a spell."

As Roy and his crooners began, Walter Lummety offered Jessica an apologetic smile. "I do hope you're having a good time, Professor Garrett."

"Oh, just peachy," she replied sweetly, wincing as the stagecoach banged into yet another rut. How had anyone ever endured travel in these wretched conveyances? she wondered. Her entire body was already sore from the jolting she'd taken.

15

Walter sighed. "I realize my cousin goes a bit far, making us don this absurd getup to ride the stage. But Woody means well, and it is an authentic Old West experience, eh?"

"Sure is," agreed Stan ruefully.

"Perhaps more authentic than I daresay a body needs," put in Harold Billingsly wryly.

Jessica wiped a grain of sand from her eye. "And how."

Stan added tactfully, "Your cousin's heart seems in the right place, even though his approach to this is eccentric."

" 'Bizarre' might be a more apt term," commented Harold. "If my students could only see me now, I'd be laughed off the campus—and likely committed, as well."

As everyone chuckled, Stan continued thoughtfully, "Still, when you think about it, some of our ancestors may have actually ridden in this very stage."

"Let's hope not while it was in the hands of Miss Lila Lullaby," quipped Harold, prompting more amusement.

"But it is an intriguing possibility," Stan contended. "Just think—a hundred or so years ago, we might have all been Old West citizens riding along together. I'd be a cowboy on my way to the next roundup, Harold an elderly wagon train master off to see his grandchildren, and Walter . . . you'd be the sheriff, of course." He grinned at Lummety. "Didn't you say one of your ancestors was actually a Colorado lawman?"

Walter nodded with pride. "Great-great-grandfather Jedediah. He even served in 'sinful' Colorado City for a time, before the town merged with Colorado Springs. We think he may have also visited relatives at Mariposa."

"Could he have been the one who arrested Lila Lullaby?" teased Harold.

"I should hope not," retorted Walter, prompting laughter.

Stan turned to Jessica. "Now, as for Professor Garrett . . . I suppose you'd be the new schoolmarm, all decked out in calico."

"Of course," she agreed demurely, smoothing down her skirts.

Jessica was actually smiling with the others when suddenly the coach hit a huge bump, sending her flying upward. She yelped in pain as her head slammed against the roof of the coach; then her dignity was doubly assaulted as something sharp poked her in the rear.

"Ouch! What on earth . . ."

Jessica winced and rubbed her head as the interior of the coach swam before her eyes. She reached behind her, digging between the seats for the object that had stabbed her. She pulled out an old-fashioned cameo brooch with an open needle-clasp. So that was what had pricked her!

Mesmerized, Jessica gazed at the lovely antique ivory oval etched with a woman's face and surrounded by gold filigree. Reality seemed to fade in and out as she watched tiny, weird flickers of light bounce off the cameo's golden edges. . . .

Chapter One

Colorado, the Past

"Young woman, are you all right?"

Jessica blinked and shook her head. Had she lost consciousness for a moment? She couldn't be sure. Feeling dizzy and disoriented, she glanced across the stage's interior, struggling to focus, frowning as she noted that the velvet upholstery appeared much newer and brighter. How strange.

Then her gaze settled on Walter Lummety, and she flinched.

Heavens! The man she was staring at *looked* like Walter Lummety. But how on earth had he managed to acquire mutton-chop whiskers, and two toy Colt pistols at his waist? Not to mention that he appeared older and heavier. And hadn't his clothing also changed? He now wore old-fashioned striped brown pants and a leather vest, and she could have sworn he'd been in black before.

And hadn't the music stopped? Again Jessica shook

her head. She felt weird, out of sync, almost as if she weren't still in the same place.

But how could that be?

"I said, are you injured, young woman?" Walter repeated.

Why was Walter calling her "young woman"? She regarded him in perplexity. "Well, I'm not sure, Professor Lummety," she muttered at last.

"It's *Sheriff* Lummety," he corrected.

Jessica rolled her eyes and touched her sore head. "Whatever."

"That's quite a bump on the head you received," he continued solicitously.

Jessica held up the cameo. "You don't know the half of it. When I landed, this brooch poked me in the—er—nether regions."

Jessica was stunned to see that Walter appeared perfectly scandalized, turning away and coughing discreetly.

As Jessica pondered this oddity, Harold reached out to pat her hand. "Bless your heart. Are you badly injured, little lady?"

Little lady, indeed! Jessica turned to Harold, only to do a double take. Somehow during the last few seconds, elderly Professor Billingsly had miraculously sprouted long white hair and a handlebar mustache that curled upward on the ends, and he'd donned a much larger hat. What was going on here? Had the men brought along these extra disguises as a practical joke? How silly! And why were both Harold and Walter suddenly talking to her in such a formal, flowery way?

"I doubt it's a fatal injury," she managed.

Stan leaned across the seats to peer at the cameo. "That's a right pretty piece, ma'am." He winked at her solemnly. "Reckon it belonged to old Lila Lullaby?"

Jessica regarded Stan in consternation. She *must* be hallucinating, for suddenly her fastidious colleague had sprouted long sideburns, and disgusting brown spittle was

19

dripping from one corner of his mouth. Since when had Stan started chewing tobacco? And talking like a hick? And when had he changed from his cowboy shirt to the Spanish-style serape he now wore?

Even as Jessica's mind reeled with these contradictions, Walter turned irately to Stan. "Lila Lullaby, indeed! Thank heaven we're rid of that Jezebel in these parts. Sir, have you no sense of decorum, to mention such a tawdry creature in the presence of a lady?"

As Jessica looked on in amazement, Stan pressed a hand to his heart and regarded her contritely. "Sorry, little lady. No offense intended."

Jessica couldn't believe her eyes and ears! This was so bizarre. Her three companions were the same, yet they *weren't* the same. Either she was dreaming or these men were pulling her leg.

She desperately hoped it was the latter. After all, hadn't Stan gotten the ball rolling by suggesting they might all have been Old West citizens riding on this very stage?

"Come on, guys," she chided. "Knock it off."

"Knock what off?" demanded a perplexed Walter. He turned to Harold. "Do you suppose the bump on her head confused her?"

Harold thoughtfully stroked his mustache. "Quite possibly."

"Oh, pleeeeze!" Jessica exclaimed. "You guys are being ridiculous, and this charade has gone quite far enough."

"What charade?" asked Walter blankly.

"*This* charade!" Losing patience, Jessica reached out and yanked on Walter's whiskers, only to recoil at his yelp of pain.

"Young woman, what do you think you're doing?" he roared.

"Sorry," Jessica muttered, laughing nervously at his look of formidable indignation. "That must be some really strong spirit gum you're using, eh? But you don't have to go ballistic about it."

Walter exchanged mystified glances with the other men.

As a tense silence ensued, Harold leaned over and picked up the cameo Jessica had dropped when she yanked on Walter's whiskers. He extended it toward her with a courtly smile. "My dear, you really must don this fine brooch. Finder's keepers, you know. And I must say the cameo bears a striking resemblance to your lovely countenance."

"Why, thank you," Jessica murmured, feeling charmed, despite herself. "My mother always did say I have an old-fashioned face." She pinned the cameo on her dress, only to blink as a strange, unreal feeling again washed over her and new, funny shimmers of light bounced off the cameo's edges. Heavens, that bump on the head had really jostled her brains!

Even as Jessica was struggling to gain her bearings, she was bemused to hear the sounds of distant hoofbeats joining the cacophony created by the horses pulling the stage.

Stan craned his neck out the window, only to groan. "Ah, hell." Ah glanced apologetically at Jessica. "No offense, ma'am."

Jessica ground her teeth. Her head was throbbing, and she was about ready to punch the next jerk who called her "ma'am" or "little lady."

"What's wrong?" inquired Walter of Stan.

Stan spat tobacco juice out the window. "Looks like outlaws chasing the stage, Sheriff."

"Outlaws?" cried Jessica.

Even as the sounds of horses grew closer, Walter was straining to get a look out his window. "Yep. It's the Reklaw Gang, all right, and them scoundrels are gaining on us."

Jessica flung her hands outward. "The Reklaw Gang? You've got to be kidding!"

Ignoring Jessica, Stan spoke urgently to Walter. "Wouldn't you know them bushwhackers would choose

21

today for their dirty doin's, when Buck's got no one ridin' shotgun for him."

Buck? Who was Buck? Jessica wondered dazedly.

Expression grim, Walter pulled out a pistol, spun the cylinder, then cocked the weapon. "Best get ready, boys."

Get ready? In disbelief, Jessica watched Stan reach beneath the seat, pull out an antique rifle, and throw the lever. As if the sight of two stuffy academics about to join in a shootout wasn't enough to unhinge Jessica, she heard with horror the sounds of approaching gunfire.

Gunfire! Wild-eyed, she dared a glance out her window, only to gasp as she observed that they were indeed being chased by five outlaws on horseback.

Outlaws! It couldn't be. Jessica blinked, but the outlandish tableau did not shift one bit. Behind the stagecoach, riding on swift horses that stirred up huge clouds of dust, were five men in Old West costumes, complete with Stetsons, kerchiefs . . . and blazing pistols.

"What *is* this?" she demanded. "Some kind of joke? A Saturday matinee, fifties style?"

Someone yanked on her wrist and hauled her back inside. "Little lady, get your pretty head down," scolded Stan. "Before it gets blowed off."

Wide-eyed, Jessica turned to Walter. "Who *are* they? The *Reklaw* Gang? Did Woody hire them?"

"You heard the man—get down!"

With those terse words, Walter Lummety grabbed Jessica by the shoulders and pressed her downward. She popped back up, only to watch mystified as Walter began returning the outlaws' fire out his window. Flinching at the loud blasts, she then observed Stan firing his rifle out the other window. Jessica's mouth fell open.

"Walter, Stan, what on earth do you think you're doing with those toy guns?" she demanded.

Walter shot her a menacing look. "Name's Jedediah, ma'am, and that there's Slim. Now hush up and lay low!"

Jedediah! Wasn't that the name of Walter's ancestor? And who was Slim? Jessica was reeling, struggling to make sense of the incomprehensible. But one thing was for certain—she was getting damn tired of the demented game her colleagues were playing.

"Walter, Stan, you stop this, right now!" she ordered furiously.

Again both men ignored her. Walter hardly missed a beat as he emptied one pistol, holstered the smoking weapon, drew out another, and resumed firing. By now, the outlaws' firing and hollering had reached a deafening crescendo, and the smell of gunsmoke was thick and acrid inside the coach.

As Stan pulled in his rifle to reload, Jessica dared another glance out her window, only to recoil as a round screamed past her nose. This was absurd. It was high time to stop this nightmare—she wanted to get off.

Yanking off her bonnet, Jessica turned to confront Walter. "Walter, that's it, I've had it! I don't care if you are department chair. Since we've been here in the Twilight Zone, I've shared my boudoir with wasps and my bed with a colony of field mice. But this is the final straw. Now you and these other morons have lost your minds, and your lunatic cousin has gone and hired outlaws to chase us." She shrieked at the sound of glass shattering on one of the lanterns outside her window. "And they're firing *real bullets* at us!"

Chapter Two

"Hold up there right now or I'll shoot you dead!"

As one of the approaching outlaws shouted the order, Jessica cautiously peered out her window. The old stage-coach rattled and groaned to a halt. Through the clouds of dust rising from the wagon wheels, she glimpsed five riders overtaking the stage and dismounting.

Heavens! What horrors lay ahead for them now?

The bandits' horses whinnied and stamped, and it seemed only seconds later that smoking pistols were shoved inside through both windows of the conveyance, and a hoarse voice commanded, "Throw out them firin' irons, fellas. Now."

Jessica watched, dumbfounded, as Walter and Stan pitched out their weapons.

The door to the stage swung open, and a masked man with light-colored eyes peered inside, his gaze pausing on Jessica in a manner that made her fight a shiver. "Now hightail it out of there. All of ya. And get them hands up high."

Struggling to forestall panic, Jessica faced down the man with bravado. "You're joking, aren't you?"

He fired his pistol into the air, and Jessica all but jumped out of her skin.

"Does it sound like I'm funnin' ya, sister?" he snarled.

With remarkable haste, Jessica clambered out of the stage and raised her hands. Her companions followed suit, though Walter moved in a halting, pained fashion that puzzled her.

Then she gulped at the sight of five armed bandits prowling about them. Daring another glance at her colleagues, she noted that Walter, Stan, and Harold all appeared pasty-faced, half ill. Not that she felt much better. Her stomach roiled violently and her heart slammed.

Who *were* these outlaws? Had Woody hired them? If so, the joke was wearing very thin.

Jessica quickly sized up their captors. All five wore kerchief masks and Stetsons, making their features difficult to discern. Aside from the fact that each man wore a different style or color of western shirt, the five were identically attired in typical cowboy garb. Three of the five were tall and lean, almost boyish in appearance; a fourth was slightly shorter and even slimmer. But it was the fifth man who most commanded Jessica's attention— he was tallest of all, broad-shouldered, more solidly built, and somehow, much more menacing. Jessica sensed at once that this man was the leader, and likely older than the rest. There was an unnerving arrogance about his stride, his stance.

Even as she struggled to make sense of things, the smallest outlaw chuckled and waved his pistol at Walter. "Well, howdy there, Sheriff. Looks like we're spoilin' your little afternoon drive, eh?"

Jessica glanced at Walter to see that his features were livid. "Young man, if you and these other cowards know what's good for you, you'll throw down your weapons and surrender to me at once."

"Surrender, eh?" the outlaw taunted, rocking on his boot heels. "Well, ain't that a hoot and a holler, boys?"

He and his cohorts all but split their sides laughing. Then the bandit waved his weapon toward Jessica. "Hey, who's the pretty girlie-girl you got there?"

As Jessica's heart lurched in fear, Walter glared. "Young man, I'll have you know this is a perfectly respectable young lady. I'll not hear you cast aspersions on her character."

The man turned to his partners. "Aspersions, eh?" he mocked, and the men guffawed.

A second man stepped forward. "All right, Billy. Enough jawing. Let's get down to business."

The smaller man turned angrily on the second outlaw. "Gabe, don't you be givin' these folks our names or, hell, I reckon we'll have to shoot 'em all."

At this casual mention of murder, the five captives cringed, and several of the bandits chuckled. Meanwhile, Gabe calmly cocked his weapon and aimed it up at the driver. "All right, pops. Throw down the strong box or I'll fill your belly full of lead."

Jessica glanced up at the driver's seat, only to go wide-eyed. Since she'd last seen him, Woody Lynch had grown a full beard and had gained at least twenty pounds. What was going on here? She couldn't even be sure this man *was* Woody.

The driver's hands were trembling. "Sorry, boys. We ain't got no strong box."

Gabe angrily strode forward. "What do you mean, you ain't got none? Get on down here, pops."

Amid the loud groaning of the stage's springs, the heavy man slid to the ground and raised his hands. Jessica did another double take, staring flabbergasted at this man who looked like Woody but wasn't Woody. Nobody could have grown a paunch like that in ten minutes!

Gabe strode about, cursing as he examined the coach

from various angles, evidently looking for cubbyholes where valuables might be stashed.

Abruptly he pointed his pistol toward the driver. "Hey, pops, what kind of sissy stage line is this, anyhow?" he demanded. "I ain't never seed no yeller stagecoach before."

A third outlaw stepped up to the door. "Hey, Gabe, lookie here. 'LL.' Ain't this Lila Lullaby's old parlor wagon?"

Gabe ambled to the door, then let out a raucous squeal. "Well, I'll be hanged. You're right, Wesley. We got us a gall-durned hussy wagon here."

Wesley turned to Jessica. "You one of Lila's gals, honey?"

As Jessica sucked in a horrified breath, Walter angrily retorted, "I already informed you contemptible scoundrels that this is a perfectly respectable young lady! Why, she's the new schoolmarm, on her way to Mariposa."

Jessica was flabbergasted. This was certainly news to her!

Gabe stepped closer, and she could see mischief gleaming in his blue eyes. "Schoolmarm, eh? Reckon she'd mind learning us boys a few lessons in earthly pleasures?"

As the outlaws howled with mirth and elbowed one another, Jessica seethed, yearning to slap the arrogant scoundrel's face. But, after Billy had discharged his weapon to scare her, she knew better.

"I told you this woman is upstanding," blustered Walter.

A fourth outlaw stepped forward to confront Walter. "Oh, yeah? Then how come she's ridin' in this here bordello on wheels?" A devilish chuckle escaped him. "You fellas are having some fun with her, ain't ya?"

As Jessica made a sound of outrage and her companions appeared mortified, Walter angrily gestured toward the driver. "That's a low-down, evil lie. Now, you boys must have heard that Buck Lynch bought this here stage, after the previous sheriff chased Miss Lila and her gals out of Colorado City." *Buck* Lynch? So Woody Lynch was

Buck Lynch now? And what was this nonsense Walter was spouting about his predecessor chasing Lila Lullaby out of Colorado City?

"Whatever, pops," drawled Billy. He pulled out a small cloth bag and extended it toward the captives. "All right, folks. Fork over your valuables. Quick like."

The captives hesitated, regarding one another with uncertainty.

"I said rattle your hocks!" Billy ordered.

In amazement, Jessica watched Walter, Stan, and Harold step forward and hand over antique pocket watches, ornate belt buckles, and a few old-fashioned bills. What had happened to her colleagues' modern wristwatches and wedding rings?

Billy extended his bag toward Jessica. "Now you, lady."

Jessica hurled the bandit a mutinous look. Since she hadn't worn a watch today, she pulled off her college ring and tossed it in. The cameo she wore was neither noticed nor requested.

Billy pawed through his treasure trove. "Aw, shit. Mostly worthless bandwagon junk." He pulled out Jessica's ring and whistled. "Well, lookie here, Luke. This is mighty peculiar."

The one named Luke stepped closer. "Yeah, look at them strange numbers. 1994. Wonder what they mean?"

"Maybe the number of notches on your bedpost, eh, little lady?" suggested Wes, and the outlaws broke up laughing.

Jessica glowered and tapped her toe.

Face red with anger, Walter Lummety took a heavy, pained step toward Billy. "Young man, I shall not tolerate any further insults to this lady."

"Oh yeah?" Again, Billy discharged his pistol in the air, causing the captives to cringe anew. "Hush up and get back in line, Sheriff. I'm sick of your lip."

Shame-faced, Walter hobbled back, while Jessica

flashed him a grateful look.

The driver cleared his throat. "You boys finished now?" he asked in a high whine. " 'Cause if'n you don't mind, think we'll just mosey on back to Colorado City and patch up this here stage."

Billy tossed Jessica's ring back in the bag. "Hell, yes, we mind, pops. Fact is, them dofunnies and ditties you folks forked over are about as worthless as a whore's smile after a busy Saturday night."

"Now, Billy, watch your language," scolded Gabe. "There's a *lady* present."

Again the outlaws roared with mirth, while Jessica was about ready to pop her cork.

Pocketing the bills, Billy contemptuously tossed the bag on the ground and cocked his pistol at the captives. "Now hand over some real money, folks, or there's gonna be some of you on your way to the bone orchard."

Amid gasps of fear, Walter protested, "But we've given you all we have, young man."

Billy shoved his pistol into Walter's chest. "Well, that just ain't satisfactory, Sheriff."

By now, Jessica had had all of the abuse she could endure from these bullies, and her outrage overrode her fear. She surged forward and shoved Billy's pistol away from Walter's chest. "You stop that right now," she ordered.

For a moment, Billy regarded Jessica in mystification; then he laughed. "Hot damn! If you ain't a feisty one."

Eyes blazing with fury, Jessica shook her finger at him. "I don't care if Woody did hire you and these other thugs."

"Who's Woody?" he asked.

"And what are thugs?" inquired Gabe.

Ignoring their questions, Jessica continued scolding Billy. "My point is, you have *real bullets* in your weapon, and you will kindly not point it at Professor Lummety."

Billy stared at her another moment, then tipped his hat with his pistol. "Why, yes, ma'am."

All of the bandits chuckled.

At last the big, silent one ambled forward, picking up the bag on his way. He fixed his dark, intent stare on Jessica, looking her over in a most insulting way, and she struggled not to shiver. Then, for the first time, he spoke, and his deep, compelling voice sent a chill down her spine.

"Time to go, boys. There's nothing more for us here."

Despite herself, Jessica was riveted by his words. Although he spoke in a drawl, he sounded better educated than the others; in fact, he possessed the deepest, sexiest masculine voice she'd ever heard. By contrast, his cohorts' nasal twangs sounded hokey and coarse. But this man's western inflections were shot through with pure sin and seduction.

Not that she wouldn't like to shoot him, anyway.

"But, Cole," protested Billy, "we can't give up yet. We ain't got no strong box."

"They don't have one, Billy," Cole replied patiently.

"But we can't go away empty-handed."

"Yeah, that ain't fair," added Gabe.

"Then what would you have us do, little brothers?"

So the five men were brothers. *Interesting*, thought Jessica.

Billy hesitated a moment, then pointed at Jessica. "I know. We'll take her."

At once, Gabe joined in with, "Yeah, let's take her!"

"Maybe we can ransom her," suggested Luke.

"Not on your life!" cried Jessica.

"Young man, I must insist you not molest this young woman," put in Professor Billingsly bravely.

"Molest?" laughed Billy. "Hell, geezer, we ain't gonna molest her. We're just aimin' to have ourselves a little fun with her. Ain't that right, Cole?"

Again Cole's dark gaze flicked over Jessica, as if she were a ripe plum he could devour in a single bite. Then he shrugged. "She's got a real mouth on her, and I say she's more trouble than she's worth. But suit yourselves."

Jessica shot the scoundrel a glare, for all the good it did her.

"Yeah," said Billy eagerly, rubbing his hands together.

Again Walter stepped forward to confront Billy. "Young man, you'll kidnap this young woman over my dead body."

Billy pointed his pistol. "My pleasure, Sheriff."

"No!" protested Jessica.

She rushed between the two men, slapping Billy's pistol away from Walter's chest. Balling her hands on her hips, she faced Billy down. "I told you not to point that weapon at him, you little jerk."

Billy chuckled. "Hell, sugar, I plumb forgot."

Ignoring new bursts of insufferable male laughter, Jessica turned to Woody. "Mr. Lynch, please, you must do something," she pleaded. "I don't care what kind of joke this is. It's *not* funny."

The poor man appeared miserable, his eyes half crazed, his lower lip trembling. "Ma'am, I don't know how to tell you this, but this ain't no joke. These here men are a'feared outlaws, wanted dead or alive in these parts, and we'd best take 'em serious."

"Oh, God," muttered Jessica, and then she felt her arm being seized.

"Come along now, sugar," coaxed Billy. "You're gonna take a nice little ride with me and the boys."

"Yeah, and then maybe a *long* ride with the rest of us," added Gabe wickedly.

Jessica threw off Billy's hand. "How dare you touch me! You men are evil, vile, and despicable. You're dangerous fugitives who obviously belong in the custody of the law."

Billy glanced helplessly at Cole. "Well, big brother, maybe she is more trouble than she's worth. Should we shoot her?"

Jessica gasped in fear as Cole started toward her, his

stride sleek and purposeful. Her heart pounded as he stared at her long and hard. But to her surprise, instead of shooting her, he brazenly grabbed her about the middle, easily hefted her up over a broad shoulder, and started walking off with her dangling there. Outraged, Jessica screamed and beat on his back. He took no note, only striding to his horse and tossing her over it. For a moment, with her derriere pointing skyward, her face to the ground, Jessica was too stunned to react. Then Cole mounted behind her, and she felt his muscled strength, his heat, and she was mortified to find her mouth shoved intimately against his hard, warm thigh. She could even smell him— leather, sweat, and pure *man*. Yet when she struggled again in earnest, his hand slammed down on her rear with enough force to make her cease her struggles at once.

"Lady," he muttered, "consider yourself in the custody of the Reklaw Gang."

All five outlaws rode off with their prize, shooting, whooping, and hollering.

Chapter Three

"Who d'ya reckon will get to kiss her first?"

As Jessica bounced along, squeezed between the saddle horn and Cole Reklaw's hard body, she could hear the men's voices, though it was more difficult to tell whose was whose. She guessed it was Gabe who had posed the question. Not that she cared, she was so miserable at the moment. Her body was jolted with each lunge of the horse. Her cheeks throbbed from the rush of blood to her face. The choking dust rising from the trail coated her hair and face, stung her eyes, and made her cough and sneeze. Of course, none of this could compare with the indignity of having her face and mouth pressed intimately against the outlaw's male thigh, in having her entire body inundated with his heat, his scent, to know the man had an unrestricted view of her rear end bobbing up and down as they barreled along. She wanted to scream, to rail against her appalling plight. Yet she dared not, or her captor might "discipline" her again. Worse yet, he might just shove her off his horse—in which case, she'd doubtless land on her head and break her neck.

What did her captors have in store for her? She shuddered to think.

Again, Jessica wondered who the bandits really were. Having seen the fear in Mr. Lynch's eyes, she could no longer rationally believe he had hired these lunatics on horseback, especially since she still couldn't make sense of the fact that all of her colleagues had somehow changed their appearances right before the outlaws had shown up. She wasn't even sure she'd left the same people she'd started out with this morning.

Nothing was making sense. Why were her colleagues suddenly sporting altered demeanors and new names? And where had the armed men come from? Were they pretending to be the Reklaw Gang, or were they real? They must be impostors, for the only other logical explanation was that the stagecoach had somehow traveled into an earlier time—and that wasn't logical at all.

On the other hand, could all of this be a dream or a hallucination? Was she actually still in the stage, lying there unconscious after having hit her head? As her captor's horse stumbled slightly, the saddle horn's jab in her side convinced her otherwise. No, if anything, this nightmare was *too* real.

The sounds of the men's agitated voices interrupted Jessica's frantic musings, and she listened, appalled, as they argued over her.

"I'm gonna kiss her first," Billy declared. "It was my idea to take her, after all."

"Hey, that ain't fair," protested Luke. "We gotta draw straws for her or somethin'."

"This is an outlaw gang, not a gall-durned knittin' circle," Billy shot back. "I'm the one that took her, so I get first dibs."

"I'll play you a hand of blackjack for her," offered Wes.

"Hell, no—you cheat, Wesley," Billy shot back.

"Do not!"

"Do so!"

"You take that back, Billy Reklaw."

"Hell, no, Wesley Reklaw, I ain't takin' nothin' back. I saw you pullin' that queen from the bottom of the deck the last time you dealt blackjack."

"That's a gall-durned lie. I may steal, but I ain't never cheated. Ma brung us up better'n that."

"Boys, give it a rest," put in Cole in his deep, commanding voice. "Any of you given a thought to what's going to happen when her people find out she's missing, or when Ma learns we brought home this—er—*lady*?"

Jessica wriggled in impotent fury at the cynical inflection in Cole's voice. She heard his low laughter, only exacerbating her ire.

"Ma won't mind," asserted Billy with bravado. "We're just aiming to have a little fun with her."

"Yeah, the *lady* here can help Ma with her woman's chores once we're done with her," suggested Wes slyly.

"And Ma's gotta understand why we took her, 'cause there weren't no strong box," argued Luke. "Fair is fair, after all, and maybe we can win a goodly ransom for her. Heck, we couldn't go away empty-handed, like a bunch of sissies."

Cole chuckled. "Whatever you boys say."

Jessica's spirits sank. So she was in the custody of a bunch of crazy men who thought they were Old West outlaws, along with their equally demented mother. The Barker Gang, complete with evil Ma.

All at once, Jessica tensed as she felt Cole's horse slowing its pace. Her body shifted forward as the group headed down an incline. Gradually, she began to hear the sounds of chickens cackling, the oinking of pigs. Then she smelled the strong odors of a barnyard, mingled with wood smoke.

The men halted their horses. Cole dismounted, then pulled Jessica to the ground with him.

Disoriented, half nauseated, she stared about her to see that all five men had removed their masks. Were she not so furious, she would have gasped aloud, for they were a handsome lot. Recognizing them from their shirts and the fact that Billy was smaller, she noted that he, Gabe, and Wes all appeared to be in their early to mid twenties. Leanly built, all three had blue eyes, the faces of angels, and thick blond hair worn longish. Luke, tall and slightly older, greatly resembled Gabe and Wes, except that his shock of shiny hair was light brown.

At last her gaze shifted to Cole, and she struggled not to flinch. He was so different from his brothers—older, closer to thirty, she judged. His frame was massive and hard-muscled, and his stance oozed arrogance. His thick dark brown hair, also worn long, shone with highlights, and his deep-set eyes were dark. His features were tanned, fiercely handsome. The hard lines around his mouth and eyes said that he truly was the leader of this gang of cutthroats, that he was a dangerous, determined man. And, from the way he was staring at Jessica, he was also sexy. Too sexy. In a very dark, smoldering way.

Jessica suddenly felt weak and defenseless. For in that moment she somehow knew she could handle all four of the younger Reklaw brothers. But this older one—this Cole—this one she *couldn't* handle.

Billy stepped forward, grinning. "Welcome to our home, little missy."

At last Jessica had the presence of mind to look at her surroundings. To her right loomed a large, old-time, native stone farmhouse with a homey swing on the porch and a high tin roof. Hanging baskets spilled flowers from the eaves, and a calico cat dozed on the steps. To her left stretched a swept yard dotted with a few brave clumps of grass and wildflowers, giving way to a cluttered barnyard. In the distance sprawled a weatherbeaten barn and a ramshackle bunkhouse, the structures hulking against a backdrop of misty Colorado mountains.

Where on earth *was* she? Perhaps she should run—but where? Beyond the homestead, she could see only raw wilderness where mule deer grazed and distant mountains where hawks circled.

She turned to Billy. "This is your home—a living farm?"

Billy chuckled. "Don't she say the most peculiar things?" he asked Gabe.

"Sure do," Gabe agreed with a grin.

Then Jessica became distracted as the door to the farmhouse swung open and a huge, scowling woman appeared carrying a broom. She was dressed in a ragged homespun dress and a badly soiled apron. Straggles of gray-brown hair dangled about the sagging jowls of her fearsomely set mouth. Dirt smeared her cheeks and nose, and her dark eyes held a predatory gleam.

She lumbered down the steps, glowered at the men, then at Jessica. "What in tarnation have you boys brung home this time?" she demanded.

"Ma, it's a girlie-girl," announced Billy proudly. "We took her off the stage we robbed. Maybe we can ransom her."

"You boys gone and done another robbery?" the woman hollered. "Oh, sweet mercy!"

"Ma, it's an honest livin'," protested Gabe, digging the toe of his boot in the dirt. "You see, there weren't no strong box, so we took her instead."

The woman swung her ferocious features on Jessica. "Who you be, honey?"

Though it wasn't easy, Jessica drew herself up with dignity and faced down the intimidating woman. "I am Professor Jessica Garrett, of Pawnee College."

"Professor?" the woman gasped. "You're some sure-enough schoolmarm?"

Schoolmarm. Hearing the word, Jessica suddenly found her instincts taking over as she remembered "Sheriff" Lummety declaring to the outlaws that she was Mariposa's expected new schoolteacher. Heck, if nothing was making sense here, she might as well join in the lunacy.

Primly straightening her cuffs and raising her chin, Jessica declared, "That is correct. I am the new schoolmarm, and was on my way to Mariposa when these scoundrels robbed the stage and abducted me."

Jessica's bold lie had more than the desired effect. Ma Reklaw appeared horrified, her huge mouth gaping open. Waving a hand in disgust, the woman turned to her sons. "Great jumping Jehoshaphat! What you boys gone and done this time, shanghaiing the new schoolmarm!"

"Ma, we didn't know," insisted Billy, while guiltily avoiding his mother's eye.

"Don't you tell me, 'Ma, we didn't know,' you lying little pipsqueak," she thundered back.

"We thought she was a Cyprian," explained Gabe.

"Hell, she was in Lila Lullaby's old pussy-wagon," added Luke.

To Jessica's amazement, the woman's face reddened in outrage; then she raised up a hand and soundly slapped Luke's face. As he recoiled, she thundered, "You rascal! Hush up that evil talk. There's a lady present, I'll have you know. I didn't raise you up to carry on like no parlorhouse flesh-peddler." She jerked a thumb toward Jessica. " 'Sides, do she look like some Cyprian?"

All five men scowled at Jessica.

"But it was a yeller stagecoach," protested Luke weakly.

"Yeah, with red velvet seats," stated Wes.

With a look of forbearance, the woman turned to Jessica and touched her arm. "Honey, you just get your sweet self up there on that porch. This here is between me and my boys."

"Yes, ma'am," replied a very relieved Jessica.

Jessica beat a hasty retreat up the steps, securing herself behind a post. From her vantage point, she was amazed to watch all five men begin backing away from their menacing mother. Meanwhile, Ma Reklaw stood clenching and unclenching her hands on her broom handle, adjusting and re-adjusting her grip, like a batter getting ready to step up to the plate. All the while, she glowered at the men with a burning vengeance that made Jessica pray that she would never cross this ferocious woman.

"Now, Ma," scolded Billy, holding up a hand, "don't you go gettin' riled."

The huge woman lifted her broom. Jessica went wide-eyed as an enraged roar welled up from the woman, making the image of a charging bear pale by comparison.

Then Ma Reklaw began to swing.

Chapter Four

"Heathens! You're just a bunch of gall-durned heathens, the lot of you!"

From the porch, Jessica watched in awe and admiration as Ma Reklaw swung her broom with a vengeance, sending chickens scurrying, the cat yowling and diving under the porch, and her own sons rushing for cover. The sight of four grown men—fearsome outlaws, to boot—stampeding like panicked sheep was comical to Jessica, as well as very satisfying. Within seconds, Billy was up a tree, Wes under the hay wagon, Luke behind the horse trough, Gabe inside a barrel. Only Cole stood his ground, resisting the urge to flee, though even he backed away and regarded his mother warily.

"Ma!" called Billy shrilly from his perch in the tree. "You stop that right now. You was aiming that broom of yours where no lady dare aim."

Ma charged toward the tree and began thrashing away, causing Billy to squeal and clamber higher. "Don't you sass me, you snot-nosed varmint. You scoundrels don't know nothin' 'bout how to treat no lady. A body would think you was all hatched up from under a rock. I've tolerated your thievin' and your whorin', your drinkin', gamblin' and shootin' up the town. But insulting a sure 'nuff lady—that I can't abide."

Gabe dared to peek out over the rim of the barrel. Wide-eyed, he whined, "Ma, she ain't no lady. Didn't we tell you she was ridin' in Lila Lullaby's old parlor wagon?"

Ma charged over and knocked over the barrel with a deft swing of her broom, prompting Gabe to scamper out and scurry away. "I'll parlor wagon you, you back-talkin' sidewinder."

"Ma, we was just tryin' to have some fun with her," put in Luke from behind the horse trough.

"Fun? How 'bout this for fun, you horse's patooty!"

Ma began thrashing at the horse trough with her broom, and although she couldn't manage to overturn it, a soaked Luke quickly dashed off for cover. Then she stalked over to the wagon and used her broom handle to poke at Wes—who went bolting off with a yelp of pain.

Jessica almost felt sorry for the men. *Almost*.

"All right, Ma, that's enough," stated a deadly calm voice.

All at once, everyone in the yard froze at the sound of Cole's stern admonition. He stood at the edge of the yard with Colt drawn, and was glaring at his mother as if he meant business.

Not daunted in the least, Ma marched over to confront her son with broom raised and ready to swing. "You! You should know better than to let your brothers carry on this way. You're the eldest, after all."

"Ma, put down that broom," he ordered.

Ma didn't even flinch. "Son, holster that shootin' iron or I swear, I'm droppin' you where you stand."

For a moment Cole hesitated. Then Jessica watched, amazed, as he holstered his weapon.

Heavens, his mother was formidable!

Especially as she ambled closer to her son and soundly slapped his face. Cole flinched slightly but otherwise held his ground. "You show some respect for your elders from now on, you hear? You think I'm a'feared of you, you little whippersnapper? Hell, I use'ta change your dirty britches."

"Ma, please," Cole pleaded, coloring deeply.

Jessica was astounded. She would have been willing to bet it would be impossible to embarrass this arrogant man. But she hadn't counted on Ma. Bless her.

Setting down her broom, Ma turned, stuffed two fingers in her mouth, and whistled loudly. "All right, get your worthless hides over here, all of you varmints." She smiled apologetically at Jessica. "You, too, ma'am. No offense, but I had to set them rascals in their places. It's a mother's call, you see."

Jessica struggled against a smile and headed down the steps. "No offense taken, Mrs. Reklaw."

The wary boys, Jessica, and Cole gathered around Ma. The younger outlaws grumbled to each other and shot Jessica resentful looks, as if she were the cause of their current troubles, rather than their own misbehavior. Cole crossed his arms over his muscled chest and pointedly ignored Jessica.

Ma was scowling fearsomely. "All right, boys, you gone and dry-gulched this here nice lady. How you gonna fix things?"

All five men appeared perplexed, scratching heads and mumbling to one another.

At last, Billy asked, "Ma, can't we just keep her around?" Watching ire rise in his mother's eyes, he hastily held up a hand. "I mean, if'n we behave ourselves?"

As Ma hesitated, Gabe wheedled, "Yeah, Ma, can't she help you out with your woman's chores? Wouldn't that be nice?"

Ma ruminated over this, then shook her head. "Nope,

boys, this ain't no stray dog you brung home, but a real honest-to-gosh lady. What you gonna do if her menfolks show up to claim her?"

As the boys scratched their heads, Jessica eagerly stepped into the gap. "Er, gents, your mother has a point. You don't want to tangle with my people, do you?" Before they could answer, she rushed on with barely disguised sarcasm. "You know, boys, it's been such a pleasure being ambushed, terrified, and abused by you. Best of luck with your deranged nineteenth-century existence and working your way to the hanging tree. But if you don't mind, think I'll just mosey on back to the Broken Buck Dude Ranch."

The men appeared confused. "Lady, they're ain't no Broken Butt Dude Ranch in these parts," said Luke.

Jessica crossed her arms over her bosom. "It's Broken *Buck*. And, whatever, I'm leaving."

Ma nodded. "Yep, you boys had best fetch her back before the posse comes after her."

"But, Ma, if we fetch her back, she'll sic the law on us," protested Billy.

"Yeah, Ma, she'll turn us in," added Wes.

Ma appeared to waver, scratching her jaw. "Well, maybe you boys got a point." She raised an eyebrow at Jessica. "Ma'am, would you give over my boys?"

Jessica crossed herself and shook her head. "Absolutely not. Honest injun. I don't even know where this place is."

"She'll turn us in," Luke insisted. "Sure as Sunday."

"Ma, purty please, let us keep her," pleaded Gabe. "After all, we deserve somethin' for our troubles, after robbin' the stage and all."

"You all deserve a kick in the pants!" roared Ma, waving a plump arm. "Here you brung home this sure-nuff lady like she's some doll for you to play with, when all five of you rascals should be settlin' down and finding respectable wives for yourselves."

The four younger men hung their heads in shame. Cole just glowered. Proudly.

All at once Billy's head shot up, and he snapped his fingers. "I know. I'll marry her, then!"

Jessica sucked in a horrified breath as Billy's three younger brothers snapped up their heads, glanced tensely at one another, then joined in.

"No, I'll marry her!" protested Luke.

"Give her to me, please, Ma," pleaded Gabe. "I promise I'll treat her right."

"Play you a hand of blackjack for her," offered Wes to Billy.

Billy stepped forward to confront Wes. "Naw, you cheat, and 'sides, it's *my* idear, so I get first dibs." He turned to his mother. "Well, Ma, what do you say? Can I have her?"

For a long, charged moment, Ma ruminated, mumbling under her breath. Jessica wrung her hands and felt half ill.

"Maybe," Ma said at last.

"What?" protested Jessica.

"Now, honey." Ma turned to flash Jessica a placating smile. "When you think about it, it could be the perfect remedy. My boys is right reluctant to let you go, lest you give 'em over to the law. So I reckon it's best you marry up with one of 'em. You ain't got no husband, do you?"

"Well, I—"

"After all, ain't that what every female wants—a husband, a home and young 'uns to care for?"

"Speak for yourself," muttered Jessica.

Ma made a sweeping gesture toward the barn, the corn crib and corral. "Honey, lookie here at all this beauty. If'n you marry up with one of my boys, after I pass, all of this will be yours."

Appalled, Jessica gazed at the cluttered barnyard, watched a pig dig in the mud, and took a deep breath of manure-fragrant air. Helplessly she beseeched the heavens. "Whatever did I do to deserve this?"

"No fair!" protested Gabe to his mother. "It ain't fair

you just give her over to Billy, and the rest of us get no chance."

"Yeah, it ain't fair," said Wes.

"Yeah," agreed Luke.

Ma mulled this over, then brightened. "I know—why don't all of you boys shape up, then all of you can court her? It can be like a contest, with the best-behaved gettin' the prize. That way, the lady here can decide for herself which one of you she wants."

Four male faces lit with grins.

"No!" protested Jessica. "I mean, no offense, ma'am, but I don't want any of these men."

Ma grew suspicious; her heavy brows drew together and thunderclouds loomed in her eyes. "Are you saying my boys ain't good enough for you, lady?"

Jessica struggled not to wince aloud. This woman was more daunting than an Amazon. And the last thing she could afford to do was to alienate her one ally here. "No, no, of course not," she hastily reassured Ma. "They're wonderful boys, princes among men. It's just that, well—I've no desire to marry at all. You see, I'm working on my dissertation—"

Ma clucked to Jessica like a mother hen reassuring a nervous chick. "Now, honey. I know my boys gave you a bad scare. But they're good boys at heart—just a mite frisky, you see." Playfully, she elbowed Jessica. "And they're handsome devils, ain't they? Why, a good, up-standing woman like you, you'll tame 'em all in no time."

"You must be joking."

"Now, honey, give it a chance. Like maybe a few weeks here. If one of my boys ain't persuaded you to the altar by then—heck, I'll have them escort you back to the Broken Butt."

"Oh, Lord," groaned Jessica.

"So do we get to court her, then?" asked Billy excitedly.

Ma shook a finger. "Proper like! Which means you and these other heathens had best put some starch in your shirts and a shine on your boots, and go fetch the lady here some candy and flowers. And while you're at it, wash all the filth out of your mouths."

The four younger men hooted and howled their victory, pounding one another across the shoulders.

"Yes, ma'am," agreed a jubilant Billy. "We'll spark her good and proper."

Jessica was left reeling. "Mrs. Reklaw, please. I *can't* do this."

"Sure you can, honey," Ma replied with a finality that made Jessica's stomach sink.

As the younger men grinned at one another, Gabe turned to Cole. "How 'bout you, big brother? You gonna compete?"

Cole sneered at Jessica. "When I want a *lady*, I don't play games."

His words brought a chill to Jessica's spine and a hot bloom to her cheeks. How she'd love to throttle the beast!

"Yippee!" cried Gabe. "Now there's more of her to go around."

As Gabe's brothers guffawed, Ma charged forward and boxed his ears. "What do you mean, more of her to go around?"

Gabe cowered. "Ma, I just meant—"

"I know what you meant, you bangtailed weasel, and I'm warning you for the last time to mind your manners. Now all of you boys get out of here and go do your chores, while I show the lady the house."

The boys rushed off, while Cole stood his ground and continued to glower at the women. Leading Jessica away, Ma jerked a thumb back toward her eldest son. "Don't mind him, honey. He's the strong, silent type."

"I've noticed," Jessica replied ruefully.

Ma wrapped an arm around Jessica's waist. "Come on in, and we'll git you settled. What did you say your name was?"

"Jessica Garrett."

Ma clucked again. "Well, Miss Jessie, my land, are you dusty. What them boys do to you, anyhow? Drag you through the dirt?"

"Something like that."

"I'll thrash 'em till they squeal. How 'bout we fix you up with a nice hot bath?"

"Yes, that sounds good. But I really can't stay."

"Now, honey, don't say that. A nice hot bath and some home-cooked vittles, and you'll be warming up to the idea of sticking 'round these parts for a spell."

"Well, maybe . . . "

On the front porch, Ma paused to regard Jessica wistfully. "Law, you're a beauteous 'un. We'll put a shine on that curly auburn hair, and some pink in them dainty cheeks." To Jessica's astonishment, the woman sniffed and even wiped away a tear with her sleeve. "I'm so glad you're here. Been right lonesome for me. You see, I ain't never had me no daughter. Only five boys, and all of 'em wilder than the devil's tail. Hell, I can't wait to sew you up some frilly new duds."

Jessica started to protest, but found she didn't have the heart to. Much as she bristled at her current bizarre plight, she couldn't help feeling touched by the woman's obvious emotion and sincerity. "How kind of you," she murmured.

As the two women headed inside, Jessica dared a last glance behind her to see Cole Reklaw still watching her. She stifled a shiver. His dark gaze was so intense that she half expected to go up in flames. . . .

Chapter Five

This woman was trouble.

That was Cole Reklaw's thought as he stood lounging against a tree, chewing on a stalk of grass and scowling at the bag of trinkets Billy had taken from the stage passengers. He pulled out the lady's ring with its odd numbers. 1994. He fought a smile as he recalled Wesley suggesting that perhaps this was the number of notches on the little lady's bedpost.

1994. The numbers confounded him. They for sure couldn't represent a date, since this was the year 1888. He held the ring up to the light and could just make out some additional small lettering: "University of New Mexico." Hmmmm. Cole knew of no such institution in New Mexico Territory, but then he was neither a widely traveled, nor a widely read, man. And hadn't the lady said she was a schoolmarm somewhere else—Pawnee College, wasn't it? Another school he'd never heard of. Plus, both she and the sheriff had claimed she was on her way to teach at Mariposa.

This little lady got around quite a bit, he mused cynically.

Who was this mysterious female and where had she come from? The fact that she'd been in Lila Lullaby's old parlor wagon had really perplexed him. Cole had known Lila well—too well, in fact—before she'd been run out of Colorado City, and seeing her old bordello wagon had stirred up mixed emotions within him.

As for the lady, she was quite a study in contradictions. She'd been dressed like a schoolmarm and was obviously well educated. But she had a peculiar manner of talking, had blessed them out with all the vehemence of a cathouse madame, and had met his eye with a boldness that should have scandalized any proper lady.

Whoever she was, Cole felt uneasy about her being here. Damn her for goading him into throwing her over his horse in the first place. Kidnapping her had been a mistake. She'd get the boys all worked up for no good cause, maybe even turn them against one another.

Hell, she already had *him* all riled up. She was a pretty one, with that curly auburn hair, those large, fiery green eyes, and that sassy, full-lipped mouth. He smiled as he recalled her feistiness when he'd brought her home. Remembering her lush curves wiggling against him, her derriere bobbing so enticingly to the rhythm of his horse, he felt himself growing hot. And he had only himself to blame for putting himself within temptation's reach.

Cole uttered a curse under his breath and spat out the stalk of grass. What had come over him that he'd allow a female to beguile him? As head of the outlaw gang, he could ill afford such luxuries as love and marriage, and he had little need of women beyond the satisfaction of his physical needs. Besides, he'd learned long ago that women weren't to be trusted. They took your money, lied to you, stole your heart with their feminine wiles, then betrayed you. The last female Cole had taken a cotton to had seduced him with her siren's body, then turned him in to the law for the reward money. It had taken all the boys' efforts to bust him out of the calaboose and save him from a certain necktie party.

No, women weren't to be trusted. He and his brothers were about a dangerous business, and they couldn't afford a potential traitor in their midst.

The problem was, his ma had taken a real shine to the lady, and so had his brothers. Cole's ma had never had a daughter, and had always wanted one; she'd also lost two good husbands at the Aspen Gulch Mines, and Cole hated to bring her another disappointment.

So they were stuck with the lady, at least for now, and that left it all to him. As the eldest, it was obviously his call to protect his family from the little temptress.

Perhaps it was time he had a word with the "lady" and set her in her place. . . .

Jessica felt rather risqué, bathing in an old-fashioned tin bathtub on the back porch. But Ma had assured her no one would dare bother her here. Though Mrs. Reklaw had taken all of Jessica's clothing to be washed, a wrapper and towel were laid out within reach on a slat-back rocker.

The porch was enclosed on two sides by exterior walls, while a row of trellises covered the third, so Jessica was afforded some measure of privacy. And she had to admit it was pleasant and picturesque here. The aroma from the lavender soap was sweet, as was the smell of honeysuckle wafting from the trellises. It felt good to cleanse the dust from her body, even though the tub was small, forcing her to sit with her knees cramped up against her chest, and the bathwater was tepid rather than hot.

Jessica shared the porch with a gray calico cat, a female by the look of her enlarged teats, who sat grooming herself nearby on a large stump of wood. Beyond the porch stretched a backyard lined with clotheslines, with sheets and towels blowing in the breeze; in the distance loomed misty blue mountains. Jessica couldn't recall the last time she'd bathed with a mountain view.

Still, the entire setting filled her with a sense of unreality. Ever since these "outlaws" had captured her, she'd seen no trace of the twentieth century. There was certainly no indoor plumbing, evidenced by the very tub in which she sat, and by the fact that Ma had filled it by hauling water in an old tin bucket.

Jessica had also been required to use an antique "chamber pot" after undressing in Ma Reklaw's bedroom. That particular boudoir had been really quaint, with its iron bedstead with feathered tick and lacy Victorian linens, its old-fashioned dressing table with beveled mirror, not to mention the antique china accessories laid out everywhere, the pomander balls in a homey wicker basket near the hearth.

Where *was* she? Were these people members of some obscure religious sect that forbade any accoutrements of the twentieth century? Or, even more horrifying, was she no longer *in* the twentieth century? Was she stranded far away from her family, her friends, from the very life she'd known before?

She carefully considered what had happened to her. One minute, she'd been riding along in the stage with her colleagues; the next, she'd hit her head and poked herself with the cameo, and everything had changed. Could the cameo have possessed magical properties? She'd have to examine it carefully when she returned to Ma's room. She smiled as she recalled that Sleeping Beauty had pricked her finger on a spindle, then had fallen asleep for a hundred years.

Of course, it hadn't been her *finger* she'd pricked.

Jessica was still smiling over this, running the soap over her arm, when abruptly the back door of the house banged open and Cole Reklaw stepped out.

Jessica recoiled in horror. Wide-eyed, she covered her bosom with her arms and watched him advance with all the arrogance of the cock of the walk.

"What do you think you're doing?" she demanded hoarsely, heart pounding frantically.

Cole didn't answer right away. With a brazenness that infuriated her, he simply strode closer, appearing daunting as hell with the intent gleam in his eyes, the powerful rhythms of his body, and especially the way his jeans molded to his muscled thighs and to the male bulge between them that was as audacious as this outlaw's entire manner.

At last he paused before her, shoving his thumbs into his pockets. "I'll be having a word with you, lady."

"The hell you will! You get out of here!" Jessica retorted. "Can't you see I'm taking a bath?"

He looked her over with an insolence that made her blush deepen. "Yeah. I can see."

"Get out of here or I'll scream."

"Go ahead. Scream," he taunted.

"Your ma will . . . "

Jessica's voice faded into a creak as she watched Cole lazily plop himself into the rocker next to her. Appalled, she watched him prop a dusty boot against her tub. Heavens, the big lug was sitting on her towel, her wrapper. The only way she could escape would be to run past him stark naked.

"My ma is out butchering chickens for your supper and she won't hear," Cole drawled, indolently lacing his fingers behind his neck. "She gets right worked up when she butchers hens. Usually sings all six stanzas of 'When the Roll Is Called Up Yonder,' as I recollect."

Jessica was mortified by his gall, his insulting familiarity. She shoved his boot off the tub. "I don't care. Get out of here, or I'll—"

He sat up straight. "You'll what, sugar? Pop up out of that tub and slap my face? Now, that's a sight I'd purely love to see."

Jessica was too mortified to respond.

From his pocket, Cole drew out a cheroot and a match. "So, what's your name, honey?"

"That's none of your business."

Striking the match on his boot heel, he slowly lit his smoke. "Now, that's a peculiar thing to say to a man while you're sitting in front of him buck naked in a bathtub."

"Jessica Garrett!" she all but spat.

"Well, Miss Jessie, I hear you're the new schoolmarm," he remarked, blowing a smoke ring at her. "What would you like to teach me?"

Jessica was so livid, she almost did bolt out of the tub. "First, to put out that disgusting cigar," she shot back. "Secondly, to get the hell off this porch."

He leaned toward her. "I'm not going anywhere, lady, so you'd best get used to it."

"You're a coward to wait until I'm alone and defenseless—"

Again Jessica's words were cut short as Cole abruptly stood, his menacing six-foot form looming just inches away from her—though she noted with satisfaction that he dropped his cheroot onto the porch and snuffed it out beneath the toe of his boot.

"So I'm a coward, am I?" he asked softly. "Lady, you sure are full of prunes, a female alone in her bath with a man who is known to be . . . well, right ruthless."

Jessica trembled in anger. "Oh! If you assault me—"

"Assault?" he repeated in disbelief. "Lady, you've already assaulted my dignity three ways to sundown, and that's why I've come here to have a word with you." Stubbornly, he crossed his arms over his chest. "And I'm not leaving till I do."

Jessica could not believe she was having this absurd conversation with this infuriating man. "Very well, then. Have your word. Then get out of my sight."

Instead of lighting into her as Jessica would have expected, he just scowled, appearing at a loss. Then the mama cat meowed plaintively, breaking the tension. Cole strode over to the cat, clucked softly to her, and stroked her ears. At once the female stood, shamelessly rubbed against Cole's thigh, and purred loudly. He stroked her flank and continued to coo to her.

Jessica's mouth went dry at the sight of this hardened outlaw displaying such tenderness. It occurred to her that a man who could behave so gently toward a cat couldn't be all bad. She dismissed the notion at once as being not the least bit helpful to her in her current plight.

Yet the sight of him petting the cat still fascinated her, and she also realized that, since this man held all the cards, it might behoove her to be civil.

She cleared her throat. "What's the cat's name?"

"Jezebel." Mischief shone in Cole's eyes as he gazed up at Jessica. "She likes catting around, and comes through with a litter at least twice a year. Got the latest batch hidden under the porch somewhere."

"Poor thing."

"What do you mean, poor thing? Isn't that a female's lot?"

Jessica harrumphed. "You would think that, like some throwback to the nineteenth century."

He appeared perplexed. "Lady, the last time I looked, this *is* the nineteenth century. It may be the year 1888, but we haven't passed the century mark yet."

Jessica was speechless. *It may be the year 1888!* Heavens, the man *must* be joking, but, with a sick, sinking feeling, Jessica somehow knew he wasn't. What on earth had happened to her? Had she died? Or was she really living in the year 1888 now?

Whatever had happened to her, it was obvious Cole Reklaw *believed* they were living in the year 1888, and there was little point arguing with him about it, or trying to convince him that she was from another time.

In the tense silence, Cole strode back toward Jessica. Then he stared again. Long and hard. Much as Jessica was outraged, she also felt extremely vulnerable, totally exposed to the whims of this powerful man. She knew he couldn't really see much of her body, not with her legs folded up against her chest as they were. But the fact that they both were well aware of her nakedness put her at a distinct disadvantage. Especially since she sensed Cole was at last gearing up to give her that promised piece of his mind.

But again, he surprised her, murmuring, "You know, you make a pretty picture sitting there, your hair all bunched up on your head and your cheeks all rosy."

At last righteous indignation overcame Jessica's fear. "Don't you dare try to compliment me, you snake. State your business."

His gaze hardened. "All right, lady, I will."

"Well?"

He shifted from boot to boot. "The truth is, I don't like you being here, even though Ma's taken a shine to you—"

"You don't like?" she mocked. "You and your brothers are the bullies who brought me here against my will. In fact, you're the jackass who threw me across his horse."

Cole was scowling at her ill-advised epithet. "That was a mistake."

She made a sound of disbelief. "Your humility astounds me."

"Yeah, and if it were up to me, I'd pitch your butt right back into the nearest arroyo," he shot back. "But the boys and Ma want you here, so I reckon I'll allow you to stay awhile."

"How generous of you. But actually, I'd much prefer to leave."

"So you can turn us over to the law?" he scoffed. "Sorry, sugar, but you don't have a say about that right now."

She glared.

He cast her a stern look. "Don't you go putting on airs and acting peeved. We both know you've got yourself a sweet deal here."

"A *sweet* deal?" she repeated, incredulous.

"Yeah. All you have to do is to bat those big green eyes of yours, and you'll have yourself a husband and a home for the taking."

Jessica was incredulous. "What gives with you people? Why do you assume every woman wants a husband and a home?"

He shook a finger at her. "You just hush up and listen. I want you to know I'm wise to you and your feminine wiles, and I don't trust you. If I get any hint you're playing loose with my brothers' affections, or giving them over to the law, I'll shoot you in your tracks. So I'm warning you to mind your p's and q's while you're here."

Jessica was fed up with him. "Thanks so much for the lovely lecture. Now go to hell."

He lunged closer, hovering over her, and spoke in a harsh whisper. "I'm warning you. And I've had about all the lip from you I can abide. Any more sass, and I'm gonna haul you up out of that tub and blister your butt, naked or not. You got that straight, lady?"

"You wouldn't dare," she raged.

"Wouldn't I?"

"Your ma would kill you."

He straightened and assumed a defiant stance. "I'm not afraid of her."

"Tell that to her broom," Jessica retorted. "Much as you and your brothers try to act like he-men, I've already learned that in the Reklaw household, 'Ma' is *the law*."

He fought a grudging smile. "Maybe I just don't cotton to shooting ladies."

"I'm so relieved to hear it."

"Don't be."

"Why not?"

His handsome, arrogant face again loomed close to her. " 'Cause I'm not convinced you're a lady, for all your stuck-up sass. I think maybe you really are some line gal, down on your luck and putting on airs. I'm not even sure you're good enough for my baby brothers."

"Oh!" Furious, Jessica slapped him.

Cole caught her wrist. Too late, she watched the anger flare in his dark eyes. Oh, Lord. He would kill her now!

Instead, he leaned over and boldly captured her lips. Jessica's strangled protest died away in her throat. Cole's kiss was hard and hot, unexpectedly provocative. And sexy as hell. When she tried to pull away, he simply caught her nape with a strong hand and continued the sensual punishment. The beast. He knew she couldn't really fight him, naked as she was.

Then abruptly he changed tactics and gentled his kiss, teasing her tongue with his own. Heavens, this was worse. A helpless shudder seized Jessica, and she clenched and unclenched her fists. His tongue pushed deeper, mating with her own, and she was left reeling.

Oh, he was ruthless, brazenly arousing her with his kiss. She hated him, but hated her traitorous body's response even more. She could feel the ecstatic singing in her blood, the tautening of her nipples, and the way desire flooded deep inside her belly. He left her no pride.

Then, just as abruptly as he had begun, he pulled away, and stared into her dazed face, his own eyes dark with desire. "Who knows, lady? I might just keep you for myself."

Jessica burned to claw his eyes out, but knew if he retaliated again, she'd be lost. "Will you please get out of my sight?" she demanded, voice trembling.

He straightened. "My pleasure, lady."

He strode for the door, and Jessica fought a groan at the view of long, beautifully muscled legs and too-cute male butt. She couldn't resist a final volley. "So when did you decide you wanted to compete?"

He whirled, and his voice came deep and husky. "When you rubbed against me on my horse. You made me hot. Made me wonder what you'd be like bobbing away to the rhythm of a man."

"You are a brute."

"Yeah," he acknowledged proudly. "And you'd best remember it."

"I thought you said you don't like playing games—"

He strode to her side again, pressing his hands on either side of the tub and leaning close, so close that she could see the sexy whiskers along his jaw, could smell his scent, and could feel the heat of his stare. "That's right, I don't play games, lady. I'm deadly serious. But I like contests. And I like winning."

Then, for the first time, Cole Reklaw grinned. Complete with dimples, wickedly gleaming eyes, and a flash of perfect white teeth. It was devastating. And even sexier than his brazen kiss.

Then he was gone, and Jessica was burning. Indeed, she was amazed to see no steam rise from her tepid bathwater.

Chapter Six

Jessica grabbed her wrapper, hastily donned it, and dashed back inside the house, entering Ma's bedroom through the door connecting it to the porch. She stood pressed against the antique armoire, breathing hard, cheeks still hot.

Oh, the nerve of that man, coming out on the porch and ogling her in her naked state, lecturing her on how to behave—as if *he* were a paragon of virtue!—then audaciously kissing her! She yearned to throttle the beast—but even more, she burned from his maddening kiss.

She felt giddy, unsettled, confused, and still couldn't make sense of anything—her apparent journey across time, the five Old West outlaws who had captured her, this primitive house they had brought her to. Where *was* she?

Jessica walked over to the dresser and picked up the old-fashioned cameo which had stuck her right before she'd made her remarkable journey. She held it up to the light, but the mysterious flickers she'd spotted before were absent now. Nonetheless, she opened it and experimentally pricked her finger, only to wince. If she'd hoped to be released from time-travel purgatory, she was sorely disappointed.

The sound of a plaintive *mrooow* distracted her, and Jessica turned to see the mama cat standing on the edge of the bed, gazing at Jessica with large green eyes, back arched expectantly as she waited to be petted.

Jessica smiled. "Well, hello, Jezebel."

Setting down the cameo, she walked over and stroked the cat; it purred and licked her hand. The contact with the animal somehow comforted and soothed her, and she scooped the feline up into her arms.

"Where are you keeping those kittens of yours, eh?" Jessica asked. "You know, Cole seems to think you and I share just about the same morals."

The cat seemed pleased at this, from her loud purring.

"Hey, want to explore the house, Jezebel?"

The cat *mrooowed* in the affirmative. Avoiding the bedroom directly ahead of her—which Ma had already informed her was Cole's room—Jessica exited through a side door and emerged into the long central hallway with its planked floors, braided rugs, and pier table near the front door.

The farmhouse was divided into two wings flanking either side of the hallway. Behind Jessica were stacked the two bedrooms; ahead stretched the parlor and kitchen.

She entered the parlor first. Though the small, square room was neat, it was crudely furnished with a ratty horsehair settee, two wing chairs with cracked leather upholstery, and a scarred Windsor rocker. A stone fireplace filled one wall, with two Winchester rifles hanging above it.

On a tea table obviously well scarred by men's boots were scattered a few books and journals. Jessica eagerly perused them, and was amazed to find several dime novels in a series entitled "The Wild West," as well as a *Farmer's Almanac* from the year 1887! A shudder swept her.

"Any idea where I really am, Jezebel?" Jessica muttered. " 'Cause I've got no clue."

Again, a contented purring was her only answer. But increasingly Jessica doubted that these sorts of accoutrements were merely props in some elaborate play staged to deceive her.

At the back of the room, an archway connected the parlor to the kitchen, and Jessica stepped down into the large stone-floored room, which was the same width as the parlor but almost twice as long. At once the cat struggled to get down; Jessica set her on the floor, and Jezebel bounded over to lap milk from a saucer.

Straightening, Jessica found her senses were besieged by a potpourri of smells: bacon fat emanating from the cast-iron stove; garlic, chives, and other spices spilling their pungent aromas from the drying rack overhead; newly cut mint and parsley adding dashes of freshness from the sideboard.

The room itself amazed her, from its huge pine trestle table with benches along the sides and chairs at either end, to the quaint pie safe with tin doors punched to admit air, to the antique pine sideboard crammed with blue pottery depicting Currier and Ives scenes.

Jessica half jumped at the sound of the back door creaking open. Then with relief she watched Ma enter bearing an enamel tub filled with several raw chickens.

"Ah, there you are, missy," Ma said, lumbering over to the sideboard and setting down her load. "Enjoy your bath?"

Jessica considering telling Ma about Cole's treachery, then thought better of it. "Yes. Quite pleasant."

Ma raised an eyebrow. "You know you shouldn't be gallivanting about the house in that risqué getup."

"But you took my clothes," Jessica protested.

Ma chuckled. "Yep, everything is washed and hung up, though I must say you have some mighty peculiar undergarments, missy. Is that what you womenfolk wear in the cities these days?"

"Er—yes," Jessica stammered.

"Well, what have times come to? Anyhow, everything should be dry before dinner."

"That's good. Thanks."

"You thirsty?"

"Actually, yes."

Ma gestured at a glass pitcher on the sideboard. "I'll get you some tea."

Realizing Ma's hands were doubtless still filthy from butchering hens, Jessica hastily offered, "No, I'll do it."

"Suit yourself. I'll get the grease to heating."

Jessica went to the sideboard. Rummaging in the cabinet above, she found a small, clean Mason jar, filled it with tea, and added a fresh mint sprig. Turning toward Ma, she grimaced at the sight of the woman ladling a huge chunk of white lard into a cast-iron frying pan.

"Have you—um—had your cholesterol checked recently?" she remarked.

"Huh?" asked an obviously befuddled Ma.

"I take it we're having fried chicken for dinner?"

"Yep." Ma wiped her hands on her filthy apron. "But first I'd best get you settled, missy, before one of the boys comes in and spots you in that scandalous getup."

Jessica took a sip of tea. "Good point."

"Come along. I'll show you where you'll be bunking."

Jessica followed Ma back through the parlor, into the hallway, and across to the front bedroom. She paused in the doorway of the pleasant room with its braided rug and pine furnishings. "Wait—isn't this Cole's room?"

Ma was already at the four-poster bed, pulling off the pillows and quilts. "Not anymore. I already met up with my eldest in the yard and gave him the news. That varmint kidnapped you, so he can give up his room for a spell and sleep with his brothers in the bunkhouse."

Jessica chuckled. "Sounds like a fitting punishment."

"Missy, would you fetch me a set of clean sheets?" Ma asked, huffing away as she pulled off more bedding. "I recollect there's one in the bottom drawer of the bureau."

"Sure." Jessica crossed the room, noting a pair of Cole's dusty boots sitting beneath the front window, his hat hung on a peg near the bureau. Setting her tea down on the dresser scarf, she leaned over, opened the bottom drawer, and pulled out a set of white, embroidered sheets scented with spicy sachet.

She crossed over and handed them to Ma. "Here you are. May I help you?"

"Sure."

Jessica watched Ma plump up the tick, sending feathers into the air. Then the two women stretched the bottom sheet over the mattress and tucked it in. They were unfolding the top sheet when Jessica heard a male throat being cleared. Both women turned to see Cole lounging in the doorway, his wickedly glinting eyes focused on Jessica. Jessica felt herself blushing at the sight of him, especially as she recalled their earlier intimacies, and quickly ascertained from his expression that his thoughts were equally decadent. Her fingers automatically moved to the top button of her wrapper, which was heavy muslin but hardly the stoutest covering.

Ma spoke first, her tone indignant. "What are you doing here, you rascal? Can't you see the lady is in a state of disarray?"

Cole chuckled, his intent gaze still focused on Jessica. "Yeah, I can see. But since you've banned me from my own room, can't I at least fetch my clothes?"

Ma waved him in. "Go ahead, varmint. But rattle your hocks. After that, this room is off-limits, you hear?"

"Oh, yes, ma'am, I hear," Cole drawled, striding arrogantly toward the dresser. He paused to regard Jessica with amusement. "My, but you scrub up nice, Miss Jessie. Enjoy your bath?"

As Jessica glared, Ma scolded, "Hush up that scandalous talk! And who told you the lady had a bath?"

Cole jerked a thumb toward Jessica. "Isn't it obvious?

63

Her skin's all rosy . . . " He paused, deliberately sniffing the air. "And I can smell your lavender soap on her."

Ma shook a finger at her son. "Enough! You and your no-good brothers have already tried my patience sorely, so don't think I won't fetch my broom again and give you your comeuppance. Quit sniffing the lady like a tomcat on the prowl and gather up your things."

"Yes, ma'am."

Tossing a last leer at Jessica, Cole busied himself at the bureau, while Ma and Jessica finished making up the bed. Smoothing down the quilt, Jessica turned to see Cole holding a large stack of folded shirts, denim pants, and longjohns, and once again staring at her boldly.

"Aren't you finished?" she asked him irritably.

"That depends," came his cocky reply.

Before Jessica could respond, Ma waved her arms. "Get out of here, you devil, and leave the lady in peace. I reckon she'll want a nap before dinner."

Cole solemnly winked at Jessica. "Yeah, she does look done in. But shouldn't I stay and show her the most comfortable spot on the bed?"

Both women gasped. Luckily, Ma was the first to hurl a pillow at Cole, or Jessica would have. As for Cole—the exasperating rogue merely ducked the missile and dashed out the door, laughing all the while.

After Ma left, Jessica took a nap on the downy feather tick. Although the sheets were clean, she could still smell Cole's essence in the bed—the scent of his skin, his hair—and this sensual presence, as well as memories of their heated kiss, rose to torment her, especially as she recalled his offering to show her the softest spot on the bed. She knew exactly what the scamp had in mind—how he would love to find that spot somewhere deep inside *herself* as he drove into her.

Oh, what had this man done to her? Her thoughts were indecent! Jessica tossed about and punched up her pillow.

What tortured her the most was the daunting truth that Cole Reklaw would doubtless be a wonderful lover, his approach as hot, raw, and virile as his searing kiss. And unfortunately, great sex wasn't exactly an everyday occurrence in Jessica's life of dull academia—in fact, it had been years since she'd experienced anything close to having her socks knocked off. If one kiss from Cole Reklaw could rattle her world so thoroughly, she couldn't even imagine the upheaval to her universe of spending a night in bed with this sexy man.

Good heavens, why was she even thinking such a thing? Giving in to Cole would be a disastrous decision, even if it was what her treacherous libido craved the most!

When Jessica awakened, her clean undergarments and starched, pressed gown were laid out at the foot of the bed. Smelling fried chicken, she realized she was famished, and remembered that she hadn't eaten since this morning—whenever *that* had been. For that matter, it was possible she hadn't eaten for over a hundred years. Shuddering at the mind-boggling possibility, she quickly dressed and combed her hair.

When Jessica stepped into the kitchen, she was literally besieged by suitors and the smell of bay rum. *Pretty boys straight in a row*, she thought ruefully as Billy, Gabe, Wes, and Luke all rushed up to greet her. To a man they were well scrubbed, in clean shirts, with neatly parted, gleaming hair and wide grins splitting their faces. All four bore gifts.

"Well, howdy, ma'am, don't you make a purty picture?" declared Billy, thrusting a bouquet under Jessica's nose.

Laughing, she accepted the spray of black-eyed susans, purple gentians, and blue columbine. "Why, thank you kindly, sir. These are lovely."

"Picked 'em myself," Billy informed her proudly, rocking on his boot heels. "Just for my lady's pleasure."

Jessica was on the verge of thanking him again when Wesley, gleaming like a new penny, thrust a small tin into her free hand.

"Here, ma'am, have some horehound candy. I've only sampled three pieces."

"Why, thanks, Wesley."

Luke took his turn, dangling a length of satiny green before Jessica's eyes. "Here, ma'am, have this purty hair ribbon. I picked it out to favor those comely eyes of yours."

Before Jessica could thank him, Ma complained loudly from the stove, "You mean you stole it from my sewing box, you slimy weasel."

At this, Wesley's brothers roared with laughter, while he colored. "Ma, please! You ain't got no call to go humiliating me that way!"

Wiping her hands on her apron, Ma stepped forward and flashed Jessica a smile. "Well, don't you look purty all starched up, Miss Jessie. Here, I'll put those in some water for you."

Jessica handed over the bouquet. "Thank you, Mrs. Reklaw."

Now Gabe strode up, extending a crude, yellowish lump toward Jessica. "Ma'am, would you care for a bar of lye soap?"

At this rather bizarre offering, Jessica giggled, and the other brothers all but split their sides laughing. Ma stormed back up, shaking a finger at Gabe. "What do you mean, you devil, offering the lady a bar of soap after she's already gone and scrubbed herself? Don't you have no idea how downright insulting that is?"

Gabe blushed miserably, his gaze darting from Ma to Jessica. "Ma, I meant no disrespect toward the lady. Only you told us to bring her some ditties, and Billy, Wes, and Luke already stole everything that weren't nailed down 'round here. This is the onliest gift I could find—leastwise, till us boys go to town."

"Well, I say a polecat has better manners," declared Ma.

"Really, it's fine," Jessica reassured Ma. "I'm honored to have the soap, Gabe."

Ma harrumphed and returned to the stove, while Gabe grinned and dropped the lump into Jessica's hand.

Now Luke dashed over to the huge table already set for seven. "Ma'am, may I pull out this bench for you?"

"Why, certainly, Luke," Jessica replied, starting forward.

Then she staggered as Billy, Gabe, and Wes all dashed into her path, all but knocking her over as they confronted Luke.

"Hey, Luke, it ain't fair *you* get to pull out the lady's bench," Billy protested.

"Yeah, it ain't fair," seconded Gabe.

But Luke stood his ground with arms akimbo and chin held high. "Too bad. I asked the lady first."

"Then Gabe and me get to sit by her," argued Billy.

"Yeah," said Gabe.

"What about me?" complained Wesley.

"Heck, I reckon you can squat by the lady's feet and lick up her crumbs," taunted Billy, prompting more mirth.

Jessica was starting toward the bench again when she spotted Cole standing in the far corner, gazing at her with sin and mischief in his dark eyes. She felt a hot blush creeping up her cheeks as she again recalled his kiss, and the brazen way he'd flirted with her in his room afterward. Lord! One would think she was a quivering virgin from the way she was responding to him! She hastily tore her gaze away and primly sat down, smoothing her skirts and murmuring a thank you to Luke. At once, Billy and Gabe vaulted into their places beside her on the bench, almost tipping it over in the process. She glared at both, but the rascals only grinned.

Wesley and Luke sat down on the bench across from her, and Cole took his seat at one end of the table. Then

Ma began bringing food to the table—a large platter heaped with a mountain of luscious-smelling fried chicken, a huge bowl of mashed potatoes, a tureen brimming with buttery cream gravy, plates of corn and biscuits. Jessica found her mouth was watering uncontrollably, and she smiled at the boys' ravenous expressions.

Before Ma was even in her chair, Billy reached out to grab a drumstick. Ma promptly slapped his hand. "Mind your manners, you little snot. Have ya already forgot we got a lady present?"

"Sorry, ma'am," Billy told Jessica sheepishly.

After Ma sat down, all waited in silent anticipation, until she nodded to Wes. "Wesley, return thanks."

While Billy and Gabe regarded each other in amazement, Wesley's mouth dropped open. "Ma, you know we don't ever—"

"I said say grace, you rascal."

"Yes, ma'am." But Wesley still appeared at a loss.

Jessica bowed her head to hide her amusement. She caught sight of Ma waving her arms. "Bow your heads, all of you heathens."

"Yes, ma'am," answered the men.

Jessica waited with the others, until Wesley loudly cleared his throat. "Dear Lord, we thank you for this here grub. And we especially thank you for this fine lady you brung us. Just make sure she marries me—all right, Lord?"

At this audacious pronouncement, pandemonium erupted at the table. Billy's head shot up first. "Hey, no fair!" he protested to Wesley. "You can't pray just for yourself like that."

"Yeah, that's taking the Almighty's name in vain," put in Gabe.

"Yeah, to be fair, you gotta pray that *all* of us gets to wed her," concluded Luke with an impassioned nod.

Then the boys flinched as Ma's fist slammed down on the table, rattling the dishes. "Hush up, all of you, before

I lose what little religion I got left! You boys is bickering worse than a passel of females fighting over a new bonnet. How dare you interrupt Wesley a'prayin'? And Wesley, that was dealing from the bottom of the deck if I ever heard it, trying to hoodwink the Almighty, no less. Any more of that, and you're out of the contest."

"Yes, ma'am," said a much sobered Wesley. Hastily, he finished. "Thank you, Lord. Amen."

"Amen," intoned Ma.

For a few moments the family passed the food and ate in silence. Jessica couldn't believe how delicious and fresh everything tasted. She devoured two pieces of chicken, a large helping of mashed potatoes, and two gravy-soaked biscuits. Occasionally she caught Cole watching her with wry amusement. Then she observed Luke and Wes snickering to one another.

She turned to Luke. "Am I doing something wrong?"

He chuckled. "You know, sugar, you ain't exactly being hanged in the morning."

Jessica was perplexed. "What do you mean?"

Grinning, Wesley explained, "It's just, we ain't used to seeing no ladies that eat like lumberjacks."

Ma harrumphed. "How many *ladies* have you two buzzards seen, anyhow?"

"We seen a few in Colorado City," asserted Luke. "And they always pick at their food like puny little kittens."

"Well, the *ladies* you two seen sure don't have hogs to slop or wood to chop at home," Ma scolded. "Rolling around in the hay with you heathens don't wear 'em out overly, I reckon."

Shame-faced, the men fell silent. Jessica lifted her napkin to hide her amusement.

A moment later, Gabe cleared his throat. "So, Miss Jessie, where are you from?"

The question washed Jessica with a chill. Where *was* she from? Perhaps the truth—or a variation thereof—would suffice.

"I'm from Greeley," she answered.

"Greeley, eh?" asked Billy as he chomped on a drumstick. "You're a fer piece from home, ain't you, sugar? You got kin there?"

Jessica felt awash in sadness as she thought of her family—wherever they were—and realized she might never see them again. "Yes, a mother and father. An older brother."

The boys exchanged worried looks. "You look right melancholy, ma'am," put in Luke. "Are you missing your kin?"

Jessica felt a new shiver course down her spine. "Of course I am—and they'll miss me as well."

"Will they send someone after you?" inquired Wesley.

"Perhaps." Sternly, Jessica added, "You know, you men really should release me."

Billy glanced nervously at Cole, and he spoke to Jessica with quiet authority. "But didn't you say you came out here to teach school, Miss Jessie?"

Jessica felt flustered. She had no idea why she was really here! She had only played along with what she'd heard the sheriff say back at the stagecoach. "Er—yes, I suppose I did say that."

"Then your people won't be expecting to hear from you any time soon, now will they?" he went on with impeccable logic.

"I suppose not," she conceded.

"Then why should we let you go?" he pursued.

"Perhaps because it's the decent thing to do?" she snapped.

Ma reached out to pat Jessica's hand. "Now, honey. Don't go getting yourself all worked up again. We'll be taking good care of you, you'll see. Why, when things settle down and you marry up with one of my boys, we'll even let you send your people a letter."

"Thanks," she muttered frozenly. "I can't wait."

Gabe leaned toward Jessica with a grin. "Speaking of

marriage, have you decided yet which one of us you favor?"

Even as Ma would have protested, Cole stepped in. "Hey, boys, she's not just picking out a new pair of dancing slippers. Give the lady some time."

Jessica regarded Cole coolly. "Thanks for defending me, Mr. Reklaw, but you're still assuming a lot. As I mentioned to your mother this afternoon, I'm not sure I want to marry at all—much less, one of you five."

"One of us *four*," corrected Billy. "Cole ain't competing."

Jessica flashed Cole a nasty smile. "Well, he could have fooled me."

Cole laughed heartily while his brothers glowered with suspicion. "Cole, have you been a'sparkin' Miss Jessie behind our backs?" demanded Gabe.

"Would I do that?" he countered innocently.

"Sure as Sunday," asserted Luke.

"Yeah, in the blinking of a hog's eye," added Gabe.

Cole only chuckled.

Meanwhile, Billy flashed Jessica his most winsome smile. "Ma'am, please, you must marry up with one of us. I promise we'll treat you just like a princess."

"Yeah, we'll even buy you your own mule if you'd like one," put in Gabe.

As male chuckles swept the table, Wesley snorted a laugh. "Gabe, have you been eating loco weed or something? What would a lady want with a mule?"

Luke elbowed Wesley. "Well, she could use that there soap Gabe gave her to scrub it."

The men had another gut-splitting laugh at Gabe's expense. Then Ma beat her fist again. "Enough of this marriage talk and sparking. Miss Jessie is right. She only just arrived here. You can't be expecting her to choose up a husband for at least a day or two."

At this pronouncement, Jessica went wide-eyed.

"And besides, Miss Jessie and I are gonna be right busy

sewing up her frilly new wardrobe," Ma continued smugly. "Why, we'll be going into town tomorrow to pick out all the fabrics and trimmings."

Luke glowered. "I don't think so, Ma. You're forgetting Miss Jessie's our prisoner. What if she gives us up to the law?"

"Miss Jessie ain't gonna do that," Ma protested. "Are you, honey?"

Jessica thought quickly. The town, wherever it was, meant possible escape. "No, of course not. My lips are sealed."

"But they're expecting her there, Ma," argued Billy. "I mean, ain't they?"

Six sets of eyes focused on Jessica; she struggled not to squirm.

"That's right," stated Luke. "Do they know your name in town, sugar?"

Jessica floundered. She had no idea how to deal with these questions. "No, I don't think so," she answered carefully.

"But how can they be expecting you, if they don't know your name?" asked a clearly perplexed Billy.

"Search me," muttered Jessica.

Billy grinned. "May I?"

Hearing Cole's insufferable chuckle, Jessica blushed, while a clearly outraged Ma tossed an ear of corn at her youngest son. "Hush up, you little toad!"

As Billy ducked the cob, Luke leaned intently toward his mother. "Ma, we still can't be sure it's safe to allow Miss Jessie to go to town."

"Yeah, she could expose us all to danger," argued Wes.

Ma appeared torn. "If she does, I'll give her a good switching."

"I won't say a word," declared Jessica. "Believe me."

Now Cole leaned forward. "Go on and take her to town, Ma. Truth to tell, if Miss Jessica should give us up, breathe even one word of our whereabouts to anyone in town, I'll be dealing with her—and it's a reckoning she won't like."

Cole's arrogant assertion made Jessica shiver, and she glared at him.

But once again his brothers weren't pleased. "How come you get to deal with her?" protested Billy.

" 'Cause I'm the eldest male in the family, and it's up to me to punish any traitors in our midst. Miss Jessie and I already have an understanding." He flashed her a lethal smile. "Don't we, sugar?"

Jessica stared daggers at him.

Gabe turned to confront his mother. "Hey, how come Cole gets to have an understanding with Miss Jessie, and reckon with her, and we don't?"

"Yeah, *I* want to reckon with her," asserted Wes.

But Ma only shook her head. "Boys, your older brother is right. It's only proper." She turned to Jessica and patted her hand. "If you betray us, honey, Cole will give you the switchin', and worse, I reckon. Won't you, son?"

"My pleasure," Cole drawled.

Jessica burned in silent outrage.

Chapter Seven

"Can I trust you to go to town with Ma tomorrow?"

Long after dinner ended, after Ma shooed the boys off to the bunkhouse, Jessica was sitting alone on the front porch swing when she heard the front door creak open, followed by Cole's deep voice. She gasped slightly as he stepped outside and slid onto the swing beside her, his weight rocking it. At once she became intensely conscious of his male scent, the heat of his body next to hers in the slight coolness of evening. She tried to scoot away, but there was no place to go.

"I didn't invite you here," she said coldly.

He shoved his boots against the floorboards, setting the swing into motion. "It's my spread, not yours, so I don't need an invite."

"It's your spread?" she asked, bemused. "Not your mother's?"

"Nope. When my pa died, it fell to me."

"Whatever. Will you leave now?"

"Nope."

She ground her teeth.

"I brought you something."

"What?"

"Here."

In the darkness, Cole took Jessica's hand, and she felt something warm and furry slide into her palm. She gasped, stroking the creature with her other hand, listening to a low purring.

"A kitten!" she cried, delighted.

"Yep, I managed to lasso one of Jezebel's latest."

Jessica held the kitten up to the moonlight; it was tiny and jet-black, with sharply pointed ears and large eyes. As she kept it aloft, it mewled pitifully. Lowering her hand, she hugged the tiny furball to her chest, feeling touched, despite herself.

"Thanks, Cole," she murmured. "She's precious. I wonder if her eyes will be yellow, or perhaps green—"

"Like yours, Miss Jessie?" he asked huskily.

Oh, he could turn a wicked phrase, making the simplest question sound sinful! Jessica's heart pounded and she felt even more rattled by his nearness.

She forced out a laugh. "So, is this *your* present for me?"

He chuckled. "Well, maybe I felt obliged to compete with my brothers a bit."

Jessica smiled at the memory. "Yes, Billy with his flowers, Wesley with his candy, Luke with his ribbon—"

"And Gabe with his soap."

They both laughed. "Yes, and offering me a mule!" Jessica declared.

Cole fell silent a moment. "I don't think a mule suits you, Miss Jessie. Matter of fact, I'd like to see you astride a palomino, riding into the wind."

The image took Jessica's breath away, conjuring a picture of the two of them riding together through a spectacular mountain pass. She forced a casual tone. "Are you offering me a horse now, Mr. Reklaw?"

He chuckled again, a low, sensual sound. "Actually,

sugar, a horse isn't quite what I've imagined offering you."

Jessica reeled. "Stop it, Cole."

"Cole," he murmured. "I like the sound of my Christian name on your lips."

"Stop tormenting me or I'll call you worse," she warned.

His lazy laugh rolled forth. "Remembering our kiss, Miss Jessie?"

"The kiss you *stole*?"

"So you are remembering it."

"Certainly not," she declared primly.

He leaned closer, and she felt his hot breath on her ear. "I think you're bluffing. And what if I call your bluff?"

Jessica jerked away. "I'd best go in now."

He grasped her wrist. "Not so fast. You haven't answered my question."

"What question?"

"Can I trust you to go into town with Ma tomorrow?"

She fell silent.

"You know she's taken quite a shine to you, wanting to make you up a new wardrobe."

"I like her, as well." Jessica sighed. "But more than that, I'd just like to leave this place—and I wish you and your brothers would simply allow me to do so."

"Don't you like us, Miss Jessie?" he teased.

"That's not my point." She gestured about them. "My heavens, I'm a captive here."

"Yeah, that's right, you're a captive," he mocked. "Sitting on the porch swing petting a kitten. Such torture."

"This is not my home," she argued. "I need to—well, be on my way."

"You mean to teach in town?"

Jessica bit her lip. She still had no idea how to answer such questions. She recovered with a bit of bravado. "My point exactly. I'm clearly wasting my time hanging around here."

"Well, sugar, I reckon we're not willing to let you go."

"I've noticed," she said tersely.

"So tell me again—can I trust you tomorrow?"

"Trust me with what?" she demanded.

"Not to run away. Not to give us up to anyone, or to let on you're expected."

She released a long breath. "You can trust me."

"I'd better be able to," he went on sternly, "because if you should betray us, break my ma's heart, even hurt her feelings, you won't like it when I'm through with you, girl."

"All right!" she cried. "You've made your feelings crystal clear."

"Not yet," he replied emphatically. "But I will."

Oh, he'd done it again, rattling her with a devilish turn of phrase. Jessica dared not speak.

Quietly, he continued. "Like it or not, for now, you're one of us, Jessie. And I demand absolute loyalty."

Unsteadily, she asked, "Look, why are you making such a big deal of this?"

"Big deal?" he repeated, sounding confused.

"Why are you turning this into a federal case? Didn't I say I'll keep mum?"

"Why?" he repeated tensely. "Because if you betray us, we could all be hanged. That answer your question?"

Jessica was growing exasperated. "You really overestimate me as a Mata Hari. I don't even know where I am, who I'm supposed to be."

His voice took on a hard edge. "Then you're not expected in town?"

Jessica groaned. She kept putting her foot in her mouth. Sure, she was confused—damn confused—but that was no excuse to dig her own grave.

When she didn't respond, he drawled cynically, "I thought that was a lot of hokum you spouted at dinner, about being expected in town but no one there knowing your name."

Again she didn't reply.

77

"Tell me the truth now," he ordered, his voice growing heated. "Don't make me find out on my own, or you'll be sorry. Are you expected or not?"

Jessica expelled a sharp breath. "All right, damn it, I'm not expected in town. Are you satisfied now?"

Cole's eyes blazed in the darkness. "Then you lied?"

"Well . . . let's say I played along."

He grasped her chin in his hand and regarded her sternly. "Quit playing with *me*, and tell the damn truth. Who are you really? And where are you from?"

The explosive seconds ticked away. Jessica had no idea what to tell Cole. Should she say she was from the year 1999, and she strongly suspected she'd somehow traveled back in time? Surely he'd never believe that! She wasn't even sure she believed it herself. But neither could she explain this bizarre nineteenth-century world in which she seemed to be existing. Perhaps she'd died and gone to heaven—or hell.

"Well?" he demanded.

The two were regarding each other tensely when abruptly both jumped at the sound of a loud *mrooow*! A split second later, Jezebel landed on Cole's thigh and growled low at Jessica.

Relieved at the distraction, Jessica flashed Cole a stiff smile and removed her fingers from the kitten's fur. "Guess Jezebel's come for her baby."

"Yeah," he muttered.

The kitten mewled plaintively; then its mother picked it up by the scruff of the neck and bounded off with it.

Another silence fell. "Cole, the kitten was sweet, but I really need to go in now—"

He grasped her wrist. "Not yet."

"Damn it—"

"Stroll with me for a minute first."

"Stroll? But I—"

"Sit here and bellyache, or get it over with," he cut in. "The point is, you're coming with me, like it or not."

Jessica ground out an expletive and Cole tugged her to her feet.

Feeling burned by his touch, Jessica pulled her hand free and started down the steps ahead of him. They wended their way across the darkened yard. A night breeze rustled through the trees, an owl hooted from its high perch, and in the distance the moon backlit the soaring silvery shapes of mountains. In the skies above, hazy stars glowed softly.

Jessica shivered slightly. "This is very pretty. Now where are we—"

"Just as far as the barn, sugar."

They strolled over to the side of the huge, hulking gray building. Jessica eyed Cole in perplexity. "What now?"

He braced a hand on the barn and leaned toward her. "Answer me something."

"Yes?"

"What kind of woman are you really?"

Pulse surging, she eyed him suspiciously. "What kind of question is that?"

He drew his lazy gaze over her. "I mean, just how innocent are you?"

"Innocent in what sense?" she mocked.

He edged closer and spoke huskily. "Are you a virgin?"

At once Jessica's blood boiled and she shoved him away. "Why, of all the asinine, insulting—"

Cole caught her by the shoulders and pinned her against the barn. "Answer my question."

"Hell, no! Why would you even ask it?"

He stroked her cheek in the moonlight. She flinched from his touch. " 'Cause ever since this afternoon, it's been eating at me that you sure don't kiss like one."

She laughed. "How many virgins have you kissed?"

"A few."

"And how do virgins kiss?" she taunted.

"Not like you do, lady."

"Well, it's none of your business."

His voice tensed. "The morality of the woman trying to marry up with my brothers is damn well my business."

"I'm not trying to marry up with them," she gritted out.

"Answer my question, anyway."

"Why? Are your brothers virgins?"

He chuckled. "I should hope not."

"Then why should they expect to marry one?"

"Because men *marry* virgins." Brazenly, he looked her over. "Now, if you're the other kind, we might just have to think up another plan for you."

"Why you . . . !" With commendable restraint, Jessica managed not to slap him. "What's the other kind, Cole? A whore?"

He grinned, and even in the darkness she could see the white flash of his teeth. "You said it."

"And you can go to hell."

Undaunted, he drawled, "I don't think you're a virgin, Miss Jessie. Oh, you may blush like one, but you sass like a seasoned line gal."

"So what if I do? It's still *none of your damned business.*"

"Like none of your lies are my business?" he countered.

"What do you expect? You're an outlaw and you kidnapped me. Stacked up against your sins, a few white lies on my part seem pretty paltry. As they say, all's fair."

"Well, I'm *making* it my business," he replied heatedly. "I'm gonna find out all about you, Miss Jessie. I'm the man who can find out."

"You are an arrogant beast."

"You know I'm really hoping you're the other kind, because, honey, I've got plans for you." He pressed his mouth to her cheek.

Jessica floundered and tried to push him away. She might as well have been shoving a wall. He was so strong, and much too close, his mouth hot and sensual on her soft cheek, raising shivers.

"Stop it, Cole."

"The hay is sweet in the barn, you know," he coaxed. "We could answer this question right quick."

At last she managed to push him away. "You are unbelievably arrogant! You expect me to just drop my drawers for the likes of you?"

He grinned. "Honey, I'm praying you will."

"Well, you can pray till hell freezes over."

He laughed.

"Just out of curiosity, what would you do if we did go to bed together, and you found out I was a virgin?"

"I'd marry you," he said cockily. "But then, I ain't worried."

Now she did try to slap him. He caught her wrist and glowered.

"You are so contemptible!" she hissed. "At least your brothers would marry me, while you want to—"

"Take you to my bed," he finished baldly. "You see, Miss Jessie, I figured you out long before you tripped yourself up with all your haywire stories tonight. You're no schoolmarm, and you're not expected in Mariposa. As for what you are—"

"Please, do tell me," she taunted.

"I think you're a liar and a charlatan. I think you're a soiled dove, putting on hoity-toity airs and playing with my brothers' affection. I'm going to give you just what you deserve—and maybe what you need, too. So now we've got that straight."

"You've got it straight. Good night."

He caught her shoulders again. "Do we have a deal about tomorrow?"

Jessica wished she could throttle him. "Do you have any idea how exasperating you are?"

He didn't answer her question, doggedly forging on. "Usually a bargain is sealed. I'll take a kiss."

"You can take your kiss and shove—"

But the rest of Jessica's remark was cut off by Cole's audacious kiss, his bold tongue, his hard body pinning hers against the barn. Somewhere in the back of her mind, Jessica knew she should be outraged, that she should fight him tooth and nail. Instead she found herself captivated by two hundred pounds of raw male sex appeal. Cole kissed like no man Jessica had ever known before—his lips rapacious, all-consuming. His tongue made love to her mouth with a wicked sensuality that wrenched a helpless moan from her. And his body pressing into hers felt so good, so hard, demanding that she give up her pride and surrender to him.

What was happening to her? It was bad enough to be hurled across time, but devastating to feel such raw, overwhelming lust for a man she should despise.

At last the kiss ended. She glared up at him, but he only smiled back and stroked her cheek again.

"Oh, Miss Jessie. We could have something good. I could make it so good for you. Stay with me, sugar."

Appalled by how very tempted she felt, Jessica pushed Cole away and fled into the night.

Moments later Jessica lay in bed, Cole's bed, staring out at the moon. The sounds of Ma's soft snores drifted in from the room next door.

She should be furious with Cole, livid at his insulting questions, his presumptuous kisses. Instead she felt weak and giddy. She could still smell him in this room. Could still taste him on her lips. And she ached with desire. Ached for Cole. She didn't know what was happening to her. Normally, caveman types weren't her cup of tea at all, but Cole Reklaw had changed all that. Not only had she run amok in time, but her hormones had gone retrograde as well. Her response to Cole conjured up images of her girlfriends back in college reading historical romance novels and saying breathlessly, "They don't make men like *that* anymore."

How true. And maybe she'd been sent to the nineteenth century to find one. She knew Cole infuriated her, insulted her, demeaned her . . . and yet she hungered for him.

She felt so confused. She didn't know where she was or what had happened to her. She didn't know how long this would last, or if she'd ever see her family or the twentieth century again. And yet never in her life had she felt so alive. . . .

Cole stood in the darkness, still tasting sweet Miss Jessie on his lips. This woman they had captured maddened and intrigued him. Her spirit, her sass, roused not just his desires but also his admiration.

He knew he shouldn't let her beguile him, but she had. He still burned from their kiss, still hungered to taste every inch of her. This girl was clearly no wide-eyed innocent but a siren well schooled in the art of love.

Who was she really? Why had she claimed to be the new schoolteacher, then all but admitted it was a lie? Clearly she was fleeing some sort of unsavory past; clearly he never should have brought her here in the first place, much less trust her to go into town with Ma tomorrow. Not that his mother wasn't equal to the task of keeping the girl in line.

He smiled. He was, too. Perhaps it wasn't essential that Jessie be trusted. There was one way to ensure her silence, her cooperation—and that was with his mouth on hers and him buried deep inside her.

Chapter Eight

Morning found Jessica in the rattletrap mule-drawn buckboard with Ma. The two women were heading for town, following the same crude road the stage had taken yesterday—whenever *that* had been. The day was balmy and slightly cool, and the landscape surrounding them looked little changed from the world Jessica had evidently left behind. Beyond them loomed a raw wilderness of blue mountain ranges interrupted by occasional homesteads and glistening lakes. Aspen, fir, and pines climbed the hillsides flanking the road, and the air was redolent with the scent of evergreen. Blue birds and gray jays flitted about lofty branches, while below, mule deer grazed on summer grasses. On a distant ridge, an abandoned sluice and gouges in the hillside gave grim evidence of rapacious mining in the region.

Nowhere were there road signs, utility poles, or automobiles that might indicate Jessica was still in the twentieth century. The reality that she had evidently traveled across time was heavily sinking in.

Ma loudly cleared her throat, interrupting Jessica's musings. "Well, before we get to Mariposa, Miss Jessie, I reckon I'd best lay down the law on a few matters."

Jessica harrumphed. "That seems to be a habit in your family. Don't worry—Cole already gave me this same lecture."

The widow slanted Jessica an apologetic look. "Now, honey, don't go getting riled. As the eldest, it's Cole's duty to protect his clan. We Reklaws must live by a strict code, else we'd all be bound to the bone orchard."

"I know," said Jessica tiredly. "I mustn't tell anyone who you really are."

"There's more to it than that. You see, in town I'm not known as Eula Reklaw, but as Eula Lively. I go by my first husband's name so as not to give away my boys."

"I see. What are the boys called when they go to town?"

"They ain't called nothing. They never show their faces in Mariposa."

"They don't? Why?"

"Well, the boys have always been right suspicious of the town. It's new, been around less than five years. Mariposa kinda sprung up like a bean sprout after the Aspen Gulch Consortium made that big strike out at the eastern branch."

"Are the boys afraid of the local sheriff?"

"Nope. The town's still smaller than a gnat's butt, so there's no lawman yet, though once in a while one of them U.S. Deputy Marshals will pass through a'huntin' for my boys."

Jessica frowned at this sobering thought. "I see."

"But I reckon Mariposa is too close for comfort, anyhow. Too many men from town work at the mines, and them's the gold shipments my boys robs."

"How contemptible of them."

Eula waved a hand. "You think I can stop 'em, honey?"

"You did a pretty good job yesterday with your broom."

Eugenia Riley

"Yeah, I can keep the varmints under control at the farm, but once they're loose, they're wild as Injuns with firewater."

Jessica groaned. "So that's all they do—hide out and rob gold shipments? Your sons have no social life?"

Eula let out a hoot. "What 'social life' they have is at the saloons and dancing parlors of Colorado City—with whores and cardsharps—even though it's a good day's ride from the ranch."

Jessica recalled her history. "Ah, yes. Colorado City is near Colorado Springs, and it's pretty much the Natchez-Under-the-Hill of old Colorado, isn't it?"

Eula appeared confused. "If you say so, honey."

Jessica struggled to digest this as more questions swirled in her mind. "Tell me a little more about your family and what brought you here. You say you had a first husband?"

Eula sniffed. "Yep, Chester Lively was one of the finest men God ever put on this earth. Way back in the fifties, we married up in Arkansas, and Cole was born our first year together. Then Chester wanted us to head Colorado way so he could seek his fortune as a miner. That's when we homesteaded our land here and started a small farm. But Chester was killed in a cave-in when Cole was still a wee thing."

Jessica's heart was filled with sympathy for both Cole and Eula. "I'm so sorry. Then Cole and the other boys don't have the same father?"

"Nope. A year later, I married Joseph Reklaw, another fine man who worked at the mines. Joseph gave me my four younger boys. And since Cole was so tiny when he lost his real pappy, he always wanted to be called 'Reklaw' like his brothers."

"That explains why he looks somewhat different from the others."

"They're all thick as thieves, anyhow."

"Indeed. But I have wondered at the differences—particularly the fact that Cole seems better-educated."

86

Eula nodded. "When he was still a young fella, a neighbor lady used to tutor Cole with her own young 'uns, learned him to read and write proper-like. Then that whole family took sick with scarlet fever and died, so my younger boys didn't have no teacher. They can barely write their own names."

Jessica fell silent, thinking of how very difficult these times were on families. "What happened to your second husband, if I may ask?"

"Joseph Reklaw was a good upstanding man, a Bible-pounder even." Ma sniffed again. "He was a fine father to all five of my boys—till miner's lung took him soon after Billy was born."

Jessica was aghast. "So you've lost two husbands to the mines?"

"Yep. And the owners wouldn't have cared if I'd lost a hundred more."

"How terrible," Jessica sympathized. "No wonder all of you are bitter toward the mining industry."

Ma's expression seethed with resentment. "It ain't the industry, honey, but the sidewinders that own the mines. Them serpents is holed up in the Springs. They be rich folk that own mines all over the state. They call themselves respectable businessmen, but they ain't nothin' but vipers in my book."

Jessica digested this. "What about your farm?"

"What about it?"

"Well, last night Cole said it's his now."

"That's right. It fell to him as Chester's son."

"Well, couldn't the boys make a go of farming instead of robbing the mines?"

Eula snorted. "When the mine owners' evil doin's have raped our hillsides, and most of our streams are poisoned by metal runoff?"

Jessica sighed. "Good Lord. Then these robber barons in Colorado Springs have seen to it that your sons can't earn a decent living off the land."

"You're beginning to get the picture, honey. They ain't doin' much for the families of Mariposa, neither."

"And your sons are helping by robbing the mines?"

Eula shook a finger at Jessica. "My boys ain't never robbed no payroll—only the gold leaving the mines."

"But aren't you afraid they'll be caught?"

Ma clucked to the mule. "Not as long as they're careful. Cole had a close call in Colorado City a few years back due to some pure-dee tomfoolery, but I think he learnt his lesson. You can bet all my boys are watching their p's and q's these days. There's no reason they'll get caught—long as we're *all* careful." She gave Jessica pointed look as she spoke the word "all."

Jessica frowned. "But if your second husband worked the mines, aren't there miners around who would remember his name—perhaps even remember you—and put two and two together?"

Ma snorted. "You're forgetting, missy, that Joseph died nigh onto twenty years ago. Just how long do you think miners live in these parts?"

"I see your point."

"There's maybe one old-timer left who remembers Joseph and knows who my boys really are—and he'll never let on."

"Meaning he approves of what they're doing?"

Ma smiled smugly.

Jessica was about to question her further when she was distracted by the sight of a wanted poster nailed to a pine tree just off the roadway. Although they were too far away to read all the small print, she could just make out the larger words: "Wanted Dead or Alive . . . The Reklaw Gang."

Pointing at the poster, she cried, "My God! Do you see that?"

"Yep, I seen posters like it a hundred times," came Ma's grim reply. "Now do you see why we have to be careful?"

Jessica nodded. Although she sympathized with the plight of the Reklaw family and could even understand why the boys had turned to a life of crime, the men were clearly bound on the wrong path, a dangerous road that could lead them only to the gallows. And, due to her own bitterness, Ma Reklaw gave her tacit consent to her sons' lawbreaking. . . .

Moments later, Jessica was gaping at the small Colorado town materializing at the crest of a rise. First they passed a small, ornate sign emblazoned with "Mariposa, Colorado, Population 204." Next they rolled past a picturesque white clapboard chapel with a sign proclaiming "Mariposa Community Church," and beyond it an equally quaint schoolhouse. Then as they continued down the rutted dirt street, Jessica stared amazed at antique storefronts flanking them on either side. It was as if they'd stepped onto a Hollywood movie set, complete with every nineteenth-century detail, from western saloon doors to delicate porch railings to frosted-glass windows to old-timey boardwalks. Everything was there—the feed store, saloon, bank, general store, the old-timers playing dominoes, the horses tied to the hitching posts, the buggies in the streets. As they passed the small hotel, an old gentleman in an elegant brown frock coat tipped his hat to them, and Jessica stared back frozenly. She went wide-eyed at the sight of two old ladies in floor-length calico dresses emerging from the post office. Then she watched a young family troop along—the father in buckskins, the wife in full-skirted gingham and matching bonnet, the little boy in overalls and straw hat, the girl in linen dress and lacy pantaloons.

Jessica glanced at Ma, who seemed to be taking everything in stride. So she really *had* traveled back in time! By now no other explanation made sense. It had been one thing to assume the Reklaws were crazy, but were all the citizens of this town demented, as well? Once again, Jessica spotted no signs of electricity, cars, modern structures, anything to indicate they were still in the twentieth century.

"Here we are," Ma said, pulling the team to a halt before the dry goods store. "Come along, Miss Jessie. We'll get you fixed right up."

The two women alighted, crossed the creaky boardwalk, and entered the store to a jangling bell. Jessica inhaled the scent of crisp fabrics and gazed at the store's charming interior—the tables stacked with bolts of cloth, the floor-to-ceiling shelves lined with clothing and notions. She saw no signs of electricity, telephones, computers, anything modern. Even the wrought-iron and frosted-glass chandelier hanging from the high ceiling appeared to be fueled by kerosene, judging from the black smudges on the glass.

A beaming middle-aged man in gartered shirt, apron, and dark pants stepped toward them. "Why, good morning, Widow Lively. How are you today?"

"I'm right fine, Mr. Granger," Eula answered cautiously.

The man's gaze settled on Jessica. "And who is this lovely young lady you have with you? Might she be the new schoolteacher, the one we've been expecting from Denver?"

Taken aback, Jessica struggled to hide her agitation, while Ma threw her a warning look. "Why, are you expecting a schoolteacher?" she asked the merchant.

"Well, as I understand it, our mayor, Mr. Polk, has a friend at the teacher's college, and he promised to send us out a graduate this summer—only so far, no one has shown up. That's why I'm wondering if it might be you."

Even as Jessica was about to reply, Ma shot back, "Nossir, it ain't her. This here lady is—er—she's kin of my dear departed husband, and she's visiting from back East."

"Ah, how nice." Mr. Granger smiled at Jessica. "And what might your name be?"

"Jessica Garrett," she answered, offering her hand.

Shaking her hand, Granger replied, "What a lovely name. Too bad you're not the new teacher, though. The young 'uns in this town could sure use one." He paused, scratching his jaw. "You know, the missus and me heard tell they're supposed to be startin' up a new stage line out of Colorado City, and we been hoping the teacher might come out on the stage. But so far, the stage ain't showed up, neither."

Taken aback by the merchant's statement, Jessica glanced tensely at Ma, only to receive another cautioning glance.

"Anyhow, miss, we welcome you to Mariposa. You really should join us at the community church. I'm one of the elders, you see."

"Why, I'd be delighted to attend."

But even as Jessica was flashing the merchant her most winsome smile, Ma snorted in disdain and gave Jessica a look hostile enough to curdle milk.

"The lady here won't be attending," Ma rudely informed Granger. "We ain't church-going folk. And now, sir, are you gonna stand there all day and palaver? Or are you ready to make some good money offen our trade?"

At Ma's diatribe, the merchant wilted. Jessica flashed him an apologetic look, and he nodded soberly to Ma. "Of course, Widow Lively. I'm always eager to serve you."

"Good. 'Cause my—er—my niece here is needing a whole new wardrobe—everything from shoes to hats, and a'course I'll be needin' to make her a heap of new dresses."

He lit up at this prospect. "You just tell me what you need. As a matter of fact, we've some spanking new Singer dress patterns in."

Jessica watched in amazement as Eula, with Granger's help, picked out several patterns for long-sleeved, floor-length frocks with bustles and lace trimmings. The garments all looked like some of the sketches Jessica had seen in old editions of *Godey's Lady's Book*. Afterward, Eula allowed Jessica to help her choose lengths of calico, gingham, linen, and muslin. Mr. Granger helped the ladies round up threads, laces, and ribbons. Then Eula and Jessica finished off the purchases by selecting an assortment of quaint hats, shoes, undergarments, and nightgowns.

The merchant totaled up the goods at the antique cash register. "Ma'am, that'll be fifteen dollars and thirty-five cents," he informed Eula.

"My land!" declared Eula, pressing a hand to her ample bosom. "I can't believe how dear everything has gotten. Why, it's highway robbery, I'm telling you."

"Yes, ma'am. Sorry."

Watching Eula grudgingly pull out her reticule and count out the money, Jessica could only shake her head. She couldn't believe Eula was actually complaining about her bill. As far as Jessica was concerned, to pay fifteen dollars for such a huge stack of clothing was ludicrous.

Then Jessica tensed as she spotted a ratty copy of *The Denver Post* on the countertop nearby. She eagerly snatched it up, only to read the date: "June 12, 1888."

In amazement, she glanced at Granger. "Sir, is this date correct?"

He glanced at the newspaper and chuckled. "Of course not."

Jessica sighed in relief. "You mean the year isn't 1888?"

He laughed again. "Certainly, the year is 1888, miss. But you must know how long it takes to get any newspapers out here. I wouldn't have this one, except a traveling salesman left it."

Jessica was growing exasperated. "I don't understand. What are you saying?"

"I'm saying it is the year 1888, but it's August now, not June."

"Oh," said Jessica dully, flashing him a frozen smile.

She barely heard Ma asking Mr. Granger to load up

their supplies in the buckboard while she and "Miss Jessie" finished their shopping next door at the general store. In a daze, she let Ma grab her by the arm and lead her toward the next shop. It was all she could do to walk on her weak knees.

So she really was living in the year 1888. There was no further denying it. She was over a hundred years removed from the life she had known before, the people she had loved . . .

They entered the general store to another clanging bell. Ma left Jessica inside the doorway and proceeded to the counter to speak with the merchant. Gradually Jessica become aware of a potpourri of scents—pickles, tobacco, beef jerky, and spices. Coming out of her daze, she glanced about the old-fashioned store with its high ceilings and glass display cases.

She strolled the sawdust-covered floor, amazed by the antique pickle barrels, the "store-bought" clothing hanging from racks, the decorative tins and apothecary jars that held foods and medicines, the barrels and bags of staples stacked everywhere—coffee, flour, beans, hardtack.

At a table laden with various giftware, Jessica marveled at a cobalt blue china tea set, a ceramic shoe, a fluted glass candy basket, a miniature hurricane lamp painted with flowers. She was particularly intrigued by a lovely, slim, leather-bound writing journal, and was examining it when she felt a tug on her skirts. She looked down to see a little blond girl with a cherubic face gazing up at her expectantly. Why, it was the same child she'd spotted outside. Wearing a lace-trimmed blue linen frock and matching bonnet, she appeared to be no more than six.

The child grinned shyly, revealing a charming gap in her front teeth. "Hello, ma'am. I see you got a book there. Would you be the new schoolteacher we been a'waitin' for? My brother Ben and me was hoping it was you."

Jessica glanced off to see the girl's brother lounging

against a syrup barrel, watching them. Catching Jessica's perusal, he blushed and stared self-consciously at his shoes.

Jessica smiled at the girl. "You know, honey, I'd love to be your schoolteacher, but—"

"She ain't one," Ma cut in.

Jessica glanced up to see that Eula, wearing a massive scowl, had joined them. Now she made a shooing motion at the child. "Now run along, young 'un, before your ma takes to frettin'."

"Yes, ma'am." Curtsying, the child rushed off.

Crestfallen, Jessica regarded Ma. "Did you have to be so harsh with her?"

"Harsh?" Ma laughed. "Shooing away a young 'un, that ain't harsh a'tall. Giving one a switchin', that's harsh."

Jessica gazed at the children, who stood with their mother at a clothing rack. "You know, I wish I could be their teacher."

"Well, you can't, so don't you go getting no highfalutin' ideas," Ma replied gruffly. She gestured at the book Jessica held. "What's that you got?"

"A writing journal."

"You favor it?"

"Well, I—"

Ma snatched the journal out of Jessica's hands. "We'll take it, and get you some pencils, too. Keep your fingers busy and your mind off palavering. Well, missy, you'd best step lively now. Mr. Allgood is ready to total us up— and see you stow the wabash this time."

Frowning, Jessica followed Ma to the counter.

As soon as they pulled out of town, Ma began scolding Jessica. "Missy, you'd best rein in that sociable mouth of yours next time we're in town. You acted much too friendly today."

Jessica frowned. "But what did I do wrong? I didn't give away anything."

"Hah!" mocked Ma. "Cozying up to Granger, getting ready to sign us all up for church, even offer yourself to teach. That all sounds pretty darn neighborly to me."

Jessica fought to retain her patience. "Wait a minute. You're going about this all wrong."

"What ya mean?"

"How can you hope to reform your sons when the only influence they have is sinful Colorado City?"

"They have you."

Jessica rolled her eyes. "Mrs. Reklaw, I hardly pack your punch with a broom, nor can I marry all of your boys. If you really hope to rehabilitate them, they need the example of a respectable community, a church to attend, decent young women to court."

"But if they go into town, they'll be caught."

"Why? Didn't you tell me the town's so new that no one knows they're actually the Reklaw Gang? And didn't you say the town doesn't even have a sheriff? Who's going to catch them?"

Ma scowled. "It's taking a risk."

"Is it? You go into town undetected. Do the townsfolk know you have children?"

Ma worked the reins. "I tell them as little about me as possible."

Jessica jerked a thumb toward the wagon bed. "With all those supplies you bought, they must know you have others living with you at the ranch."

Ma shrugged. "They likely think the grub is for my hired help."

"But what if the boys got all cleaned up and came into town with us?" Jessica went on. "Who would suspect that five handsome, strapping young farmers are really outlaws?"

Ma was still scowling. "Well, I'll give it some thought."

"If you want to reform your sons, you'd better," Jessica replied adamantly.

Chapter Nine

As the buckboard drew closer to the farm, Jessica found her mind was churning with all that had happened to her today, all she had learned. She considered her bizarre situation. She was now clearly living in the year 1888, and might never find her way back to the present, and to the family, friends, and colleagues she'd abandoned there. What was worse, she didn't even have a way to get a message back through, and surely her loved ones were very worried over her strange disappearance. Thank heaven she hadn't left behind a husband or children, but her elderly parents and older brother must be frantic.

On the other hand, if she truly was stranded in another time, then perhaps she was here for a purpose. She might as well try to make the best of things. And she'd begin by trying to reform the five outlaw brothers. Already she liked them all, even the exasperating Cole, and she couldn't bear the thought of any of them swinging at the end of a hangman's rope.

Jessica also realized she'd been granted a wonderful opportunity to experience firsthand life in the Old West. In just one day, she'd learned much that wasn't in the history books—seeing how people really lived, learning of the hardships they endured. She resolved to make good use of the journal Ma had bought her by keeping a detailed account of all her experiences. Perhaps her diary could somehow be preserved for posterity. Moreover, if she ever did make her way back to the twentieth century—something she was beginning to doubt—her journal could prove a priceless resource.

But how could she reform the Reklaw boys? If they were to turn away from a life of crime, she must offer them something better in exchange. Of course, Mariposa was the perfect answer. There the brothers could find a sense of community, a church to attend, perhaps even respectable young women to court.

And although Ma had resisted this idea, Jessica felt confident that in time she could wear Eula down. If she could get Ma on her side, and also convince the boys to clean up their language and appearance, if she could teach the unruly outlaws to act and talk more like gentlemen, then surely no one would guess that the "Lively" brothers were actually the hardened Reklaw Gang. After all, families with half a dozen sons were not uncommon in these times.

Jessica was still immersed in thought as the buckboard crested a rise and rattled down the hillside toward the farm house. Jessica frowned as she spotted the five brothers in front of the barn saddling their horses. All of them waved at the approaching buckboard, then began striding toward the house. Jessica noted all five wore hats, chaps, and gun belts.

Not a good sign!

Jessica turned to Ma. "What are they up to?"

Ma pulled the buckboard to a halt before the house. "Off to more of the devil's doin's, no doubt."

Billy arrived first at the conveyance, tipping his hat to Jessica. "Howdy, Miss Jessie. How was your outing?"

"Fine, thank you. And it appears you're about to embark on one of your own."

Before Billy could respond, Luke ambled up, offering Jessica a hand. "May I help you down, ma'am? Golly, that's a purdy book you got there."

"Thanks." Accepting his assistance down, Jessica added, "Your mother very kindly bought it for me in town."

Gabe joined them, gallantly offering Jessica his arm. "May I escort you into the house?"

Ma snorted loudly from the buckboard. "Which one of you sidewinders is gonna help *me* down, and bring in the supplies?"

"Ma, we're all headin' out," protested Wesley.

"Headin' out where?" asked Ma.

"Here, Ma, let me help you," offered Cole.

He stepped forward and assisted his mother out of the buckboard. Then his dark gaze settled on Jessica. She fought a shiver, feeling intensely conscious of his strong, virile presence, especially as she remembered him kissing her so audaciously beside the barn last night. She couldn't help noticing how his shirt hugged the muscular contours of his arms and shoulders, how his chaps molded his powerful thighs. Not to mention how deep-set and sexy his eyes were, how sensual his mouth, how stubborn the set of his handsome jaw.

His gaze still lingering on her, Cole remarked to Eula, "We just got word of a gold shipment leaving the Aspen Gulch Mines. Reckon we'll go relieve them of a bit of the heavy stuff."

"Another robbery?" Ma shrieked. "Ain't you boys got in enough trouble?"

"Yes, you men should be ashamed of yourselves," seconded Jessica.

"But, ladies, there weren't no strong box yesterday, so we gotta make up for lost time," whined Billy.

"Yeah," seconded Gabe.

"You boys already got enough gold stashed away to pave a road halfways to hell," groused Ma.

Cole lifted an eyebrow at Jessica. "And we'll need everything we've got if we're ever found out, if we have to pull up stakes and move on. Now if you ladies will excuse us—"

"But I don't excuse you," Jessica retorted crisply. As Cole swung about, glowering at her, inspiration dawned. "In fact, I'm going to come along and take notes."

Jessica's bravado had the desired effect. All five of the men appeared stunned. Billy stood with his mouth gaping open. Luke and Wesley exchanged horrified glances. Gabe stared bug-eyed at Jessica. Cole glared.

At last Billy sputtered, "Y-you's gonna turn us in, ma'am?"

Before Jessica could answer, Luke spun angrily on Cole. "I just knew it. This Jezebel's gonna give us over to the law!"

Cole stared hard at Jessica. "That true?"

"No! I haven't done anything to betray you, nor do I intend to! Just ask your mother how I behaved in town."

As five sets of suspicious male eyes turned to Ma, she nodded. "Miss Jessie did right well, other than being a mite too friendly gossiping with Mr. Granger about church and such."

Wesley stalked forward and stabbed at Jessica's journal with a forefinger. "Then how come you want to put what we're doin' in that there book?"

She drew herself up with dignity. "I—I shall record your exploits for posterity."

Those words drew outraged mutterings from the men, and brought Billy surging forward. "You'd better watch your mouth, sister. I've shot men for lesser insults."

Jessica giggled, which did not at all improve the men's dispositions. "No, you misunderstand. I want to write down what you're doing for history."

Billy's face lit up. "You mean like in dime novels?"

"Yeah, like Billy the Kid, and them Clanton boys?" Gabe inquired excitedly. "Cole reads to us about 'em."

"Well, something like that," Jessica conceded, struggling not to feel charmed at the mention of Cole reading to his younger brothers.

Billy stuck his thumbs in his trouser pockets and preened like a peacock. "How 'bout that, boys? We's gonna be famous."

Billy's brothers also laughed and bragged to each other, with the exception of Cole, who was still scowling. "You boys considered that there just might be some drawbacks to our being—er—*in*famous?"

Jessica turned to him with cool defiance. "If you're worried about my turning over my journal to the law, don't be. I'm doing this strictly for the sake of pos—of future generations. You'll be dead by the time any of it is published, assuming it ever is."

Cole smiled nastily. "You planning to be around after we're dead, sugar? Oh maybe you're the one aimin' to do us in."

"You know what I mean," she shot back.

"Frankly, I don't."

"Aw, come on, Cole, let the lady come along," suggested Gabe. "I see no harm in it."

"I can see a *lot* of harm in taking along our own witness for the prosecution. It's the most haywire notion I've ever heard."

"Then we'll make her marry up with one of us," declared Billy. "Ain't there a law that a wife can't testify against her husband?"

"It's a thought," agreed Cole, scratching his jaw and eyeing Jessica in a lewd manner that made her heart lurch.

Meanwhile Ma waved a hand in frustration. "Aw, boys, quit your palavering and let the woman go along. You're fussin' worse than old biddies at a rummage sale. You may as well make up your minds—either you're gonna trust her or ya ain't."

Cole stared hard at Jessica. "Yeah, Ma, you're right. The lady can come with us. It's just as well we keep an eye on her. Besides, if I didn't trust her, she'd be dead by now."

Just the way he said it made Jessica shudder as she watched him swing about and stride over to his horse.

While the men unloaded the buckboard, Jessica rushed off with Ma to change. Digging through a trunk, Ma managed to find Jessica an old pair of overalls, a red checked shirt, a pair of boots, and a straw hat, all of which had belonged to Billy when he was a boy and were small enough to fit her. She changed into the getup, and was pleased to find that her journal and a pencil fit nicely in one of the huge front pockets of the overalls. Donning the hat, she giggled at her image in the mirror. With the brim pulled low and her hair pinned up, she looked like a farmer. All she needed was a stalk of hay to chew on.

By the time she went rushing back into the yard, Cole had saddled her a palomino and stood waiting with the reins in hand. He regarded her attire in amusement. The other men, sitting on their own mounts, snickered to one another.

Observing Cole with the horse, Jessica felt her cheeks heating as she remembered his saying last night, "I'd like to see you astride a palomino, riding into the wind." She glanced at his expressive face and wondered if he, too, was remembering his provocative comment. Not that she'd make a very dramatic sight right now, since she'd never been on a horse in her life!

Cole broke the silence with a chuckle. "Well, don't you look fetching, Miss Jessie. Come on. Mount up."

Rolling her eyes at him, Jessica stared skeptically at the horse. The palomino was huge, its shoulders massive, its back level with her own forehead, its large white tail batting at flies. Although the animal was beautiful with its

101

Eugenia Riley

gold coat, flowing white mane, and white blaze, its eyes
appeared dark and wary. No doubt the animal sensed that
she had no experience on horseback—although she wasn't
about to admit this to Cole. Still, even the thought of
mounting the beast was daunting.

"Something wrong, sugar?" Cole pressed.

"No. Just help me mount."

"You need help?" he mocked.

She balled her hands on her hips. "In case you haven't
noticed, this is a very large horse, and I'm not six feet tall
like you are."

Cole grinned lazily. "Oh, honey, I've noticed."

"Stow the charm and give me a hand."

"Yes, ma'am. Just put your foot in the stirrup and I'll
give you a lift."

Tossing him a resentful glance, Jessica turned back to
the horse. The animal snorted and eyed her balefully,
hardly putting her at ease. Trying to remember what she
could about equestrienne procedures from old western
movies she'd watched, Jessica stuck her left foot in the
stirrup and grabbed the saddle horn with her right hand.

Then she was horrified to feel Cole's hand positioned
intimately on her bottom as he gave her a massive push.
She landed in the saddle with face flaming. The horse
gave a neigh, and she glowered down at Cole. "You crude
jerk."

Though he appeared somewhat bemused at her termi-
nology, he tipped his hat. "My pleasure, ma'am. And you
did ask."

He had her to rights there, and she could hear his brothers chuckling. "Hey, Cole, quit sparking the lady and let's
ride," urged Luke. "Time's a'wasting."

"I'm ready," Cole replied with ill humor, striding to his
chestnut horse and mounting with fluid grace. "You're
the ones who insisted we bring the *lady* along."

There it was again—that derogatory inflection on
"lady." Jessica's blood boiled.

Gabe let out a whistle. "All right, gentlemen. Head out!"

Watching the men gallop away, Jessica panicked as she realized she had no idea how to mobilize her own horse. The animal evidently recognized her ineptitude and fear. When she nudged its sides with her thighs, it only snorted. When she yanked on the reins, it neighed and stamped a hoof, then turned its head around and tried to bite her! Hastily she lifted her foot to avoid the animal's teeth.

"Stop that!" Jessica scolded, prompting only an indignant whinny. Then the beast lowered its head and began chewing on grass and ignoring her.

Meanwhile, the men were already yards ahead! Jessica felt her face flaming. She was mortified, defeated by a mere beast of burden. Humiliating though it was, she knew she had to ask for help. Cupping a hand around her mouth, she yelled at the departing cloud of dust, "Hey! Wait for me!"

The men wheeled their horses and regarded Jessica in consternation. "What ails you, woman?" Wesley called out. "Ain't you never been on a horse before?"

"Nope," Jessica admitted cheerfully.

Laughter erupted. "Well, I'll be hanged," said Billy.

"A gall-durned greenhorn," scoffed Gabe.

Meanwhile, Cole spurred his horse and galloped back to Jessica's side. "You might have told us," he drawled.

She glowered.

He grabbed her reins. "Hold on tight now."

Jessica's eyes widened. "To what?"

"The saddle horn."

Jessica had no sooner gripped it than Cole galloped off, her horse lurching into motion behind his, prompting her to squeal in fear. It was all she could do to hang on, her bottom bouncing hard in the saddle as they bounded along. Then she felt herself slipping to one side, and shrieked bloody murder.

103

"S-stop!" she stammered. "Please stop! I'm falling off the d-damn horse!"

The men pulled up again, all appearing disgusted. "Lady, you're a pain in the butt," declared Luke.

"Females," scoffed Wesley. "All useless sissies. We should have left you behind."

But Cole, appearing amused, only shrugged. "The lady can ride double with me."

"W-with you?" Jessica stammered.

"Hey, how come you get her?" protested Gabe.

"Didn't you boys just ask to leave her behind?" Cole reasoned. "Besides, it's *my* idea this time."

The boys grumbled to one another, but didn't protest further to Cole. Jessica realized the boys had developed something of a code for dealing with her. The first man to come up with an idea got "dibs"—whether it was to pull out her chair or to ride double with her.

However, since Cole had been the first one to baldly proclaim he would bed her, the knowledge of their "system" didn't exactly comfort her now.

Cole edged his mount close to Jessica's. "All right, sugar. Hop on behind me."

"Hop on—where?"

"You heard me." He slid forward in the saddle, patiently waiting.

Somehow, Jessica managed to clamber on behind him. She restrained a groan at the feel of Cole's muscled back against her breasts, her thighs nestled close to his own, and the male scent of him tempting her senses. "All right. I'm here."

"Yeah, you sure are," he agreed huskily.

"Cole—"

"Hold on tight."

Biting back her frustration, Jessica was forced to place her arms around Cole's trim waist, only enhancing their proximity.

"Ah, sugar, that feels good," he murmured.

"Shut up."

Chuckling, Cole wheeled his horse about, then slapped the riderless palomino across its rump. "Hee-ah! Head home."

The horse whinnied, turned, and galloped homeward.

"All right, boys," Cole said. "We've wasted enough time."

As the group rode off, Jessica began bobbing in the saddle again, her bottom taking a pounding, her breasts rubbing provocatively against Cole's back.

She heard his low, suggestive chuckle. "You need some riding lessons, sugar."

"And you're the man to teach me?"

"As a matter of fact, yes," came his cocky reply. "I'm the man who can teach you just about everything you need to know."

Jessica was on the verge of issuing a sharp retort when she bounced hard, then heard Cole's moan of pleasure as her breasts collided with his back. Oh, she was going to be black and blue before the day was over!

Then as she bobbed once more, Cole spoke in a slow, sexy drawl. "Actually, sugar, why don't you just keep on doing what you're doing? It feels fine."

Jessica could have killed him.

Chapter Ten

"If you look, sugar, you can see the mine from here."

Breathless, Jessica was still clinging to Cole's waist as the group of outlaws at last halted on top of a high, dramatic ridge. Below them, down a rugged plunge of wooded hillside, a narrow dirt road snaked its way through the canyon. Next to the road, a stream rushed by, its waters tinged a grayish yellow by metal runoff. In the distance to the west, Jessica could just make out the hazy outline of the mines—a group of rambling gray buildings sprawled in a mountain pass, with gouges in the hillside above, and a sluice emptying into the stream below.

"Is that the mine where your father worked?" she asked.

Cole twisted about in the saddle, raising an eyebrow.

"Your ma told me about your family history this morning."

He grunted. "Nope, both my pa's worked in the old western branch of the mines, which the owners over-tunneled and closed down years ago, after too many cave-ins. This eastern branch was opened up when they hit a major vein five years ago."

Jessica snapped her fingers. "That's right. Your mother explained that the town of Mariposa was formed soon after that strike occurred."

"Now they have this mine tunneled out, too, and on the verge of collapse," he added grimly.

Jessica was about to comment when, next to them, Billy pointed at the gorge and whispered tensely, "Hey, Cole, lookie there! I see the dray!"

Jessica strained in the saddle to peer over Cole's shoulder. She spotted the heavily laden wagon, pulled by a team of workhorses, just appearing on the road to the west of them and plodding slowly toward them.

"That's what you're going to rob?" she asked Cole.

"Yep." He viewed the scene with a hand shading his eyes, then grinned at Billy. "Only a driver and one old poke riding shotgun. You'd think they'd have learned better by now."

"Easy pickins'," agreed Billy. "Like shootin' fish in a barrel."

Puzzled, Jessica glanced at Billy. "How did you boys know this shipment would be coming through this afternoon?"

Billy pressed a finger to his mouth. "Trade secret, ma'am."

She smiled nastily. "Do you have a spy at the mines?"

As the boys exchanged alarmed glances, Cole twisted about again, glowering at Jessica. "Lady, you'd best stow the curiosity before it takes you straight to the bone orchard."

"Oh, spare me your melodramatics. I'm not impressed."

Perplexed, Cole glanced at Billy, who gave a shrug and said, "Don't bellyache to me. You wanted her along." Billy turned to the other brothers. "Ready to ride, boys?"

Eager nods greeted his question.

"All right, let's do it!" Billy declared.

"Wait a minute," Cole put in. As the other men reined in their horses, he swung to the ground, then offered Jessica his hand. "Get down. You're waiting here."

"No!" she protested. "I'm along for the ride—for everything."

"Yeah, and if you get shot, Ma'll never forgive us."

"What about you?" Jessica mocked. "Would you care?"

Cole reached up, grabbed her about the waist, and slid her to the ground, letting her body rub slowly, sensuously against his own. Jessica stifled a moan and glared at him.

Ignoring her surly look, he drawled, "Don't count on it, sister. And you're fixin' to get your hide blistered if you don't start minding a sight better."

"I'm not some puppy you can order about."

"You're going to do what I say, anyhow."

"Yeah, lady, Cole is right," remarked Gabe. "It's too dangerous to take you along. You could trip us up."

Though exasperated, Jessica realized it was futile to argue further; she couldn't win against all five of them. "Very well. Besides, if I remain here, I'll be able to take lots of notes."

All five men chuckled. "See you do," mocked Cole, tipping his hat and swinging back up into the saddle.

Jessica watched with bated breath as the men rode off, heading down the tricky incline. Soon they were obscured in the wooded hillside, and she didn't see them again until the dray was rounding a bend. Suddenly Cole, Billy, and Gabe materialized in front of the dray, firing their weapons into the air and causing the confused workhorses to buck and stamp. Luke and Wes attacked the wagon from the rear.

Confuse and conquer, Jessica thought grimly. The outlaws were good at their nefarious work. Within seconds, the dray had been halted and both driver and guard had thrown down their weapons and surrendered.

Jessica had to shake her head at the outlaws' ingenuity

108

and audacity as they tied up the two men and threw them into the back of the dray. Quickly the four younger boys loaded their saddlebags with gold bars, while Cole tied the remaining sacks of gold to the backs of the two workhorses. Within minutes, the group rode off, leading the workhorses and hooting their victory.

Soon the desperadoes arrived back in the clearing, faces aglow with victory. Jessica strode forward to face them with hands balled on her hips. "It's shameful the delight you men take in your sinful doings."

Cole swung down to grin at her. "Sin is always fun, sugar. How 'bout a victory kiss?"

Before Jessica could protest, Cole hauled her close and soundly smacked her lips, while his brothers hooted catcalls.

Her face was flaming. "You thief."

Cole grinned unabashedly. "I'm a bandit, sugar, and I take what I want."

"Hey, no fair!" protested Gabe. "How come we don't git no victory kisses from the lady?"

"Yeah, how come?" asked Billy.

Cole swung around. "Because if we don't hightail it, someone's bound to come along and discover us. Let's ride, boys. We can fight over the lady later."

Within seconds, Jessica was again mounted behind Cole on his horse, her breasts once more rubbing sinfully against his muscled back, her lips still throbbing from his brazen kiss. . . .

The ride home made Jessica acutely conscious of how sore her bottom was getting. Eager to distract herself, she spoke to Cole. "I'm curious about something."

"Not again," he complained.

"Why was the dray hauling gold bars, and not ore?"

He laughed. "The Aspen Gulch Mines is a fully contained operation, one of the few in the state with its own stamping mill. That way, the few miners the consortium doesn't kill underground can be poisoned by fumes from the acids used to separate the metals."

She whistled. "You sound very bitter. Not that I can really blame you, after listening to your mother this morning."

He grunted. "I think my ma's been runnin' off at the mouth too much."

That remark chafed Jessica's pride. "Meaning, you want me to be your captive, but you don't want me to get to know you?"

"Well, I'd be happy for you to 'know' me in the biblical sense," he teased back.

Jessica pounded him on the back, but the devil only laughed.

About a mile from the farm house, Cole held up his hand to halt the group. "You boys go on and see to our business. I think it's best I take Jessie back to the house."

"All right, Cole," agreed Billy, then raised an eyebrow meaningfully. "Just see you mind your manners with the lady."

"Of course," he drawled.

The four boys rode off to the east, leading the heavily laden workhorses. Cole spurred his mount on toward the house.

"So, are your brothers going to stash the gold at your hideout?" Jessica inquired sweetly.

Cole shook his head. "Jessie, you're too smart—and too curious—for your own good."

"Count on it," she retorted crisply. "But I take it you don't want me to see your secret cache, either?"

"Yeah. Then I *would* have to shoot you."

They fell into an uneasy silence until Cole paused his horse beneath a shade tree next to a stream. He dismounted and pulled Jessica to the ground. "We'll let old Red rest a spell. He's been carrying quite a load."

"Sure," Jessica said.

Actually she was grateful for the respite, since her rear was very sore and it had been much too long since she'd visited the "necessary" back at the farm house. Muttering an "excuse me" to Cole, she ducked into some trees to see to her needs.

When she emerged, Cole was sitting on a log sipping water from his canteen. The sight of him quickened Jessica's pulse. Despite the fact that she was thoroughly exasperated with him, he just looked so handsome in the fading light, with his beautifully honed features in profile, his massive body in repose.

Spotting her, he stood. "You want to sit here?"

"No thanks," she replied gruffly. "But please, go ahead."

He walked closer, extending the canteen. "Saddle sore, eh?"

Rolling her eyes, she accepted the canteen and took a long drink. "Thanks," she said, returning it to him.

He strode back to the log and resumed his seat. Capping his canteen and setting it on the ground, he asked, "Well, sugar, what did you think of our exploits today? Did you take lots of notes in that journal of yours?"

She harrumphed. "I'll do that when we get back. But if you want my initial impression—"

"I do."

She crossed her arms over her chest. "I think you and your brothers should be ashamed of yourselves."

Although he appeared amused, his tone was challenging. "Should we? After the mine owners saw to it that our streams are poisoned, and we can't earn an income through honest means?"

"Ah, so you're an environmentalist," she mocked.

He glowered. "*What* did you call me, woman?"

She waved him off. "Don't pop your cork. I didn't insult you, and besides, I've had entirely enough *machismo* for one day."

He shook his head, appearing bemused.

111

"What I'm saying is you must see yourself as having some kind of higher purpose—like a latter-day Robin Hood."

"Robin Hood," Cole repeated thoughtfully. "Yeah, I like the sound of that."

"I suppose you give to the poor as well?"

"Nope."

Expression indignant, she began to pace. "Well! Here you are trying to convince me your motives are noble—"

Cole was watching her intently as she moved, obviously savoring the motions of her body. "Am I?"

"When they're not noble at all."

He grinned unrepentantly. "You got me to rights there."

She shook a finger at him. "You could damn well earn an honest income if you wanted to."

"Maybe I don't want to." He shook his head and eyed her admiringly. "So full of sass, you are."

Jessica waved her hands. "Quit trying to be charming. I can't believe how short-sighted you are."

He whistled. "I am?"

"What about your brothers?" she ranted. "Their futures? Don't any of you want to settle down, have wives, children?"

His expression turned downright sinful. "You aimin' to give me those young 'uns, woman?"

She colored, her voice trembling badly. "Will you get your mind into decent territory for once?"

"Now what have I done? You brought up children."

"And you've twisted everything I said to make it lewd."

He appeared amazed. "Is having children lewd, woman?"

"The way you'd go about it? Yes!"

Cole roared with laughter.

Jessica stormed up to him. "Don't you dare laugh at me—"

Her words were smothered as Cole pulled her down into his lap. She winced as her sore bottom landed against his hard thigh. But his proximity, the sexy heat and scent of him, were even more unnerving.

"Just what do you think you're doing?" she demanded, the words breathless.

"Clipping your wings, woman," he replied gruffly. "You're making me hot, strutting about in those trousers."

She gasped.

Abruptly, he pulled off her hat and sank his fingers into her hair, sending pins flying and her auburn locks tumbling down upon her shoulders. Jessica couldn't have felt more unnerved if he'd stripped her naked.

"Damn, if you don't look a sight in that boy's getup, with your tumbled hair," he said huskily. "Not to mention what you're doing to me sitting in my lap. Lord, if there wasn't all this cloth between us, I'd give you a riding that would put any horse to shame."

Jessica was sinking fast. "Damn it, Cole, let me up."

"No. You want to have a serious talk. So let's have it." His hand at her nape urged her face closer, until she was forced to meet his dark, burning gaze. "Eyeball to eyeball."

"Cole, please, I'm sore."

He dimpled. "Want me to kiss you where you're sore?"

"Stop it!"

"I'm not gonna stop it, so you might as well quit your bellyaching and say your piece now. You're staying right here till it's said, anyhow."

Jessica was left groaning. "Very well. I'll say it. You need to set a better example for your brothers."

Cole laughed and released her nape. "Do I?"

"Yes. They need to be exposed to a respectable town, decent women—"

"Like you?"

"Yes, like me," she snapped.

He flicked his wicked gaze over her curves. "Then let's find out. My deal's still good, sugar. Let's strip off those britches of yours and roll around in the sweet grass. If I'm your first, you'll be my wife by sundown. If not—hell, honey, you're mine, anyway."

At last Jessica managed to spring out of his lap. She trembled before him. "You stop that! Right now."

The rascal only grinned. "You're shaking, honey. You want it, too."

"Maybe you're scaring me," she shot back. "Have you considered that?"

He adamantly shook his head. "Nope, I don't think so. That's one thing I like about you, Jessie. You don't scare easy. Now c'mere."

"No."

"Why not?"

"My God, your ego is incredible," she declared. "You hardly know me, Cole, but you think you've got me pegged, don't you?"

"Yeah, I do."

"Well, let me tell you something. I'm wise to *you*. I haven't known you for long, but I know you're one of those conceited fools who's in love with himself and thinks he's God's gift to women. You're like one great big gland walking around."

He blanched. "What does *that* mean?"

"It means all you want me for is sex."

"So?" he asked.

Jessica could have thrown something at him. "Do you have any idea how demeaning that is?"

He squinted at her. "Huh?"

"You don't care about me as a person. You don't want your mother telling me about your past. You don't want me knowing your wicked little outlaw secrets. You don't trust me, even though I've made no move to escape, or to betray you. You don't respect me. You want sex—end of case."

As she finished her diatribe with chest heaving, he had the grace to appear guilty, and flashed her a cajoling smile. "Ah, sugar, that's not true. I do respect you. I do

114

want to know you." Watching ire shoot into her eyes, he held up a hand. "Other than in the biblical sense. 'Sides, do you think I'd be so hot for you if you didn't have all that spunk and sass?"

She glowered.

He stood and took a step toward her. "They're all part of *you*, Jessie, and it's not just a body I want." His gaze slid over her. "Not that I've ever seen one quite as tempting as yours."

She fought a smile.

He edged closer. "Honey, I didn't mean to insult you. So how 'bout we quit fighting and make up?"

She eyed him in disbelief. "You must be joking."

"Pretty please?" he wheedled, flashing his most winsome grin.

Jessica had to laugh at Cole's contrite expression; he could be a charming devil. And she did need to get him on her side. She extended her hand. "Very well. Truce."

"Truce," he agreed.

But when Cole caught Jessica's hand, instead of shaking it he pulled her close, lowered his face to hers, and claimed her lips. But this time Jessica found she couldn't mind because his kiss was sweet and gentle, a giving of trust rather than a claiming of her will. Still, the touch of his mouth on hers was more tempting and sexy than she could abide.

She broke away and cleared her throat. "So, are you going to let me talk to you now, person to person?"

"I'd rather have another kiss," he teased.

"Cole!"

He chuckled. "All right, sugar. Person to person."

She regarded him soberly. "Cole, you need to start thinking about your brothers' futures."

He set his arms akimbo and frowned. "I'm listening."

"Your ma showed me Mariposa today, and it's such a nice town. If only the whole family could go there, perhaps for church—"

"Church?" he cut in, wild-eyed. "Have you gone haywire, woman? That's the fastest route to the gallows for us all."

"But why? There's no sheriff in town. Your mother is already known locally as Eula Lively. All of you could adopt new names—perhaps similar to those you have now to avoid confusion—and no one will be the wiser."

He snorted. "That's the most loco notion I've ever heard."

"Why? Why is it loco?"

"Because we've survived so far by laying low."

"Really?" she mocked. "You mean by cavorting in dancing parlors and bedding whores?"

His mouth dropped open. "Ma told you that, too?"

"She sure did. And if you can gambol in Colorado City, there's no reason you can't attend church in Mariposa."

"It's different."

"Why?"

"Too many miners in town might guess who we are."

"Don't be silly. No one should guess your real identities if you act respectable." She touched his arm. "If you care for your brothers, you'll give my suggestions some serious thought."

Although the look in his eyes showed he was wavering, he tightened his jaw. "Why?"

"Cole, have you ever been wounded?"

"In the past, Billy and Gabe have both taken flesh wounds. But they recovered."

"Have you ever been arrested? Seems like your ma mentioned something."

Cole paled. "I was. Three years back in Colorado City. But the boys sprung me."

"Then you already know the risks involved in your line of work. You and your brothers have been lucky so far. But sooner or later your luck will run out. You know as well as I do that the inevitable fate of every outlaw is a bullet in the head—or the gallows. You may be willing to risk that for

116

yourself, but don't foist that fate off on your brothers. Please, Cole."

He appeared genuinely swayed by her passionate words. "What are you suggesting?"

"We must expose your brothers to a different kind of life. A respectable life. One they'll want."

Cole scratched his jaw. "Maybe."

She sighed. "I can't do this without your help. Think about it, will you?"

"All right."

Jessica flashed Cole a grateful smile and walked off to retrieve the canteen. Cole watched her, admiring the sexy sway of her hips. He felt so torn. Jessie was so beautiful, and he desired her so much.

But she'd been right to criticize him for lusting after her. At first, the thought of bedding Jessie had been little more than a challenge to him. But she'd stood up to him repeatedly, insisting he respect her. And it was working. Not that he wasn't just as determined to woo her. But something deeper was also developing between them, that first small bond of understanding and trust. Remembering her passionate face when she'd pleaded with him about reforming the gang, he couldn't doubt that her motives were genuine, that this woman honestly wanted to help him and his brothers.

And this scared him badly. Cole had lived a hard life and was unaccustomed to kindness in others, particularly women. It was simple to bed females, complicated as hell when they got under his skin. And Jessie was managing to do that. On the one hand, his instincts urged him to trust her—to open up to her and tell her about his feelings and his past, make himself vulnerable. Yet the last time he had really trusted a female, it had all but gotten him killed. Jessie might mean well, but her good intentions could still send them all straight down the road to hell.

Chapter Eleven

At home, Jessica spent some time with Ma, who took her measurements for her new wardrobe. Afterward, in her room, she wrote up a detailed account of the day's exploits in her journal. She included her encounter with Cole—her frustration at his roguish behavior, her sense of being charmed despite it all. At least he was listening to her point of view, if not really agreeing or cooperating yet.

Still, she had to wonder poignantly if she would ever make it back to her own time, if she'd ever be able to show her journal to those she'd left behind. Even if she did manage to move across time again, would anyone ever believe what had happened to her?

Afterward, Jessica wandered out to the kitchen and volunteered to help Ma chop vegetables for supper. The two women stood at the crude sideboard working and talking.

"Well, I hear tell from Wesley you had quite an adventure this afternoon," Ma commented, hacking an onion.

"Doesn't it bother you when your boys break the law?" Jessica asked, delicately cubing a raw potato.

" 'Course it bedevils me no end," came Ma's indignant response. "That's why I want you to lay down the law to my boys."

Jessica sighed. "You know how I feel about that. We must be able to offer them something better in exchange."

Ma fell grimly silent.

Jessica squared her shoulders. "Tell you what. Let's start this with baby steps."

"Baby steps?"

"Before your boys can have a better life, they must learn to act and behave like gentlemen."

Ma nodded. "I agree. They's wild as March hares."

"You spoke today about how Cole benefited from having a teacher."

"Yeah?" Ma prodded.

"Well, why don't I begin by teaching your four younger boys to read and write?"

A soft gasp escaped Ma and she appeared genuinely moved, her softening expression revealing a mother's tenderness. "You would do that, Miss Jessie?"

"Of course. Everyone should have a right to a basic education. What I need to know is, will you support me in this, see that the boys cooperate when I try to teach them?"

"Will I?" Ma declared, features rapt. "I'll do ya better'n that, honey. I'll beat them little snots senseless if'n they don't toe the mark. Not that we have to worry, 'cause they's all as lovestruck over you as dogs baying at the moon. They'll be buzzing about you like bees to honey."

"That's what I'm afraid of," Jessica replied soberly. "I'll need them polite and attentive, not flirting with me and bickering with each other."

Ma nodded. "You just leave that up to me, honey, and worry about your teachin'."

"That's another matter," Jessica went on with a frown. "I'm going to have to wing this, since I don't have any texts or supplies—much less, visual aids."

Although Ma scowled over the term "visual aids," she soon grinned and snapped her fingers. "I know. I think I still have one or two of Cole's old primers in my storage chest."

"Oh, that will be wonderful!"

"I'll dig 'em up for you tonight."

Jessica glanced about at the sunny room. "And this kitchen will be perfect as a classroom. So it's decided, then. School will begin in the morning."

"Boys, I'd like to have a word with you."

The following morning, Jessica sat in the kitchen, one of Cole's old McGuffey's Readers in her lap, with the four younger brothers gathered across from her, seated in a row of chairs. All regarded her with slicked-back hair and eager smiles. Ma was at the sideboard working dough, and Cole lounged in the back doorway with arms akimbo. His powerful body backlit by sparkling morning sunshine, he appeared the epitome of arrogant, cynical male.

"Why'd you gather us up, ma'am?" Billy asked. "Are you ready to announce which one of us you favor?"

Gabe elbowed him. "Naw, she told us the other night she ain't ready yet."

"Well, she's had two nights to think it over, ain't she?" Billy shot back.

"That's true," chimed in Wesley. "You ready, ma'am?"

Catching sight of Cole fighting laughter, Jessica squared her shoulders. "No, I'm not ready." She opened the primer. "But I am prepared to give you boys a few lessons."

"Lessons in what?" asked Gabe with a lecherous wiggle of his eyebrows.

"Yeah," agreed Luke, rubbing his hands together. "Just what you got there, ma'am?"

"One of Cole's old primers that your mother lent me."

All four men groaned. "Just what are you aimin' to teach us with that there primer?" asked Gabe.

"Well, to begin with, how to read and write—then how to speak like gentlemen."

Indignant looks greeted this statement. "You saying we don't talk like gentlemen?" demanded Billy.

"I'm saying precisely that."

Gabe swung about to his mother. "Ma! You hear that? This here lady is insultin' us!"

Ma waved her rolling pin. "That there lady is right!"

Silence and grumpy looks met Ma's pronouncement.

"How come you want to teach us to talk like gentlemen?" Wesley pursued.

"So you'll be accepted by the community," Jessica replied.

"Huh?" Billy asked, scratching his head.

"What community?" pressed Luke.

Setting down the primer, Jessica stood. "Have you boys given any thought to your futures?"

"Futures?" Gabe echoed with a blank look.

"Yes, your futures. You can't just rob gold shipments all your lives."

"We can't?" Luke asked. "Why not?"

"Because sooner or later you'll want to settle down."

"We will?" Wesley asked.

"Yes. Sociologists tell us that criminal behavior is mainly confined to younger men."

The boys appeared flabbergasted. Billy whispered to Gabe, "You got any idear what the Sam Hill she's talking about?"

"Nope," Gabe answered. "You got any notion, Wesley?"

"Nope. You, Luke?"

Before Luke could put in his two cents' worth, Jessica waved a hand. "Please, listen to me, all of you!"

The ranks snapped to attention.

"What I'm saying is, before long you'll all want to get married and have families."

Billy guffawed. "Oh, that! Why didn't you just say so, sugar?"

121

Jessica balled her hands on her hips. "Well, how do any of you expect to marry decent women if you don't improve your manners?"

"But, sugar, we ain't interested in no decent women," Billy declared smugly. "We want you."

Catching a glimpse of Cole holding his sides, Jessica glowered at the boys. "Are you implying I'm not decent?"

Billy paled. "Oh, no, ma'am."

As Billy's brothers needled him, Ma bristled from the stove, "Yeah, you'd best mind your manners, William Tyler Reklaw, else I'll be making me up some outlaw stew for supper, if you know what I mean."

Billy appeared thoroughly chagrined. "Yes, Ma." He flashed Jessica a lame smile. "Sorry, ma'am. No offense. I was just trying to point out that it's you we're all interested in. You're the apple of our eyes. Right, boys?"

A chorus of eager "Yeah!"s greeted Billy's question.

"But you can't *all* marry me," Jessica contended.

That pronouncement gave the men pause; then Gabe snapped his fingers. "How come? Ain't that what them Mormons do? We'll just all convert and share you, eh, boys?"

The men roared with delight, hooting catcalls and punching one another.

Then Ma charged over and began swinging her rolling pin over her son's heads, prompting them to duck and cringe. "You devils! Hush up that heathen talk. I'll not hear you making a mockery of your religion or that of other folks."

"But, Ma, we ain't got no religion," Billy protested.

Ma glanced him across the head with the back of her hand. "That's just what I mean, you addlebrained pissant! You're managing to make a mockery of it, anyhow."

"Yes, ma'am," said her much-sobered son.

Ma waved her rolling pin toward Jessica. "Carry on, now, ma'am. I'll whip these varmints into line if they insult you again."

"Thanks so much," Jessica responded with a gracious smile. She returned her attention to the now sullen boys and clapped her hands. "Now, where were we?"

"Ma'am, why do you want to learn us to read and write?" Gabe demanded.

"*Teach* you," Jessica said. "I want to teach you. And none of you will ever get far in life, much less find decent wives, if you remain illiterate."

The boys didn't comment, but still appeared morose and unconvinced.

Jessica cleared her throat. "Now, since we only have this one book, we'll need to arrange three chairs in a semicircle. Perhaps I could sit in the middle, with Billy and Gabe on either side of me. Wesley and Luke, you can stand behind us and look over our shoulders."

Gabe and Billy grinned, while Wesley glowered. "Hey, how come me and Luke don't get to sit beside you?"

"Yeah, how come?" Luke seconded.

Exasperated, Jessica said, "Well, we'll switch places from time to time. How's that?"

Wes considered this with a frown, then brightened. "All right with me, I reckon. It'll be like musical chairs, eh?"

"Yeah, like musical chairs," Luke echoed.

"Yes, something like that," Jessica muttered. "Now, boys, if you'll just arrange the chairs . . . "

In the near-fracas that ensued, Jessica struggled to hold onto her patience and Cole all but died laughing as his four brothers scrambled to arrange the chairs, overturning them, punching each other, and growling in the process.

At last Billy motioned to the new arrangement. "Have a seat, ma'am."

"Thank you," Jessica said wearily. With primer in hand, she sat down, only to have Billy and Gabe rush to grab their seats beside her, while Wesley and Luke fell into place at her rear, bending over her as eagerly as dogs with their tongues hanging out.

Squeezed between four strapping, grinning males, Jessica felt as if she were drowning in a sea of spicy pomade and muscled male flesh. She wiggled. "Must you all press in so close?"

"If we don't, we can't see, ma'am," Billy pointed out solemnly, though his eyes gleamed with mischief.

"Very well." Grimacing, she opened the primer, smiling poignantly as she saw the name "Cole" inscribed in childish print on the flyleaf. She flipped a page or two, until she found a listing of the alphabet. "Guess we'll begin with the alphabet."

"What's that?" asked Gabe.

"It's what I'm about to explain," Jessica replied through gritted teeth, "if you men will kindly quit interrupting and listen for a change!"

"Yes, ma'am," said her chastened student.

"Now . . . the alphabet. Do you boys know anything about letters?"

Blank looks greeted her question, and then Billy replied, "Don't recollect we've received any mail of late, ma'am."

"No, I mean *letters,* the alphabet—you know, ABC's."

Gabe snapped his fingers. "Yeah. ABC's. We know about them."

"What do you know?" Jessica pressed.

"Well, when we was little, Ma taught us all how to write our names," Gabe explained. "Ain't that right, Ma?"

"Sure is," Ma replied, chopping away. "I may not know much, but I sure as Sunday can spell all my boys' names."

"Great. That's a beginning." Jessica glanced at the boys. "Do you know anything beyond your names?"

" 'Fraid not, ma'am," Billy said.

"Well, no matter, at least we have a good starting point. Now, Billy, we shall begin with you."

He straightened his spine. "Yes, ma'am."

"Look at this page with the alpha—that is, the ABC's."

"Yes, ma'am."

"These twenty-six letters are symbols—consonants

124

and vowels, that in various combinations make up all the words we use."

Billy appeared mystified and impressed. "Well, hot damn, ma'am."

"None of that language now!" Ma interjected.

"Yes, Ma. Sorry." Billy flashed Jessica a sheepish look.

"Now, I know this seems complicated, but it really is simple." Jessica pulled her pencil out from behind her ear. "First, I shall point to each letter and say it aloud, and I want all of you to repeat it."

The boys dutifully followed Jessica's cues and recited the alphabet.

"Very good," Jessica pronounced afterward. "Now, Billy, I'm going to write your name here in the top margin—"

"Hey, how come Billy gets his name writ first?" asked Gabe.

"For heaven's sake, you'll all get a turn!" Jessica declared, almost losing her patience. "But any more bickering and this lesson is over!"

"Yes, ma'am," said a subdued Gabe.

Jessica began to print Billy's name. "Okay, here we go. B-i-l-l-y. Now, Billy, I'm going to hand you my pencil, and I want you to circle all the letters in the alphabet that are found in your name."

"Hey, that's easy!" Billy quickly went about the task, then frowned at the letter "l." "Hey, ma'am that there letter is used twice in my name. Do I get to circle it twice?"

"Sure, why not." After Billy finished, Jessica printed Gabe's name. "Now you, Gabe."

With Jessica's help, Gabe picked out the letters for his name.

"Hey, it's time for us to switch places now," chimed in Wesley.

"Yeah, so me'n Wes can pick out our names," Luke added.

"Very well," Jessica conceded. "We'll change."

She endured renewed pandemonium as the men moved about, deliberately shoving one another and muttering insults. Then she helped Wesley and Luke pick out their names.

"What next, ma'am?" chimed in Gabe from over her shoulder.

"Next we move again," Billy suggested gleefully.

"No—not again!" implored Jessica.

"Then, what?" asked Wesley. "We're tired of letters."

"Then we'll try a few words, okay?"

The men grumbled but didn't protest too much as she explained the sound each letter represented.

Next she flipped to a page of simple text. "Okay, here we are." She pointed at a word placed beneath an illustration of a dog. "Wes, I bet you can read this word."

Wes scowled. "Well, lemme see. D-O-G."

"Hey, that's a dog!" chimed in Luke.

Wes scowled at his brother. "I was supposed to say it!"

"Well, you spelled it."

"That don't count. It ain't the same as saying it."

"So say it!" cried Jessica.

"*Dog*," Wes uttered proudly.

The other boys laughed. "Guess that must mean old Wesley's a dog," suggested Billy wryly.

Amid more mirth, Wesley twisted about to glare at his brother. "I ain't no dog!"

"Wait a minute!" Jessica shouted, raising a hand. "Wes, please continue. Try reading the simple sentence below the illustration."

Wes scowled. "T-H-E . . . "

When he hesitated, she prompted him. "The."

"D-O-G. *Dog*. R-A-N. *Ran*." He snapped his fingers and grinned. " 'The dog ran.' "

"Excellent," praised Jessica, clapping her hands.

At the sideboard, Ma let out a whoop of joy, pressed hands to her bosom, and gazed heavenward. "My son's reading! He's sure 'nuff reading! Oh, thank you, Lord!"

126

"Yeah, Wes can read just like a four-year-old," jeered Billy.

Wes shot to his feet to confront his brother, punching a finger at Billy's chest. "You take that back, you little runt."

"Will not! You're reading like a baby."

Wes smacked Billy's arm with the book. "And you can't read a'tall. You're plumb ignorant as a cow turd."

Now Billy grew angry, shoving Wes. "You take that back, Wesley Reklaw!"

"Will not!"

"Will so, or by damn, I'll—"

"Stop it!" Just as the men were on the verge of swinging at each other, Jessica surged to her feet and shoved them apart. "That's enough! Both of you!"

Wearing a massive scowl, Wes thrust the book into Jessica's hands. "I ain't reading no more. That there's a baby book."

"And I say you're both *acting* like babies."

"Well, babies or not, we're through with larnin'," Wes retorted.

Jessica was at her wits' end. "Oh, give me a break, will you? I've dealt with two-year-olds who were more reasonable than you four. It's bad enough that the Fates sent me across time. Now I've been cursed with the task of teaching four grown men with attention deficit disorder!"

Total silence fell at these words, the men exchanging bewildered glances. Finally Luke whispered to Gabe, "You got any idear what she's babbling about?"

"Nope." Billy twisted around to face his mother. "Ma, you'd best check the lady here for a fever."

Ma turned furiously on her sons. "Well, if she has one, I'm sure it's you varmints that gave it to her, bedeviling her at every turn." She lumbered toward the men, drying her hands on her apron. "Go on, you rascals, get out of here. School's out for the day. Give the poor schoolmarm a rest."

"Yes, ma'am," replied Billy.

The four men all but tore out the door. That was when Cole, still wearing his look of cynical amusement, sauntered in to join the women. But even as he opened his mouth to speak, his mother hurled him a blistering look and waved a fist. "And not a word out of you, neither, you heathen! You hightail it with the rest of them villains or I'll take my rolling pin to ya!"

"Yes, ma'am," Cole drawled back. Winking at Jessica, he strode out the door.

Jessica sighed in frustration. "Guess I'm not much of a teacher."

Ma patted Jessica's hand. "Now, honey, you're doing just fine. It's just them rascals is a real handful."

"Tell me about it." Her expression discouraged, Jessica held up the primer. "But they're right that this book is way too juvenile for them—much as I do appreciate your lending it to me."

Ma nodded. "Our neighbor lady used to tutor Cole when he was only knee-high to a toadstool."

"Well, the primer is about on the level of a five-year-old, so I can't really blame the boys for calling it a 'baby' book. If only I had a more adult text. And I could use some chalk and a blackboard—guess you'd call it a slate here."

Ma nodded. "Tell you what, honey. Let's go into town again tomorrow morning and see what we can find."

"You mean it?"

"You betcha," Ma said with renewed vigor. "If you're aimin' to improve them rascals of mine, I'm going to help you every way I can."

Chapter Twelve

That night, Jessica was drifting off to sleep when she heard the rocker by the window creaking, followed by a feeble "meow," and realized she wasn't alone.

Gasping, she sat up in bed to see Cole sitting in the rocker, his hard-muscled form outlined by moonlight as he held and petted her kitten. Half afraid she was dreaming, she shook her head, but his image didn't waver one bit. She also couldn't hear the usual rhythmic grunts of Ma's snoring, and she realized Cole must have shut the door between the bedrooms.

"What are you doing here?" she gasped.

"Your kitten missed you," he drawled back.

"I'll just bet!"

"So we decided to come for a visit."

Jessica struggled not to feel charmed. "Don't make excuses. You have to be the nerviest man I've ever known, Cole Reklaw."

He chuckled. "Don't you want to come pet your kitten?"

"Don't try to sweet-talk me. And get out of here—now."

"And if I don't?"

"I'll call your mother."

"Will you? I had to shut her door just so we could hear each other over her snores. Waking the dead would be a lot easier, I reckon."

Jessica ground her teeth in frustration. She was tired and not up to another confrontation. "Please don't make me waken her."

"Will you?" he pressed.

She sighed. "No. I don't relish watching her skin you alive. Okay?"

He laughed.

"Now will you please leave?"

"No."

"Damn it, Cole—"

"We have things to discuss first."

"Do we? Like what?"

"Like the rough time you're having trying to educate my brothers."

"Don't remind me," she said wearily. "And you weren't helping at all, standing there laughing like the very devil."

"You should give up on that bunch."

"Why? You jealous?"

"Maybe."

"Well, forget it. I don't give up that easily."

"Maybe I don't, either," he replied softly.

She groaned. Lord, she had asked for that one.

"You could use a little schooling yourself, sugar."

Sure where he was heading, she protested, "Cole—"

"Like in how to properly sit a horse."

Pleasantly surprised, she laughed. "You've got me to rights there."

"Where are you from that you have no notion of horse-back riding?"

"You wouldn't believe me if I told you."

"Ah, so you're being a lady of mystery again. That's mighty tempting to a man."

"And you have to be the most easily tempted man I've ever met."

He chuckled. "Lord, you're sassy. I'll have to give you some riding lessons, though."

"Yes, that might be useful," she replied tightly.

He fell silent for a moment, and all she could hear was the creaking of the rocker. Then he continued in more thoughtful tones, "You know, I've been thinking about what you said yesterday, Jessie. How I don't respect you."

"Indeed," she agreed. "Case in point, you are sitting in my bedroom right this minute, like a great big lug—despite the fact that I've repeatedly asked you to leave."

Ignoring her complaint, he murmured, "I do respect you, Jessie. I even respect your trying to reform those wayward brothers of mine. It means a lot to my ma, you know."

For once Jessica couldn't doubt his sincerity. "Thank you."

"I've been thinking about what else you said—how I don't want you knowing my secrets."

"Have you come to share them?" she taunted.

"Maybe I'll tell you one," he replied.

"Really?"

"Yeah. Today when you were teaching the boys, it did bring back memories of when I was just five, and was tutored by the neighbor lady, Mrs. Joiner. That was one of the best years of my childhood. Mrs. Joiner was from back East, well educated, and she had two of the prettiest little blond daughters you've ever seen in your life. I learned a lot in the time we had together, and the girls and me had a lot of fun playing." He sighed. "Then that whole family caught scarlet fever, and all four of them died. Why I was spared, I'll never know."

As he paused for a moment, obviously struggling against emotion, she whispered, "I'm glad you were."

"Are you, sugar?" For once Cole's words lacked the

usual blatant insinuation. "I'll never forget my ma at the funeral, sobbing over those two little caskets. 'They're angels,' she cried. 'Angels gone straight to heaven.' "

Jessica's heart twisted at the image. "I'm truly sorry, Cole."

"Well, you know what these times are like," he went on more philosophically. "I've lost two fathers, countless friends. Surely you've lost some of your own people."

That statement gave Jessica pause. She might well have lost her "people" forever. The thought made her throat tighten with emotion, and made her feel closer to Cole than she wanted to feel.

"Yes, I've lost a lot," she managed. "Like both sets of grandparents when I was younger."

"And when you lose folks, you must realize how important it is to grab what pleasure we can in the here and now."

"Ah," she murmured cynically. "Why do I suspect a new turn down the primrose path? You're not much of a sagebrush philosopher, Cole—not with motives so transparent."

He chuckled again. "I may be more of a thinker than you know, sugar. You've already got me ready to admit I haven't been a very good example to my brothers."

"No!" she exclaimed in mock disbelief, and they both laughed.

"I admire what you're doing, Jessie, even though I fear the path you're taking us down is more dangerous than the one we're bound on now. I respect you, anyhow—and I still want you. Have no doubt about that."

Feeling aroused despite herself, she shook her head. "Cole, you're such a contradiction, trying to convince me your motives are noble, then all but admitting they're not."

"Jessie, any man who's not six feet under is gonna want you. As Billy is fond of saying, 'that's just the facts, ma'am.' Would you find me more noble if I dressed up

132

my desires behind candy, flowers, and sugary compliments, maybe eloquent proposals of marriage? Truth is, those that want you, including my brothers, all want the same thing as me. I'm the only one being honest about it."

"And that's why I'm so little impressed with the motives of any of you." She eyed him in supplication. "Cole, I'm tired. Will you leave?"

"No, we got other matters to discuss."

"Like what?"

He inclined his head toward the open window. "Like maybe what a fine sight the stars are, and how pleasing the new moon is. If you listen, you can hear a screech owl hooting, and the wind rustling the pines."

Treacherously charmed, she cleared her throat. "Thanks for the lessons on night sounds—"

"Oh, far as *night sounds* go, I haven't even begun to teach you, sugar."

His words set her trembling. "Will you please go?"

He fell quiet, and the kitten mewled again. "Not till you come pet your kitten. It's downright mean of you to ignore her."

"Very well." Jessica got out of bed, hastily shimmied into her wrapper, and crossed the room. Heart thumping at Cole's nearness, she reached out and scratched the kitten's head, smiling as she heard the tiny creature purr. "There."

His fingers closed over her wrist. "That isn't enough. She needs a slow, gentle stroking."

"Cole, stop it."

"Stop what?"

"You know what!"

His voice was deep, wicked. "Pet her right."

"Oh, very well." For a few moments she stroked the kitten and listened to the rising crescendo of her purring.

"She needs a name, you know."

Startled, she glanced up, and her eyes met his vibrant, dark gaze. "She what?"

Eugenia Riley

"What are you aiming to call her?"

"Well, I hadn't thought."

"You're not a very responsible kitten owner."

"I never asked to be a pet owner."

"Well, you are one now. And you need to name her."

Jessica thought for a moment. "If I name her, will you leave?"

"Maybe."

She sighed. "Very well. I'll call her Inkspot."

"What kind of name is that?"

"I think it's a fine name, and it suits her."

"Spell it."

"What?"

"You spelled out my brothers' names today. Now you can spell out the name of your kitten."

"If you aren't the most exasperating—"

"*Spell it.*"

"All right! I-N-K-S-P-O-T. Now will you kindly leave?"

He grinned. "Sure, sugar. Just as soon as you kiss me good night."

"What? That's not fair. You said you would leave—"

"I said maybe."

"Well, forget it."

But even as she started off, he grabbed a handful of her wrapper. "Hold it."

"Cole!" Fuming, she twisted about to face him.

He extended the ball of fur. "Take the kitten."

"No."

"Take her."

Jessica took the kitten.

His voice turned husky. "Now c'mere, darlin'."

Jessica almost dissolved at his sexy words, so sinfully drawled, but still she managed to stammer, "N-no."

He pulled her down into his lap.

The sensation was unbearably erotic, being hauled down against Cole's hard body, with only two flimsy lay-

134

ers of handkerchief linen separating them. His scent was thrilling her senses and his strong arms holding her captive. The breeze wafting through the window was cool and fragrant with night scents, urging her to cuddle against his warm strength. And the kitten purred loudly, only adding to the sensual ambiance.

When Cole's seductive lips just brushed her cheek, Jessica thought she would come unglued. "Cole, please let me up."

His large hand gently stroked her middle, sending heat radiating downward. "Your voice is trembling, sugar. Am I getting you all rattled?"

"I said let me up!"

"Not till you kiss me good night."

"Damn you!"

His voice held a note of sadness. "Jessie, why do you always fight me, when you know you want me, too?"

That question compelled an honest response. "Not everything I want is best for me."

"Oh, honey," he murmured in silky tones that left her melting deep inside, "you're wrong."

Her resistance in tatters, Jessica looked up at Cole, only to wince at the blaze of passion in his eyes.

"I'm waiting, sugar."

Drowning in frustration and desire, Jessica lifted her lips toward his.

It was all the encouragement Cole needed. His mouth closed over hers in a kiss of raw sweetness. When his tongue eased between her lips, then plunged deep to ravish her mouth, rapture surged through her in torrid waves that staggered her as she felt her control spinning away.

Breathlessly she pulled away. "Cole, please—"

"Jessie, admit you want more. Want *me*."

"No."

"Really?"

Cole's large hand cupped her breast, and Jessica was

staggered with desire. She could not summon the will to fight him.

"That's not what your tight little nipple is telling me," he whispered. "It's telling me it wants my mouth, my tongue. Wants *me* inside you."

Her words shuddered forth. "Only if you force this, Cole."

He sighed. "Darlin', I'm not forcing anything on you that you don't want."

"Then you'll go," she stated quietly.

He hesitated for a long moment, then conceded her point with a groan. "Give me one more kiss, then I'll tuck you and the kitten into bed."

"I'll do no such thing."

"One more kiss," he repeated obdurately.

Arguing with this stubborn man proved impossible. Jessica pressed her lips to Cole's even as his mouth captured hers again, so pleasurably. Then he set the rocker into slow motion, rolling Jessica's bottom against the hardness of his aroused manhood and sending hot needles of desire shooting upward. His hand remained gently cupped around her breast, and his mouth devoured hers without restraint. It was torture beyond bearing, pleasure beyond belief. Jessica moaned and clung to him.

She hardly noticed a moment later when Cole rose and carried her and the kitten to the bed, laid them down and covered her.

"Want some company, sugar?" he whispered.

"Cole, please, I can't."

His hard knee moved between hers. "If I stayed, you wouldn't fight me."

"But you wouldn't have my consent, either."

He regarded her sadly. "You're right. And I don't just want your consent, Jessie. I want your *surrender*. And I'm going to get it."

As he turned and left her struggling with frustrated desire, Jessica didn't doubt him. She knew Cole Reklaw was all wrong for her. But every time he wooed her, charmed her, kissed her, she found herself closer to losing control.

Leaving the house and striding across the cool, moonlit yard toward the bunkhouse, Cole struggled with mixed emotions. He had gone to Jessie's room tonight intent on seducing her, yet instead a part of himself had been exposed.

He had shared with her experiences, feelings from his childhood. He had admitted his admiration and respect for her. It wasn't like him to bare his feelings that way to a woman, to put himself at risk of being hurt or betrayed.

Yet Jessie was different. Increasingly it was not just her tempting body he wanted, but her—her spirit, her intelligence, her wit. He realized in awe that he'd finally met a woman who was his equal, a woman who stood her ground and refused to be bullied by him. And he wanted her coming to him in spirit, not just in body. It was not just a physical coupling he craved but a more emotional sharing.

Could he afford to risk his heart again? Every time he tried to penetrate Jessica's defenses, he found more of his own barriers being stripped away.

Chapter Thirteen

"Will there be anything else, Mrs. Lively?" Mr. Allgood asked.

"Reckon that'll do," Ma Reklaw replied.

At Allgood's General Store late the next morning, Jessica stood with Ma at the counter, a heap of goods piled before them—everything from a slate and chalk to bundles of pencils and sheaves of papers.

Mr. Allgood, a rotund little man with thinning brown hair, winked at Jessica. "Looks like someone's fixin' to hold school."

Before Jessica could reply, Ma countered, "What makes you say that?"

"Well, the writing supplies, the slate."

Ma harrumphed. "Cousin Jessie here just aims to help me polish up my three R's a bit."

The merchant appeared mystified.

Jessica quickly stepped in. "Actually, Mrs. Lively hates to brag, but she has five sons—my, er, cousins—and they're the ones I'm planning to tutor."

While Ma shot Jessica a withering look, a clearly surprised Allgood remarked, "You have sons, Mrs. Lively? Why, I had no idea. Although you do seem to buy a lot of supplies for just one person—so I assumed you must have help out at your farm."

"Yes, I have sons," Ma shot back, hurling Jessica another blistering look.

"Why haven't we seen them in town?"

"Because they're too busy working the farm!" Ma retorted. "They're a sober, hardworking lot, I'll have you know."

Allgood paled at her hostile tone. "Oh, I'm sure they are, Mrs. Lively. I had no intention of hinting otherwise. And we here in the town would love to meet them."

"Yes, wouldn't that be wonderful?" Jessica agreed, clapping her hands. "As a matter of fact, I was just telling Ma—that is, Aunt Eula—that the whole family should come in to church."

"Oh, you'd all be most welcome," Allgood replied.

Ma made a sound of contempt. "Well, you know how these highfalutin' cousins from back East are, always trying to give the whole family religion, and educate the lot, to boot."

Allgood smiled at Jessica. "There are plenty of children here in town that could use some learning." He snapped his fingers. "And you know, Mayor Polk has spoken of needing an educated person to write our town's history for the Founders' Day celebration next month."

"Why, that sounds fascinating," Jessica commented.

"If you want to volunteer, you could speak with Mayor Polk about it at church this Sunday."

Before Jessica could reply, Ma snorted loudly. "Can we settle up with you now? The day ain't gettin' no younger, and we'd best be on our way."

The merchant's expression sagged. "Yes, ma'am."

Once the two women were in the buckboard driving away, Ma lit into Jessica again. "How come you were spoutin' off at the mouth 'bout my boys to Merchant All-good? Last time you was spillin' your beans to Granger, and today was worse!"

"Didn't we agree that your sons need more exposure to the town?" Jessica countered.

"Well, maybe *you* agreed."

"Come on now, Mrs. Reklaw. You said you would support me."

"I said I would support you *learnin'* 'em. I think you really want me 'supporting' 'em all the way to the hanging tree. You had no call telling that man about my boys."

"But why not, if we're careful? I've thought this through. I have a plan for introducing your sons to the town, a plan that will ensure no one will guess their true identities."

Ma shook a finger. "Your plans are gonna land us all in deep trouble."

"I disagree. In fact, I think your performance with Mr. Allgood was inspired."

Ma was perplexed. "Huh?"

"It was very *smart*, what you said to him."

"How so?"

"Well, you mentioned that I'm trying to get your boys educated and attending church. When you think about it, my arrival here is the perfect excuse for introducing your sons to the community. I'm your niece from back East, and I'm insisting the entire family socialize more." She patted Ma's arm. "It makes perfect sense. Thanks again for your brilliant ploy."

"If you say so," Eula mumbled. But a grudging smile proved she was charmed by Jessica's praise.

Jessica fell silent as they passed Mariposa's weather-beaten, small gray schoolhouse on the outskirts of town. A couple of young girls were jumping rope on the sagging front porch. "You know, these people really do need a schoolteacher."

Ma's look was virulent. "Now, don't you go getting no

more fancy ideas, missy. You've already got this family headin' straight down a blind trail into a box canyon."

Jessica didn't press her point further. She knew she'd have to be satisfied with making only small steps toward progress with this stubborn, willful family.

At home, Jessica sat on her bed with the various school supplies arranged around her. She wondered how she could effectively teach the four younger Reklaw brothers. Talk about fighting an uphill battle!

And it seemed everyone was thwarting her efforts, including Ma and Cole. But her more immediate problem was, how could she teach the four younger boys to read and write, when they were determined not to learn from a "baby" primer?

Maybe she needed to develop her own teaching materials. After all, if she was capable of writing a dissertation, surely she could draft an adult-level basic primer. But how? She had no computer here, not even a typewriter, much less a Xerox machine.

She'd just have to make do with the supplies she had, and find some way to make the materials hold the interest of four grown men—who were bad boys, to boot.

That was a tall order, unless . . . Jessica smiled as a devilishly clever idea struck her. She picked up the slate, put it in her lap, stacked papers on it, grabbed a pencil, and began to write. . . .

"Good morning, gentlemen. Please, come right in and take your places."

The next morning, as the four younger brothers filed into the kitchen to join Jessica, she was prepared, sitting with her primer—a collection of folded papers tied together with twine—in her lap. She'd stayed up past midnight writing and illustrating her own text for today's lesson. Behind her, her slate was displayed against the pie safe, the wooden knobs holding it upright. Cole wasn't present this morning, but Ma was sitting in a far corner, rocking and sewing a seam in some purple gingham for one of Jessica's new frocks.

Wesley scowled at the pages in Jessica's lap. "You aimin' to teach us with another baby book?"

"No, not at all," she responded pleasantly. "I think you'll find today's lesson most intriguing."

The boys appeared confused, muttering to one another. "What ya mean by that?" Billy asked.

"Sit down and find out."

After the inevitable battles over arranging the chairs in a semicircle, and who would get to sit by Jessica, the men took their places. Jessica deliberately put Wes and Luke on either side of her, since they seemed the more serious of the four brothers. Wearing frowns that bespoke their displeasure, Billy and Gabe stood behind Jessica.

Wesley scowled at the "cover" of Jessica's book, which showed a cowboy smiling at a lady in a pretty dress, with lettering scrawled beneath. "What you got there, ma'am?"

"Why, this is a story I wrote for the four of you."

Behind her, Gabe gasped. "You wrote us a sure 'nuff story, ma'am? Will you read it to us?"

"Of course I won't read it," came Jessica's crisp response. "I wrote it so you boys can read it."

"But, ma'am, we don't know how to read!" protested Billy.

"My point exactly—and the very reason I wrote the story. You're going to use it to *learn* to read—and I think we'll begin with Luke."

"Me?" he asked, pressing a hand to his chest.

"Yes, you. Now, Luke, take a look at the writing below the pictures and see if you recognize anything."

He scowled at Jessica's neat lettering. "T-h-e." Abruptly he grinned. "Would that be 'the,' ma'am?"

"Precisely! See how easy this is?"

"Yeah, but look at the next word," Wesley pointed out, grimacing. "Longer than the devil's tail."

Fighting laughter, Jessica said, "Then I think you're the man to tackle it."

"Me?"

"Come on. Courage."

Wes scowled at the letters. "Well, ma'am, would that first one be an 'a'?"

"Right."

"But I don't know the next one."

"It's a 'd'!" declared Gabe.

Jessica twisted about to smile up at Gabe. "Right you are. Now who can guess the next letter?"

The men started to have fun, like children trying to solve a puzzle. With a little help from her, they managed to sound out the word "adventures."

" 'The adventures,' " pronounced Luke proudly. "But the adventures of what, ma'am?"

Jessica clapped her hands. "Luke, that's splendid! You just guessed the next word! It's 'of.' "

"Well, hot damn," he declared proudly.

"Yeah, but look at that next word," put in Wes with a troubled frown. "W-i-n . . . "

"Windbag!" guessed Billy.

"Naw, winding!" suggested Gabe.

"Hold it!" Jessica scolded. "*Look* at the letters and try to sound out the word. Don't just guess."

There was a moment of dead silence, then Luke mused, "Looks like a name to me."

"Yeah—Wilfred," suggested Gabe.

"Close—but not quite," Jessica said.

Wes snapped his fingers. "Winfield."

"Closer yet, but still no cigar."

All at once Billy hooted. "I know! It's Whinny-furd."

Jessica struggled not to laugh. "*Winifred.*"

"Right," Billy said. "Just what I said, teacher.

'Whinny-furd.' Them there's 'The Adventures of Whinny-furd and C-L-Y . . . ''

"Clyde!" exclaimed Gabe. " 'The Adventures of Whinny-furd and Clyde'!"

"Yes. Exactly right."

"Are we sure 'nuff reading, ma'am?" Wesley inquired raptly.

"Sure enough," Jessica pronounced.

The boys were grinning and congratulating one another when abruptly all were distracted by the sounds of loud sobbing. All watched as Ma got up from her rocker, wiping tears on her sleeve.

She crossed over, giving Jessica a bear hug. Straightening, she clasped her hands to her bosom, her expression ecstatic. "My boys is sure 'nuff readin'. Not just words, but bunches of 'em. And here I was thinkin' they was all lost souls and plumb ignorant. Thank you, ma'am. For as long as I live, I won't forget this. It's more joy than I can abide."

"You're welcome, Mrs. Reklaw," Jessica said sincerely.

Sniffing tears, Eula lumbered out of the kitchen.

"Teach us more!" ordered Billy.

"Of course," Jessica said brightly. "But before we go further, I want to tell you that I intend this primer to be a text not only for your education but also for your social enlightenment."

"Huh?" Gabe asked.

"Social *what*?" asked Billy.

"I intend for it to teach you how to act while out in polite society. You'll learn some—er—manners, through reading about the adventures of Winifred and Clyde."

Dubious silence greeted this pronouncement.

Jessica flipped a page. "Here we have Chapter One, where Winifred and Clyde will meet. Luke, will you begin?"

"Yes, ma'am. Only I have a question. Is this Whinny-furd a man or a woman?"

Gabe punched him. "Why she's a female, a'course, idjut. You think old Clyde would be adventurin' with another fella?"

"Well, I didn't know," Luke said defensively.

"Yes, Winifred is a woman," Jessica confirmed. "A *lady*."

"And what's Clyde?" asked a deep voice from across the room.

At the sound of the new voice, everyone glanced up to see Cole standing in the doorway, eyes gleaming with merriment.

Jessica smiled back brightly. "Why, Mr. Reklaw, how kind of you to join us. To answer your question, *Clyde* is a scoundrel."

"Oh, is he?"

"Yes, he's a stage robber."

"Like us?" cried Billy.

Jessica didn't take her eyes off Cole. "Precisely. Just like you."

A cynical smile curving his mouth, Cole stepped inside, seating himself on a bench nearby. "Then this is one story I've got to hear."

"Yes, ma'am!" agreed Gabe. "Let's read."

Through the laborious efforts of all four men, they were able to make out the words on Jessica's first page: "Once upon a time in the old West . . . "

Then Jessica turned a page, revealing the first of many illustrations, and that was when pandemonium erupted.

"Well, lookie there!" declared Billy, pointing at the first picture. "There's Miss Whinny-furd in a stagecoach. You can see her pretty face in the winder. Why, ma'am, she looks just like you on the day we met."

"Doesn't she now?" Jessica agreed smugly.

Gabe pointed at the next illustration. "And that there must be Clyde chasing the stage, a'firin' away! Hot damn, if he don't look like Cole."

"Correct once again." Jessica glanced at Cole to see

him scowling now. She flashed him a brilliant smile.

Wes reached out and flipped the next page. "There's Clyde stopping the stage!"

Luke howled with laughter. "And there's Miss Whinny-furd a' boxin' Clyde's ears!"

"And Clyde crawling away like a clobbered snake," declared Gabe.

"Boys!" Jessica protested. "You're supposed to *read*, not just look at the pictures and guess. Why, you've already come to the end of Chapter One."

But her admonition came too late, as Billy flipped another page. "And there's Miss Whinny-furd . . . Heck, now the stagecoach is gone and so is Clyde. Looks like she's a'prayin'."

"She's in church," Jessica explained.

"And here comes old Clyde," put in Luke. "Why, he's a'kissin' Miss Whinny-furd's hand. And sharing her hymnal."

"Now they're eatin' fried chicken together," pronounced Billy.

"Ma'am, what does all this mean?" asked Wes.

Jessica sighed. "Well, you were supposed to read about it, but—"

"Please, ma'am, tell us!" implored Luke.

"Very well." Again glancing straight at Cole, whose expression now smoldered, Jessica spoke vehemently. "What it means is, if you want to meet a proper lady, don't kidnap her off a stagecoach, but meet her at church."

At this pronouncement, Cole smiled slightly, a nasty smile. The boys fell silent and exchanged guilty looks.

Jessica flipped back to the first page. "Now that you've had your fun, boys, we're going to go back and learn to read *every single word*. Is that clear?"

"Yes, ma'am," replied four subdued voices in unison.

Cole left long before Jessica's "lesson" was completed. But as she was leaving the kitchen after finally dismissing the boys, she felt her arm being grabbed. Before she could protest, Cole wordlessly pulled her across the porch and around to the back of the house. Grabbing her by the shoulders, he pressed her body against the cool stone and stared down at her forbiddingly. From his dark and brooding expression, Jessica was sure she was in trouble, but she refused to cringe from him.

"What do you want?" she asked irritably.

"Seems to me the teacher is telling tales out of school," he remarked with deliberate menace.

"So what if I am?" she countered recklessly. "If it gets the message across to your brothers, so be it."

"Well, maybe I say the teacher needs to be punished for breaking the rules."

"And I say, why don't you just go choke and die?"

Cole shook his head. "You sure are feisty for a woman who's cornered."

"Cornered?" she mocked. "That's a laugh. One false move, mister, and I'm screaming bloody murder. We'll see how 'cornered' I am when Ma comes running with her broom."

Cole backed away slightly, anger tightening his features. "Do it, Jessie, and I'll make you sorry."

"For heaven's sake! What do you want?"

He regarded her belligerently. "You made fun of me in there, Jessie, and after I shared things with you. I want you to take your medicine."

"Be serious!"

"I am serious." He edged closer, until she could feel his hot breath on her cheek. "Now, just how do we punish the teacher? Maybe rap her knuckles?" As Jessica gasped, Cole lifted one of her hands, his dark gaze burning into hers as he slowly kissed each knuckle. "Naw, they're too pretty."

"Cole!" Jessica snatched her hand away.

Abruptly he pushed her back into the wall with his hard body. His soft voice sent chills down her spine. "How 'bout we give her a spanking?"

"Stop it!"

"A tempting notion, but I think I have a better idea."

"You can take your idea and—"

But the rest of her comment was smothered as Cole kissed her passionately. She tried to resist, turning her head, but Cole seized her face in his hands, forcing her to yield to his demanding lips and rapacious tongue. He continued to kiss her ruthlessly until she quit fighting and her lips softened against his own. To her horror, she felt herself responding, softening deep inside.

At last, breathless, she shoved him away. "Cole, stop it. You're violating me against my will—"

"I'm what?"

"Kissing me without my consent."

"And you ridiculed me without mine," he shot back. "So we're even. How's it feel, honey?"

Jessica was fuming. "Lord, I can't believe how arrogant and conceited you are! You need to quit taking yourself so damn seriously."

"Oh, do I?"

"Yes! Furthermore, as far as the lessons go, you know I'm performing a valuable function—"

"You were mocking me," he cut in darkly, "and you do so at your peril."

"My God, you're unbelievable. Cole, your brothers need to learn that if they want to meet a lady they can marry, they should do so at church, not by bushwhacking her off a stage."

"Are you so sure?"

"I'm sure you're a man with anything but marriage on *his* mind."

Surprising her, Cole grinned. "Oh, yeah? Then maybe you still don't know how tempting I find you."

Jessica was totally caught off-guard by his comment, and her mouth fell open. Cole took advantage of the situation by kissing her again.

* * *

After Cole released Jessica, he watched her go running back inside the house without a backward glance. Lord, this woman had his head in a spin. After tasting her again, he was burning with frustrated passion.

Was Jessie just a tease? The other night he had shared with her, risked his feelings with her; then today she had mocked him, needling his pride. It made him wonder if her motives were so upstanding, after all.

Hell. Through it all he just wanted her. Wanted to unravel her mysteries and level her pride. Wanted her in his bed, wanted to set her in her place.

Or did he? Truth to tell, maybe it was the challenge of her he craved most of all. . . .

Safe in her room, Jessica leaned against the wall, breathing hard, trembling. The nerve of that man, taking her to task for trying to educate his brothers, brazenly kissing her, even hinting he was willing to marry her to get her in his bed. Again she was angry at herself for allowing Cole Reklaw to rattle her.

Yet wasn't his behavior also proof that she was getting under his skin? She smiled. Yes, it seemed she was penetrating his defenses, chafing his pride, even forcing him to think.

Cole might have power over her, but she also had control over him—perhaps even the means to make this hardened outlaw change.

Chapter Fourteen

Over the next few days, Jessica continued to tutor her four charges, with great success, even as Ma busied herself with Jessica's new wardrobe. Soon, Jessica had two new dresses, one of purple gingham and one of yellow muslin. Ma was quite a skilled seamstress, and when Jessica wore her frocks, she caught appreciative looks from all the men, Cole included. She often wore her hair down or tied with a ribbon at her nape, and began to feel decidedly old-fashioned.

She faithfully recorded all her experiences in her journal, often taking a few moments to jot down the day's impressions as the boys were practicing their penmanship. And while she continued to miss her family in the present, she became more accepting of her fate, and her existence in the nineteenth century. After all, there was nothing she could do to change things—at least, not as far as she knew.

Her greatest achievement was in teaching the "boys." Enchanted by "The Adventures of Winifred and Clyde," the four younger brothers were soon able to read simple sentences. Jessica also corrected their grammar—and their manners—at every juncture, trying to shape them into polished young gentlemen.

Cole occasionally stopped by to monitor the lessons, but soon lost interest. Then one morning just as Jessica was ready to begin class, he strode into the kitchen. Dressed for the trail in chaps, jacket, and a western hat, he assumed an arrogant stance, hands shoved in his trouser pockets. He appeared all daunting outlaw, especially with the shadow of whiskers along his handsome jaw.

"I need Billy today," he announced.

"But we're just beginning the day's lessons," she protested.

"Yeah, and Miss Jessie says I get to read first today," put in Billy with obvious disappointment.

Cole made a sound of contempt. "You want to learn your ABC's like a baby or come with me to Colorado City to take care of business?"

Billy lit up. "Colorado City? Well, why didn't you just say so in the first place, big brother? Will we get to visit the dancing parlors, too?"

"And can the rest of us come along?" asked Luke.

"Nope, you men know the rules," Cole replied firmly. "Never more than two of us can go to Colorado City or the Springs, not since the incident. If all five of us show up together we might be recognized."

The other brothers fell glumly silent.

"So, you coming, Billy?" he asked.

Billy popped up. "You betcha. The rest of you boys have fun readin' to Miss Jessie. Cole and me—"

"*I,*" Jessica corrected. "Cole and I."

Billy grinned. "Cole and I may just go find us a *real* Whinny-furd!"

At this, the men broke up laughing. Jessica regarded Cole coolly; he raised an eyebrow arrogantly.

Jessica rose and cleared her throat. "Mr. Reklaw, may I have a word with you before you leave?"

He dipped into a mocking bow. "Why, of course, ma'am." He gestured for her to precede him outside.

On the back porch, he took a moment to eye her appreciatively. "That's a mighty pretty dress, sugar."

Though annoyed with him, she couldn't insult his mother. "Thank you. You're mother's a marvel with a needle and thread."

"So she is." His voice dipped to husky note. "I especially like that low, lace-trimmed bodice and tight waist."

She defensively crossed her arms over her bosom. "You an expert on ladies' fashions now?"

He chuckled. "So what's on your mind, sugar?"

"I don't like you taking my student away from class."

"You jealous?"

"Don't flatter yourself."

"Not even curious?" he teased.

"As a matter of fact, I am curious. Why are you and Billy bound for Colorado City? And what was the 'incident' you mentioned? Were you referring to the time you were arrested?"

He rocked on his boot heels. "Sorry, sugar, it's gang business."

"Gang business, my butt," she retorted.

He laughed. "You *are* jealous."

She slanted him a chiding glance. "Try disappointed. Especially that you're so blatantly undermining my efforts."

He slowly shook his head. "Jessie, you know what I am."

"Yes, I know."

The two were regarding each other tensely when Billy stepped out onto the porch, fastening on his gun belt. "So, big brother, you ready to hightail it yet? Or are you gonna spend the whole day sparkin' Miss Jessie?"

Cole winked at Jessica. "Later, sugar."

She didn't reply, her expression turbulent.

Jessica hated to admit it, but, over the next day and a half, she did a slow burn at the thought of Cole and Billy being off in "sinful" Colorado City. After lessons with the boys, she sat on the front porch, petting her kitten, trying to tell herself she was angry because Cole had disrupted her lesson and was thwarting her efforts to reform his brothers. But she also couldn't help remembering his fiery kisses and sexy words, and she finally had to admit the real reason she was upset. She *was* jealous—jealous as hell at the thought of him spending the night in bed with some Jezebel, while she sat here fuming. How could he tease her and woo her, then brazenly ride off to consort with some whore?

Cole and Billy didn't arrive home until supper time the following day, both appearing tired and subdued when they joined the family at the dinner table. Gabe, Wes, and Luke made up for their reticence.

"Billy, you got no idear what you missed today," Gabe related. "Do you know there ain't no such word as ain't?"

"Yeah, ain't that a hoot!" seconded Wes.

"And today old Clyde tried to steal a kiss from Miss Whinny-furd behind the barn," added Luke.

"And Miss Whinny-furd lit poor old Clyde's britches on fire!" finished Gabe. "Why, it was almost more carrying on than the three of us could abide."

Cole glanced sharply at Jessica. "Yep, sounds like Miss Winifred could light a fire in just about any man."

Jessica flashed him a long-suffering look.

Ma spoke up. "So, what sin was you and Billy into over at Colorado City? Did you feather some hurty-gurty gal's nest?"

Cole chuckled. "Not quite. But we found out some interesting information."

"Yeah?" Ma prompted.

Cole glanced at Jessica. "Perhaps we should discuss this later."

While Jessica regarded Cole coolly, Ma snorted. "Are you thinkin' you'll be keeping your little secrets from Jessie here? You think she's so plumb ignorant she won't

153

figure it out? 'Sides, you know your brothers'll spill the beans to her."

He sighed. "I just thought it might be in Jessie's best interests not to know—"

"From the man who has my best interests at heart," Jessica finished cynically, prompting laughter from Cole's brothers.

"Very well," he said wearily. "I'll tell you. You'll find out soon enough, anyway. Billy and I learned that Elijah Miser and his cronies are coming out tomorrow to inspect the mines."

"Who's Elijah Miser?" Jessica asked.

"He and his associates from Colorado Springs make up the Aspen Gulch Consortium that owns the mines. Miser is president."

"And he and his den of snakes suck up the lifeblood of the menfolks in these parts," Ma put in, eyes gleaming vengefully. "That bastard sent two husbands of mine to the grave."

Flashing Ma a sympathetic smile, Jessica still felt needles of suspicion. "How did you get this information about Elijah Miser? Don't tell me he hangs out in Sin City?"

"No, but his secretary, Calvin Stickles, likes to visit a little line gal over on Colorado Avenue," Billy replied.

Ma gasped. "Why, you two heathens! So you was visitin' the red light district!"

"Only to get information, Ma," Cole protested.

"I'll believe that when a weasel sprouts wings," Ma spat.

Jessica was tempted to add "amen," but restrained herself and glowered at the two prodigals instead.

Ignoring his mother's outburst and Jessica's harsh look, Cole continued. "Anyway, boys, the entire consortium is visiting the mines tomorrow, and I say we give them a welcoming party."

"Yeah!" seconded Gabe. "We'll set *their* britches on fire!"

"I say we string 'em up!" put in Wes.

But Cole held up a hand. "Boys, you know we draw the line at murder. But I think we can get our message across to those jackals that they're not welcome in these parts."

"Yeah!" agreed Gabe, pounding a fist.

While the men exuberantly plotted their exploits, Jessica glanced at Ma, who ruefully shook her head. Jessica excused herself, set her dishes on the sideboard, grabbed a shawl, and strolled outside onto the front porch. Standing by the railing, she noted the day had cooled down and the wind had picked up slightly; the red-gold sunset was spectacular; the sinking sun painted the misty white mountain peaks in soft rosy pastels. She watched an eagle soar in the distance above the trees.

Despite the awe-inspiring setting, she felt down. She didn't know why she was here—but it was certain that she wasn't doing this family a bit of good.

"Sugar?" called a familiar voice.

She turned to frown at Cole, who stepped out to join her. If anything, the time on the trail had only made him look more handsome and rugged. Tempting though he was, Jessica remained miffed.

"Do you mind? I came out here for a moment of solitude."

He whistled. "How come you got your feathers in such a ruffle? I thought you set great store by your manners."

"And I thought you set great store by your word."

"What word?"

"See what I mean? Just days ago, you admitted to me that you haven't been a good example for your brothers. Now you go off carousing in Colorado City, and planning God knows what else."

"Jessie, you know I never promised you anything."

"That's right," she rejoined bitterly. "You sure haven't."

"Sugar, what do you expect? We still gotta earn a living."

"Look, why don't you go? I'm tired of your lame excuses."

155

He eyed her thoughtfully. "You look melancholy, sugar."

"And not because I've been pining away for you, so don't get any ideas."

He raised a hand. "All right. I won't. Guess I was a bit hard on you a few days ago."

Surprised, she muttered, "Yes, you were."

"A man doesn't take kindly to being mocked by his woman."

"I'm not your woman."

He edged closer. "Wanna kiss and make up?"

"Cole—"

Surprising her, he said, "Come on, let's go for a ride."

"What?" she asked, taken aback.

"Well, why should you just stand here feeling sorry for yourself? You need to take your mind off your troubles."

"Cole, it's much too late in the day for a ride."

But Cole was already tugging her down the steps. "Nope, it isn't. We've got close to an hour of light left. 'Sides, we won't go far."

She dug in her heels. "You're forgetting I can't ride."

He tugged her on again. "No, I'm not. That's why I'm fixin' to teach you. 'Sides, if you plan to ride with us again tomorrow, you'll need some practice."

She stopped again. "Why are you trusting me all of a sudden?"

He gave a shrug. "It's like Ma said at dinner. You're part of the family now, and if I don't tell you what the gang is doing, you're bound to find out on your own. And won't you insist on coming along again tomorrow?"

"I presume I will," she conceded.

"What were you expecting to do? Ride double with me again?"

Jessica succumbed to a smile. "I see your point. Very well, bring on the riding lesson."

Inside the barn, Jessica waited patiently as Cole saddled up two horses, his own chestnut gelding, and for her,

156

a smaller dappled gray. Glancing at the palomino in a nearby stall, she asked, "Why aren't you saddling the same horse for me again?"

" 'Cause Belle's a mite more docile," he replied, adjusting the mare's cinch.

"Then why didn't you give her to me in the first place?"

Straightening, he tweaked Jessica's nose. " 'Cause you plumb forgot to tell me you're such a greenhorn."

Charmed despite herself, she smiled. "Guess I should go change into trousers."

"Naw. Who'll see you?"

"You will!"

He shrugged. "Just bunch up your skirts real good. You womenfolk wear so damn many layers, it's a wonder most husbands don't just give up on the notion of having young 'uns."

She blushed. "I hardly see why that should concern you."

"And why not?"

"Because you're a will-o'-the-wisp. An outlaw."

He raised an eyebrow. "I want to tell you something, Jessie."

"I'm breathlessly waiting."

Eyeing her solemnly, he murmured, "In Colorado City, I was tempted by a line gal or two. But I resisted, 'cause none of them can hold a candle to you, girl."

She rolled her eyes. "If you think I'm flattered, you're delusional."

Chuckling, he reached out to toy with a curl at her temple. "God, you've got such a mouth on you, woman. That's one thing I like about you. But you know there's a time when a real woman needs to stow her sass and get ready for some serious loving."

"Don't hold your breath."

Cole roared with laughter.

Moments later, he showed her how to lead her horse

outside by its bridle. Then he pointed. "Now just put your foot in the stirrup and hoist yourself up into the saddle."

Thinking of what he might see when she "hoisted," Jessica colored. "Turn away."

"Jessie—"

"Turn away!"

With a groan, he displayed his broad back to her.

Holding the horse by its bridle and grasping the saddle horn, Jessica put her toe in the stirrup and tried to climb up. But the horse, sensing her hesitation, began to whinny and sidestep.

Doing a one-footed dance to keep up with the skittering beast, Jessica was exasperated. "Damn it, horse, will you *pleeeeze* cooperate?"

Then she froze as she felt a hand slide up her skirts. Once again, Cole grasped her bottom and boosted her into the saddle. She landed with face burning.

"Damn it, Cole! How can I learn if you keep doing that?"

He appeared delighted. "Well, I had to do something before you spooked the poor nag into pitching you off."

"Sure."

He mounted his horse. "All right, woman. We'll start out real slow. Just nudge the horse with pressure from your thighs."

She glanced at him in perplexity.

"You know all about that kind of pressure, don't you, sugar?" he teased.

"You go straight to hell, Cole Reklaw." But she said it with a smile.

"Sugar, you've got too short a fuse. But that's all right with me, I reckon. I figure if you're that hot-tempered riding horses, you're also that hot in—"

"Stop it, Cole!"

"Yes, ma'am," he said with a mock salute. "All right, then, let's try a few turns around the barnyard first. Hold your reins firm but not too tight, and give her a nudge."

Jessica nudged the little gray, and felt pleased when she ambled into motion. For a few minutes, she and Cole circled the barnyard. She followed Cole's instructions on how to turn, rein in, and halt her horse. She found the gray was much gentler and more cooperative than the palomino had been, and she felt much more comfortable in the saddle, especially at this slow pace.

After a while, Cole held up his hand and they both reined in their mounts. "Good. Now we'll try trottin' down the road a piece."

"Are you sure?" Jessica asked skeptically.

"You can do it, honey."

Cole spurred his horse ahead, and stronger pressure from Jessica's thighs was all the encouragement Belle needed to spring into step behind the other horse. At the brisker pace, Jessica tensed in fear, her bottom bobbing in the saddle.

Cole noticed. "Just relax, honey, you're doing fine. But you need to learn to move with the horse, not against it."

"Yeah—tell me about it," she retorted dryly.

Still, as they proceeded, she found herself growing more attuned to the rhythms of the horse and not bobbing quite as violently. She even began to enjoy the ride—the powerful movements of the horse, the deepening red splendor of the sunset, the coolness of evening, the thrill of having Cole riding along beside her . . .

Catching her perusal, he remarked, "Tell me something."

"What do you want to know?"

"I was just wondering why none of your kinfolk have come looking for you yet."

Taken aback, she murmured, "Guess I'm kind of lost."

"You mean like a lost woman?" he teased. "A soiled dove?"

"You're one to talk after visiting Sin City."

"Seriously, though, sugar. Seems to me it's odd that a

159

lady like you would disappear, and no one comes looking for her."

"Maybe I'm an orphan," she suggested.

"Somehow I doubt that. Just as I doubt you came out to Mariposa to teach school. Why don't you tell me the truth? I shared with you."

"You didn't exactly bare your soul." At his chiding glance, she admitted, "Okay, you shared a little."

"Are you gonna tell me now?"

"You gonna make me?" she responded sweetly.

"Hey, Jessie, that's not fair," he scolded. "You want my help with my brothers, but you won't be honest with me."

She laughed ironically. "You haven't helped me much."

As they crested a rise overlooking a wooded hillside and rushing stream, he held up a hand. "Let's rest a spell."

She reined in her mount. "Suits me fine."

Cole dismounted and assisted Jessica to the ground. "What is it you want of me, Jessie?"

She smoothed down her skirts and gathered her thoughts. "Funny you should ask that. I was just about to request your support in getting the boys into town to church—"

"Church again?" he cut in, glowering.

"Yes, church. Why, just yesterday, I was thinking the boys will soon be presentable enough to take into town. Then you pulled that juvenile stunt, going off with Billy to Colorado City. Now you're no doubt planning more nefarious doings for tomorrow, which will obliterate all my progress."

Cole appeared unmoved. "I say taking the boys to town would be a huge mistake."

"I say it's their only possible salvation. But if you aren't going to support me, why should I tell you anything you want to know?"

Cole fell broodingly silent, then dug in his pocket. To her surprise, he pulled out her college ring, took her right hand, and slipped it on. "Maybe because of this?"

Jessica couldn't help feeling delighted. The presence of the familiar ring on her finger comforted her somehow, a physical symbol of the world from which she'd been so arbitrarily removed. "My ring! I was sure your brothers sold it soon after you kidnapped me."

For once, Cole spoke tenderly. "I wouldn't let them sell your ring, Jessie."

Jessica was amazed to find herself blinking at a tear. "Thanks, Cole."

"I've looked at that ring a dozen times since you've been here," he admitted quietly, "and I want you to tell me what it means. The name, 'University of New Mexico.' And the number, '1994.' "

Jessica felt at a loss. She didn't know any way to explain her time-travel experience to Cole without convincing him she was delusional. At last she said simply, "The University of New Mexico is where I went to school. As for the number 1994, I don't think I can explain it to you in a way you'll understand."

He appeared keenly disappointed. "You're learning all about us, sugar, all about me, but you still don't trust me in return."

"That's not true, Cole," she replied. "You're the one who doesn't really trust me, and you know it."

"I'm trying to, Jessie." His frown betraying his guilt and torn feelings, he gazed off into the distance for a long moment. "You know, the sunset's right fine."

Though his words tugged at her senses, Jessica soberly replied, "How much longer do you think you and your brothers will enjoy these sunsets if you continue with your wild ways?"

"That's a low blow, woman," he scolded.

"It's the truth. How long? Days? Months? A year or two if you're really lucky? Don't you want more for your brothers than that?"

He groaned. "What do you want me to do?"

"You know what."

He fought a smile. "Church, eh?"

"Church."

"I'll think on it," he conceded.

"Good. And Cole, if you do agree, I promise I'll think of a way to disguise the boys' identities, to ensure we won't blow your cover."

Cole shook his head cynically. "Woman, you may think you're prodding us all down the road to redemption, but it's ruination you're really taking us to." He stroked her cheek. "But what can I say? You've bewitched me."

Much as his touch stirred her, Jessica still felt troubled. "Cole, I don't want you cooperating because of my presumed feminine wiles. I want you in harmony with me—"

Abruptly Cole pulled her close. "And I want you in harmony with me, Jessie."

Traitorous longing swept Jessica at being in Cole's strong arms again. This time he didn't try to force kisses on her, but only held her, pressing his lips to her hair. Somehow his gentleness was far more devastating than his earlier aggression.

"How much longer do you think we can resist this, Jessie?"

The soulful question tortured her, especially since they both knew the answer. *Not long.* Every time they were together, the attraction became stronger—almost overwhelming now.

She managed to pull away. "We—we'd best head back now," she whispered.

Silently, Cole followed her back to the horses.

Chapter Fifteen

Jessica spent a fitful night, remembering her moments in Cole's arms and longing for more. Like him, she wondered how much longer either of them could resist this powerful attraction. Despite her misgivings, she felt closer to the edge each time she was with him.

She was given an opportunity to put her riding lessons to the test the next morning, when the men left on their planned foray to waylay and rob the Aspen Gulch Consortium. Again dressed in Billy's old overalls, her hair pinned beneath her hat, Jessica rode at the rear of the band, her expression fraught with frustration because once again she'd been unable to dissuade the men from their nefarious plans.

At the crest of a rise overlooking the road from Colorado Springs, Cole held up his hand, halting the group. He pointed to the east. "There they come now, those sidewinders, in their fine carriage."

Shading a hand over her eyes, Jessica followed Cole's gaze. A sense of *déjà vu* swept her as she stared at a scene reminiscent of the day she'd crossed time. The handsome black coach approached them, the horses' hooves and wagon wheels stirring up clouds of dust.

"How do you know it's their carriage?" she asked Cole.

"The little lady in Colorado Springs described it."

Jessica shot him a resentful look, then glanced downward. "Is this the same canyon where you kidnapped me?"

"Nope," he replied, "you and the others never made it out this far. Haunted Gorge is back further to the east."

"Haunted Gorge?" Jessica repeated, dumbfounded. "I thought it was called Reklaw Gorge."

Cole winked. "Who knows? Maybe it will be from now on."

"Cole," whined Billy, "hadn't we best get a move on? Them fellas is gonna make a clean getaway while you're palavering."

"Right," Cole concurred, lifting his kerchief over his nose and pulling down the brim of his hat. "You stay here, Jessie."

"But—I'd like to come this time," she protested.

"Ladies can't come with us!" Gabe shot back.

"Why not?" Jessica countered. "Where is it written that females can't ride with outlaws? Haven't you ever heard of Belle Starr? Besides, I'd like to judge for myself these men of the consortium who you say have ruined your lives."

Clearly perplexed, Gabe deferred to Cole. "You want her along?"

Although he scowled, Cole pulled another kerchief from his shirt pocket and tossed it to Jessica. "If you want to see the snakes up close, wait till they surrender and we get everything secured, then ride down to join us. Tie this over your face and make sure that hair stays under your hat. No sense them knowing you're a lady."

Jessica took the kerchief. "Aye, aye, sir."

He eyed her askance. "Mess up our timing and you'll be sorry."

"Oh, I wouldn't dream of messing up your timing," she responded sweetly, only to blush when all of the men laughed.

Jessica watched tensely as the men descended to the gorge and hid themselves in some trees. When the coach moved into view, they swarmed around it, whooping, hollering, and firing their pistols. The man riding shotgun on top of the coach put up a valiant effort—until Cole shot his weapon out of his hands! Jessica could only shake her head in grudging admiration.

Within minutes the driver surrendered and pulled the team to a halt. Jessica watched the gang work like a well-oiled machine. The brothers quickly dismounted, forced the driver and guard to the ground, then threw open the door and gestured for the occupants to alight. Amazed, she watched four men in old-fashioned suits and beaver hats step out.

She figured this was her cue. Quickly she donned her kerchief, then nudged Belle into motion. Although it made Jessica nervous to descend the steep, rugged hillside, the little gray horse was equal to the task and picked her way downward, remaining calm even when her hooves skidded on loose rocks.

When Jessica rode into the clearing, the four men with their hands raised regarded her suspiciously. They were a comical Mutt and Jeff assortment, complete with handlebar mustaches and steel-rimmed spectacles. The expressions of frozen horror on their faces made them seem even more droll. As she dismounted, Cole greeted her with a wave of his pistol. "Nice of you to join us, Butch."

Amused by the nickname, Jessica used her lowest voice. "Yes, sir."

He chuckled. "Now, Butch, I'd like to introduce you to the four slimiest weasels these parts have ever seen." He pointed to each man in turn. "That tall skinny fella with the beady eyes is none other than Elijah Miser himself, head of the Aspen Gulch Consortium. Next to him, the little weasel with the blond mustache and snooty expression is his secretary, Calvin Stickles. The red-faced, ugly one is Hiram Yapp. The one with the pug nose and pot belly is Willard Peavy."

Jessica nodded at the men. "Gents."

In a shrill, unpleasant voice, Elijah Miser spoke up. "Sir, I don't know who you and these other blackguards are, but I'd advise you to release us at once or rue the consequences."

"And I'm telling you you'll *rue the consequences* if you flap off your mouth again," Cole retorted.

Miser sucked in an outraged breath. "Just who do you think you're dealing with, sir?"

"The cruelest dog this side of the Mississippi," Cole drawled back.

"How dare you!"

Cole strode closer to the man and spoke with angry menace. "How dare I? How dare you exploit the good folk of Mariposa with your shoddy mining operation—even stealing the lives of many of their menfolk."

As Stickles and Yapp trembled in fear, Miser protested, "I'll have you know we run a fair operation—"

"Fair?" Cole cut in incredulously. "Were you fair to the twenty miners who died in that cave-in two years ago?"

Miser colored. "Those are just—the dangers of mining—"

"Hokum and hogwash," Cole cut in. "What I hear is you kept right on digging, even after your engineers warned you the tunnel was unstable, and that's how you murdered those men."

"Murder? Why, that's an outrageous lie—"

"Tell it to someone who'll believe you," Cole cut in darkly.

"Yeah!" seconded Billy.

Cole pointed his pistol around the group. "For now, I think it's high time for you men to learn how it feels to lose everything. To be victimized and abandoned."

Miser's eyes burned with fire. "Sir, if you so much as—"

Cole cocked his pistol, stopping the other man cold. "Shut your yap or I'll shoot you."

Miser gulped and clamped shut his mouth. All four consortium members trembled in fear.

Now the driver spoke up. "Please, sir, I beg you not to shoot anyone."

Cole turned to the man, who stood nearby with the guard, both with raised hands and pale faces. "Relax, gentlemen. My argument isn't with the two of you."

Looking relieved, the men nodded back to Cole.

Cole's gaze shifted back to the consortium members. "But as for the rest of you scoundrels, take out your wallets and jewelry—slow like—and hand them over to Butch here."

Flabbergasted, Jessica pressed a hand to her heart. "Me?"

"You would rob us?" demanded Miser.

"Shut up," retorted Cole. He swung around to Jessica, and the gleam in his eyes told her he meant business. "That's right, Butch. You wanted to learn how the gang operates, so here's your chance."

Jessica approached him and whispered tensely, "I can't, Cole. You know I'm only along to take notes."

Adamantly, he replied, "You can, sugar. You're here, and that makes you as guilty as the rest of us. If we're caught, we're all gonna swing, and that means you, too."

She gulped. "I suppose you've got a point."

He turned. "Gabe, give Butch here that sack you got."

Gabe strode forward and handed Jessica the cloth sack. Although she accepted it hesitantly, as she turned to see the four men regarding her with trepidation, her confidence built. Suddenly she liked the thought of stealing from these greedy jackals who had victimized the citizens of Mariposa and taken two husbands from poor Eula Reklaw.

Eugenia Riley

As she strode toward the men, they were already pulling out ornate pocket watches and thick wallets. "All right, fellas," she ordered in her deep voice. "Fork it over."

The men grudgingly threw in their valuables. Jessica backed away with her booty.

Cole ordered, "Now take off those fancy suits."

As Jessica struggled not to laugh at Cole's outrageous directive, Miser cried, "You expect us to strip?"

"Right down to your union suits."

"We'll die first."

Cole fired several shots near Miser's feet, causing him to dance about and yelp in terror. "You sure of that?"

With commendable haste, all four men began tearing off their suits. Within a minute, the four stood there looking utterly ridiculous in their union suits, boots, and hats.

"Pitch off the hats and boots, too," Cole ordered.

After the men complied, Cole nodded to Billy and Gabe. "Gather up the clothing."

Hooting their victory, the brothers scooped up the finery.

"Now, Luke and Wes, tie up all of them inside the carriage."

"You'll be sorry for this!" Miser warned.

"You're gonna be sorry sooner," Cole shot back. "And in case it hasn't gotten through to you yet, you fellas have worn out your welcome in these parts. You'd best remember it."

Luke and Wes tied up the four men, as well as the driver and guard, and shoved all six of them inside the cab of the coach. Then they unharnessed the two black horses from the carriage and tethered each to one of their own mounts. Soon the group was on its way again, whooping and hollering.

Once they were a safe distance away, Cole turned to Jessica. "You're quiet, sugar."

"Will they be all right, tied up like that?"

"You're worried about them?"

"Frankly, yes."

Cole gave a shrug. "It's a fairly busy road. Someone should be along in a day or so to release them."

"A day or so? Lord, I hope so."

Once they were back at the farm, the boys had a great time playing with their plunder. They paraded around the yard wearing the jackets and hats of the men. Ma looked on disapprovingly from the porch and scrubbed under-wear in the washtub. Jessica sat, frowning, on the porch swing. Cole lounged against a pillar and watched his brothers with a forbearing smile.

In the yard, Luke pulled a cigar from the pocket of his elegant jacket and lit up. "Look at us, Ma, Miss Jessie. Why, we're all set to go to church now, just like Clyde."

Ma shook her head at Jessica. "They're all wound up, strutting about like peacocks and bragging about their evil doins'. They'll likely be off a'whoring in Colorado City before the night is out."

Ma's words left Jessica feeling both uneasy and guilty. Uneasy because the boys were backsliding—largely thanks to Cole. Guilty because she'd been perhaps a too willing participant in the day's shenanigans.

She rose and crossed over to Cole. "Want to go for a walk?"

He smiled in pleased surprise. "What brought this about?"

"We need to talk."

"Whatever you say, sugar."

They walked about a hundred yards from the house, through the trees into a clearing with a large stump at its center. Cole turned to face Jessica. "What's on your mind, sugar?"

She crossed her arms over her chest and eyed him in re-proach. "Your continuing bad influence on your brothers."

"That's to be expected." He dimpled. "What I'm still hoping is I'll be a bad influence on you."

"Cole, be serious for once."

"I am." He reached out, straightening one of the straps on her overalls. "Jessie, do you have to spoil all the boys' fun? Those sidewinders we robbed deserved what they got. Can't you let my brothers revel in their exploits a little?"

"So you think I'm just a big spoilsport?"

"I think you mean well, but you need to loosen up on the reins a bit."

She sighed. "Actually, on that very subject, I have—well, a confession to make."

"Ah. I'm fascinated. Tell me."

Her guilty gaze locked with his amused one. "What we did today was wrong—there's no doubt about it. Nevertheless, I enjoyed today's exploits more than I should have."

He howled with laughter. "Hot damn! I knew it. I *am* a bad influence on you."

She shot him a chiding glance. "Speaking of bad, I have a very bad feeling about what we did."

"Why? Why would you have any sympathy for those snakes?"

"Because you're only getting them all worked up, Cole. Now they'll probably hire bounty hunters to track you."

He shrugged. "We're not afraid."

"You should be. What about the danger to your brothers, your mother—to me?"

He pulled her close. "Sugar, you're safe with me. And, damn, do I love how you look in those trousers. Give me a kiss."

She shoved him away. "Stop it."

"Why are you so riled?"

"Because you're not helping."

"Oh, I'll help you a lot when you do what I want."

"That's what I'm afraid of." Jessica began to pace. "Cole, all this lawbreaking has got to stop. I think we should begin by going to church—and we should start this Sunday."

He groaned. "Not church again."

She shook a fist at him. "You promised you would help me."

"No, I said I would think about it. I have, and I've decided we should have nothing to do with Mariposa."

Crestfallen and angry, she turned. "But why?"

He squared his jaw stubbornly. "My mind's made up."

"Not good enough," she retorted. "You must tell me why."

Now anger sparked in his eyes. "Because three years ago, I let my guard down over at Colorado City. As a result, I got thrown in the hoosegow, and if the boys hadn't sprung me, I would have been hanged."

"Cole, I'm sorry about that. But you're making no sense. There's no sheriff in Mariposa."

"Which still doesn't give us leave to get cozy with the town."

"But you still go to Colorado City, which, from what you're telling me, must be even more dangerous."

"It's different."

"How is it different?"

"The old sheriff is gone now."

She laughed ruefully. "You're still taking one hell of a risk."

"It's not the same, Jessie. In Colorado City, I know where to go and how to watch my back. I don't get too friendly with anyone, much less sit around gabbing and eating fried chicken like you want us to do. And I don't trust anyone. Especially not females."

"Maybe you don't trust *me*," she accused.

He hesitated, then admitted, "Maybe I don't. Not completely."

"Well, thanks a lot!"

He shook a finger. "Look, you asked me to be honest, and now I have. I sure don't trust what you're suggesting. You're going to have us cozying up with that town, inviting everyone to mind our business, and you're going to get us all hanged."

"And I say you just don't want to give up your life of crime."

"Maybe I don't," he retorted.

Fuming, Jessica stalked away a few paces, then turned. "That's it, then," she declared, waving a hand. "I give up on you."

Cole sat down on the tree stump and eyed her with concern. "Uh—Jessie, I think you'd best move."

Assuming he was ordering her about again, she retorted, "No."

He raised an eyebrow. "Uh, sugar, you'd best come here if you know what's good for you."

"No."

"Woman, you'd best rattle your hocks," he ordered harshly.

"What's wrong with you?" she shot back. "Why are you all of a sudden turning so belligerent, giving me orders and—"

Her words ended in a muffled scream as Cole leaped up and made a dive for her, grabbing her about the waist and hauling her back to the stump with him. She kicked and screamed as he threw her face-down across his lap.

"What in the hell are you—"

Her words ended in another cry as Cole began thrashing at her legs and tearing off her overalls! Even as she struggled, outraged at his brazen actions, he yanked off her boots and then her britches.

Livid, stripped down to her shirt and drawers, she somehow managed to grab his pistol. She felt him freeze just as she leaped to her feet.

Trembling, she pointed the weapon at Cole's chest and hoarsely ordered, "Stop it right now, you bastard, or I'm blowing off something *very* essential."

Cole stared white-faced at the pistol quivering in Jessica's hands. His voice was deadly calm. "Jessie, give me that gun—*now*—before you hurt one of us."

"No!" she shouted. "What in hell were you just trying to do? Spank me? Rape me?"

Cole nodded soberly at the pile of her discarded clothing. "How 'bout get the blamed ants off your britches?"

Jessica glanced down, only to shriek in horror at the sight of large red ants swarming all over her boots and overalls. She glanced at herself, screaming at the sight of yet more ants crawling on her drawers and her bare flesh beneath. Then she yelped as the ants began to bite her.

"Ouch!" she wailed, dropping the pistol and frantically beating at her drawers. "Cole, please, help me."

At once Cole fell to his knees, his hands shooting up under Jessica's shirt and yanking at the waist of her drawers.

She screeched. "No, Cole, you can't take off my—"

"Damn it, Jessie, quit fighting."

Though Jessica was mortified, further resistance proved futile as Cole had already managed to pull the drawers down around her ankles.

"Step out of 'em!" he ordered.

Jessica gratefully hopped out of the drawers, and she and Cole frantically slapped away the remaining ants on her legs and feet.

Suddenly it was all over, and Jessica stood totally defenseless, all but nude, with only a skimpy shirt to hide her nakedness from Cole, and with him so close that he could see all her charms if he wanted to. One look into his eyes made her wince as she glimpsed an anger and lust that made her shudder.

Oh, God, she was in deep, deep trouble.

"Cole—" she whispered, trying to back away.

He grabbed her knee, preventing escape. "Don't you have something to say to me, woman?"

His touch burned her. His voice sent shivers down her spine. She nodded convulsively. "Of course. Lord, Cole, I'm sorry. So sorry. I didn't know about the ants, honest to God. Will you please let me go?"

He glanced up, eyes smoldering. "No. Jessie, you've got to be the most stubborn woman I've ever met. I tried to warn you, but obstinate you, you had to go stand smack dab in the middle of the biggest anthill I've ever seen in my life."

Jessica twisted around to look at the anthill, grimacing at the sight of thousands of ants swarming about. She turned to face Cole, intensely conscious of the heat of his strong, rough fingers gripping her flesh, and the passion burning in his eyes. "You're right. Again, I'm sorry."

"You were going to shoot me," he accused.

"No. I mean, I don't think I was. I misunderstood."

"This has got to stop, Jessie."

Alarmed, she asked, "What do you mean?"

"You know what I mean," he whispered, looking her over in slow, scorching fashion. "We're gonna have us a reckoning, you and me."

Sensing his meaning, Jessica panicked. "Cole, please, isn't it enough that I got bitten?"

His fingers reached upward to stroke a welt just above her knee. "Yeah, sugar, you sure did." Abruptly he hooked an arm about her thigh and pressed his mouth to the welt.

At the touch of his hot lips, Jessica's senses went wild, needles of desire shooting up between her thighs and piercing her with stunning intensity. "Oh, God, Cole, please don't—"

It was too late. His mouth was on her thigh, kissing her tenderly, while his other hand slid brazenly up her bare leg coming to rest on her bottom. "My God, do you have any idea how soft your bottom is?"

Jessica was on the verge of collapsing against him. "Cole, please, I can't take this."

His mouth continued its relentless ascent. "I can't either. I'm on my knees, sugar. And I want you down on your knees beside me. It's time, Jessie."

Half collapsing, Jessica fell to the ground beside him. He stared into her dazed face, his hand touching her cheek. "Lord, you look so lovely, cheeks flushed, hair tumbled—"

"Cole, this is crazy—"

"Yeah." He began unbuttoning her shirt. "You're driving me crazy, woman. You already have."

"I feel—"

His hand closed over her bare breast. "What do you feel, sugar?"

Wincing, she blinked back tears. "I feel powerless over this. I can't fight it anymore. You've got me, Cole. Please don't press it."

His voice was rough. "Sorry, sugar, but I'm not in a mood to give quarter."

Then his hard mouth closed hungrily over hers, and she would have screamed with the sheer rapture of it had she been able to.

Cole clutched her closer, his hands moving freely down her body, kneading her breasts. When he boldly stroked her between her thighs, she sobbed at the keen, aching pleasure that shot through her. Her hands ripped at the buttons on his shirt. She caressed the smooth, muscled flesh with its covering of coarse hair. Abruptly he pushed open the folds of her shirt and held her so her bared breasts brushed against him. "Feel me, love."

Jessica groaned helplessly and bit his shoulder.

His hand took her wrist, pressing her fingers to his engorged manhood. "Unbutton the rest of me."

"Cole, we mustn't—"

"*Unbutton me*. Now."

Helplessly she complied, reaching inside his trousers to touch him, her fingers curling about him almost greedily. Her caress was rewarded by a drowning kiss. Heavens, he felt huge, smooth, so warm, so hard. Though she wasn't a virgin, she shuddered at the prospect of having all of him sunk to the hilt inside her. And his wicked tongue in her mouth left no doubt as to the brazen coupling he desired.

175

He lowered her to the ground, smiling into her eyes, watching her reactions as he parted her thighs and stroked her again until she shuddered. Then he replaced his fingers with his manhood and pressed inside her. Jessica was in heaven, as if she'd waited forever to feel him like this, to feel herself opening up to his passion. Her soft gasp snapped his control; his mouth ravaged hers and he thrust upward powerfully.

Jessica moaned, reeling at the sheer power of Cole inside her. She was bursting with pleasure, filled to unbearable aching with his solid heat. He eased back and plunged, his strokes consuming and ravenous, rocking her deeper, sweeping her away on waves of riveting pleasure. Jessica cried out, her fingernails digging into his back as he staggered her with one shattering thrust after another. Then his mouth was melting into hers, and hers into his, as his last masterful strokes brought them both to a climax of blinding fervor.

Chapter Sixteen

As unexpectedly as it had come, the storm of passion subsided. Jessica couldn't believe she had succumbed to Cole.

The confrontation between them had started out angry and intense and ended up hot and very passionate. Her fatal mistake had been pointing the gun at him; she'd been overwhelmed to realize she'd actually endangered his life when he'd only been trying to help her. When he had tenderly pressed his mouth to the welt on her thigh, when he'd stroked her bottom, she'd lost control, her defenses decimated.

And she realized the day's activities had also contributed to her descent into sin. Guilty pleasures, she thought. First, the guilty pleasure of joining the Reklaw Gang in the robbery. Then the guiltier pleasure of succumbing to Cole. The fact that he was the sexiest man alive had only hastened her downfall. Their lovemaking had been raw, intense, mindblowing . . .

And a huge mistake.

It didn't help at all that he was now sitting on the tree stump, watching her as she dressed. His gaze smoldered as he observed her donning her drawers, overalls, and boots.

And repairing herself wasn't exactly an easy task. In his haste to get the ants off her, Cole had ripped a button off her overalls, and she was forced to tie the straps together as best she could. Luckily she did have a comb in one of the large pockets, so she could rake some order through her mussed hair. Yet her fingers trembled as she pulled at snarls. Why wouldn't he take his eyes off her?

Cole was indeed savoring Jessica's every movement. Their lovemaking had thrilled him deeply, even though she hadn't been a virgin, just as he'd suspected. Still, she'd been so tight, so hot and passionate, her surrender so sweet. Already he wanted more. He wanted his Jessie all the time, not sneaking around as they were now. He wanted to make love to her in a soft bed, with neither of them having a stitch on. He wanted to part her smooth thighs, to throw those shapely legs over his shoulders, and taste her thoroughly with his mouth. He wanted to make her crazy with desire. And just when she couldn't bear any more, just when she begged him for mercy, he wanted to thrust into her hot depths again—slowly this time, making sure she reached every peak of delicious pleasure his body could deliver.

Most of all, he didn't want to share her. Ever again. Especially not with his brothers. If this were indeed a contest, then Cole was ready to be declared the winner. He wanted Jessie to be his alone.

Of course, he clearly had a long way to go in convincing the lady. But he was ready to do some passionate persuading. Jessie looked so uncertain, so vulnerable, and so appealing standing across from him. He hungered to pull her into his arms and reassure her that everything would be all right, that he was in charge.

Of course, that was the problem. The lady still wanted

to wear the pants. She was a feisty, strong-willed female who wouldn't trust him with her future without a fight. But it would be a good fight, even sweet. He'd see to it.

At last, done with her primping, she flashed him a tremulous smile. "Remind me never to point a gun at you again."

Although she'd obviously meant to lighten the mood with a touch of humor, Cole didn't smile back. "I didn't force you, honey."

Now she appeared intensely frustrated, even torn. "I know that!" she whispered miserably. "Why do you think I'm so angry at myself?"

Cole quickly crossed the distance between them and pulled Jessica close, feeling her soft body trembling against him. He buried his lips in her hair. "Shhhhhh," he soothed. "Don't be mad at yourself, sugar. You know you wanted me as much as I wanted you. Tell you what—why don't we get married?"

Wild-eyed, she sprang apart from him. "What?"

Cole grinned. "You heard me, you little siren. I want to marry you. Even though you weren't a virgin and I don't have to."

Cole was unprepared for Jessica's reaction. With a cry of outrage, she attacked him with her fists. "You big jerk!"

Laughing, Cole caught her wrists. "Why so feisty, Jessie? I might just have to cool you down again."

She flung off his hands and her eyes snapped fire at him. "What does my virginity, or the lack thereof, have to do with this?"

"Just what I was saying," he stated calmly. "I want to marry you anyway."

She made a strangled sound. "You are nuts."

"Why?"

"You're an outlaw. You don't intend to change. I . . . " She gestured helplessly. "I have problems of my own."

He eyed her tenderly. "We're good together, Jessie."

179

Her chin came up in defiance. "You mean in bed."

"Oh, honey, we haven't been in bed yet," he replied huskily. "But we will be."

He knew he was getting to her, from the way she trembled, the way color stained her cheeks. "You know damn well what I mean," she said.

"Yeah, I know." He stepped closer, planting his hands on her shoulders. "Come on, darlin', don't be so stubborn. You've already given yourself to me, so it's a bit late to be coy. Why not get hitched?"

She was shaking her head in disbelief. "Do you propose to every woman you go to bed with?"

"No. You're the first. And that oughta tell you something," he added meaningfully.

"It tells me you're not thinking with your *brain*," she retorted. "You're probably only proposing because you want to win the contest with your brothers."

That remark stung. "That's not true, Jessie, and you know it. But you're right that I'm declaring the contest closed. And, by the way, you invited *me* here today."

"So I did, but I sure didn't invite *this*." She drew a convulsive breath. "Cole, this just happened too soon. You caught me in a weak moment. I wasn't ready, and I suspect you weren't either."

"Speak for yourself."

"My point is, we're not in love, and you don't really trust me. Our getting together was a mistake."

Cole was stunned by how much her words hurt. He reached for her. "Jessie—"

She backed off, vehemently shaking her head. "Cole, please, don't. I can't take any more of this right now."

Cole wanted to reassure her, but stopped cold when he spotted tears of pain and confusion in her eyes. Clearly, she *wasn't* ready for this discussion. "I don't know what to say, Jessie. Tell me how I can help."

She wiped away a tear. "I'm going back to the house now."

Wordlessly, Cole followed her.

When Jessica stepped in the kitchen door with Cole close on her heels, she grimaced at the sight of Ma and the boys, who were already seated and in the middle of dinner. The scents of fried beefsteak and greens cooked in bacon fat wafted over her.

"Where you two been and what you been up to?" Ma demanded grumpily. "I hollered for you till I was hoarse; then we all went ahead with supper."

Jessica felt color shooting up her face; she heard Cole reply, "Jessie and me were having a talk."

"What were you *talking* about?" Gabe asked suggestively.

"Yeah, and what happened to Jessie's buttons?" inquired Billy with a perplexed frown.

"That's none of your damned business," Cole shot back.

At the venom in Cole's tone, the boys fell silent and Ma gasped.

As Jessica proceeded tentatively into the room, Billy and Gabe shot up from their bench. "Here, ma'am, have a seat between Gabe and me," Billy offered.

But even as Jessica moved forward to comply, Cole grabbed a chair from the corner and shoved it toward the table. "No, Jessie, sit here by me. I'm tired of watching the boys trying to squeeze you into a hoecake."

Gabe and Billy exchanged a mystified look. Jessica glanced sharply at Cole and started to protest, but his brooding expression convinced her she would only cause a scene if she refused. She sat down in the chair he had indicated. After pushing her in, Cole took his place and unfolded his napkin.

For a moment tense silence gripped the table; then Wesley asked, "Hey, big brother, why are you so ornery?"

Before Cole could respond, Luke suggested, "Bet he asked Jessie for a kiss and she refused."

Amid the boys' laughter, Gabe asked, "That true, Cole?"

Using his fork, Cole speared a beefsteak on the platter Luke had passed him. "Enough of this joshing. There are going to be some changes around here."

Blank looks greeted this pronouncement.

"Such as?" pressed Luke.

Cole glanced at Jessica, his gaze softening. "Such as, we're all going to church on Sunday."

Stunned, Jessica could only stare back at him.

Billy clapped his hands. "We are? Sure 'nuff church?"

"Son, are you sure you want to do this?" Ma asked skeptically.

Cole nodded firmly, still staring at Jessica. "I think Jessie is right. We can't all marry her, and if we're all going to have wives and children someday, we need to begin churchgoing."

"Well, hot damn," Billy said to Jessica, passing her the biscuits. "What do you think of that, sugar?"

"Sounds great to me," she replied with a forced smile. She took a biscuit and busied herself buttering it. By now, Cole was staring at her so intently, she was grateful for the distraction.

"What changed your mind about church, Cole?"

After dinner, Cole was standing on the front porch in the darkness when he heard the front door creak open, followed by Jessica's voice. He turned to see her beautiful face outlined in moonlight.

"Jessie," he whispered, starting toward her.

But she held up a hand. "Cole, please, come any closer and I'm going in."

At the fear in her eyes, disappointment seared him. "Afraid of me now, Jessie? I thought you weren't afraid of anything."

"I'm not afraid, but confused." After a moment, she quietly admitted, "Well, I guess I am afraid of what I'm feeling."

Touched by her honesty, he whispered, "Then you need to give in to those feelings, honey."

"I already did. That's why I'm confused."

He sighed. "You know I'm not going to force you, Jessie. I didn't today, you know."

"Yes, I know." Her voice trembled, rife with emotion. "But I can't have you touching me again right now. I just can't."

Anguish and longing assailed Cole, but he tightly replied, "All right, honey."

"So tell me—what changed your mind about church?" Almost bitterly, she added, "Is it my reward for letting you have your way?"

Wounded, he asked, "Jessie, how can you ask that?"

Her voice trembled. "I know you, Cole. Are you actually going to pretend to be noble now?"

"I offered to marry you, Jessie. Wasn't that noble?"

She laughed bitterly. "You weren't really thinking things through. You want me in your bed. You've made that clear from the beginning. With marriage, you can possess me and also win against your brothers."

Again her words stabbed him. He slowly shook his head. "If your opinion of me is so low, why should I argue?"

She lifted her chin, revealing eyes bright with unshed tears. "Tell me the truth about church, Cole. You owe me that much."

He sighed. "I want us to go 'cause of what you said— the boys might meet some decent women there."

"Ah—so your reasons *are* self-serving."

"What do you mean?"

"You want them to go to church not to save their souls but so they'll become interested in other young ladies— and won't compete for me."

Now Cole was angry. "Damn right, I do! How do you expect me to feel after today? Should I want my brothers touching you, kissing you?"

"You're thinking of yourself, Cole—not your brothers' best interests."

"Oh, I have their best interests at heart," he stated harshly. "And it's definitely *not* in their best interests to be murdered by me."

She shuddered. "You needn't fear I'll succumb to one of them. I shouldn't even have succumbed to you."

That comment hurt even more. "I didn't think we 'succumbed' to each other today. I thought we shared what we felt. I know I gave part of myself to you. Did you give part of yourself to me?"

"You know I did," she admitted in a small, tortured voice.

His voice was tormented, too. "Then why are we having this discussion? Why aren't you here in my arms?"

"You know why, Cole."

"No, I don't."

But even as Cole reached for Jessica, she stepped back and held up a hand again in warning. "I just want you to know that, whatever your reasons, I'm glad you changed your mind about church, Cole."

Then she fled back inside the house. Cole stood grinding his teeth till his jaw hurt. Then he muttered every curse he knew, and invented a few more.

He felt so frustrated, his emotions so torn. Jessie had given herself to him, then pulled away. It hurt like hell.

What did she want of him? It wasn't enough that he'd offered to marry her. Obviously he had to change for her, too, really change. Could he do it? And could he really trust her with his feelings and his heart?

Jessica sat in her room, rocking in the darkness, unable to get the day's events out of her mind. She felt so torn about succumbing to Cole—like an alcoholic who'd had a massive slip. And she wasn't even a drinker!

Her conduct had been rash and foolish. What if she

were pregnant? She realized with relief that it was unlikely she would conceive so close to her period. And *that* should be great fun here.

Despite all her misgivings, she couldn't deny how deeply drawn she was to Cole Reklaw, how moved she'd been by their lovemaking. Even now she ached to be in his arms again. Resisting him on the porch had been hell, especially as she sensed that his emotions were also in turmoil. Could his feelings for her run deeper than she had assumed?

And Lord, was she falling in love with the wrong man?

For Cole did seem wrong for her in any time. She was well educated, he a man of the land. She was upstanding, he a lawbreaker. Worse yet, she doubted she could ever trust him with her feelings, trust him not to hurt her. Just before they'd made love, he'd admitted he didn't trust her.

Still, there *must* be a reason why she was here, perhaps to show Cole and his brothers the right path . . . before he corrupted her beyond salvation.

Chapter Seventeen

On Sunday morning, Jessica sat wedged between Cole and his mother on the front seat of the family's buckboard as it plodded through a canyon passageway on the narrow dirt road to Mariposa. The four younger Reklaw brothers were squeezed on the seat behind them. The late August morning was balmy and scented of evergreen; a bald eagle circled in the clear blue skies overhead. On the mountainside beyond, Jessica spotted two mule deer munching grass, as well as a big-horned sheep warily watching them from his perch on a high rock. In the fir and aspen trees along the canyon walls, colorful bluebirds and larks flitted about.

As they passed the familiar "Wanted Dead or Alive" poster, Jessica felt her confidence lagging. Would today's masquerade work? She prayed they weren't on a fool's errand.

At least appearance-wise, they should pass muster. All seven occupants of the conveyance were attired in "Sunday best," and the scents of pomade, talcum, and perfume

186

were heavy in the air. Ma and Jessica were ensconced in starched calico dresses and matching bonnets. Ma's ensemble was dark brown and high-necked; she wore crocheted gloves and clutched the well-worn family Bible in her lap. Jessica's frock was a pleasing light blue, with long sleeves and a lace-trimmed, rounded neckline; white gloves and a blue knitted reticule completed her ensemble.

Glancing behind her at the boys, Jessica noted how very handsome and solemn they looked, all clean-shaven, wearing the various brown and black suits, starched linen shirts, black string cravats, and dress western hats that she and Ma had purchased for them in town. Much as the boys had begged to wear some of the finery they'd stripped from the men of the Aspen Gulch Consortium, Jessica and Ma had prevailed on them to avoid such foolish conduct, which might well be an invitation to be arrested.

Turning back around, Jessica glanced at Cole and stifled a surge of longing. A strong, silent stranger sat beside her in his elegant black suit and matching western hat. Expression stoic, Cole stared ahead and worked the reins. Although Jessica could feel the hardness of his muscled thigh next to hers, could even smell his spicy, enticing scent, emotionally he seemed a world apart. Ever since their lovemaking and her emotional retreat afterward, Cole had become a different man, cold and remote, hardly the hot-blooded, charming rogue she remembered.

His distance now made her ache for him all the more . . .

The rest of their week had been tense, with lots of hot, accusatory looks between her and Cole. The few conversations they'd had had been strained and impersonal. But he hadn't made any further moves to touch her, for which she was grateful.

If he had, she likely would have been lost.

Still, she wondered at his reserve. Was it possible she had actually hurt more than his pride? Perhaps she hadn't given him enough credit; perhaps his feelings for her ran deeper than she'd realized. Under the circumstances, it had been gentlemanly of him to propose marriage. But even if he had proposed out of genuine caring, and not just to win the contest and bed her, their relationship was still wrong, wrong, wrong. He was an outlaw—and she might not even belong in this time.

"Miss Jessie?" prodded Billy, breaking into her thoughts.

Jessica turned to face him. "Yes?"

"What did you say our new names was, ma'am?"

"*Were*. What did I say your new names *were*."

"Yes, ma'am, that's just what I asked."

Biting back her frustration, Jessica regarded all four boys soberly. "All right, we'll go over it again. You must all go by different names in town or else risk discovery. Your ma is already known as 'Mrs. Lively,' so all of you will assume 'Lively' as your surname. As for your Christian names, the new ones I've chosen for you are different from your actual names, but also similar enough so you can readily remember them."

"Will you tell us them again, ma'am?" pressed Gabe.

"I was just getting to that. Gabe, you'll be Gill. Billy, you're Bobby. Luke, you'll be Lyle, Wesley will be Walt, and Cole, you'll be Clay."

Cole made a sound of contempt. "And you really think those silly monikers are gonna fool anyone?"

"The new names should be adequate to cover your actual identities. They're subtle enough."

"Yeah, about as subtle as a peddler's red bandwagon."

"Well, what do you propose?" Jessica demanded. "If I were to suggest names vastly different from the ones I've already chosen for the boys, they'd only get confused."

"Yeah, they're pretty damn stupid, my brothers."

Jessica felt her hackles rising. "That's *not* what I said. I'm just trying to keep things simple."

"Simple?" he mocked. "What I say is we should abandon this whole haywire scheme of going to church."

Jessica was mystified. "B-but the other night, you said you were supporting me in this!"

As Ma and the boys looked on intently, Cole shot her a heated look which for once revealed some depth of emotion. "Well, maybe I've reconsidered. Maybe females aren't the *only* ones who can change their minds about what it is they want."

Jessica knew exactly what Cole was referring to, knew he'd made his remark strictly to bedevil her—and he'd succeeded. She felt hot color flooding her cheeks. She wondered if he really had given in on church just to soften her up. Maybe now that his ploy wasn't working, he was retaliating. The scoundrel.

But before she could respond, Ma intervened. "Hush up, you two. I say I'm glad Miss Jessie put her foot down and made us all go to the meeting house. 'Bout time you rascals turned away from the devil's doin's, even if it's just for the Lord's day. 'Sides, I haven't darkened the door of a church since I wed my Joseph, and I've missed the sermons, the hymns, and the praying. So I'm thankful."

Ma got the final word on the subject. Cole grudgingly fell silent.

Moments later they pulled into town and approached the small white frame church. Jessica noted the church-yard was crammed with conveyances; a young family was climbing the front steps together, while other members milled about in the yard.

Sobered by the sight and the reality of all they were risking, Jessica turned to the boys. "Remember, you're farmers, not bandits. No talk of lawbreaking, or even of hell-raising in Colorado City. Is that clear?"

"Yes, ma'am," the men replied in unison.

Cole parked the conveyance, hopped down, and came around to help the ladies out. He assisted his mother to the ground, then offered Jessica his hand, helping her step out. She felt rather disappointed that he didn't grab her about the waist and swing her to the ground as he normally did.

189

Crossing the churchyard, the entire group remained hushed. They caught curious looks from several men. The sounds of "Shall We Gather at the River," played on an off-key piano, spilled out from the church beyond.

As the group paused before the steps, Ma hugged her Bible to her chest and flashed the others an ecstatic smile. "Ah, that heavenly music. How I've missed it. Come on, sons, Miss Jessie. Let's not be shy in the Lord's house."

With Ma proudly taking the lead, they all trooped up the steps. Inside the foyer, they were greeted by Merchant Allgood; the short, portly man wore a brown striped suit, and his thinning hair was slicked back. "Why, Widow Lively, Miss Garrett," he greeted pleasantly. "What a pleasure to have you both here to worship with us today."

"Merchant Allgood," Eula acknowledged, briefly pumping his hand. "I reckoned we'd see you today."

"Indeed, I never miss a Sunday." He smiled at Jessica. "How lovely you look, Miss Garrett."

She smiled and shook his hand. "Thanks, Mr. Allgood."

He glanced at the men. "Mrs. Lively, are these your sons?"

"Yeah," Eula replied. "Their names is—"

Terrified Ma might fumble, Jessica announced, "Clay, Lyle, Gill, Walt, and Bobby."

Although Allgood appeared perplexed at Jessica's outburst, he soon recovered his composure. "Pleased to have you with us, gentlemen, though I do wonder why we're never seen you before."

"They's been busy working the farm, just like I told ya," Eula responded in no-nonsense tones. "And I'm sure you'll also recollect how I said Cousin Jessie here put her foot down and made us all come in to church."

"Oh, of course," Allgood replied with a nervous laugh.

"Very devout, Cousin Jessie is," Eula added.

"Indeed." Allgood gestured toward the sanctuary. "By all means, come right in, folks, and take a pew."

As they all paraded down the aisle of the almost

packed sanctuary, Jessica noted that most every eye seemed glued to them. The churchgoers appeared neatly dressed but hardly prosperous; their garments ranged from neat muslin and calico for the women and girls to ofttimes threadbare wool and broadcloth suits for the men. The group also ran the gamut age-wise, ranging from squalling infants to white-haired geriatrics. Jessica noted a couple of young women dressed in black, each with several small children in tow, and wondered sadly if these ladies were mine widows.

Unfortunately, the only vacant seats left were at the front, so Jessica and the others were compelled to walk the full length of the sanctuary. Jessica was pleased to note a rowful of pretty girls bedecked in lovely hues of gingham and calico. There were three brunettes, an auburn-haired beauty, and a plump though attractive blonde—and all of them were already making eyes at the boys. Like ants spotting spilled honey, the younger Reklaw brothers were quick to take note and pause, grin, and tip their hats, until Ma sent each boy on his way with a scolding look or a less-than-gentle nudge. The six Reklaws and Jessica seated themselves in the front row just as the choir trooped in, singing, "Bringing in the Sheaves." Cole and his brothers listened stoically. Ma was so affected, she dabbed at tears.

Soon, the tall, gaunt, gray-haired minister appeared. The congregation stood as he ascended the pulpit. At the conclusion of the hymn, he held up a broad hand.

"Brethren, heed these words from the book of Joshua: 'The Lord your God, He it is that fighteth for you.' Shall we pray."

There followed the usual succession of prayers, hymns, scripture readings, and a lengthy, passionate sermon. Although Jessica had expected a preacher from this time to spew forth fire and brimstone, she was rather surprised when the reverend's approach was more inspirational, when he expounded on several uplifting biblical themes, including an encouraging verse from the Psalms: "Sit thou at My right hand, until I make thine enemies thy footstool." The rousing closing hymn, "A Mighty Fortress Is Thy God," left all of the attendees with smiles on their faces.

As soon as the group began to disperse, Mr. Allgood strode forward, escorting a thin, gray-haired lady in black silk. "Mrs. Lively, Miss Garrett, gentlemen, I'd like you to meet my widowed mother, Mrs. Allgood."

Ma shook the hand of the frail lady. "Howdy do, ma'am."

The other woman smiled back. "Horace tells me you're also a mine widow, Mrs. Lively."

"Sure am," Eula replied.

"My sympathies. There are a number of us in the church. In fact, we have a little quilting society you might want to join."

"Why, sure," Ma said eagerly. "I love needlework."

"We're working on several quilts which we'll be selling at the Founders' Day bazaar, and we could sure use your help."

"Count me in," said Eula.

Mrs. Allgood turned to Jessica, offering her hand. "And Horace has told me about you, that you're a refined, well-educated young lady. Welcome to Mariposa."

"Why, thank you." Jessica shook the woman's thin hand.

Mrs. Allgood winked at the boys. "And such handsome young gentlemen. Wonderful additions to our congregation."

Cole spoke for the brothers. "Thank you, ma'am. We're pleased to be here."

Now another family joined them. The husband and wife were both dark-haired and attractive, as well as better dressed than most of the other churchgoers; the woman wore an elegant full-length coatdress and a large hat lavishly tiered with egret feathers; the man wore a

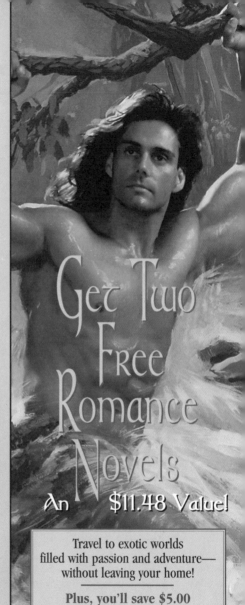

Thrill to the most sensual, adventure-filled Romances on the market today...

FROM  LOVE SPELL BOOKS

As a home subscriber to the Love Spell Romance Book Club, you'll enjoy the best in today's BRAND-NEW Time Travel, Futuristic, Legendary Lovers, Perfect Heroes and other genre romance fiction. For five years, Love Spell has brought you the award-winning, high-quality authors you know and love to read. Each Love Spell romance will sweep you away to a world of high adventure...and intimate romance. Discover for yourself all the passion and excitement millions of readers thrill to each and every month.

Save $5.00 Each Time You Buy!

Every other month, the Love Spell Romance Book Club brings you four brand-new titles from Love Spell Books. EACH PACKAGE WILL SAVE YOU AT LEAST $5.00 FROM THE BOOK-STORE PRICE! And you'll never miss a new title with our convenient home delivery service.

Here's how we do it: Each package will carry a FREE 10-DAY EXAMINATION privilege. At the end of that time, if you decide to keep your books, simply pay the low invoice price of $17.96, no shipping or handling charges added. HOME DELIVERY IS ALWAYS FREE. With today's top romance novels selling for $5.99 and higher, our price SAVES YOU AT LEAST $5.00 with each shipment.

AND YOUR FIRST TWO-BOOK SHIP-MENT IS TOTALLY FREE!

IT'S A BARGAIN YOU CAN'T BEAT! A SUPER $11.48 Value!

Love Spell  A Division of Dorchester Publishing Co., Inc.

Get Two Books Totally
FREE —
An $11.48 Value!

▼ Tear Here and Mail Your FREE Book Card Today! ▼

PLEASE RUSH
MY TWO FREE
BOOKS TO ME
RIGHT AWAY!

Love Spell Romance Book Club
P.O. Box 6613
Edison, NJ 08818-6613

beautifully cut gray suit and an elegant top hat. The three children, two boys and a girl, were also smartly attired.

Turning to the newcomers, Allgood said, "Folks, I'd like you to meet the mayor of Mariposa, Willard Polk, his wife, Mary, and their three children, Mildred, William, and Mathew."

Jessica and the others shook hands with the Polks. "Miss Garrett, Mr. Allgood has been telling us all about you," Mary remarked eagerly. "Is it possible you might be able to teach our children?"

Before Jessica could speak, one of the children, William, addressed her. "Would you teach us, ma'am? Millie and Matt and me really need us a teacher."

"Now, Will, don't be pushy," scolded the mother.

Will lowered his gaze. "Sorry, ma'am."

"Please, no need to apologize," Jessica reassured the boy.

"We do so badly need a teacher," Mrs. Polk continued. "Willard has a friend at the teachers' college in Denver, and he promised to send us someone, but so far no one has arrived."

"Yes, I heard about that," Jessica murmured.

"I've been able to tutor my children a bit," Mrs. Polk added. She gestured toward the two women in black whom Jessica had noticed earlier. "But poor Chila Clutter and Rose Pritchett are widows with several young ones to educate. They're too busy hiring out as maids or scrubwoman to do much for their own."

Jessica sadly regarded the others. "What a shame."

Mary touched Jessica's hand. "Think about it, dear."

"I will," Jessica promised.

Now Polk addressed Jessica. "We'd love to have you, Miss Garrett. And Merchant Allgood also mentioned that you might be willing to write up our town's history for the coming Founders' Day celebration."

"I'd be happy to assist." From the corner of her eye, Jessica caught Cole frowning at her, but ignored him.

Eugenia Riley

"Indeed?" Polk clapped his hands together in pleasure. "If you can come by my office, Miss Garrett, I have some materials that could help you—and we can discuss the matter further."

"I'll try to get by this week," Jessica promised.

As soon as the Polks moved on, the bevy of five pretty young ladies rushed up. As the four younger boys plucked off their hats and grinned at the girls, the plump one tugged at Mrs. Allgood's sleeve. "Ma'am, would you introduce us to the gents?"

All the boys appeared pleased as punch at the prospect, and Jessica had to admire the girl for speaking up so boldly. Dressed in yellow gingham, she was stout but also lovely, with bright blue eyes, an upturned nose, and long, thick, curling blond hair. Jessica sensed she had a lot of spunk.

Mrs. Allgood frowned. "Dumpling, your mother should teach you better manners than to be so forward around the menfolk."

As the girl lowered her head, Billy said to Mrs. Allgood, "Ah, ma'am, I don't think the young lady means nothing by it. She's just being friendly." He elbowed Gabe. "We sure ain't offended, are we, boys?"

"Nope!" replied the other three, all grinning ear to ear.

Dumpling grinned back, then turned again to the dowager. "Sorry, Mrs. Allgood, but we just want to welcome these folks to the church, like the gent says. Ain't that right, girls?"

The other girls nodded, giggling behind their fans.

"Very well," Mrs. Allgood conceded wearily. Gesturing at the various girls, she said to the "Livelys," "Folks, these are the Holler sisters—Maybelle, Minerva, and Beatrice—and their cousins, the Hicks sisters—Peaches and Dumpling."

Jessica sized up the rest of the girls. Maybelle, Minerva, and Beatrice were all pretty, slender brunettes. Peaches was an auburn-haired beauty who somewhat re-

194

sembled her sister Dumpling, but wasn't plump. All five of the girls appeared wholesome and pleasing. Jessica quickly decided they would do nicely as romantic prospects for the boys. There were even enough of them for Cole to have one.

Why did that prospect fill her with jealousy?

Meanwhile, Ma was announcing to the girls, "Pleased to meet you, ladies. And these are my sons—er—"

"Clay, Lyle, Gill, Walt, and Bobby," Jessica supplied.

The girls giggled at this. "Which one of you fellas is which?" Dumpling asked.

Grinning with pride, Billy spoke up. "Ma'am, I'm Bibby—I mean Bobby, and this here is . . . uh—"

"Lyle!" popped up Luke as he shook Minerva's hand.

"Yeah, Lyle," Billy repeated, sounding intensely relieved.

Wes stepped forward to shake hands with Maybelle. "And I'm—er—Walt."

"Pleased to meet you, Walt," Maybelle said.

Gabe winked at Peaches. "I'm Gill, ma'am."

"Gill," Peaches repeated, licking her lips. "I just love that name."

Dumpling clapped her hands. "Well, you folks staying for the covered dish dinner?"

Jessica and Ma exchanged perplexed looks, then Ma sputtered, "Well, we didn't know there was no dinner today, or we would have brung something. Seeing's we didn't, it ain't fair we impose."

Peaches would not take no for an answer. "It's no imposition at all, is it, Mrs. Allgood?"

"Heavens, no," declared the dowager. "There's always plenty of food, and we want our visitors to become better acquainted with our congregation."

"Just wait till you taste Dumpling's cooking," put in Beatrice.

"You got us convinced, ma'am," said Billy with such an eager grin that everyone laughed.

Peaches clapped her hands. "Will you boys help us unload the food from our wagons?"

"Why, ma'am, we'd be honored to," Gabe declared.

The four boys trooped off with the five girls. But Dumpling lagged behind, turning to Cole. "Ain't you coming, Clay?"

He winked. "Looks to me like you girls have enough help."

Dumpling shrugged, then followed the others out. Jessica couldn't believe how relieved she felt. Cole had every right to flirt with the girls, but she was so glad he'd chosen not to.

She was getting in deep, deep trouble!

Now the minister stepped up with his plump wife. "Welcome, folks. I'm Reverend Bliss and this is my dear Matilda. Who might you folks be?"

Another round of introductions followed. After the minister and his wife also urged the newcomers to stay for the dinner, Ma relented. The three followed the others outside and sat down on benches placed beside a long picnic table draped with oilcloth and shaded by a thatched awning. Several ladies busied themselves laying out food and glasses of tea.

Sitting between Ma and Cole toward one end of the table, Jessica smiled and watched the girls maneuver themselves next to the boys a few feet beyond her. Minerva sat down next to Luke, Maybelle with Wes, Peaches next to Billy. As for Gabe, he stood beyond talking to Beatrice, clearly flirting with the pretty young woman. Then Jessica was rather perplexed to watch Beatrice shy away, moving over to join a dark-haired couple, most likely her parents, who were seated down the table from Jessica and Cole. Appearing at a loss, Gabe sat down next to Peaches at the end of the table.

As for Dumpling, she was left odd woman out; she finally sat down across from Gabe and next to Maybelle.

Jessica felt sorry for Dumpling; indeed, it became obvious that Dumpling's sister Peaches was the center of attention as two young men with straw-colored hair strode up to flirt with her. But when Peaches only cast the two a haughty look and flipped her hair, the boys stalked away.

Once everyone was seated and all the covered dishes were in place, Reverend Bliss said grace, then made a point of introducing the "Lively" family and Jessica to the congregation. Jessica was warmed to note many smiles and nods.

For a few moments, most of the conversation involved passing the food. Then a stocky blond man sitting across from them offered Cole his hand. "I'm Joshua Hicks and this is my wife, Wilma." He gestured down the table. "We're the parents of those two young ladies, Peaches and Dumpling, who are sitting with your brothers, and we'd like to welcome you folks to our church."

Cole shook Joshua's hand. "Thanks much. You've all certainly given us a warm reception."

"You folks farm?" Joshua asked.

"We try our hand at it."

An old-timer, seated between them and the boys, called out, "What can you folks farm, with most of our streams p'isoned by runoff from the mines?"

At this, Billy stepped in, declaring, "Cotton."

Gabe quickly followed with, "Watermelons."

Luke added, "Persimmons."

As laughter erupted, Jessica groaned, while the old-timer turned fiery eyes on the boys. "You gentlemen joshing me?"

"Yeah, they are," Cole called out.

"Then what do you farm, sonny?" the codger demanded.

"We try our hand at corn and wheat, some livestock," Cole answered modestly.

"Well, it's a wonder you can raise anything with all the runoff from the mines," Joshua commented to Cole. "But it's a pleasure to have some new blood in our church."

"Thank you," said Cole.

"Especially young men," added Wilma, a pretty auburn-haired woman who resembled Peaches. "Several of our best young men were killed in that cave-in two years ago." She inclined her head down the table, then lowered her voice. "Including poor Beatrice's fiancé."

Jessica felt a surge of sympathy for the girl, who sat with eyes downcast. No wonder she had shied away from Gabe—she was obviously still grieving over her lost love.

Down the table, a younger man remarked, "I say damn Miser and his consortium for killing off half the good men in this town. Those of us still working the mines may not be with you much longer if things don't change."

"Yeah," put in another man, "makes me want to shake the hand of the Reklaw Gang for terrorizing them low-down snakes."

At this pronouncement, Cole raised an eyebrow at Jessica, and she demurely sipped her tea.

Another man laughed. "Hey, you boys hear what them Reklaws did the other day? Stopped old Miser and his cronies in their fancy carriage, robbed 'em and made 'em strip down to their longjohns."

As more merriment erupted, Reverend Bliss held up a hand. "Gentlemen, please, I think we've heard quite enough of this indelicate talk. There are ladies present, after all. And we Christians must never endorse the ways of lawbreakers."

"But, Reverend, the Reklaws are standing up for us, battling the consortium," Joshua argued. "Surely you gotta agree. Didn't you say today that the Good Lord will vanquish our enemies?"

"He'll vanquish them through His justice, not through the breaking of the laws of man."

The men fell glumly silent, deferring to the reverend. But Jessica noted that Cole, Joshua, and several other men soon got up and strode off to talk in a huddle beneath an oak tree.

Noting that Ma was happily involved in a conversation

with Mrs. Allgood and several other matrons, Jessica talked with Wilma, but mostly had fun watching the boys.

Luke and Wes were happily flirting with Minerva and Maybelle. Billy and Gabe were competing over Peaches. Dumpling was still being ignored, and was now pouting.

Then at last the plump, vivacious blonde went into action. She flounced up, grabbed a platter of chicken, then shoved it under Billy's nose. "Honey, have you tried my fried chicken?"

Billy grinned. "No, ma'am, but I'd be right proud to." He grabbed a leg, took a bite, and licked his lips. "Hot damn, ma'am, that's wonderful. And you cooked it yourself?"

"Sure did," Dumpling simpered. "But you ain't seen nothin' yet."

Dumpling sashayed off, soon returning with another plate. Leaning over, she all but shoved her ample bosom in Billy's face as she brandished the new platter just inches from his nose. "Try my biscuits, honey."

Billy's gaze was riveted to Dumpling's generous breasts, and his voice held a telltale quiver. "Yes, ma'am." Reaching up, he grabbed a biscuit, took a bite, gazed at Dumpling's staggering attributes, and looked ecstatic enough to faint.

"Well, what do you say, honey?" Dumpling pressed.

Billy grinned at Dumpling, then turned to Peaches and Gabe and loudly cleared his throat. "Hey, folks, would you scoot down a bit? I think Miss Dumpling would like to set a spell."

Peaches and Gabe scooted down, and Dumpling happily seated herself next to Billy. Billy appeared thoroughly bedazzled, and Jessica struggled not to laugh aloud. She had to hand it to Dumpling—she was quite a little operator.

On the way home, Billy's brothers teased him. "Billy's got a dumpling for a girlfriend," jeered Gabe.

"Yeah, and he's gonna need a wheelbarrow to carry her around," taunted Luke.

"Who knows, maybe she'll fatten him up a mite with that cookin' of hers," added Wes.

Even as Billy appeared ready to pop his cork, Ma turned wrathfully on her sons. "Hush up that mean talk, right now, varmints. Miss Dumpling can't help it if'n she's hefty. This unseemly talk makes me wonder what you vipers must say about your own ma behind her back."

"Ma, we don't say nothin'," protested Billy.

"Hush up!" she scolded. "A little pipsqueak like you, you don't deserve a fine woman like Miss Dumpling."

"But Ma, I didn't say nothin' against her!" Billy protested. "Why are ya blessing me out?"

" 'Cause the good Lord told me to," Ma shot back. "You was thinkin' evil thoughts, I just know it."

Billy rolled his eyes.

After a moment, Cole spoke up sternly. "You know, you boys need to watch your mouths. That business about growing watermelons just about did us in."

"But everyone knew we was joshing," protested Billy.

"You weren't. You were acting like the ignorant hicks you are."

The boys grumbled to one another.

"Well, no harm done, and you set everyone straight, Cole," Gabe remarked. " 'Sides, we don't know nothin' about farming."

"That's obvious. And the more we're around these people, the more suspicious they're going to become."

"Come on, Cole, don't be such a spoilsport," put in Jessica.

He shot her a resentful look, but refrained from further comment.

"Hey, Miss Jessie, ain't them women beauteous?" asked Billy.

"*Weren't those* women *beautiful*. And yes, they were."

" 'Course we're not through competing for you," he quickly added.

"Of course," she agreed solemnly.

Cole shot Jessica a glare.

From the back of the buckboard, Wes spoke up. "Ma, can we go back for prayer meeting on Wednesday night? Miss Maybelle and the others, they'll be a'comin."

Ma turned to regard her younger sons in amazement. "Well, I'll be hanged. Prayer meeting, is it? There may be hope for you heathens, after all."

Chapter Eighteen

At home, Jessica felt the need to speak with Cole, to thank him for his cooperation today. Although she didn't want to encourage him, she hoped she might get their relationship back on a more civil basis. She couldn't really blame him for being miffed and angry. She'd given herself to him in a moment of weakness, then had cut him off. For men, these matters were always so simple, and every problem could be resolved in bed. For her, the issues were far more complex.

She didn't find Cole around the house or in its immediate environs. Then the sounds of gunfire prompted her to walk past the barnyard toward an abandoned chicken coop. That was where she spotted him, shooting at bottles lined up on the ledge of the old shed. Her heart automatically hammered at the sight of him; he looked so sexy, still wearing his fine white linen shirt and dark trousers, especially with the intent look on his tanned face as he fired his Colt, shattering bottle after bottle.

She questioned the wisdom of speaking with him alone

this way. She remembered all too well what had happened to her the last time they'd been alone. But they were much closer to the house this time and she doubted Cole would try anything; there was too much risk of discovery.

Once he stopped to reload, she stepped into the clearing. "You pretending those bottles are me, Cole?"

Startled, he turned to her. "Well, hello, Miss Jessie. Nice afternoon, isn't it?"

She moved closer, crossing her arms over her bosom. "Yes, nice afternoon. But you haven't answered my question."

Cole grimly turned to fire, blowing apart another bottle. "Now, why would I want to pretend those bottles are you?"

Jessica laughed ruefully. "Oh, I can think of lots of reasons." She moved closer. "But for now, let's start with the fact that you're not pleased with me for insisting everyone go to church today, even though you offered your support."

He cocked an eyebrow. "Actually, I found the outing rather educational, especially talking to the miners who were there. Seems there's a lot of backing for what the gang is doing."

"The people of the church are frustrated and angry. But that doesn't make what you're doing right."

He merely shrugged and fired another shot.

"You know, Cole, if you really were an authentic Robin Hood, you'd give some of your proceeds to the church, to the people in the town whom the consortium is harming."

"That's a thought," he conceded, firing again.

"So what are you doing here—practicing for your next robbery?"

His answer was punctuated by more gunshots. "Anyone living in these parts who isn't schooled in self-defense is a fool."

"Then I'm a fool?"

Cole turned, shoving the pistol into his waist. "You pointed a loaded gun at me and didn't know the first thing about firing it. What do you think that makes *you*, Jessie?"

She felt wounded by his harsh words. "You're still mad about that?"

He moved closer, breath hot on her cheek, eyes blazing into hers. "You know damn well what I'm mad about."

"Yes, I suppose I do," she conceded.

"You're a tease, Jessie."

"I am not!" she protested.

"Really?" he mocked. "You gave yourself to me, then you pulled away. That's a tease in my book."

Wretchedly, she twisted a bit of her skirt fabric. "Cole, I didn't mean to."

"Mean to what? Give yourself to me—or pull away?"

She swallowed hard. "Don't you know I feel torn about this, too? I—I just wanted to thank you for your cooperation today. And I was hoping we might become—well, friends again."

"Friends?" He seized her by the shoulders. "I'm not going to be your friend, Jessie. *Ever.* You got that straight?"

She nodded vigorously.

He turned, grimly reloading his pistol, then firing off another round.

"Guess I'll go, then."

He turned. "Wait."

"Yes?"

"You know, it wouldn't hurt you to learn to fire a pistol—and a rifle, too. Ma knows how."

"I'm shocked she needs anything besides her broom." At last he smiled.

"Cole . . ." Feeling a bit encouraged, she asked, "Were you at least pleased with your brothers' progress today?"

"Progress? You mean with the ladies?"

"Yes. They need the influence of respectable women."

"And you're not jealous?"

"Of course not. I'm relieved. You know I never wanted you and your brothers to compete for me."

His expression darkened and he didn't comment.

She stepped closer. "Look, there's something else I want."

"Yes?"

She bravely met his eye. "I want to teach the children in town."

He shook his head. "Jessie, you're gonna dig our graves with all this socializing."

"I disagree! After seeing the needs of the children in Mariposa, I must insist on going in to teach—at least a couple of days a week."

"And if I say no?"

She touched his arm, watched a muscle work in his jaw. "You had the privilege of a basic education. Now your brothers are benefiting from the same. Would you deny that to the town's children?"

He sighed. "You sure like to turn the knife, don't you?"

"It's the truth."

He glanced away toward the trees, his expression tense. "Just what is it you want to do?"

"Well, for starters, I need to go into town to speak with the mayor—about the school and also about writing up the town's history for Founders' Day."

"Founders' Day?"

"Didn't you hear your ma volunteer to help make quilts for the bazaar?"

He flung a hand outward. "Damn it, Jessie, what are you going to have all of us do next? Make lace tatting?"

"Cole, please."

He continued to frown for a long moment. "Very well," he conceded at last. "Guess I still have a soft spot when you wheedle, woman. I'll take you to town."

"I can go myself."

"Really?" he mocked. "You don't even know how to defend yourself."

"I'll borrow Ma's broom."

He chuckled. "Not good enough."

Laughing herself, she nodded toward his pistol. "Then why don't you show me?"

His suddenly sensual gaze caught hers. "Show you what?"

She eyed him in reproach. "How to use the pistol, of course."

He dipped into a mocking bow. "Yes, ma'am."

She watched Cole stride off to a barrel filled with discarded bottles, then position several more on top of the coop. He sauntered back, turned, and pointed the pistol toward the coop.

"Now watch," he directed. "Here's how you hold the pistol . . . Here's how you cock it . . . Here's how you shoot." After discharging a round, he asked, "Want to try?"

"Sure."

He moved closer, putting the heavy pistol in her hand. "Now don't tense up."

She raised an eyebrow at him. "A little hard when one is holding an instrument of death."

"I'll help." Cole moved behind her, curling his body around hers, placing his hand over hers on the pistol. "Now just relax. Point the pistol. Cock it. Now shoot."

Though it was hard to concentrate with him so temptingly close, Jessica complied, wincing and recoiling as the first shot rang out. Although she missed the bottles, she did hit the coop.

"Not bad," Cole commented. "But just like I told you, you're too tense. Try again."

Jessica struggled to relax, and succeeded in not flinching as she fired off several more rounds, each one striking closer to the bottles themselves. Meanwhile, she felt Cole's lips moving to her cheek—and was stunned at the torrent of emotion his mouth stirred in her.

"Cole, please don't."

"Just trying to relax you, honey."

"Well, you're not succeeding." She fired another round, this time shattering a glass.

"Bravo, you're getting better." He was nuzzling her neck.

Jessica's voice trembled badly. "And you shouldn't be putting the moves on a woman holding a loaded gun."

"Tell me about it," he agreed dryly.

Abruptly Cole seized the pistol from Jessica's fingers and shoved it back in his waist. Then he turned her into his arms and crushed her close.

"Cole—"

"I miss you, Jessie," he whispered against her hair.

His words, his nearness, were pure torture. Jessica shut her eyes tightly, trying to hold back a floodtide of emotion. But she couldn't stop her senses from reacting to his exciting nearness, especially his tenderness and lack of aggression. It would be so easy to give in, and she wanted him so badly. But it would be another huge mistake.

"I know, Cole," she whispered at last. "I miss you, too."

"Do you, honey?" His arms tightened. "I miss the smell of your hair, your kisses, the little sounds you made when I was inside you. You want me inside you again, don't you, honey?"

His words were sensual torture. "Please, Cole, stop."

"Why?"

She pulled back, miserably meeting his gaze. "Because you'll get us both in trouble, get me pregnant."

He sighed heavily. "Are you so afraid to trust me?"

She stepped out of his arms. "It's not just trust, Cole. You have to change. And despite all your sweet-talk, you're really not willing to do so, are you?"

His silence was ample answer. With a resigned expression, she turned and walked away.

Cole watched her leave in anguish. His heart urged him to run after her, but his pride held him back. For hadn't she spoken the truth? He'd offered to marry her, but could he really give her all the love and devotion a husband should, much less a safe and secure future? Was he ready to make sacrifices for her, to change for her? He wanted her, wanted to make love to her, but was he really ready to share his life with her in the most profound sense? He still hadn't shared with her his deepest hurts and feelings.

He wanted her all right, but on his own terms. He realized sadly that his terms might never be good enough for her. She needed and deserved much more.

Chapter Nineteen

On Monday, Jessica started her period, and Ma helped her see to her needs, giving her boiled rags to use. Although Jessica felt relieved that her lapse with Cole hadn't produced a child, she was also surprised to find herself feeling melancholy. She missed Cole—his arms, his nearness. Even the prospect of bearing his child filled her with longing. But she continued to feel that the price of giving herself to him was too great.

On Tuesday, Cole took Jessica into town to see the mayor. In the cluttered back office of the feed store Polk owned, the mayor greeted the couple warmly, found them chairs, then began digging in a cabinet for the materials he'd promised Jessica.

"Ah, here we are—our town's historical papers," he declared. Carrying a small, crude wooden box, Polk strode to Jessica's side and handed her the box. "Actually, we had a town historian, Mrs. Agnes Agee, but the poor soul passed away last year. However, the materials she left should suffice for you to write up our history."

"Indeed." Jessica sifted through the contents of the box, which included the town's original charter, Agnes Agee's numerous notes on events over the years, and even a faded daguerreotype photo of the mayor and Merchant Allgood at the ground-breaking ceremony for the town five years ago.

She smiled at Polk. "These will be fine, and I'll take great care with them. What length do you have in mind?"

He waved a hand. "Oh, ten pages or so will do nicely."

"And when is Founders' Day?"

Polk took his seat. "The last Saturday in September. That will give you almost a month."

"That sounds adequate." If she was even here that long!

"And would you be willing to read a summary at the celebration?" Polk asked.

"Of course."

The mayor leaned back in his chair. "The ladies of the church are already busy making up quilts, canned goods, and other items to sell at the bazaar. All proceeds will benefit the school fund."

"I'd be delighted to help out with the bazaar, as well," Jessica offered.

"You just write up the history. That will be ample contribution." Polk flashed her an encouraging grin. "Now, about the schoolteacher position . . . Are you interested?"

"I might be."

"Splendid. Could you tell me a little more about your background?"

Having expected this question, Jessica gave Polk a vague account of having received her degree from a university in New Mexico, and having taught at the college level in Greeley. Luckily, the mayor didn't press her for details, instead listening with a broad smile.

Afterward, he stated, "Miss Garrett, I'm quite impressed, as well as deeply honored that you're offering your services to the children of our town. We haven't had a schoolteacher in these parts for several years." He paused, frowning. "But didn't Mr. Allgood mention you're only here for a visit?"

Jessica glanced uneasily at Cole, but he only raised an eyebrow as if to say, *This is your pickle, not mine*. She turned back to Polk. "Well, it could be an extended visit. I'll be happy to teach the children for as long as I can. And besides, aren't you expecting another teacher?"

"Indeed, we were," Polk replied, frowning. "My professor friend in Denver promised months ago that he would dispatch us a suitable graduate—but so far no one has come."

"Then it's possible I'll be able to fill in until the other teacher arrives."

"We'll hope so. Will you be available to teach every day?"

Catching Cole's dark look, Jessica hedged. "Well, I thought perhaps two days a week to begin with."

Polk sighed. "I suppose we must be grateful for whatever we can get. By the way, are you aware that you may have as many as two dozen students? Do you think you can handle that number?"

"Of course."

"What did you have in mind for a salary?"

"Well, I hadn't really thought."

"The town can afford to be fairly generous. How does twenty dollars a month sound?"

Jessica had to quash a smile. "Sounds fine to me."

"Good." Polk reached behind him, taking down a large key from a peg on the wall. "I'll show you folks the schoolhouse—such as it is."

The three left the feed store and walked several blocks to the tiny schoolhouse, which stood with an abandoned air, front porch sagging and shutters hanging askew. Mayor Polk unlocked and pushed open the creaky door. Jessica sneezed at the dust as the three entered a murky expanse of rattletrap desks, scattered textbooks, cobwebs, and bits of debris.

Opening a window, Polk dusted off his hands and said, "The place needs a lot of work. The roof's leaking, several of the desks are missing legs, not to mention the shattered windowpanes and sagging floorboards. Some refurbishing must be done before students can be received here—but I'm sure the town will pitch in."

Jessica addressed Cole. "Perhaps you and the boys can help."

Cole slanted her a skeptical look.

"We can raise the issue at prayer meeting tomorrow night," Polk suggested. "You folks will be attending, won't you? I'll have Reverend Bliss ask for volunteers."

Cole glanced with distaste at the decrepit structure. "I can hardly wait," he muttered dryly.

Prayer meeting on Wednesday night proved a rousing event, complete with gospel readings and inspiring hymns. During the service, the four younger Reklaw boys again made eyes at the Hicks and Holler daughters, who simpered back and waved.

Following the benediction, Reverend Bliss announced, "Ladies and gentlemen, before we disperse, I'm pleased to inform you that Miss Jessica Garrett has graciously consented to teach the children of our town."

Applause and cheers sounded out. Jessica blushed.

"Miss Garrett also needs some help fixing up the schoolhouse."

Billy popped up. "I'll help."

"Me, too," declared Gabe.

Soon, a chorus of other men volunteered.

"Very good," said Bliss. "All of you just show up at the schoolhouse tomorrow morning, and bring what tools and construction supplies you can spare. I'm sure you'll want to speak with Miss Garrett during the ice cream social outside in the pavilion. The Women's Society is treating us tonight." He paused, snapping his fingers. "But the Quilting Widows shall remain behind in the sanctuary, to continue working on their offerings for Founders' Day."

As the group dispersed, Mrs. Allgood came up to greet the Reklaws and Jessica. "Miss Garrett, we're so glad you'll be teaching our children."

"Thank you," Jessica replied. "It's my pleasure."

The old woman turned to Eula. "Mrs. Lively, would you care to meet the Quilting Widows?"

"Meet 'em?" Ma declared with a grin. "Why, I'm ready to join 'em. Got my best needles and some cloth swatches right here in my reticule."

Jessica happily watched Ma and Mrs. Allgood walk off to join the other widows. Glancing about, she noted the boys following the girls outside. Then she turned to see Cole staring at her with amusement.

He offered her his arm. "Ice cream, sugar?"

She smiled and took his arm. "Don't mind if I do."

Cole escorted her outside to the pavilion area, where several matrons were dipping ice cream from old-fashioned machines, serving church members who trooped by. Off to one side, an old-timer played a poignant refrain of "In the Sweet Bye and Bye" on his harmonica.

Cole fetched Jessica a bowl of peach ice cream, then went off to chat with the men, leaving Jessica to converse with Mrs. Hicks and Mrs. Holler.

"Miss Garrett, we're so grateful you're willing to teach our children," remarked Wilma Hicks.

"It's my pleasure."

"Have you taught school before?" asked Millie Holler, who was an older, slightly graying version of her three brunette daughters.

"Indeed I have. Even at the university level."

"Oh, how wonderful," declared Wilma. "You know, much as I love Mariposa, we've had to do without so much here. No school, no sheriff. I've tried to persuade my cousin Jedediah to come out here and be our lawman. I'm sure Mr. Polk would be happy to hire him. But I just can't budge my cousin."

As Wilma spoke, a chill washed over Jessica. Could "Jedediah" be the Jedediah she'd met on the stage weeks ago?

"Um—Mrs. Hicks, are you speaking of Jedediah Lummety?"

Wilma's face lit up. "Why, yes. He's sheriff of Colorado City. Do you know him?"

"I—uh—believe I may have heard someone else mention him."

Wilma sighed. "The last time we saw Jed in Colorado City, he promised he'd come out for a visit as soon as the new stage line started up. I worry about him, since he's a widower with grown children that have moved away. But so far Jed hasn't come—and neither has the stage."

A new shiver streaked down Jessica's spine. "Er—couldn't your cousin ride out to see you?"

Wilma waved her off. "Jed can't ride that far, not with his lumbago. He's somewhat older than I am, you see. Thank heaven he has his deputies, or he could never hold down his job in Colorado City. That's one rowdy town, another reason we want him to move out here. I even wrote him about it—but, of course, like a typical man, he never answers my letters."

Thank God, Jessica thought to herself.

As the two women chatted about ordering some dress patterns, Jessica found her attention wandering. Wilma's comment had really set her mind to churning. She didn't know what anything meant—how she had managed to travel across time, and land in Buck Lynch's stagecoach with "Sheriff" Lummety, or why he and the other men she'd ended up with had assumed she was the new schoolteacher, on her way to Mariposa. There was something spooky about the whole scenario. Would any other schoolteacher be coming out from Denver? Somehow she doubted this. In a weird sense, it was almost as if she had stepped into someone else's life. It all defied comprehension.

Worse yet, Jedediah Lummety, who had seen all five outlaw brothers on the day she'd arrived here, was Wilma's cousin and would presumably try to visit Mariposa again at some point! What then? Would he recognize the "Lively" brothers as the actual Reklaw Gang and haul them all off to a certain hanging? Should she warn the brothers?

And risk losing all her dearly gained progress?

Hearing laughter, she turned to watch the boys "sparking" their women. Minerva and Luke were sharing ice cream from the same bowl; Wes and Maybelle stood close together listening to the harmonica music.

But otherwise, there seemed trouble in paradise. Dumpling Hicks was trying to flirt with Billy, but he was ignoring her and conversing with Mayor Polk. And Peaches had been lured away from Gabe by her old straw-haired boyfriend. Gabe stood in the shadows, glowering and watching the other two flirt.

Jessica went over to join him. "Something wrong?"

Gabe's jaw tightened. "Looks like Miss Peaches favors her old flame over me."

"I'm sorry," Jessica commiserated. She glanced around the pavilion, her gaze settling on a lovely dark-haired young woman in a burgundy-colored muslin dress. "But you know, I think the prettiest girl here is Beatrice Holler, and she's sitting all alone. But she'd be thrilled if some nice fella brought her some ice cream."

Gazing at Beatrice, Gabe swallowed hard. "Yeah, she's mighty pleasing, but I had no luck with her on Sunday. Heard Miss Dumpling say she's still grieving over her dead fiancé."

"And I say you're giving up too easily," Jessica admonished.

He glowered.

"Maybe she felt guilty when you first approached her.

215

But she could have had second thoughts by now."

"Ya think?" The worry in Gabe's expression had lightened somewhat as he continued to stare at the young woman. Beatrice, seeming to sense his perusal, glanced in his direction, then shyly glanced away. "I don't know, ma'am. She still looks 'bout as spooked as a new colt."

"You just need to be a little more subtle, Gabe," Jessica advised. "You probably caught her off guard on Sunday. I'm sure she hadn't even considered having a new beau. Why not give it one more chance now that she's had time to think it over?"

Though his expression remained uncertain, Gabe nodded. "All right, ma'am. If you say so."

He sauntered off, fetched a bowl of ice cream and took it over, solemnly offering it to Beatrice. Watching the girl greet Gabe with a shy smile, Jessica breathed a sigh of relief. Within moments, the two were seated together, quietly talking.

"Ma'am?"

Jessica turned to see Dumpling standing in front of her. Although the girl tried to put on a brave front, Jessica could see the disappointment in her lovely blue eyes. "Well, hi, Dumpling, how are you doing?"

Dumpling twisted her pudgy fingers together. "Fine, I reckon. Anyhow, ma'am, I just wanted to tell you I'd be happy to help out tomorrow."

"Great. You know the boys, and Bi—that is, Bobby—will also be there."

The girl sniffed and glanced away.

Jessica touched her arm. "Something wrong, dear? I'm a good listener, you know."

Dumpling shuddered, appearing close to tears. "It don't make no never mind whether Bobby's comin' tomorrow or not. He don't cotton to me."

"What makes you say that?"

Dumpling glanced with longing at Billy, who was now

216

happily joking with Luke, Wes, Minerva, and Maybelle. "I've tried to be friendly, but Bobby gave me the cold shoulder."

"Oh, men sometimes get all caught up on their pride. I'm sure he likes you."

Dumpling shook her head and sniffed. "He don't, 'cause I'm a fat cow."

Jessica was crestfallen. "Dumpling, no! How can you say that about yourself? You're lovely!"

Dumpling fell silent, lower lip trembling.

"You know, Bobby has been talking about how wonderful your cooking is."

Dumpling brightened a bit. "He has?"

"Indeed." Jessica winked. "Why not bring a few samples to the school tomorrow, around lunchtime?"

Dumpling's features lit with new hope. "Oh, yes, ma'am! I'll bring biscuits, and stew, and chicken and dumplings."

"Now you're talking."

"Thank you, ma'am!"

Watching the girl waltz off with a smile on her face, Jessica felt encouraged.

"Having fun with your matchmaking, sugar?"

Jessica turned to see Cole regarding her with cynical amusement. "Don't mind admitting that I am."

"So I guess we're all coming in to town tomorrow to help fix up the school."

"Guess so. You mean you're willing, too?"

Cole gave a self-deprecating smile. "Jessie, after being around these folks Sunday and tonight . . . Well, I'll have to admit it's something good you're doing."

Jessica pressed a hand to her breast in mock amazement. "Mr. Lively! Such humility coming from you!"

He chuckled. "Not that I completely approve. The risk still bothers me."

Jessica glanced away guiltily. If Cole only knew what she'd learned tonight, he'd call off this charade—now.

"But it's still a worthwhile thing to do."

"Thanks, Cole." She eyed him quizzically. "What put you in such a reflective mood?"

"Oh, talking with the men, learning more about the harsh conditions at the mines. Several miners have even offered to take me on a tour, show me just how bad things are."

"My heaven, is that allowed?"

"It'll be our secret, on Sunday afternoon. Believe me, the consortium will never get wind of it."

"But what persuaded the men to take you there?"

"They know I'm concerned, that I want to help. Hell, Ma's a mine widow just like so many others in the church. What other incentive do they need?"

She nodded. "You're right, of course. And it's good of you to take an interest."

A sheepish look drifted over Cole's features. "I've also promised a generous contribution to the Mine Widows and Orphans Fund—and to the church."

Jessica laughed. "Why, Mr. Lively, I *am* reforming you."

Cole leaned close, eyes gleaming wickedly. "Not a chance, woman. When it comes to you, my mind is always in the devil's territory."

Chapter Twenty

The next morning when Cole and Jessica arrived at the schoolhouse, a contingent of help greeted them on the sagging front steps. As Jessica approached the building, with Cole close behind carrying an armload of tools, Mrs. Clutter and Mrs. Pritchett stood awaiting them with cleaning supplies at their feet and children in tow. Both families were pitifully attired, their garments filthy and tattered.

"Good morning, ma'am," greeted Mrs. Pritchett, a frail, dark-haired woman of about thirty. She gestured about her. "Chila and me, and the kids, we've come to help with the school."

"How kind of you," Jessica replied graciously. She turned to Mrs. Clutter, who was slightly plumper, with stringy brown hair and a wary expression on her sallow face. "Thank you, too, Mrs. Clutter."

The woman nodded stiffly, appearing embarrassed. "Yes, ma'am."

"We can certainly use the help, can't we, Mr. Lively?"

"Yes, indeed," Cole agreed.

Jessica smiled at the children, all of whom appeared pale, undernourished, and rather dejected. "And who have we here?"

Mrs. Pritchett gestured in turn at boys who appeared to be about eleven and ten. "My boys, Abe and Ben. Abe's the eldest—he's thirteen, and Ben is twelve."

Jessica had to struggle not to gasp aloud as she noted how underdeveloped these children were for their ages. She shuddered to think of the deprivations they must endure.

"Pleased to meet you, boys," she said.

Both boys tipped their straw hats and murmured in unison, "Ma'am."

"And these four is mine," Chila Clutter added awkwardly. "Hazel is nine, Caleb eight, Polly seven, and Rachel six."

Jessica smiled at the four little stairsteps who, again, appeared much too small and sad for their ages.

"It's wonderful to have all of you. Shall we go in?"

Inside the dusty building, the group went to work, opening windows, sweeping, cleaning. With the boys as helpers, Cole began repairing the ramshackle desks; the mothers and daughters scrubbed scarred floorboards, while Jessica tried to organize and rearrange the pitiful assortment of books that served for the school's library.

Afterward, she walked over to join the two mothers, who were on their knees scouring a corner, while their daughters worked nearby. "May I help you?"

"No, ma'am," answered Chila Clutter. "Rose and me have this in hand. You're the teacher, and have better things to do with your hands than scrubbing."

Jessica cleared her throat. "I can't help but notice how small your children are."

Both women stopped their labors to regard her suspiciously.

"I don't mean this to criticize," Jessica quickly added.

220

"I realize how difficult it must be for you, widow ladies on your own, trying to keep growing children fed."

"We make out best we can," Rose replied tightly.

"But I want to help," Jessica remarked. "I mean, I'd like to donate my salary to your two families."

Jessica was stunned by the widows' response. Both women scrambled to their feet to regard her angrily.

"We don't need your charity, ma'am," declared Rose, pride burning in her pale eyes.

"Yeah, and we'll be on our way," added Chila.

And before Jessica's horrified eyes, and heedless of her protests, the two women grabbed their children and left.

Jessica followed the group to the door. "Please, I meant no offense. You don't have to leave."

Without a backward glance, both women dragged their children down the steps. Only a couple of the children dared to glance back, features stark with sadness and disappointment.

"What have you done now, woman?"

Jessica turned to see Cole regarding her in consternation. She threw up her hands. "I don't know. Guess I insulted them. I tried to give them some money."

Cole whistled. "Where are you from, woman? Don't you know people here have their pride? Joshua Hicks told me those two won't even accept assistance from the Mine Widows and Orphans Fund."

"Well, you might have told me, Cole."

He waved a hand in exasperation. "Maybe I figured you'd have more common sense than that. Most folks around here figure they have to work for what they get."

She lowered her voice and balled her hands on her hips. "Except for certain scoundrels who feel they're entitled to rob stages and gold shipments for a living."

He grinned. "That's work, too, sugar."

"Oh, you're impossible." Growing increasingly agitated, she flung several stray tendrils of hair from her

221

forehead. "Look, hold down the fort for a minute. I'm going to see if I can't catch them and apologize."

"Sure." Cole strode back to the desk he'd been repairing.

Jessica rushed outside, relieved to see that the women's wagon still hadn't pulled away—although everyone had boarded and Rose appeared ready to snap the reins attached to the scraggly-looking mule.

She rushed up. "Wait! Please, won't you wait a moment?"

Her expression tight, Rose Pritchett glanced down at Jessica. "What is it, ma'am? We need to be on our way."

"But won't you stay awhile? I really do need your help."

Rose glanced at Chila; both women appeared to be wavering. Then Caleb called out from the bed of the wagon, "Please, Mama, can't we help Teacher? We was having fun."

Rose gave Jessica a hard look. "We won't tolerate no more talk of charity. We take care of our own."

Jessica held up a hand. "I understand entirely. In fact, I really put my foot in my mouth—I mean, I misspoke. What I really meant to say was that I need to hire you both."

"Hire us?" Chila repeated, glowering suspiciously.

"That's right. You see, Mayor Polk has warned me that I may have as many as two dozen students, and I can't possibly handle all of them by myself, especially since they'll be all different ages. I'll need to hire at least two teacher's aides."

The two women exchanged a perplexed look, then lowered their heads in shame.

"Please, what is the problem?" Jessica protested. "If I've insulted you again, I didn't mean to."

At last Chila's gaze, filled with pride, met Jessica's. "Ma'am, we ain't educated," she admitted miserably.

"But that shouldn't make a difference," Jessica hastily reassured the women. "You can both still help, can't you?

You can quiet rowdy children, wipe runny noses, supervise recess. Plus, you can learn. You're both older, more mature. As you learn to read and write, you can teach the youngest ones. And think of how you'll eventually be able to tutor your own children with their homework."

The two women consulted each other with wary glances.

"Of course, under these circumstances, I'd have to pay you," Jessica rushed on. "I mean, I know you're two very smart women, and you're not going to let anyone exploit you without compensation, are you?"

Though Jessica suspected neither woman fully understood the words "exploit" or "compensation," her implication sank in. "No, ma'am, we ain't workin' without wages," agreed Chila with a firm bob of her chin.

"Then do we have a deal?" Jessica asked hopefully.

Again the two consulted each other, then Rose nodded. "Yes, ma'am, you got yourself some hired help."

High spirits prevailed as the families returned. Jessica was intensely grateful that she'd managed to smooth things over.

And, to her delight, more members of the community soon arrived. Merchant Allgood delivered half a dozen panes of window glass he was donating to the school, and helped Cole putty them in to replace the broken panes. Mrs. Polk brought by a box of her own children's books that she was donating.

At mid-morning, Ma arrived with the rest of the boys, everyone carrying in tools and baskets of food. Mrs. Allgood and another elderly widow came bearing sewing baskets and bolts of gingham they were donating for curtains. Ma settled down with the widows, helping them measure, cut, and sew.

The Holler and Hicks families appeared soon afterward, the women bearing more covered dishes and pies, the men with donated roofing supplies. Jessica had to smile as she once again watched the boys and girls flirt: Maybelle handed Wes nails as he stood on a ladder repairing a sagging wall plank; Minerva chatted with Luke as he solemnly sawed a piece of lumber; Gabe and Beatrice quietly conversed as they swept cobwebs from the corners. Yet Billy, repairing furniture, was still resisting Dumpling's attentions as she tried to tempt him with a cup of iced tea or a damp rag to wipe his sweaty brow.

Watching the girl trudge off wearing a downcast expression, Jessica approached Billy; he had a rickety bench upended on the teacher's desk and was trying to reinforce its sides with nails.

Continuing to hammer, he grinned at her. "Well, howdy, Miss Jessica, are we doing you proud?"

"Proud?" she repeated reproachfully. "I don't think so."

Billy set down the hammer, wrapped an arm around Jessica's shoulders, and flashed her a charming grin. "What's wrong, sugar? Ain't we giving you enough attention?"

"*Aren't*, Billy."

"*Aren't* we giving you enough attention?"

She pulled away, casting him a scolding look. Glancing about to make sure no one was close enough to hear her using his real name, she scolded, "Billy, I'll have you know I'm a grown woman and I don't stand around pouting like a schoolgirl, expecting all of you men to fawn at my feet. However, I do think I'd pout if you treated me as rudely and shabbily as you've just treated Miss Dumpling."

Billy blanched. He glanced at Dumpling, who was sitting by herself in a corner. "Oh."

"Oh? Is that all you have to say for yourself?"

His guilty gaze met hers. "What do you expect me to say?"

"Well, for one thing, why were you so rude? I know you must like her."

Billy stared at the scuffed toe of his boot. "Yeah, I do."

"Then why are you giving her the cold shoulder?"

Billy glanced up, tension and pride clenching his features. "Well, the boys have been joshing me about having a hippopotamus for a sweetheart."

"Oh, how mean of them!" Jessica declared, indignant. "I'll give them a piece of my mind."

"Yeah. You do." He stared at his toe again.

"And what about you?"

He didn't glance up. "What about me?"

She tapped his chest with her index finger. "Are you going to act like a baby who does what his brothers tell him to, or a man who goes after what he wants?"

Billy glanced up, eyes blazing now. "I ain't no baby."

"Then start acting like a man."

Jessica flounced away, praying Billy would heed her scolding. Stealing a glance at him over her shoulder, she was relieved to see him staring at Dumpling again, his features a mixture of pride and longing. She wondered what he was thinking. . . .

Watching Jessica storm away in a flash of gingham skirts, Billy Reklaw was left frowning over her lecture. Hot damn—that was one feisty female. When he and his brothers had first captured Jessie, he'd been all but convinced he was in love with her, and he'd cheerfully joined in the competition with Gabe, Luke, and Wes. Now he wasn't so sure.

His gaze drifted with longing to Dumpling. He'd never fancied himself wanting a plump woman, but, Lordy, this girl enticed him. She was a pretty one, with that curly blond hair he longed to sink his fingers into, those pert dimples, that cute little nose and kissable mouth. And the rest of her—a rounded, ample bottom to sink his hands into, and breasts large enough to make a man sure he'd died and gone to heaven. And she could cook, and laugh, and what a smile! She made him hungry enough to take a big bite out of her.

Only, why did his brothers have to bedevil him so about her? Calling Miss Dumpling a watermelon and him a beanpole. And why did he even care? Wasn't Miss

Jessie right? Wasn't it time for him to decide whether he was really a man, or a baby?

And just look at poor Miss Dumpling sitting in that corner all by herself, like a big, sad flower waiting to be plucked.

His decision made, Billy strode across the room to her. "Howdy, Miss Dumpling."

Spotting him, Dumpling gave a little gasp. Then she surged to her feet. "Well, hey, Bobby."

He flashed his most charming grin. "What's a purty thing like you doin' all alone?"

She dimpled. "Don't look like I'm alone no more, do it?"

"No, ma'am." He gestured toward the desk. "You know, I could use some help with that bench I'm repairing."

She laced her arm through his. "Why, sure, sugar." Lowering her voice to a husky purr, she confided, "You know I was a'watchin' you drivin' them nails."

Billy all but swallowed his tongue. "Y-you were?"

Dumpling licked her lips. "Ain't never seen no man do it better."

Billy gulped. "Well, hot damn, sugar."

"You getting hungry?" she added suggestively.

"Yes, ma'am," he replied just as eagerly.

"Well, wait till you see my basket—I brung stew, and biscuits." She wiggled her eyebrows suggestively. "And even chicken and *dumplings*."

Billy's grin all but split his face. "Hey, honey, I just love dumplings. Can't wait to dive into 'em."

"I'm counting on it, sugar—that is, after you pound nails."

"Yeah!"

"Then what are we waitin' for? You hammer the nails—"

"And you show me your basket."

Across the room, Jessica was relieved to watch Billy and Dumpling pair off together, Dumpling holding the bench for him while he hammered. They continued to work together, laughing, for the balance of the morning, ignoring the occasional snickers they received from Wes, Luke, and Gabe.

At high noon, Reverend Bliss stopped by just in time to pronounce grace before everyone sat down to eat. Sitting next to Cole at an old desk, Jessica glanced about happily; already the schoolhouse looked so much better. The steps, sagging walls, and floorboards had all been shored up, the roof repaired. This afternoon they would begin whitewashing the walls—and by tomorrow, the curtains would be hung. The little place was starting to look like a real school, after all.

When the meal was over, young Caleb pulled out a harmonica and treated those gathered to a jaunty rendition of "Nellie Bly." While the townsfolk looked on and clapped, Wes and Maybelle got up to dance, soon followed by Minerva and Luke, Gabe and Beatrice. Jessica felt disheartened when Billy and Dumpling didn't join the others right away.

However, once the three couples retired from the floor and Caleb started up a new tune, "Flow Gently, Sweet Afton," Jessica was pleased to see Billy proudly escort Dumpling out to dance. Dumpling was grinning from ear to ear as the two waltzed; Billy was smiling shyly. Everything went fine until Dumpling stumbled onto Billy's instep and he jerked back with a yelp of pain.

That was when his three brothers, standing along the sidelines with the Holler girls, erupted into laughter and began to point and jeer. Billy glowered at the others while Dumpling blushed and hung her head. The Holler girls appeared embarrassed by the boys' obnoxious behavior, while others present, including Dumpling's parents, looked on, frowning their disapproval.

Outraged, Jessica turned to Cole. "*Do* something."

"My pleasure," he replied grimly.

Cole strode off, grabbing the three culprits and taking them off to a corner. She watched as he soundly scolded his brothers. Cole behaved as a true hero of the down-trodden. Watching his angry gestures, observing the look of fierce recrimination on his face, Jessica felt proud of him. And his lecture worked. She smiled as she watched three male faces dissolve in guilt. Good for Cole!

She glanced back at Billy and Dumpling, relieved to see them dancing again, this time with no taunts from the sidelines. Both of them looked happy. She was making real progress here, reforming all of the brothers, perhaps even Cole. Perhaps *this* was the true reason she'd been brought across time.

Wilma Hicks and Millie Holler now strolled up to join her. "Well, Miss Garrett, looks like there's romance in the air," declared Wilma. "My Dumpling talks of nothing but Bobby."

Jessica eyed the woman contritely. "I'm so sorry about the way Bobby's brothers just acted toward your daughter. I'm going to skin them all alive once we get home."

Wilma sighed. "I know, but it looks like their older brother already took them to task. Anyhow, boys will be boys, and poor Dumpling has always been teased about her size. Don't you worry, now—my daughter's a strong-willed young woman who can hold her own with those boys."

"And her cousins will help, too," put in Millie Holler. "My three girls are really taken with Walt, Lyle, and Gill. I'm sure they'll insist the boys mind their manners around Cousin Dumpling."

"Good for them," Jessica replied gratefully.

She was touched by the women's support. It seemed she now had extensive help in her mission to redeem the brothers. Suddenly her world felt filled with happiness.

Jessica's bubble burst in mid-afternoon, when the group arrived home and the five brothers began gathering their pistols and saddling their horses. She confronted them out in the yard.

"Where do you think you're going?" she demanded.

Standing next to his horse, Billy answered, "There's a new shipment of gold coming down the mine road this afternoon. Reckon we'll go relieve 'em of it."

"My God!" Jessica cried. "But I thought all of you were changing, becoming reformed."

"We are," answered Gabe. "We all had a meeting and decided we're giving part of today's take to the school, and part to the church."

Jessica was flabbergasted. "Has it never occurred to you that churchgoing folks don't steal?"

The boys exchanged perplexed looks, then Luke spoke up. "That makes no sense, ma'am. Don't the church need money to run it just like anything else?"

She beseeched Cole. "Please, do something."

But he, too, proved immovable. "It's the way we live our lives, sugar."

"Well, it stinks."

"Want to join us?" he asked.

Remembering what had happened following their last robbery, Jessica felt weak. To cover her discomfiture, she crossed her arms over her bosom and glowered. "Think I'll pass this time."

Cole edged closer to her, and from the ardent look in his eyes, Jessica suspected he was also remembering that torrid episode. "Don't be mad, Jessie. It's what we do."

"Don't give me that hogwash."

"It's the only way to stop Miser."

"You haven't stopped him yet. And, by the way, how do you find out about all these shipments? Do you have a spy at the mines?"

Cole's features tightened. "Sorry, trade secret."

Jessica watched glumly as Cole swung about; then he and the others mounted their horses and rode off. Ma came out, sweeping the porch and humming "Bringing in the Sheaves."

"Can't you do something?" Jessica beseeched, gesturing at the departing riders.

"Well, honey, I could have told you a skunk don't change its stripes," Ma muttered to Jessica.

"No kidding," she replied.

Chapter Twenty-one

On Sunday afternoon, Cole galloped into the yard of the Aspen Gulch Mines, a collection of ramshackle buildings, sluices, and piles of tailings, all sprawled amid gouges in the mountainside.

Cole was eager to see evidence of what he and his brothers were fighting for—especially after their escapade the other day. Though he hadn't admitted this to Jessica, the last gold shipment robbery hadn't been the usual easy pickings—the guard had been unexpectedly tripled. A spirited gun battle had ensued between the guards and the gang, and the guards hadn't surrendered until one of them had been winged by a gang bullet. Even though no one had been seriously hurt, the incident bothered Cole. Robbing gold shipments was one matter; wounding or even killing people was another.

Cole dismounted to face four miners from church milling about in the yard—Joshua Hicks, Henry Holler, Gideon Mayhew and Thaddeous Jeter. At the back of the group stood a fifth man, a white-haired old-timer, a familiar stranger to Cole. Beyond the group yawned the black entrance to the mine, with an empty ore car sitting outside on the narrow tracks.

Cole tethered Red to a hitching post and strode toward the group. "Afternoon, gents."

Joshua Hicks shook Cole's hand. "Clay, you know most everyone from church. But I don't expect you've met old Jeremiah Crane, since he doesn't attend."

Cole approached the thin old man, whose features were wizened and sallow. He wore the tattered flannel shirt and filthy canvas Levi's typical of hard rock miners. Offering his hand, he said, "Mr. Crane. Clay Lively."

Humor gleamed in the old-timer's gray eyes. "Pleased to meet you, Mr. Lively," he rasped back, shaking Cole's hand.

"Jeremiah's the only miner left in these parts who was around when the first mine opened over thirty years ago," put in Henry Holler.

"Really?" asked Cole. "Mr. Crane, I don't suppose you would have known my pa, Chester Lively?"

"Yep, I knew him," replied Jeremiah solemnly, telltale merriment again sparkling in his eyes. "A pity we lost him in that cave-in back in '59 at the old western branch."

Cole nodded. "My ma still hasn't gotten over it."

"Yeah, them Aspen Gulch boys kept on tunnelin' out that hillside till the blame thing collapsed," Jeremiah related bitterly.

Henry clapped Cole across the shoulders in a gesture of reassurance. "And Clay's ma is not the only woman in these parts to lose a good man in one of Elijah Miser's hell-holes."

"Yeah," agreed Jeremiah. "If cave-ins don't do us in, it's miner's lung." He paused, coughing hard, then straining for his next breath. "I reckon it'll put me under before spring."

Thaddeous Jeter waved off the old man. "Ah, Jeremiah, you've been promising to die on us for ten years now. I reckon you'll outlive us all."

All six men laughed at this much needed bit of levity. Then Joshua continued more soberly to Cole, "We do lose a lot of men to lung disease, especially our drillers like Jeremiah." He pointed to a huge, rambling shed off to the west. "But we lose more due to the cyanide and acid fumes used in the stamping mill. I'll have to hand it to Miser and his cronies—they're damned shrewd to have such a self-contained operation, so they can just ship the gold bullion off to their fat coffers in Colorado Springs."

"Yeah, but they didn't count on the Reklaw boys unloading their booty along the way," put in Henry, and again the men erupted in laughter.

Joshua clapped his hands. "Ready to see the mine, Clay?"

Cole hesitated. "Are you sure it's safe for us to be snooping around? Isn't there a chance we'll be discovered?"

Joshua chuckled. "Not with Gideon here pulling guard duty today. And Jeremiah will help him out."

Cole turned to Gideon, a tall, thin man with carroty hair. "Thanks, neighbor."

Gideon grinned back. "Long as you fellas don't try no high-grading, reckon we'll be all right."

Perplexed, Cole asked, "What's high-grading?"

"Oh, it's a custom certain miners have of pocketing the highest grade gold ore," Gideon explained. "At most mines, any man caught loses his job. Out here, a guilty fella more likely will disappear down some unused shaft."

Cole whistled. "You must be jesting."

Jeremiah answered the question. "Nope, sonny, we're pretty sure it happened to Clive Kitchell back in '82. We all knew he was high-grading, then one day he just up and disappeared."

Cole shook his head. "Maybe he left for better parts."

Joshua's bitter laugh rang out. "Without his wife and year-old baby? We reckon not."

"It's a harsh life, isn't it?"

Joshua nodded. "Doesn't your family know that as well as anyone else?" Since a reply seemed unnecessary, he gestured toward the mine opening. "All right, men, time to go down the hole."

As the others began striding off, Cole again shook Jeremiah's hand. "Good to meet you."

Jeremiah nodded. "Take care down in the mine, sonny."

"You bet."

Joshua spoke to Gideon. "You two keep an eye out, now."

Gideon touched a pistol at his waist. "Sure will."

Cole and the other three men entered a tunnel cluttered with debris. Joshua paused to light a lantern. "You ever been in a mine before, Clay?"

In the dank, cool interior, Cole gazed about at rock walls, clutter and machinery parked everywhere. The mine shaft itself was marked by a crude elevator at the end of the cave. "Well, a neighbor took me down into one when I was little, but it's been a while."

Nodding, Joshua led the others over to a large, grimy engine. "That's the steam engine powering the hoist," he explained. "We'll fire her up, then Thaddeous will operate the hoist and lower us down. He's our hoistman."

Cole helped the other men load the firebox with wood and start the fire. "The fire heats the tubes overhead," Joshua explained, pointing to a network of piping above the engine. "They have water in 'em, and that turns into the steam that drives the pistons."

Cole waited with the others as the fire roared, the steam began to sputter and sing in the pipes, and eventually, the pistons began to clang. Thaddeous then assumed the hoistman's seat and grabbed the lever controls.

"All right, boys, we can get in the cage," Joshua said.

The remaining three men proceeded to the elevator shaft. Because the inside of the cage was so tiny, Joshua extinguished his lantern. The three men squeezed inside together, then Henry fastened the gate. With a whoosh, they descended.

Cole found the ride down in total darkness downright eerie, with only the whistle of the cage slicing the air as it sped past the close walls. The atmosphere grew cooler and clammier the deeper they descended.

Finally the basket jerked to a halt at the bottom. Joshua stepped out first and relit the lantern. Cole found they were in a vast round room with stone walls heavily streaked with gold—and signs of carving and blasting everywhere.

"Well, this is it," Joshua explained. "The glory hole."

Cole was amazed by the vast size of the dig, almost big enough for a small church. "Isn't this a rather large excavation this far under?"

"Tell that to Mr. Miser," Joshua said cynically. "He found this heavy vein of ore and he's milking it for all he can get. Come along and I'll show you more."

Joshua led them down a dank tunnel to their left. "This here is a 'drift,' a tunnel off the main, tapping an offshoot of a major vein. It's intersected by a 'cross-cut' here, another tunnel for ventilation."

Inside yet another tunnel Joshua paused where hammers and drills were propped against stone walls. "You can see the drilling holes they're working on," he said, pointing at crevices in the stone. "We'll be blasting a new tunnel next week."

"Isn't that dangerous work?" Cole asked.

"You bet," answered Henry. "We lost three men last autumn when the dynamite was placed wrong and sent the force of the blast back inside the tunnel. And the drilling itself is dangerous work. Knox Joiner had to quit after his partner accidentally crushed his wrist with a hammer last week. He's useless now, will never be back. That's one reason they call the job a 'widowmaker'—also because the dust from the drilling can eat away a man's lungs."

Cole thought of poor Jeremiah. "What a brutal way to make a living."

"Yeah—especially when a man is only making two dollars a day," said Henry.

"That's a worse crime."

Joshua continued to lead them through a labyrinth of tunnels. "This place is like a maze," Cole said.

"It's overdrilled," Joshua stated bluntly. "We've already had several minor cave-ins. One of these days this entire hillside is gonna give way just like what happened at the old western branch."

"Yeah, my pa died in one of the earlier cave-ins there," Cole stated quietly. "You'd think the owners would have learned."

"Miser learn? Never," Joshua replied bitterly.

Cole fell silent for a moment, thinking of how frightened his own father must have been almost thirty years ago, to be trapped hundreds of feet below the surface in pitch darkness, most likely in excruciating pain and dying slowly, knowing rescue would never come. He tried to imagine these good men suffering that same harrowing fate, and their families torn apart by grief.

"Is there nothing that can be done?" he asked at last.

Henry and Joshua exchanged a cautious look, then Joshua spoke up. "Well, Henry and me have thought of coming out here some night with a box of dynamite and blowing the place to kingdom come."

"But if we did, none of us would have jobs," Henry added.

"Mainly, we'll just have to hope we're not here when the mine collapses," Joshua added.

Cole didn't reply. No one needed to state the obvious—that the mine was far more likely to collapse while the miners were here, working and blasting.

"Surely something can be done to make conditions safer," he muttered.

Joshua laughed. "With Miser and his crew? Now that's funny."

Cole remained lost in thought as the threesome made

their way back to the cage. He realized Jessica was right. He'd been taking his revenge on the owners of the consortium, but not really considering the fates of the miners. Men like his father and stepfather. Good men with families to support, who desperately needed the pitiful dollars they earned.

He felt a deep sense of shame, knowing that the best way to honor his father's memory would be to help these people, *really* help them. And somehow, he must find a way to do so.

Chapter Twenty-two

The next couple of weeks were busy and happy ones for Jessica. She taught the children in town two days a week, and tutored the boys several hours a day on the other three. At night she wrote in her journal or worked on the history of the town of Mariposa for Founders' Day.

The whole Reklaw crew as well as Jessica attended prayer meeting on Wednesday night and church on Sundays. To Jessica's immense satisfaction, both Ma and Cole had softened their attitudes on the family's developing ties with the community.

And of course the boys didn't protest at all, being so happily occupied courting the girls in town. The young women even visited the farm, Millie Holler and her three daughters stopping by to drop off some snap beans from their garden, Peaches and Dumpling Hicks bringing by pies they had baked. Dumpling in particular soon became a fixture around the farm, and she and Billy spent long hours walking about the property or conversing on the front porch swing.

The four younger Reklaw brothers definitely had their minds on romance, while Jessica strongly suspected Cole still had his mind on sex. Every time she caught him staring at her in his intense, smoldering way, she was reminded of the intimacies they'd shared, of how much she missed him. In her quieter moments, sitting petting her kitten, Jessica had to admit that she remained thoroughly beguiled by him. But somehow, she managed to hold the line. She was relieved that he no longer seemed so angry at her—indeed, he more often flirted, though she maintained her prim control.

On a couple of occasions, Cole gave her additional shooting lessons, teaching her how to fire a rifle as well as a pistol. When she pressed him on why he was practicing so much, he admitted that the gang's last robbery had been difficult, that the consortium had increased the guard on the shipment. However, when Jessica pleaded that he and his brothers must cease their foolhardy, dangerous activities, he turned a deaf ear.

His brothers proved equally stubborn. Three weeks after the family started attending church, the gang went on yet another foray to rob a gold shipment.

Jessica tried to address this when she tutored the boys the next day. By now, all four were fairly adept at elementary reading, and she'd written up for them another adventure of Winifred and Clyde.

Billy began the reading with, "Whinny-furd and Clyde was walking down the street."

"*Were* walking," Jessica corrected.

"Yes, ma'am . . . *were* walking down the street when they found a ten-dollar gold piece in the dirt."

"Very good, Billy," Jessica said. "Now, Wes, you continue."

Taking the crudely bound pages from his brother, Wes read, "Clyde picked up the gold piece and handed it to Miss Whinny-furd." He paused, grinning. "Good for Clyde."

"We'll see if it's *really* good for Clyde," Jessica pronounced soberly. "Gabe, your turn."

"Down the street, an old lady was a'screamin', 'Where's my gold piece?' And old Clyde said to Miss Whinny-furd, 'You keep it, honey.' "

"Hey, good for Clyde!" chimed in Luke.

"Really?" Jessica asked, raising an eyebrow. "Why don't you read the rest for us, then?"

Luke took the pages from Gabe and cleared his throat. "Miss Whinny-furd got mad. She told Clyde to come back when he had some manners, and some morals. Then Miss Whinny-furd gave the gold piece to the old lady. And Clyde broke out bawling, just like a baby."

Slowly shaking his head, Luke finished reading, and Jessica stared at four devastated male faces.

"Well, boys, what do you think?" Jessica asked.

"It's terrible!" cried Billy.

"Yeah, Miss Jessie, you can't do that to poor Clyde, showin' him up in front of Miss Whinny-furd, when he ain't done nothin' wrong," protested Gabe.

"That's not true," corrected Jessica. "Clyde *was* wrong. And he got what he deserved. He did it to himself."

"Huh?" questioned Wes.

"Clyde was wrong in giving the gold piece to Winifred, when he knew it really belonged to the old lady. And Winifred had enough integrity not to accept something that wasn't hers." Pausing for dramatic emphasis, she finished, "She knew accepting the gold piece would be just like stealing."

"Wait a minute!" protested Luke. "Are you trying to teach us a lesson or somethin'?"

"I sure am. If you want to impress women, don't steal."

"But, ma'am, we gotta earn a living," Billy protested.

"Don't give me that hogwash," Jessica said stoutly. "You've probably already stashed away enough gold to support yourselves, plus wives and children, for the rest of your lives. You could quit if you wanted to."

"Well, maybe we kind of enjoy it," Gabe confessed.

"Oh, yeah?" Jessica mocked. "Well, tell me this: What decent woman will want to marry a wanted man? Have you thought about what your women would think if they knew the truth?"

"Ma'am, you ain't gonna tell 'em, are you?" Billy asked.

"Of course not. But do you think the truth would please them?"

The boys exchanged guilty glances. Then Wes asked, "Ma'am, how do we please our women?"

"Start by not stealing."

"Aside from that," put in Gabe.

She shot him a chiding look.

"Please, ma'am, you've made your opinion clear," said Billy. "We just need a little help on how to melt a woman's heart."

Jessica sighed, realizing she'd done about as much moralizing today as she could afford. She didn't want to risk losing the boys' goodwill, and had to be satisfied with influencing them where, when, and how she could.

"The way to a woman's heart . . . " she murmured, laying a finger alongside her cheek. "Well, you must be caring, gentle, tender. Aware of her feelings. Ask her what she thinks about things—don't just make assumptions. Bring her gifts—stationery, flowers, candy—"

"Yeah, and if'n it's Billy, he'd best bring the whole candy store for Miss Dumpling," taunted Gabe, prompting Luke and Wes to guffaw.

Livid, Billy shot to his feet and hauled out his pistol. "Didn't I warn you varmints not to scorn Miss Dumpling?"

Noting that the other boys appeared white-faced, and Billy on the verge of shooting them, Jessica ordered, "Billy, holster that weapon at once! I won't allow gunplay in this classroom."

Though his expression was mutinous, Billy holstered

his pistol, hurled a glare at his brothers, then resumed his seat. "Yes, ma'am."

Jessica cast an admonishing glance at the other three. "You know, boys, Billy is right. It's terrible of you to cast aspersions on Dumpling. It'll make your ladies think you're coarse and ill-mannered. Remember how embarrassed Maybelle, Minerva, and Beatrice were that day when you made fun of their cousin at the schoolhouse?"

The three culprits stared contritely at their laps and muttered, "Yes'um."

Satisfied she'd managed to shame the boys, Jessica pulled out a dime novel she'd found in the living room and handed it to Billy. "Now, boys, I think you're ready to try a few sentences from *Dastardly Dave's Daring Deed.*"

"Yes, ma'am," said Billy, taking the book. "But first, I have a question."

"Yes?"

Solemnly, he inquired, "Do you mind that the four of us is no longer courting you, that we've dropped out of the contest?"

"No, I don't mind at all," Jessica said happily.

"Good," Billy said with a relieved smile.

" 'Sides," Gabe added, "we all know Cole's the one that really wants you. And the four of us have decided he can have you."

Now Jessica shot to her feet. "What? I'm not some damn prize the four of you can raffle off!"

"And why not?" came a deep, arrogant voice from the doorway.

Jessica whirled to face Cole, who was standing there grinning like the very devil.

"If my brothers have dropped out," he drawled, "don't I get you by default?"

She strode over to face him. "You'll get your ears boxed by default, if anything."

Even as the boys broke up laughing, Cole chuckled. "Settle down, sugar. My brothers have decided, so why fight it?" He looked her over and winked. " 'Sides, what can you do about it?"

That invitation proved irresistible. Jessica stomped down hard on Cole's instep, smiling at his yelp of pain as she swept out the door.

The next morning found Jessica at the little schoolhouse in Mariposa. The desks were filled with her twenty-two happy students, fourteen boys and eight girls, who ranged in age from five to thirteen and were all dressed in neat but modest homespun clothing. It was music hour, and Jessica stood in front of her desk, leading the youngsters in the song "This Old Man" in order to teach them their numbers, while her aides, Chila and Rose, stood on either side of the room. They were also singing and holding up cards with numbers.

They had reached the final chorus when Jessica became aware that she was being watched. Glancing at the back of the schoolhouse, she spotted Cole standing there, just as he'd appeared when she'd tutored the boys at home yesterday. What on earth was he doing in town? And looking so dapper in his Sunday suit and hat? Struggling not to betray any signs of agitation, she finished leading the tune.

Afterward the children noticed Cole, pointing and snickering among themselves. Chila and Rose had also spotted the newcomer, and Rose said to Jessica, "Ma'am, looks like you got a visitor. You want Chila and me to see to the young 'uns' lunches?"

"Yes, thank you. Children, you may get out your lunch pails."

Amid the clang of metal pails on the desks, Jessica walked back to join Cole. "What are you doing here?"

He grinned. "Thought I'd buy you dinner at the hotel."

She rolled her eyes. "But I'm teaching."

Cole ignored her, turning to tip his hat to Chila and Rose. "Howdy, ladies. Do you think you can handle these

243

children for an hour while Miss Garrett and I see to some business?"

" 'Course, sir," answered Chila.

That was when one of the boys, mischievous Willie Pickens, called out, "Miss Garrett's got a sweetheart!" and the entire classroom erupted in giggles.

Jessica faced the children forbiddingly. "That is enough."

Twenty-two faces at once sobered.

Feeling a stab of guilt for being so severe, Jessica added less vehemently, "Now be good and enjoy your lunches. Any of you who misbehaves while I am gone will miss recess. Is that clear?"

Two dozen heads nodded.

As she stepped outside into the cool sunshine with Cole, he whistled. "You're really hard on those young 'uns."

"Thanks to you. What are you doing here, Cole?"

"Didn't you hear? I'm your sweetheart."

"Stop it, Cole." But Jessica repressed a smile.

They strolled down the boardwalk to Mariposa's small hotel. In the cozy dining room, the owner's young, smiling wife seated them at a small, gingham-draped table near the front windows, and brought them both glasses of tea and plates filled with biscuits and chicken fricassee.

Sipping her tea, Jessica glanced at Cole's angular, handsome face, trying to assess how much mischief was lurking in the depths of his dark, sexy eyes. "All right, we'll begin again. Why did you come get me?"

"I need to tell you some things."

"Yes?"

Surprising Jessica, Cole turned solemn. "First of all, I've been wanting to tell you that I'm glad you made us go to church, Jessie. I'm glad because I've been able to learn something, things I should know. You were right about the people of this town. The mining families. They do need our help. I especially realized this when I visited the mines."

She frowned. "It's bad?"

He nodded. "If they go on drilling, there's bound to be a major collapse—and a lot more widows in this town."

"What can we do?"

"Maybe if the gang harasses the owners enough, they'll shut the mine down."

"Then the miners will have no livelihood."

"I know. That's what several of the men have already pointed out. But isn't it better to be out of work than dead?"

"I suppose."

Thoughtfully, he murmured, "Maybe there is something we can do."

"What?" she asked.

He flashed her a stiff smile. "I really can't say anything more about that now. But I need to discuss another matter with you. Billy and I have to be away for a few days."

She frowned.

"Now, we're not going whoring," he quickly added. "Or gambling or drinkin'. It's business."

"You're going to pull off a robbery somewhere else."

"No, sugar. We're not robbing anyone."

"Then what?"

"It's business," he reiterated. "Every couple of months, we have to tend to it."

Jessica waved a hand. "This is beginning to sound like that movie *The Godfather*, when Al Pacino told Diane Keaton not to ask him about his business."

"Huh?" Cole asked, clearly bewildered.

"Never mind. You're not going to tell me, are you?"

"Nope."

"You scoundrel."

He smiled at that. "Gonna miss me, sugar?"

Jessica stared daggers at him, but her flaming cheeks gave her away. "You wish."

He leaned closer, ardor gleaming in his eyes, and spoke huskily. "Give me your hand, Jessie."

Horrified, Jessica glanced about, and saw the owner's wife smiling at them as she wiped glasses. Wide-eyed, she turned back to Cole. "Have you lost your mind?"

"No." He extended his own large hand across the table and repeated, "Your hand, sugar."

"No!" She shoved her hand into her lap.

He reached under the table and firmly grasped it.

She struggled to pull her fingers free. "Stop it, Cole!"

His strong fingers tightened over hers. "Keep resisting and I'm gonna cause a scene you'll regret."

She ground her teeth.

Cole opened her tight fist and began sensuously stroking her wrist, her palm. "Come on, sugar. Settle down."

Jessica fought his insidious assault on her senses, even as the passionate look in his eyes thoroughly rattled her. "You trying to humor me now?"

"Don't you miss me at all, sugar?" he asked tenderly.

The words, his sensual caresses, further weakened her embattled defenses. She gave a tremulous laugh. "Miss you? You're here, aren't you?"

"You know what I mean. Exactly what I mean."

Jessica gulped. "Yes. I know."

"I sure miss you, sugar," he whispered.

Jessica shut her eyes and groaned.

"I know you feel we got the cart before the horse," he went on gently. "And that's why I've tried to be patient. But don't you want me anymore?"

Her eyes flew open. "Of course I do," she acknowledged miserably.

He smiled a smile that brightened even his eyes. "Then why do you keep me at arm's length?"

"Because we still have problems to address."

"And we're gonna work them out apart?"

"We sure didn't work them out together."

His thumb drew suggestive circles on her sensitive palm. "We were good, sugar."

Jessica was coming unglued. "That's not what I meant."

"We can work out the rest."

"Cole!" she exclaimed. "You have your entire life to work out!"

"I know. Maybe I'm starting to do that."

"How?"

"We'll talk about that more when I get back. For now, I want you to promise me you won't run away while I'm gone."

"Why would I run?"

He stared straight into her eyes with an intensity that made her stomach curl. "I think you know why. You want to run away from me, Jessie. From us. From what you're feeling."

Oh, he'd spoken the truth. Jessica turned away, as if the passion radiating from his eyes might burn her.

"Promise me you won't leave," he reiterated. "It would drive me crazy if I lost you, darlin'."

She shuddered. "Cole, stop tormenting me."

"Promise."

Miserably, she met his gaze. "All right. I promise."

"Good." Pleasure shone in his expression. "Do you want me to come to your bed tonight, before I go?"

Jessica felt as if her heart had climbed into her mouth. "Cole! Of course not!"

"Really?" he teased. "You may say that, but your blush says different, that and the way your pulse is beating against my thumb. Where else am I making you throb?"

Oh, he was killing her, an unbearable death by inches, in public, no less! Jessica felt wet, weak, as if she might dissolve in a puddle. "Cole, please, no more. Have you forgotten I have to go back to the school and teach?"

Undaunted, he replied steadily, "When I get back, sugar, we're settling this. I'm through waiting for you, Jessie, so you'd best be ready." In a voice raspy with passion, he added, "I'm claiming that other pulse of yours, the one deep inside you."

Breathless, she could only stare at him.

"Now kiss me."

"Absolutely not!"

Cole leaned over the table and claimed Jessica's lips in a brief, tender kiss. Afterward, as she eyed him raptly, his voice held a note of steel. "When I get back, Jessie . . . "

He stood and offered her his hand.

Jessica's expression betrayed her torn feelings. "Damn you! Why did you make me promise I'd stay first?"

Cole only grinned, and as they left the restaurant together, Jessica noted a broad smile on the face of the owner's wife.

Chapter Twenty-three

Dressed in his best Sunday suit, Billy Reklaw sat on a fine silk brocade and rosewood settee in the large, lavish second-story parlor of the Teller House Hotel in Central City, known to the locals as "Central." He was smoking an expensive cigar and sipping the fine brandy brought to him by the room's hostess as he and the others waited to be called for luncheon. The strains of a waltz drifted in from the piano in the music room as people chatted and milled about him—two lovely ladies in bustled silk gowns admiring a richly carved table at the center of the room, a dapper elderly gent peering into a glittering diamond-dust mirror, and nearby, two couples sitting at a small table, engaged in a game of cards. The hostess had informed Billy that one of the couples was none other than Horace Tabor and his second wife, Baby Doe, the creature who had scandalized all of Colorado by breaking up Tabor's first marriage. The lovely woman with her lush, curly hair and classic features caught Billy's perusal and glanced briefly in his direction before lowering her gaze to the cards she held.

Billy smiled to himself. Baby Doe was every bit as beautiful as her reputation alleged, but his thoughts and feelings were firmly focused on another. Dumpling. How he missed that girl—her spirit and sass, even her big, lush body. When he was around her, he found himself lost in those cornflower blue eyes, beguiled by her dimpled smile, and dreaming of things he'd never before imagined—marriage, young ones, even giving up his life of crime. For what would Dumpling think if she knew what he and his brothers really did for a living? Surely she'd be just as riled as Jessica was, for she was a respectable woman from a good family. For so long Billy and his brothers had assumed they were pursuing a just cause. Now he wasn't so sure.

"May I get you anything else, sir?"

Billy set his cigar in an ashtray and glanced up at the smiling middle-aged hostess in her black silk gown. "No, thank you, ma'am. I'm just waiting for my brother to return from Little Kingdom Bank."

The woman nodded. "You two staying for the show at the Opera House tonight?"

"What show is that?"

The hostess laughed. "You didn't know that Buffalo Bill Cody and his troupe are expected in town later today? Most of them are staying right here at the Teller House. Why do you think the Tabors have come down from Denver? Cody's troupe is performing a melodrama at the Opera House tonight to help interest the townsfolk in their Wild West Show tomorrow. Why, you and your brother should try to attend."

"Why, thank you, ma'am. I'll mention the shows to him." Glancing toward the archway, he laughed. "And speaking of the devil . . ."

As the woman moved on, Billy watched his eldest brother stride into the room, wearing a black suit. He motioned for Cole to join him, and Cole folded his large frame into the chair next to Billy's.

Billy lifted his brandy in a salute to Cole. "Want a drink, brother? You just missed the nice hostess lady."

Cole shook his head abstractedly. "No, I'm fine."

Billy lowered his voice. "Get our business taken care of?"

"Yep."

Billy chuckled. "You know, big brother, we've got bank accounts, and safety deposit boxes stuffed with gold, all over Colorado now. Pretty soon we're gonna run out of banks."

Cole smiled cynically. "Pretty soon we're going to run out of a lot more than banks, I'd say."

"What do you mean?"

Cole sighed. "Billy, have you thought about how much longer we can keep up this—er, life of crime—without being arrested?"

His expression troubled, Billy sipped his brandy. "Yeah, it does seem we're on the verge of wearing out our welcome around Mariposa."

"We've been lucky so far. Too lucky."

"Yeah." Billy scowled. "Matter of fact, I was just thinking about the gang—and Dumpling. You know what her people would think if they knew."

"It's a grim prospect," agreed Cole.

"I reckon you've been thinkin' about Jessie, eh?"

Cole nodded tightly. "I have."

"So what do you think we should do, big brother?"

Cole leaned forward, lacing his fingers together. "I'm thinking it's time we pull up stakes, move much further west."

"Pull up stakes?" Billy was aghast. "What about our women?"

"Well, maybe we should take them with us."

Billy mulled this over. "Maybe. If they'll go."

"We gotta start thinking ahead, Billy."

"Yeah, I suppose."

"I mean, what if we should stay put? What if you marry

your Dumpling, or I marry Jessie? What do you picture your son saying some day? 'My daddy's an outlaw'?"

Billy shuddered. "The thought does give a man pause." He brightened. "So you think I should marry Miss Dumpling?"

"Billy, that decision is yours."

Billy's jaw tightened. "Wes, Gabe, and Luke still tease me about her—you know, her size and all."

"They also tease you about being the runt of the litter," Cole remarked. "How does that make you feel?"

"Like murderin' all three of 'em."

"And how do you think Miss Dumpling feels when people tease her about her size?"

Billy ruminated for a long moment. "Are you saying Dumpling and me have something in common?"

"Could be. But what I'm really telling you, little brother, is that it's high time for you to become a man and quit fretting about what your brothers think. It's what *you* think that counts."

"Yeah," Billy agreed.

"So what do you think of Miss Dumpling?"

Billy grinned from ear to ear. "I think that lady's a pure-dee piece of heaven—and a big piece at that."

Cole chuckled. "Then there's your answer."

Billy licked his lips with relish. "Yeah, her and me go together just like chicken and dumplings. Hell, she makes me feel like the cock of the walk."

Cole shook with laughter.

"So what about you and Jessie?" Billy added.

Cole's expression turned thoughtful. "I think I'd marry the woman in a minute if she'd have me."

"So she's another reason you want us to give up the gang?"

"Sure is."

"You know, our brothers seem plenty serious about their own sweethearts. Maybe we should all marry up, pack up Ma and our wives, move west, and get a fresh start. Maybe it could work."

But even as Billy was pondering the prospect, Cole's expression sobered. "I wish it were all that simple."

Billy was taken aback. "It ain't?"

"What about Mariposa?"

"What about it?"

"The miners, Billy. The men and their families, the people we're *supposed* to be helping."

"Oh. You mean, we still ain't convinced Miser to shut down the mines?"

"Right."

Billy snapped his fingers. "Well, we could buy the mines, couldn't we? Then shut 'em down?"

Cole violently shook his head. "Why should we give that villain Miser one plug nickel? Besides, even if we did somehow manage to close the mines, the people of Mariposa would still be left destitute."

Billy scowled at Cole's word. "Huh?"

"Dirt poor, little brother."

"Oh." Billy nodded gloomily. "Reckon you're right."

"I have a much better idea. In fact, I've already set the wheels into motion. I just spoke with the banker about setting up a trust fund for the miners of Mariposa. It'll be a special account to be used to see to the needs of the various families after we leave the area."

"But why would we do that?"

Cole was irate. "Why? Wasn't the entire purpose of our life of crime to help those families?"

Billy grimaced guiltily. "Well, yeah, I guess."

"We've been kidding ourselves, Billy. We haven't really helped them at all. We've just been raising hell at the expense of those good people. In fact, indirectly, we've been robbing them."

Billy's features twisted in perplexity. "Robbing? Well, I reckon that don't sound right."

"That's why I'm setting up the trust. And I've arranged for all of our assets from Trinidad, Georgetown, and Silver Plume to be transferred here, as well."

Billy whistled. "Hey, that's most of our money, Cole."

Cole laughed, then spoke in a whisper. "We already have enough stashed away at our hideout to buy half the Territory of Wyoming, and you know it."

"I reckon so."

"Anyway, the banker will have all the paperwork ready for me to sign tomorrow. He'll begin administering the trust sometime after we're all out of the state, when I notify him by mail."

"You have this all planned out, then."

"I do."

Frowning, Billy glanced about the parlor. "So does that mean we have to hang around Central till tomorrow?"

"Yeah, that's how it looks." Cole elbowed his brother. "Guess you'd rather be back with Dumpling, eh?"

"Yeah. Guess you'd rather be back with Jessie."

"Yeah." Cole flashed his brother a wistful smile. "I'm just hoping she misses me as much."

Jessica missed him.

Much as she hated to admit it, while Cole was gone her thoughts were centered almost exclusively on him. Where was he, and with whom? When would he return? Had he told her the truth, or was he even now in the arms of another woman?

Such thoughts obsessed her when she was holding school in town or at the farm. When she watched an Inca dove fly off in a flash of flame-tinged underwings. When she observed a mule deer romping through a meadow with its mate.

Memories of his lovemaking enticed her. The promise of his passion enthralled her. He'd vowed to settle things between them when he returned, leaving no doubt as to what he expected.

Did he presume he would rape her? This she could never believe. Overwhelm her? He already had.

And while she still harbored doubts, she could no longer deny that her feelings toward him were deepening, her resistance softening. After all, from the things he'd said before he'd left, he was beginning to think seriously about the dangerous game the gang was playing, about the fates of the miners, perhaps even about changing and living his life differently. Was it so important that she continue to resist him when he might at last be willing to meet her halfway? And when she wanted him so badly?

If only she could be certain he was sincere, and not off misbehaving. But so little was certain in love—or in life. Her own adventure in time was certainly proof of that.

On a morning two days after the men left, Jessica sat on the front porch swing, missing Cole, petting Inkspot, and watching a hen and a rooster battle in the barnyard. She was smiling over the sight when Dumpling pulled up in a buckboard, looking ready to meet her sweetheart in starched blue gingham and a straw hat with jaunty silk flowers.

"Howdy, ma'am," the girl called. "Is Bobby around?"

" 'Fraid not. Come sit with me a minute."

Wearing an expression of intense disappointment, the girl clambered down from the buckboard and lumbered up the steps. Breathing hard, she sat down heavily next to Jessica, vigorously rocking the swing.

Dumpling fanned her face with a plump hand. "Where did Bobby go?"

"He and Co—that is, Clay—went off for a few days on business."

Dumpling scowled. "Business? What business?"

"They didn't say."

Dumpling harrumphed. "When men don't say, it's for sure they're up to mischief."

Jessica fought a smile. This girl was no dummy. "You think so?"

"Yep." Dumpling reached out and petted the kitten. "I'm thinkin' Bobby's off chasing some other gal—especially since his brothers keep funnin' him about me. He'll probably never be seen in these parts again."

"Oh, no, I'm sure that's not true," Jessica reassured the girl. "Clay promised me they'll be back in a few days, and I'm sure he'll keep his word."

Dumpling struggled to her feet. "When Bobby does return, he'll have some explaining to do. If he's been sparking another gal, I ain't taking him back. I have my pride, after all."

Don't we all? Jessica thought. She reached out to squeeze Dumpling's hand. "I can't blame you at all, but I'm sure Bobby has been true to you. Why, he talks of you constantly."

Dumpling brightened. "Does he?"

"You bet."

The girl's smile faded. "Still, he'd best come back with a pretty good story, or I'm fixin' his britches."

Amen, Jessica thought, watching Dumpling march back down the steps with head held high.

Several long, excruciating days passed. On Saturday afternoon, Ma was off in town buying supplies, and Jessica was in the barn, hunting for eggs the hens had hidden, when she heard the door creak open.

"Jessie? You in here?"

He was back! The deep baritone of Cole Reklaw's voice was music to Jessica's ears. "Cole!" she called, almost dropping her basket in her haste to cross the barn.

He stood in the doorway, holding his hat, looking a bit trailworn but glorious, with a shaft of sunlight spilling in from behind him and outlining his tall body. He wore a green checked shirt that was stretched taut over the muscles of his chest and arms, and denim trousers that clung to his hard thighs and long legs. A sexy stubble of whiskers darkened his jaw, and his hair gleamed.

Bolting forward, Jessica all but collided with him. He laughed and caught her close, then leaned over, quickly kissing her, his warm lips thrilling her senses. Absorbing his heat and strength, breathing in his exciting male scent, Jessica felt as if in heaven. She looked up to see him gazing down at her with tender amusement in his dark eyes.

"So you missed me, woman?" he teased.

Realizing how forward she must have seemed, Jessica stepped back. She felt color creeping up her face. "Well, you've been gone five days. I was concerned."

"Counting the days, eh?"

"Oh, hush."

He chuckled.

Forcing a casual tone, she asked, "Was your trip successful?"

"Very."

"Where did you go, Cole? And what did you do?"

"We saw a Wild West Show up in Central—Buffalo Bill Cody himself."

"Did you? What else did you do?"

He shook a finger at her. "Oh, no, I'm not going to let you bait me."

"Bait you?" she countered indignantly. "You disappear for five days, and I have no right to know?"

He closed the door and leaned against the wall, lazily crossing one leg over the other. "Well, that depends."

"On what?"

"On what we mean to each other, Jessie."

Feeling a new surge of heat, Jessica knew just what he meant. "So you're not going to tell me."

He shrugged. "It was business."

"Business with another woman?"

He dimpled. "Kiss me, sugar, and maybe I'll tell you."

Instead she punched him in the arm. "Oh! I might have known you'd never change." She turned to leave.

He caught her arm. "Just where do you think you're going?"

"Out."

His expression was darkly determined. "Oh, no, you don't. I told you we were settling this when I got back. No more games, Jessie."

"No more games? You're the one playing games here, Cole, refusing to answer my questions."

He pulled her close and ran his fingertips teasingly up and down her spine. "Very well. I wasn't in another woman's bed, and that's all that should concern you."

Much as his statement relieved her, she struggled to break free. "You're so arrogant. Let me go, Cole."

He only locked his arms around her spine, until she could feel the hardness of his desire rising between them.

"Do you want me to let you go, Jessie?" he asked huskily.

Jessica could only stare at him helplessly. Lord, she had missed him so much—devil that he was! By now his eyes were burning into hers even as the nearness of his body inflamed her. She felt so vulnerable to him.

"Do you want me to?" he repeated softly.

"No," she admitted.

A sigh of longing escaped her; then Cole was kissing her. Long, deep, almost punishingly. And she was clinging to him, loving it, mating her tongue with his, running her fingertips over the muscles of his back.

At last they broke apart, both breathing hard. "Miss me?" Cole asked.

"Yes."

"Want me?"

She gazed at him in anguish. "Oh, yes." But even as he

reached for the buttons on her bodice, she pushed his fingers away. "But you don't want me."

He glowered. "What do you mean, I don't want you? What do you think I've been dreaming of these past five days?"

She lifted her chin. "You want sex—not me."

"Sex? Sex I could have with any woman."

"Then why me, Cole?" she pressed passionately. "You still don't completely trust me—or share with me."

He smiled contritely. "Jessie, maybe it started out that way, when I first saw you. But not anymore. You make me want to trust again, to share. There's so much I've missed about you—your spirit, your smile. Every word you say. Always something different, always unpredictable. You fascinate me, girl."

She stared at him, desperately wanting to believe him.

"But I'm not ashamed to admit I want your body, too," he continued huskily, raking his gaze over her. "After all, loving you is my only real way to demonstrate my feelings. I want the sexy sway of your hips. I want to look into those proud eyes of yours and watch 'em melt as I drive into you . . . again."

Jessica gazed at him, sinking fast.

"And another thing—we're going to have us a serious talk about getting hitched," he went on sternly. "After a little loving." Grinning roguishly, he leaned over and kissed the pulse at the base of her throat. "Make that a *lot* of loving."

Jessica moaned ecstatically. Why couldn't she seem to resist him? "Cole, please—"

But he only gripped her hand. "Come along, sugar. The waiting's over."

Cole tugged her into a nearby empty stall and pulled her down to her knees with him in the soft hay. Her weak protest was drowned out by his lips, his ravenous tongue. Then she was lost. This time his fingers made quick work of the buttons at her bodice. His hot mouth took her nipple, his tongue lapping eagerly, and Jessica almost screamed at the pleasure.

"Easy, sugar, easy," he whispered. "It'll be so good. Just you wait."

Jessica was transported, clinging to Cole, thrusting her breast eagerly into his hot mouth. "I missed you, Cole," she admitted achingly. "Really missed you."

"I know, sugar. Me, too. I missed this . . . " He demonstrated by nipping her lightly.

Desire staggered Jessica. She sank her fingers into Cole's hair and let him devour her breasts with his rapacious mouth. His hands cupped her bottom, fingers kneading through her skirts. Hot filaments of passion threaded their way deep inside her, tormenting her.

It was going to happen, she realized. They were about to have hot, uninhibited sex again, and she was powerless to do anything about it. Indeed, she was so overwhelmed by her need of him that she suspected she would shoot just about anyone who might try to stop them.

His strong hands tugged her dress down about her waist. She moaned and kissed him eagerly. Her fingers slid between their bodies to touch his arousal. Oh, he was rock-hard, so delicious, and she wanted him inside her so badly . . .

Then suddenly they both froze at the sound of a high, raucous female cackle out in the yard. Jessica glanced wildly at Cole to find him scowling murderously.

"Who is *that*?" she demanded in a hoarse whisper. "It can't be your ma, and it sure doesn't sound like one of the boys' sweethearts."

"Yeah, you're right. I don't know who it is, either," Cole responded tensely. Already he was tugging up Jessica's dress and buttoning her bodice.

He had no sooner pulled her to her feet, and she was still smoothing down her hair and frock, when the barn door banged open. As she and Cole stepped out of the stall, Jessica stared in horror at a tawdry creature in purple satin who stood there with a cigarette dangling from her rouged lips.

Like Cole, the woman appeared trailworn, her dress soiled and ripped in places, her coiffure ratty. She was clearly a prostitute, with her heavily painted face and brassy dyed hair. Behind the woman out in the yard, Jessica caught sight of three other gaudy women, and Cole's brothers lounging there talking to them. An unfamiliar buckboard was parked beyond.

"Well, well," the intruder purred in her whiskey voice. "What have you two been doing?"

Jessica glanced at Cole to see him regarding the woman with scorn. "Cole, who *is* she?"

"Yeah, Cole, honey, tell the lady who I am," the creature taunted.

Grimly Cole turned to Jessica. "Jessie, meet Lila Lullaby."

Jessica received this pronouncement with a gasp. Then she turned and slapped Cole's face.

Chapter Twenty-four

Flinching at the sting of Jessica's hand, Cole caught her wrist and glowered. "Ouch! What in hell do you think you're doing, woman?"

"You brought her here!" Jessica accused, yanking free.

"I what? Like hell I did. And where'd you get that haywire notion, anyway?"

"Don't lie to me!" Jessica ranted. "Do you think I was born yesterday? You just arrived, Cole." Jerking a thumb toward the hussy who stood grinning beyond them, Jessica added nastily, "*She* just arrived."

Cole glared at Lila, who smirked back. He turned back to Jessica and rolled his eyes. "Oh, that. That's just a coincidence."

"Coincidence, hell. I can put two and two together."

Cole waved a hand in exasperation. "Well, you've come up with six, woman. I didn't bring her here." Heatedly he turned to Lila. "Tell her."

"Tell her what?" Lila teased back, puffing away.

To Jessica's horror, Cole whipped out his pistol. "Damn it, Lila, tell Jessie the truth about how you got here."

Lila held up a hand. "All right, sugar. You don't have to go off half-cocked." With a look of disgust screwing up her rouged face, she said to Jessica, "Yeah, Cole's right, he didn't bring us here. Me and the girls, we followed him and Billy."

Cole's mouth fell open. "You *what*?"

"Now, Cole, honey, simmer down," Lila cajoled, batting her eyelashes at him. "Where's your manners?"

Cole sneered. "I lost 'em the last time I saw you."

Lila cackled. "Ain't you even gonna properly introduce me to your ladylove here?"

"Her name's Jessie Garrett," came the terse response, "and you'd best remember she *is* a lady."

With a cynical smile, Lila took in Jessica's slightly disheveled air. "Not from how it looks—but then, you never did know how to treat a lady, Cole."

As Cole glared, Jessica's anger spiked. "Of all the nerve!"

"How come she's here, anyhow?" Lila asked Cole.

"Not that it's any of your damn business," he replied, "but she's my cousin from back East."

Lila harrumphed. "Looks to me like she's a kissing cousin. Or were you just helping her adjust her cinch when I come in?"

While Jessica made a sound of outrage, Cole waved his pistol. "Enough, Lila. Outside. Let's find out what's really going on here."

"Sure, honey."

Swaying ample, satin-draped hips, Lila sashayed out. Without even glancing at Cole, Jessica followed, choking on Lila's acrid cigarette smoke and cheap perfume.

Out in the yard, she took in the scene; Cole's grinning younger brothers stood laughing with three more scarlet women. All three were dressed similarly to Lila, in cheap, flashy satin gowns heavily stained by dirt and perspiration. All were coarsely rouged, and two of the women even sported gaudy dyed feathers in their hair.

Pointing in turn to a brunette, a blonde, and a third woman with raven hair, Lila announced to Cole, "Meet Dolly, Clover, and Ernestine."

Cole nodded to each. "Ladies," he drawled.

"Ain't it great, Cole?" asked Billy, stepping forward with a grin. "Lila and her gals have come a'visitin'."

"Oh, yeah, it'll be just peachy keen till Ma finds out," replied Cole. He lifted an eyebrow at Lila. "All right. What's the story? Why are you women here and how did you follow us?"

"Well, me and the girls are on the run," Lila began.

"Again?" he asked.

The whore wrung her hands and assumed a pathetic air. "Yeah. Well, you see, sugar, after we was run out of Colorado City, we holed up in Trinidad. But now the sheriff run us out of there. We left in something of a hurry, if you know what I mean."

Cole glanced ruefully about the group. "Looks to me like you gals left smack dab in the middle of a busy night."

Clover cackled and jiggled her breasts. "You got that right, sugar."

At the creature's crude demonstration, the boys broke up laughing. Jessica glowered at Cole, and he frowned back.

Dolly spoke up. "Truth to tell, we got no money and no place to stay."

"Is that so?" Cole asked Lila softly. "The last time I saw you, seems like you had just come into a windfall."

Lila's garish features twisted with guilt. "Sugar, surely you ain't holding that against us after all this time."

Cole clenched his jaw. "Go on with your story."

Lila twisted her fingers together. "We're on our way west. Figured it's high time we clear out of Colorado. Only we're down on our luck, so I figured we'd stop off and see you and the boys first. We knew your farm was near Mariposa, but we wasn't exactly sure where, and we wasn't too eager to stop off and ask for directions, if you know what I mean. Then this afternoon we caught sight of you and Billy on the trail ahead of us—so we just laid low and followed your tracks to the farm."

"So you tracked us like a passel of foxes. What do you want?"

In a rustle of satin skirts, Lila sashayed closer to Cole and flashed him her most beguiling smile. "A place to stay, sugar—just for tonight—and maybe a grubstake?"

His gaze was hard. "I don't know, Lila."

"But, Cole," protested Billy, "how can you say no? I mean, don't we owe it to them, for old times' sake?"

"Yeah, Cole, what's the harm of allowing the ladies to stay for just one night?" pressed Gabe.

Before Cole could reply, everyone tensed as Ma's buckboard appeared over the rise in a cloud of dust.

"Ah, hell," groaned Wes. "Now our gooses are cooked."

Appearing concerned, Lila asked Cole, "That your ma?"

"Yep."

"She don't take kindly to our sort?"

"Nope." Cole's mouth twisted. "She doesn't take kindly to *whores.*"

At this harsh statement, Lila flinched and Jessica actually felt sorry for the woman. Then Lila became distracted as Ma pulled the buckboard to a halt just feet away from them.

Jessica grimaced, watching Ma all but leap from the conveyance, grab a shotgun from beneath the seat, then point it at the newcomers. As the painted ladies cringed in fear, she demanded, "What in purple sin hell is going on here?"

"Ma, put down that shotgun," scolded Cole.

"Not till you tell me what evil you rascals have been up to with these—these harlots! Sweet Savior, I can't believe it—harlots on my land! Did you and Billy bring home these cathouse kittens? If ya did, I'll beat ya both till you're dead. Are you fornicatin' with 'em beneath my very roof?"

"Ma, it ain't like that a'tall," Billy protested. "They followed us home."

"A likely story," Ma scoffed.

Lila stepped forward. "It's true, ma'am."

Ma stared murder at the woman. "Who in hell are you?"

"Lila Lullaby, and this here's Ernestine, Dolly, and Clover. We's on the run, you see, and Cole—well, he's an old friend."

"I'll just bet he is," Ma snarled. "Well, what do you want, *hussies*?"

Cole replied, "Ma, they just want a place to stay for one night."

"Not while I live and breathe."

Cole strode forward and calmly pushed the barrel of his mother's gun downward. "Ma, what can we do? The sheriff ran them out of Trinidad. They don't have any money, and it'll be dark in a few hours."

Ma glowered. "Lila Lullaby . . . Why does that name sound familiar?"

"She and the gals used to hang out in Colorado City."

Ma gasped, eyes growing huge. "You mean she's the one . . . ?"

"Yep," Cole replied grimly.

Ma struggled to lift her shotgun. "Then why ain't you shootin' her, son, or stringing 'em all up?"

Even as a couple of the whores gasped, Cole wrenched the shotgun from his mother's hands. "Because I don't shoot ladies."

266

Ma regarded the painted women in disbelief. "So?"

"I mean, I don't shoot *females*," Cole amended. With a weary air, he added, "Ma, please, only for one night."

Ma glared at the soiled doves for a long moment, while the women twitched and avoided her blistering perusal. At last, with a great sigh, she relented. "Well, son, I reckon if you can abide 'em . . . I suppose we got a Christian duty to give 'em food and shelter before we send 'em on their way, even if they is Jezebels."

"Thanks, Ma."

Her expression ferocious, Ma turned to the women and wagged a finger. "All right, you *females* can have the bunkhouse—one night only. Boys, you'll be bunking in the barn. And no hanky-panky, any of you heathens, or I'll boil up the lot of you up for supper. Is that clear?"

"*Yes, ma'am*," came a chorus of male and female voices.

Muttering to herself, Ma stalked away to the house, and Lila rushed up to hug Cole. "Thanks, sugar."

He pushed her away. His voice was hard, his gaze glittering with anger. "You heard my ma—bed and board *only*. One night. That's all you're getting, Lila."

"Sure, sugar," she said, winking.

Jessica moved forward to join them. "Mind telling me something?" she asked Lila.

Lila looked her over in disdain. "Sure—if I can."

Jessica gestured toward the buckboard. "Didn't you used to have a stagecoach with your initials on the door?"

Lila cackled and drew on the stub of her cigarette. "Yeah, we sure did, but we sold that broken-down rig to Buck Lynch right before we girls left Colorado City. You know, we heard tell old Buck finally patched up that rattletrap chariot and started up a stage line—only he quit after some gang robbed him."

Jessica glanced meaningfully at Cole. "Wonder what gang that might have been?"

Cole's expression darkened. "Ladies, if you'll excuse us . . ."

Not waiting for a reply, Cole grabbed Jessica's hand and pulled her away with him. She struggled to break free.

Beneath a tree, he paused, turning to her sternly and gripping her by the shoulders. "Don't you dare go embarrassing me again, or I may just set you in your place in front of everyone."

Jessica was incredulous. "Embarrassing *you*? Just what have I done to you?"

"Don't you go telling Lila my business."

"You mean she doesn't know you're an outlaw?"

"That's not what I said."

"If you're so suspicious of her, why did you let her stay?"

He glanced toward Lila. "I had to let them stay, Jessie. Four women traveling alone like that—it could be dangerous, even if they are whores. All along you've wanted to reform me—now you can't go getting mad at me for doing something decent."

Jessica was at once contrite. "You're right," she admitted. "But who are they and what do they mean to you? And what's the bad blood between you and Lila?"

"Maybe I'll tell you later. For now, would you help me tidy up the bunkhouse? It's quite a pigsty, and I'd feel sorry even for a whore having to sleep there."

"Sure, Cole."

Jessica glanced back to see Lila gazing after them, licking her lips like a cat anticipating cream. She didn't like the way *that woman* was staring at Cole. And what on earth had gone on between the two of them previously? It was clear to her that Cole disliked and distrusted Lila.

It was also clear that Lila and Cole had once been lovers, and Jessica was stunned at the hot waves of jealousy this revelation stirred.

* * *

The bunkhouse was indeed filthy. Jessica swept the floor while Cole aired bedding, cleaned off the crude table, and dusted the rickety chairs. Meanwhile the boys helped the line girls bring in what few belongings they had, clothing and toiletries crammed in several ratty carpetbags.

Then Dolly strutted in, holding aloft two bottles of whiskey, squealing and jiggling her ample hips. "Hey, you boys ready to play?"

While Wes and Gabe grinned, Clover, standing just behind Dolly in the doorway, hooted exuberantly and waved two packs of cards. "Yeah, boys, I got the decks right here."

Jessica noted with pride that Billy appeared uncertain. "I don't know, ma'am," he replied soberly to Clover. "It don't seem fittin', and Ma'll skin us all alive if she finds out."

Clover slinked over to Billy, devouring him with her sultry gaze. "Aw, honey, show some grit, will ya? What are you anyhow, a man or a mama's boy?"

Billy's brothers howled derisively, and Billy colored deeply. At last he unsteadily replied, "I reckon we'll play."

"Billy!" scolded Jessica.

He offered her a lame smile. "Sorry, Jessie, but it ain't your decision."

"What would Dumpling say?"

Clover hooted a laugh. "Dumpling!" she exclaimed to Billy. "Who's that, sugar?"

Though his face darkened, Billy managed to toss Jessica a surly look. "Dumpling's got nothing to do with this. It's just a game of cards."

"Yeah, sure," Jessica mocked.

Clover glanced about the room. "Looks like there's enough of us for two games." She lifted an eyebrow at Jessica. "You playin'?"

Jessica could feel Cole staring at her, but her own gaze

shifted to Lila as she in turn ogled Cole. She quickly decided she didn't want to risk leaving him alone with these tawdry creatures. "Sure, I'll play," she told Clover. "Why not?"

She glanced at Cole just in time to watch his mouth drop open. Then he recovered with a cough. "Yeah, I'm in, too."

The women fetched glasses and poured whiskey for everyone but Jessica, who demurred. Then the group split up into two games, Billy, Wes, Luke, Dolly, and Clover taking up one end of the long table, Gabe, Cole, Lila, Ernestine, and Jessica at the other.

Cole settled in next to Jessica, leaning over to whisper in her ear. "Playing the devil's game, Jessie? I'm surprised at you."

She shrugged. "I have to make sure the boys behave."

He comically wiggled his eyebrows. "Just the boys?"

Although she could feel her face heating, she maintained a steady tone. "All my progress will be lost if your ma kills them."

"True," he conceded with a chuckle.

With a new cigarette dangling from her rouged mouth, Lila dealt the first hand of five-card stud. "So, Cole," she murmured, slapping down cards, "do you remember when we used to play strip poker over at Colorado City?"

"I remember how you used to lose," he drawled back.

Lila laughed ribaldly, and Jessica kicked Cole under the table.

After throwing Jessica a belligerent look, Cole turned to Lila and offered the liquor bottle. "More whiskey?"

"Why, sure, honey," Lila purred. "Why not?"

Cole grinned and poured the liquor, and Jessica could have shaken him.

The game continued, the atmosphere growing bawdy as the others imbibed more freely. Jessica noted that Ernestine's hand kept slipping under the table in the direction of Gabe's thigh; the woman was up to no good, from the way Gabe first went bug-eyed, then colored, then even moaned.

Down the table affairs were no better. Dolly was flirting heavily with both Wes and Luke, and Clover had climbed into Billy's lap. Billy was ogling the whore like a love-struck puppy. Good grief! Jessica could only hope that things wouldn't proceed too far as long as she was here. At least Cole was behaving, although the hot looks he and Lila kept exchanging made her uneasy. She suspected passion on Lila's part, anger on Cole's, and realized the two emotions were far too closely allied for comfort.

Down the table, Clover, winning a hand, shrieked and smacked Billy's cheek, making him blush like a virgin. She was tossing her cards into the air and hugging his neck when all at once a new, irate female voice exclaimed, "Why, you low-down snake!"

Utter silence fell. Everyone turned to see Dumpling Hicks standing in the doorway, hands balled on her hips, features purple, the very picture of outraged female vanity.

Where had she come from? Jessica wondered wildly.

Soon this question receded in her fascination at Billy's reaction—which was downright comical. First he turned pale as a ghost. Then he flinched as if poked by a cattle prod. Then he summarily shoved Clover off his lap. As the whore landed on her butt with an indignant yelp, he shot to his feet.

"Dumpling, darlin', what are you doing here?"

"What are *you* doing, you cheatin' little pipsqueak?" Dumpling yelled back. "And to think I brought you my Jenny Lind cake that I baked myself, and here you are cavortin' with"— she paused, chest heaving, staring about the table in disgust—"with gall-durned Cyprians."

"Honey, they's just some old friends who stopped by for a visit," Billy protested, his face still white as a boiled shirt. "And I sure would love some of your cake, honey."

Amid wicked cackles from the women, Dumpling shot back, "They's whores, and if I had that cake in my hands right now, I'd shove your lying face in it, you little snot. I'm sure your ma'll do it for me once you get back to the house."

Billy rushed up to Dumpling. "Honey, can't we talk?"

Dumpling slapped his face, hard, setting him spinning even as his brothers and the whores roared with laughter. Tears of humiliation in her eyes, Dumpling said bitterly, "Play with your harlots. I'm leaving, and if you ever set foot on my pa's farm, I'll have him shoot you on sight like the low-down snake you are."

Dumpling turned with dignity and marched out the door, while Billy watched, aghast. The others, except for Jessica and Cole, were still holding their sides and laughing. Billy stood with a hand on his cheek, his expression stunned.

"Well, your goose is cooked now, brother," Wes jeered.

"Come on back in and play," teased Gabe. "These women are prettier than that heifer, anyway."

Even as Jessica burned to throttle Gabe, Billy whirled and struck him across the cheek. As his brother glared back, Billy spoke with such vehemence that several of the women gasped. "I told you, brother, that I'll hear no more of that loose, insulting talk about Miss Dumpling. She's a lady—a *fine* lady, and, meaning no offense to our guests today, these here females *ain't*. And all of you oughta be ashamed of yourselves."

"Hey, brother, we didn't mean no harm," protested Luke.

"Oh, yeah?" Billy countered. "Then you just tell me what your Miss Minerva would say if she could see you carrying on like you are. And Gabe, have you given one thought to Miss Beatrice as you paw that Jezebel? Wes, have you forgot all about Miss Maybelle? Why, I say to hell with the lot of you. You ain't no brothers of mine—

272

not anymore. It's just like Ma said—you're a bunch of dad-blamed heathens."

Utter silence fell as Billy turned and walked out the door. Jessica stared at the other brothers to find their faces deadly sober and guilt-stricken. Then, to her amazement, they got up, one by one, and filed out of the building.

Jessica glanced at Cole to see him grinning at her. A treacherous warmth seeped into her heart as she realized he was as pleased as she was regarding this show of maturity and solidarity from his brothers. Perhaps she was making progress, after all. Indeed, Jessica realized she might have just watched the four younger Reklaw brothers grow up.

Chapter Twenty-five

Dinner was a somber occasion, mainly because Ma kept an eagle-eye over the gathering. She marched about the table, slapping mashed potatoes on each plate, mumbling, "Guess it's my Christian duty to feed you, even if you is fallen women."

Little else was said as roast beef, gravy, fried okra, and biscuits were passed. Billy in particular looked so forlorn that Jessica actually felt sorry for him. Cole and Lila kept exchanging odd, intense glances, increasing Jessica's anxiety.

At the end of the meal, a hush fell over the gathering as Ma came forward with a beautiful iced cake. As the others eyed it greedily, Ma stepped up to Billy and all but purred. "I almost forgot, son. Miss Dumpling left this here cake for you."

"Yeah, I know," Billy muttered, regarding her skeptically.

Ma flashed him a simpering smile. "You want it, honey?"

Billy gulped. "Reckon I wouldn't mind a piece."

"Then it's yours."

Without further ado, Ma slammed the cake smack into Billy's face. For a moment he sat transfixed, looking ridiculous with hunks of cake and icing globbed on his face and hair. Laughter shook the table.

Ma waved a fist and yelled at her son, "That's what you get, you little toad, for cheating on a fine woman like Miss Dumpling—and with *whores*!"

Ma stalked away from the table. Billy sputtered and wiped the sticky mess from his face, while the hussies cackled and the boys held their sides. Jessica and Cole looked on soberly.

Once the revelry died down, Cole stood and picked up one of three lit hurricane lanterns on the table. "Ladies, I'll escort you back to the bunkhouse now."

"All right!" agreed Lila, clapping her hands.

Casting her a chiding glance, he turned to Jessica. "That all right with you?"

Although seething inwardly, Jessica jerked her chin in the affirmative.

"And see you're quick about it," Ma scolded from the sideboard. "We got church on the morrow, after these *sirens* is on their way."

Lila shot Ma a cool look; Clover yawned, and Dolly and Ernestine giggled.

Cole glanced about the table. "Ready, ladies?"

"Sure," Lila said, standing and tossing down her napkin. She nodded to Ma. "Thank you kindly, ma'am."

"You ain't welcome," Ma replied.

As the whores filed toward the door, Cole leaned over and whispered in Jessica's ear. "I won't be long. Wait for me on the porch."

Watching Cole leave, Jessica felt tempted to throw something at him. He was so arrogant, expecting her to wait for him, when it was clear there was something going on between him and Lila. Perhaps one woman wasn't enough to satisfy the rogue.

Nonetheless, after she helped Ma tidy up, Jessica ventured out onto the porch, where she was greeted by a new moon and a crisp night breeze scented of pine and cedar. She arrived at the railing just in time to watch Cole's dark figure emerge from the bunkhouse and stride back toward the house. Not wanting to seem too eager, she retreated to the porch swing.

He soon joined her. "Thanks for waiting for me, sugar."

"You're not welcome."

Cole chuckled. "Are you taking lessons from my ma now? You want to shove my face in a cake?"

"Sounds lovely," she replied sweetly, smoothing her skirts.

"God—you females when you're riled."

"You males when you prowl."

His voice tensed. "Wait a minute, honey, that's not true."

"Yeah, sure."

"I mean it, Jessie." Cole curled his arm around Jessica's shoulders. When she flinched, he pulled her closer, then spoke in a husky drawl. "Why are you so mad, when I haven't even done anything wrong?"

She shot him a withering look. "Maybe it's what you're thinking. What's really going on between you and Lila?"

"Nothing—not now." He toyed with her earlobe.

She pushed his fingers away. "What went on before?"

"Damn it, Jessie." Cole sprang out of the swing and stood facing her with hands shoved in his pockets. "I don't want to talk about Lila anymore. I want to get back to you and me—before she interrupted us."

Jessica's voice trembled. "You don't understand—she's come between us now."

Cole grabbed Jessica's hand and hauled her up into his arms. "Nothing's going to come between us, woman, unless you let it."

Jessica reeled at his passionate words and the hard heat

of his body pressing into hers. Then Cole's rough hand gripped her chin, forcing her face up to meet his. He leaned over, tenderly pressing his mouth to hers . . .

All restraint evaporated. Cole clutched her close and plunged his tongue into her mouth. Jessica groaned and coiled her arms about his neck, thrusting her breasts into his chest. Lord, she had missed him so much. It was as if she had waited forever for this moment. She was on fire with him, her insides hurting to feel his heat—even though she still wanted to murder him.

"Take me inside with you, Jessie," Cole whispered in anguished tones. "Take me inside *you*."

Reeling at his brazen suggestion, she still managed to push him away. "No—not yet."

"Why?" he asked darkly. "What ails you now, woman?"

Jessica waved a hand and spoke hoarsely. "I don't know. You have me so confused. I don't know if you really want me—or if being around those scarlet women is just making you hot."

He laughed. "You're jealous."

"Maybe I am." She tapped his chest with a fingertip. "And I want you to tell me the truth."

"What happened was in the past, woman. This is now."

"If that's so, then the past is now, too."

Cole made a sound of frustration. "Why do you have to know what went on between Lila and me? Do you want to punish me for it? I didn't even know you then."

She drew a seething breath. "That's not my point, Cole. You're keeping things from me, secrets that prove you still don't completely trust me. In other ways, you still have blinders on. As far as darling Lila is concerned, that woman has the hots for you—and I suspect the feeling may be mutual."

He ground his teeth. "Damn it, Jessie—"

"Why don't you come back when you really want *me*?" Jessica rushed inside the house.

Cole remained on the porch, feeling hurt and confused. Why on earth was Jessie so mad at him now? Was it his fault Lila and her line gals had followed him and Billy home?

Perhaps indirectly, it was. He realized he had some fences to mend with Jessie. And the hell of it was, he had missed her terribly, for days dreaming of nothing but taking her in his arms again. Kissing her in the barn had been heavenly, until Lila had interrupted, ruining everything. Now Jessie was ready to roast his chops. How was he going to get out of this pickle? Hell, he might be falling in love with the woman.

He also realized Jessie had made some valid points. He was withholding himself from her in a lot of important ways; he still wasn't ready to share his past with her, or the truth about him and Lila—perhaps because he still hadn't fully reckoned with Lila himself.

He needed to settle things with Lila once and for all. Indeed, Lila was likely the reason he couldn't trust Jessie—or any woman—completely. It was time for him to let go of the past and start building a future with Jessie.

In her bedroom, Jessica tossed and turned, missing Cole but feeling too proud to go to him. The sight of him with the hussies had driven her wild. She was still dying to know what had really gone on between him and Lila. Would Cole go to the woman tonight, hold her in his arms, make love to her?

She turned, tears in her eyes, her belly tight. Cole had been right—the very prospect of him with Lila made her crazy with jealousy. She had missed him so desperately, wanted nothing more than to be with him. Now this— more evidence that they were wrong for each other.

She wanted him with a fierceness that hurt . . .

Much later, the sounds of distant muffled laughter drifted in through the window, awakening her. She grabbed her robe and tiptoed to the window—and was appalled to spot Cole and Lila strolling together not far from the house!

Jessica quickly donned her underclothes, dress, and shoes, then rushed out onto the porch, freezing at the sight of Cole and Lila embracing about twenty feet away. Anger and hurt churned within her with a vehemence that was physically painful. She heard Lila's low cackle as Cole released her and watched the whore sashay back toward the bunkhouse. Murderous thoughts blackened her mind.

Jessica rushed down the steps, joining Cole in the yard. He regarded her in surprise. "Why, hello again, sugar."

She slapped his face, hard. "You liar."

Cole caught her wrist. "Jessie, you hit me again and by damn, I'm going to strip off your drawers and blister your butt."

"You try it and I'll gouge out your eyes."

He released her hand and eyed her in disbelief. "What's wrong with you now?"

"What's wrong? You said there was nothing between you and Lila, yet there you were kissing her, you bastard! Are you planning to join her in the bunkhouse now?"

"You really are jealous!"

"You go to hell!"

Even as Jessica turned to march away, Cole grabbed her by the shoulders and hauled her close. "Jessie, listen to me. It isn't easy for me to discuss this, since it's a very painful subject—"

Her eyes blazed at him. "You better 'fess up, mister, or I'll show you pain."

He smiled. "All right, I'll tell you the truth. Three years ago, Lila and I were lovers. I used to visit her bordello in Colorado City. Then Sheriff Pitts, the lawman before Sheriff Lummety, arrested Lila and her girls for prostitution. She had to find a way to get herself out of trouble."

Jessica mulled this over, then snapped her fingers. "You're talking about the time you were thrown in jail, aren't you? Did Lila turn you in to the law?"

Cole grimly nodded. "Lila connived with the sheriff to entrap me. I was arrested in her bed, then thrown into jail.

Although my brothers broke me out of the calaboose before morning, I've hated Lila ever since for betraying me. And she sure didn't hesitate to pocket the reward money, either."

Jessica's expression was awed. "No wonder you're suspicious of women. I'm surprised Lila had the courage to show up here."

Cole sighed. "Seems Lila came to the ranch mainly to apologize, and to explain that she betrayed me before because the sheriff threatened her, claiming her girls would rot in prison if she didn't give over the leader of the Reklaw Gang. When the sheriff promised that the whores would be allowed to leave Colorado City free and clear if Lila would only cooperate, she felt she had no choice but to conspire with the sheriff."

"She could have chosen a different path in life to begin with," Jessica pointed out harshly.

"To be fair, so could I," Cole admitted. "You know, it took a lot of spunk for Lila to show up here and make her peace with me. That's why I hugged her—and we weren't kissing."

Jessica regarded him in turmoil.

"Lila won't ever be my woman again, but I'm really glad she came, 'cause now I can understand. Lila was only protecting her own." He stroked her cheek tenderly. "Now do you understand, sugar?"

"Yes, I understand," Jessie whispered back. Indeed, she had had all of the emotional upheaval she could abide—Cole with Lila, Cole apart from her. Drawing a shaky breath, she added, "And maybe I need to protect my own, too." Then she grabbed Cole and kissed him hard enough to pop his eyes out.

His response was immediate and fierce. He crushed her body close, lifted her, and pressed her into a nearby tree. His hands roved all over her body, squeezing her breasts, kneading her bottom, as his mouth devoured hers with a voracious intimacy that left her reeling. She felt almost small and helpless in his powerful embrace, and reveled in the feeling.

"Jessie, Jessie," he whispered, his hot lips roving down her throat. "Woman, I'm on fire for you."

"Me, too," she replied achingly, stretching on tiptoe to press her mouth into his.

His voice shook with passion. "We're not stopping this time, you hear me?"

"Try to stop and I'll kill you," came her fierce reply.

He groaned in pleasure. A moment later, he lifted her into his strong arms, his gaze burning into hers. "Now let me show you who I *really* want, sugar."

Chapter Twenty-six

"Cole, you shouldn't be doing this," Jessica pleaded as he strode across the darkened yard with her in his arms, heading straight for the front porch.

"Damn right, I should."

"No, I mean taking me into the house, with your mother there."

He chuckled. "But, sugar, you should know by now that I'm a man who likes to live dangerously."

She fell silent as he climbed the steps, opened the front door, and slipped inside. "Cole, she'll wake up."

Cole didn't reply as he stepped inside Jessica's dark bedroom, crossed the room to the bed, and set her down on the soft feather tick. A loud sawing sound could be heard from the adjoining room. "Hear that snoring?" he whispered. "A box full of dynamite couldn't wake her up."

"Cole—"

Cole leaned over, silencing Jessica with his lips, and she was lost. After a moment he whispered, "Hold on, sugar."

She lay in the darkness, watching his shadowy form cross the room. She heard a soft click as he shut the door to his mother's room. As he returned to her side, a breeze ruffled the curtains and she could hear leaves rustling outside. The sound seemed sexy. Then Cole was leaning over her again, kissing her urgently, tangling his fingers in her hair.

"I've wanted to do this for so long, since the day we first made love," he murmured. "And I'm not waiting any longer."

"Me, too." Indeed, Jessica was through waiting. She kissed him feverishly, holding his face to hers.

Abruptly he moved away from her, standing at the side of the bed. His eyes burned into hers as he began unbuttoning his shirt. "I want you naked, Jessie," he said hoarsely. "I want nothing between us as we lie together."

At his sexy words, waves of desire flooded Jessica, along with torrid memories of their previous lovemaking. Yet the fire now burning in Cole's eyes told her he intended to love her with an intensity that would make that experience pale by comparison.

With trembling fingers, she began unbuttoning her dress. Meanwhile Cole all but flung off the rest of his clothing, and soon stood proudly naked before her. At the sight of him, Jessica went weak, no longer able to continue disrobing. He appeared so glorious in the moonlight, his body all hard, sexy muscles and angles, his manhood engorged with passion. Instinctively, she reached out and touched him.

His reaction was violent. He groaned, then tumbled her beneath him on the bed, overwhelming her with a shattering kiss. "I said nothing, Jessie. Nothing."

And he began tearing at her clothing, stripping her naked with a dispatch that took her breath away—until a feather rising from the tick made her sneeze.

She heard him chuckle in the darkness. "Bless you, sugar." He rose to his knees and spread her legs, staring down at her. "You're so beautiful, Jessie," he whispered, tracing a teasing finger over her face.

Shamelessly aroused to have him viewing her so intimately, Jessica sucked Cole's finger into her mouth. He groaned and pulled it away, trailing it seductively down her throat.

"That face of yours, your eyes," he whispered. "So damn beautiful and big."

"I have big eyes for you."

"And your breasts are enchanting." Cole glanced downward and grinned. "You've got a feather on one of 'em, sugar."

She writhed. "Yes, I can feel it tickling."

"Can you?" Cole grasped the small feather and trailed it seductively over Jessica's breasts. She moaned, and felt herself break out in shivers, her nipples hardening pleasurably, even as desire for Cole throbbed in her womanhood.

The feather lingered teasingly on a taut nipple. "Look how tight you are, love. Do you want to feel my mouth there?"

She drew his entire rough, huge hand to her breast. "Oh, yes."

Yet Cole pulled his hand away and continued the feather's tormenting descent, moving it down her belly, until he tickled the curls between her thighs. Jessica tossed her head and whimpered.

A muscle worked in Cole's jaw. He let go of the feather, and his fingers found the center of her desire, parting her, caressing so boldly, so pleasurably.

"Oh, Cole." She moved with him, panting softly.

"You're so hot, so wet and ready." He pushed his finger inside her.

Jessica gasped, writhing her hips, unwittingly increasing the exquisite pressure inside her. Cole continued to ply her passions, stroking her with his thumb as his finger probed deeper.

She sobbed.

He froze. "What's wrong, sugar?"

"I . . . nothing. I just can't stand . . . I want . . . " Gasping, she held out her arms to him.

He smiled, his hand sweetly torturing her. "No, Jessie, not yet. This time we're going to savor it—and I'm going to taste every inch of you."

He covered her, his hot hard chest crushing her breasts, his mouth passionately ravishing hers, even as his fingers moved more boldly between her thighs, coaxing an overwhelming response. Jessica couldn't help herself. With a low cry, she began to climax. Cole drowned her with his tongue until she tumbled over the edge.

Afterward, he pulled back and stared into her eyes. His expression was awed. "Just how I want you, Jessie. Flushed. Open to me. All mine."

Then his lips began following the same path the feather had taken. Jessica could not bear the frustration. "Please, Cole, I want you—"

"Not yet."

His hot tongue licked at her breasts, and she screamed softly. When his lips followed, his hot mouth sucking in her nipple, she could bear no more. She reached between their bodies and grasped his manhood, squeezing roughly.

He groaned violently. "Jessie, damn it—"

She spoke hoarsely. "Inside me. Now. Please."

She got her wish as Cole surged upward and plunged deep, filling her tight womanhood with hot, pulsing pleasure. The rapture was so intense, she moaned. When he began to move, the pressure and friction were unbearably sweet. She writhed beneath him, digging her fingers into his spine, unable to contain the waves of rapture swelling and peaking inside her. She raised her hips into his and met his deep, virile thrusts.

Cole's mouth took hers in a crushing kiss. He gripped her bottom and pumped into her until incredible torrents of pleasure consumed them both, sending them spinning away to paradise. They clung together, joyous and deliriously sated.

By the time Jessica awakened, her room was flooded with light and Cole was gone. Sitting up in bed, she smiled, recalling how he had claimed her two more times during the night. Although she was uncertain as to what all this meant, she was all but convinced now that she loved him, and knew it was futile to continue fighting the attraction between them.

She quickly saw to her toilette and dressed for breakfast. Combing her hair, she spotted the cameo on her dresser scarf, the piece she'd found in the stagecoach just before she'd traveled across time. Fingering it, she wondered if the brooch had previously belonged to Lila. Perhaps she should return it.

Then doubts seeped in. What if the cameo were indeed blessed with mystical properties, and held the key both to her traveling across time in the first place, and to her possible return to the future?

But did she want to leave this time? Her throat ached. Much as she remained conflicted about the life she'd left behind, Jessica found the thought of leaving Cole devastating.

Jessica held the cameo up to the light. She spotted none of the unusual sparkles of light she'd seen that first day. Perhaps the piece had lost its magical properties, if indeed it had ever had them. Perhaps she should return it to Lila.

Resolving that she would decide the matter later on, she slipped the brooch into her pocket.

When Jessica walked into the kitchen, everyone was present drinking coffee, Lila and her girls still in their jaded, tawdry costumes. Wearing an expression of martyrdom, Ma was at the stove stirring a pot of grits. The air was redolent with the smells of coffee, bacon, stale tobacco and liquor, and cheap perfume.

Cole at once jumped to his feet, smiling at Jessica as he pulled out her chair. "Good morning, sugar."

Noting the mixture of mischief and tenderness in his expression, Jessica felt her heart fluttering, and resolved not to give away too much. "Good morning," she returned with a smile.

Meanwhile, Lila eyed Jessica suspiciously. "You look awfully happy this morning, Miss Jessie." Lifting a brow at Cole, she continued, "Maybe you fared better than the rest of us last night, huh?"

Jessica groaned. So much for her attempt to keep her and Cole's secret. While the other whores tittered and the boys exchanged curious glances, Ma surged forward with the pot in one hand, a wooden spoon in the other. She frowned murderously at Lila.

"What do you mean, she fared better?" Ma ranted, waving her spoon. "Hush, up, Jezebel, before I make grits outta you. If Miss Jessie looks happy, it's because she has a pure heart, unlike you creatures of Sodom."

Jessica felt relieved to discern that Ma hadn't over-heard her and Cole. While her female cronies tittered, Lila squelched an amused look. "Yes, ma'am, whatever you say."

After hurling the fallen woman another fulminating look, Ma stalked around the table, slapping grits down on each plate with a vehemence that made several of the women cringe. "Eat up, harlots, then it's on your way with you. And ain't you got nothin' to wear but them hurty-gurty gowns?"

"No, ma'am," Lila answered. "This is all we got."

"May as well paint a sign on your buckboard saying, 'Traveling Sin Wagon,' " Ma grumbled.

Lila winked at Cole. "We used to have one of them."

Ma glared, Cole chuckled, and Jessica tossed him a scolding look. At once he sobered up.

"No more of your lip, missy," Ma scolded Lila. She turned to her youngest son. "Billy, after the vittles, you

287

and Gabe see if'n you can scare up some old britches and shirts for these . . . *females*."

"Yes, ma'am," Billy said.

"We'd be obliged," Lila said with a simpering look at Billy.

Ma harrumphed. "You ain't welcome."

An hour later, Ma, Jessica, Cole, and the boys saw the women off in the yard. Jessica's jealousy spiked anew as Cole lifted the overall-clad Lila onto the wagon seat and handed her a wad of folded bills. "You girls take care, now. Buy yourselves some respectable duds, and try to make a fresh start."

"Sure, sugar—and thanks," Lila purred back to Cole. Glancing at Jessica, Lila for once appeared sincere. "Good to meet you, ma'am. Take care of our man, now."

Cole grinned at Jessica, and she felt her cheeks heating as she caught curious looks from Ma and the boys.

"I—I will," she replied awkwardly. On impulse, she stepped forward, dug in her pocket, then handed Lila the cameo. "Here's a going-away present."

"My cameo!" Lila gasped, staring at the brooch. "Where did you find this?"

Jessica glanced at Cole to see his lips twitching. "I found it between the seats of Buck Lynch's stage."

"You did? Well, I'll be hanged." Lila turned to Cole. "What was she doing in Buck Lynch's stage?"

Cole coughed. "It's a long story."

Gabe stepped forward, grinning. "Hey, Lila, honey, what was *you* doing there when you lost it?"

Amid guffaws from the others, Ma emitted a howl of outrage and batted Gabe across the shoulders. "Hush up that lewd talk, you godless infidel!"

Gabe cringed. "Yes 'um."

Cole eyed Lila sternly. "You girls had best be going."

"Sure, honey." Lila smiled at Jessica. "Thanks for the cameo, ma'am."

"You're welcome. Good luck."

Lila worked the reins and the wagon rattled off, the other whores shouting out goodbyes to the boys and blowing kisses. Soon the men, Jessica, and Ma were left alone in the yard.

Ma brushed off her hands in a gesture of disgust. "Good riddance, is what I say. Now all of you go find your go-to-meeting clothes. I say some redemption is in order."

"But, Ma, we didn't do nothing," protested Billy.

Ma charged on her youngest son. "Don't lie to me, you little pissant. 'Sides, your day of judgment is at hand."

"Ma, quit blustering," Billy scolded.

"Blustering?" Ma yelled, waving a fist. "You think I'm funnin' you, you horse's patooty? It plumb slipped my mind yesterday owing to all the excitement, but I heard tell in town that some Pinkerton boys been asking questions about the Reklaw Gang—there, and at the mines. Yessir." Ma nodded in violent emphasis.

At this revelation, Jessica gasped, and Cole and his brothers exchanged anxious glances. Cole addressed his mother. "Ma, is that really true?"

"Hell, yes, it's true. You think I'm just making it up to whip you sidewinders into line? Them Pinkertons have been spotted hereabouts. If you don't believe me, you can ask whilst we're at church today."

"Yes, ma'am, I will," said Cole. He glanced at Jessica, and she shook her head ominously.

"Now go get dressed, the lot of you," Ma ordered. "Maybe it ain't too late for you to seek salvation."

While Luke, Wes, and Gabe stared guiltily at their feet, Billy faced down his mother. "I ain't going today, Ma, Pinkertons or not. I got other business to attend to."

Ma snorted. "Other business, eh? I know what you're conjurin' up, you varmint. You think you can win back Miss Dumpling after your evil doin's yesterday. Well, you'll be rewarded with britches full of her daddy's buckshot for your trouble."

Billy stubbornly crossed his arms. "I said, I got other business to attend to."

Ma waved him off. "Aw, get out of here. You're bound for hell, anyhow. Come along, Jessie, I'll fix your hair."

As the boys dispersed, Jessica started to follow Ma, but Cole caught her hand. "Ma, she'll be along in a minute."

Ma waved a hand in disgust and lumbered up the stairs.

Cole smiled at Jessica. "Come with me for a walk first. We've got stuff to talk over."

"All right," she said.

They strolled off into the pines to the west of the homestead. The morning was clear and crisp, and Jessica could hear mourning doves cooing. A brisk wind blew, tossing about pine needles and wafting the scent of evergreen.

She glanced at Cole, noting the abstracted look on his handsome face, and again remembered their beautiful lovemaking, as well as Lila's departure moments earlier.

"Tell me something, Cole," she murmured.

"Sure."

"Did you tell Lila about us?"

He grinned. "I told her you're my woman now. You mind?"

She frowned. "Well, I wish you'd consulted me before making such announcements."

He didn't comment, though his smile faded.

"So what's on your mind now?" she pressed. "The Pinkertons?"

He sighed. "It's a worry—but not unexpected. I knew Miser was bound to hire 'em sooner or later."

"What are you going to do, then?"

"Reckon we'll have to be more careful."

"That's all?"

Unexpectedly, he turned to her and grinned. "How 'bout we get hitched?"

She was stunned. "Just like that?"

"It's not like it's the first time I've asked you," he pointed out. "And I'd say it's pretty natural under the circumstances." He placed his hands on her shoulders. "I'm saying I want us to be husband and wife, Jessie. To live together every day, and sleep together at night."

Though thrilled, Jessica also felt troubled. "Not everything can be resolved in bed, Cole."

He reached out to pluck a pine needle from her hair. "No? Seems like we've gone a pretty good job so far."

"Nothing was settled."

"You're not convinced yet?" Eyes gleaming wickedly, he ran his hand over her bottom.

"Cole, no," she said breathlessly. "We can't just do this again and again. I could become pregnant."

The unabashed scoundrel only chuckled. "Isn't that the point of the exercise?"

"Not for two people who aren't married!"

He grinned. "Well?"

"Oh, you're impossible." She pushed him away and started off again, though a telltale smile tugged at her lips.

He fell into step beside her. "Jessie, why are you so dead set against marrying me?"

She shook her head in disbelief. "You can ask that after what your mother just revealed? I can think of a million reasons."

"Such as?"

"Such as you're an outlaw—one being hunted by the Pinkerton Detective Agency."

"My occupation might change."

"Oh, really?" she mocked. "You sure haven't shown any such tendency so far."

"Which doesn't mean I won't. Why else won't you marry me?"

She released a long, troubled sigh. "We're different, Cole. In so many ways. I'm . . . " Lamely she finished, "I'm not from here."

"I know you're not from here—and I don't care."

"You don't understand. I'm *really* not from here."

He frowned. "Explain that."

Jessica felt at a loss. How could she explain? Even if she told Cole the truth, would he ever believe her? But wasn't it time she offered him some explanation, whether he comprehended it or not? Didn't she owe him that much?

Glancing at the class ring on her finger, she made her decision. Lifting her hand, she asked, "Cole, do you remember this ring?"

" 'Course I do, sugar. My brothers stole it from you the day we kidnapped you, and later I gave it back."

"That's right. Do you remember the day you gave it back—how you asked me about the University of New Mexico, and what the number 1994 means?"

"Yes." He grinned. "I knew it couldn't be the number of notches on your bedpost, as Wesley had teased." He reached out to caress her cheek. "And we sure know better than that now, don't we, sugar? You might not be a virgin, but you're no seasoned line gal, either."

Jessica cast him a chiding look. "Spare me your fascination with my sexual prowess. My point is, those numbers *weren't* equal to the notches on my bedpost—"

"Isn't that what I just said?"

Jessica took a bracing breath. "Cole, the numbers were a year. The *year* 1994. The year I graduated from college. From the University of New Mexico."

Cole frowned over this a moment, then howled with laughter. "The *year* 1994? Why, that's the craziest notion I've ever heard. Everyone knows the *year* 1994 is over a hundred years in the future."

"That's right," she stated calmly. "I'm from the future—from one hundred and eleven years in the future to be exact—the year 1999."

Cole's gaze implored the heavens, then he hooted another laugh. "And I'm from the Dark Ages, honey."

"You don't believe me!"

He waved a hand. "Do you blame me? You're talking hokum and hogwash!"

She faced him earnestly, continuing in an impassioned rush. "Cole, you must believe me. I'm from the year 1999, and I don't know how I got here, except that I was in an antique stagecoach with some colleagues from the university where I taught; then we passed through Reklaw Gorge; then I hit my head; then everything changed. Before I knew it, the men I was riding with became their own ancestors, the year became 1888, and you and the others rode up and kidnapped me."

He felt her forehead. "You have a fever, sugar?"

She stamped her foot. "Cole, damn it, listen to me."

"I can't. You're jabbering like a lunatic."

"It's the truth. I tell you I'm from the future. You've wondered why my people haven't come after me—well, they can't, because my real family exists in another time. I left behind a mother and father there, an older brother, a job, a life. I don't know why I was brought here—but perhaps it was to reform you and your brothers, to save you from the hangman's tree. But I do know that if I can't even figure out how I got here, or why, then how can I ever be sure I'll be allowed to stay here? Under the circumstances, of course I can't marry you."

Cole's expression hardened. "You finished?"

"Actually, no. There's much more."

He held up a hand. "I don't want to hear it."

"Why?"

He gave a bitter laugh. "Why? Because if you wanted to say no, Jessica, why didn't you just say no?"

"You still don't believe me."

"Not a single word," he retorted.

She groaned. "There are other reasons, too, Cole."

"I'm not sure I can bear to hear this."

"You—you've never mentioned love," she said.

Cole grasped her chin in his hand, and hurt shone in his eyes. "And what if I did, Jessie? Would that change anything for you? Or would you just keep on lying to me to keep us apart?"

"Cole, I'm *not* lying."

"Sure, you aren't. Just like you haven't invented a hundred other excuses to shove me away."

Jessica could only stare at him, miserably torn, until he dropped his hand and walked away. She clenched her fists in frustration. Ever since she had arrived in this mystifying nineteenth-century world, nothing had really made sense to her. Now she had told Cole the truth, hoping to improve things between them . . . and she had only made things much worse.

Returning to the bunkhouse, Cole felt equally hurt and torn. He had opened up to Jessie, sharing his heart and soul, trusting her completely. And how had he been rewarded? By her throwing up new barriers between them, even inventing crazy stories to keep them apart.

She was from the year 1999? Hell, that was just plain crazy. Was she crazy? He doubted it. Maybe she was just too smart. What he couldn't doubt was that she was determined for them never to marry, or even to have a real, lasting relationship.

Maybe he'd been wrong ever to trust her in the first place.

Chapter Twenty-seven

Billy Reklaw was perched on a rise, anxiously watching the Hicks house in the hollow beneath him. For more than two hours, he'd been waiting to catch a glimpse of his sweetheart, and his patience was wearing thin.

Like the Reklaws, the Hicks lived on a farm. Their property was smaller, but the main house, a story-and-a-half white frame structure, was much larger. Since Billy had been here, he'd watched Peaches Hicks appear to feed the chickens, her ma come outside and pump water, and her pa hitch up the buckboard near the steps of the house. Yet after Mr. Hicks had gone back inside, no one had emerged for at least twenty minutes.

All at once Billy tensed at the distant, muffled creak of the front door. He watched Mr. and Mrs. Hicks troop out, both dressed in Sunday best—Mrs. Hicks holding a Bible and her husband carrying food baskets. A starched, bonneted Peaches appeared next, followed by his darling Dumpling in crisp green muslin and jaunty feathered hat. Billy strained to get a better glimpse of her. Lord, she

Eugenia Riley

looked pretty in that full-skirted gown, with those feathers and her shapely hips bobbing as she went down the steps. He couldn't make out her expression this far away, but he knew her face was downcast.

Damnation, it looked like the whole family was heading off to church, which meant he'd have no chance to speak with Dumpling alone. If only she'd been the one to feed the chickens or fetch the water. But now his goose was cooked. If he tried to approach her, her pa would no doubt fill his britches with buckshot, just as Ma had warned.

The family headed for the buckboard, Dumpling lagging behind. Abruptly Dumpling stopped, then began to shriek and stamp her foot. Billy went wide-eyed. He watched his sweetheart wave her plump arms and heard her shout, "I can't, Mama!" Then she went racing back up the steps. Mrs. Hicks rushed after her, while Peaches and her pa waited.

A few moments later, Mrs. Hicks emerged from the house alone. She approached her husband, gesturing in frustration. The parents spoke tensely for a moment or two, then they and Peaches climbed in the wagon and headed off.

"Hot damn!" Billy exclaimed. "So the little vixen is alone, after all!"

Quickly he mounted his horse and galloped down into the valley. . . .

Dumpling Hicks sat sobbing on her mother's horsehair settee. She was so mad at Bobby Lively, she could spit nails at him. She'd gone to all the trouble of baking him a cake, had driven out to his farm to deliver it, only to find him betraying her with a cheap floozy. She'd bawled about it all night long, till she'd soaked her sheets.

She should have known Bobby was no good, especially from the way his brothers always teased them both. He couldn't be the only good apple in that rotten bunch. She'd been a fool to allow herself to fall in love with him.

296

But fall in love with him she had, and now he'd betrayed her. How she'd love to get her hands on the little rascal and shake him till he was dead.

Why did she have to miss him so? Her heart felt as if it were busted in two. She pulled out a handkerchief and loudly blew her nose.

All at once she tensed as she heard the sound of hoofbeats. Had Ma and Pa returned already? Had they forgot their Bible?

No, the sound was not of a team but of a single rider.

Dumpling rushed to the front door and pushed aside the sash curtain just in time to see Bobby Lively marching up her steps. Oh, the nerve of him! Quickly she threw the lock, brushed the curtain back into place, and retreated into the hallway.

Now he was banging on her door—and yelling! "Dumpling, I know you're in there! Let me in!"

"Go away!"

"Let me in or, by damn, I'll break down this door!"

"Go ahead!"

"Oh, yeah? What will your pa say when he comes home?"

"You go away, Bobby Lively, or I'll shoot you!"

"You'll *what*?"

"I'm going for the shotgun now!"

Dumpling raced across the living room and grabbed her daddy's shotgun hanging over the fireplace. She was attempting to throw the lever when she heard the front door blast open, and then Bobby Lively raced inside and vaulted across the room. A split second later they were struggling over the weapon.

"Put that down, you crazy woman!" Billy ordered, wild-eyed.

"Not till I shoot you dead, I won't!" Dumpling vowed, trying to yank the weapon free of his strong fingers.

"Damn it, woman, put the gun down before you kill us both!"

On they struggled, Dumpling gripping the shotgun with all her might, Billy trying to wrench it away from her. Then both flinched as the weapon discharged and buckshot sprayed the ceiling.

Smoke filled the room, and flecks of ceiling plaster fell down on their heads. Dumpling dropped the gun and stared, horrified, at Bobby. He'd gone deathly pale.

"Bobby, I'm sorry . . . "

His eyes burned with anger, and his voice sent a chill down her spine. "You've done it now, woman. And I'm flat gonna wear you out."

For a moment Dumpling could only stare at him. Then, as the import of his statement sank in, she was off with a gasp, racing for the stairs.

His expression grim, Billy followed Dumpling, quickly climbing the stairs. He could not believe this fool female had actually tried to shoot him! Well, she'd be sitting on pillows for a month after he was finished with her!

He arrived on the upstairs landing in time to watch a flash of skirts disappear around the corner, and to hear a door slam.

He stalked around the corner to her door, tried the knob, and found it locked. Infuriated, he began to pound. "Damn it, woman, don't make me break down another door! We're gonna have this out—now!"

"I have another gun!" Dumpling yelled.

Rage blinded Billy. "By God, you do and—" The rest of his statement was drowned out as he kicked open the door. He heard Dumpling scream, and his gaze darted to her. To his relief, he saw that she didn't have another weapon. Instead she was cowering on her bed, curled up in a ball with her back to the wall and her hands over her face.

Well, she should be shrinking away, after almost killing him!

"Not so brave now, eh?" he jeered, starting toward her and unbuckling his belt.

He heard a muffled sob; then Dumpling moved aside

her hands and whimpered at the sight of him whipping off his belt. "Bobby, please don't beat me."

"Turn over, woman, and take your medicine," came his obdurate reply.

"*Please*, Bobby."

He heard the tears in her voice and cursed as conflicting emotions warred within him. Pausing before her bed, he gazed down at her stricken, tear-streaked face, and tenderness filled him. For a long moment he struggled to contain his anger.

"Woman, you almost killed me," he said at last.

"I know. I'm sorry."

Billy hesitated, the belt still in his hand.

Her gaze beseeched him. "Please, I'm really sorry."

With a groan, Billy hooked the belt back around his slim waist. "Will you talk to me now, you stubborn female?"

She nodded.

"Calmly?"

Though her features were clenched up with pride, Dumpling replied, "Yeah. Calmly."

Billy sat down beside her on the bed. When she flinched, he reached out to stroke her cheek, which was hot from exertion and wet with tears. "Easy, sugar, I ain't gonna hurt you. In fact, I'm sorry, too."

At that, Dumpling appeared amazed, sitting up on the bed. But hurt stained her features and tears choked her voice. "Sorry? Are you really? You was kissing a whore, Bobby Lively."

Billy groaned. "I wasn't kissing her. She was sitting in my lap."

"Same difference."

"Look, them women were just some old friends of Co—of Clay's that was passing through."

She sniffed. "So you just had to paw 'em, eh?"

"I didn't paw the woman. She sat down in my lap."

"And you're too puny to shove her off, huh?"

Billy reached out to brush a wisp of hair from

Dumpling's forehead. "You're right, sugar. I should have dumped the Jezebel right on her butt the moment she came close."

Dumpling struggled against a smile.

"Dumpling, look at me."

She did, eyeing him warily.

"Honey, nothing happened."

She struggled for a moment, then hiccoughed. "I don't believe you."

"Why in hell not?"

She was shuddering. " 'Cause I ain't pretty like them. And they ain't fat like me."

Billy clutched Dumpling's hand and stared at her with his heart in his eyes. "Honey, I think you're as pretty as a meadow full of spring flowers."

She stared, her expression uncertain.

"You know, I waited outside for hours this morning, just to catch a glimpse of you," he went on cajolingly. "Then when I thought you was leaving with your folks for church, it plumb broke my heart, you looked so delicious in that purty gown."

Dumpling's face was rapt with hope. "Oh, Bobby."

"I was so grateful, sugar, when you run back inside the house."

"Was you really?"

"Yeah, I was happy because I knew I would be able to see you, and we could talk."

She bit her lip.

"Don't you believe me yet, sugar?"

She pulled her fingers away. "I don't know."

He eyed her sternly. "Give me back your hand, woman."

Hesitantly, she complied.

Billy leaned closer, until he could smell the sweetness of her rosewater cologne, the womanly scent of her. "Honey, I'm going to tell you again: Nothing happened. And here's the proof." Billy stared solemnly into Dumpling's eyes and pressed her fingers to his crotch.

At his bold move, Dumpling's eyes grew even larger than Billy *felt*. She struggled to pull free. "Bobby, no!"

But his grip was like iron and he wouldn't release her fingers, instead deliberately running them up and down his aching shaft. Though it was torture to speak, he managed. "I've been saving this for you, sugar."

A little gasp proved she was aroused, too. Nonetheless, she sputtered, "Bobby, don't, this is—"

"What, honey? Scandalous? Bad? Are you ashamed of what you do to me? 'Cause, honey, I ain't. And there ain't no other woman on God's earth who can do *this* to me."

Now Dumpling didn't speak. She merely gulped.

"Come 'ere."

"Bobby!"

Billy hauled Dumpling close and ardently kissed her. When she trembled sweetly in his arms, he couldn't bear it. He plunged his tongue deep inside her mouth, loving the sounds of her muffled whimpers. His hand reached for her big, soft breast, and he tumbled her beneath him on the bed. Feeling her nipple harden beneath his fingers, he was in heaven.

As both of them came up for air, she gasped, "Bobby, what are you doing?"

Still kneading her breast, he whispered huskily, "Loving you, sugar. You gonna fight me?"

Dumpling groaned in helpless abandon. "I can't. Lord knows. I should, but I can't. I just want you so much, too."

"Oh, sugar. I'm so glad. And don't worry. It'll be so good."

Billy planted little kisses all over Dumpling's hot cheeks, her soft throat, delighting to her little gasps of pleasure, and the look in her eyes—so sweetly trusting, so vulnerable. Encouraged, he began unbuttoning the bodice of her gown. When she tried to resist, he merely kissed her fingers away and firmly continued. Soon her large, ripe breasts with their taut, rose-tinged nipples were exposed to his scrutiny. She was breathless beneath him, her chest rising and falling.

"Oh, sugar, I just died and went to heaven," he breathed.

"Have you?" Shamelessly, Dumpling threw her arms about Billy's neck. He kissed her lingeringly, then buried his head between her breasts. She screamed in delight as his hungry mouth took her nipple.

By now she was writhing beneath him. "Oh, Bobby, Bobby, we're being so wicked. On a Sunday, no less."

"Naw, honey, we're being *good*."

"I ain't never felt nothin' like this."

He struggled to keep his mouth attached to her breast. "Easy, sugar, you're flat gonna pitch me off."

"Oh, Bobby, I just can't stand it. You make me want to move."

"That does it," Billy said, feverishly reaching beneath her skirts, pulling down her drawers, touching her wetness.

Dumpling froze. "Bobby, this is going too fast—"

Billy smiled tenderly into her eyes. "Don't you trust me, sugar?"

"Oh, yes!"

"Just hold on to me tight, then. And call me Billy."

"Billy?"

"Billy. Yeah, Billy. It's my nickname. But only when we're alone."

"All right . . . Billy."

"Ah, you make me wild when you call me that."

His merest stroking made her wilder yet. Billy tried to hold Dumpling still as he caught her lips in a sweet, tender kiss. When he felt her relaxing, responding, felt the wetness spreading between her thighs, he thought he might explode right then and there, his passion for her was so overpowering. Struggling to keep control, he eased his fingers away and mounted her. She panicked and clenched her thighs together.

"Billy!"

He smiled down into her eyes. "Let me in, darling.

Spread those thighs. Come on, now. There, that's so good . . . "

Dumpling complied, only to cry out as Billy began to penetrate her. "Billy—oh, it smarts."

"I know, angel, but not for long." Smiling, he positioned himself firmly between her thighs, so she wouldn't be able to close on him again. "You know you're a big woman where it matters, and just as small where it counts."

Dumpling smiled then, only to scream softly as Billy penetrated her fully. Even as shudders shook them both, she tossed her head and bit a fist. "Oh, Billy, Billy. Oh, it hurts, but so damn good!"

Billy was beyond replying, totally focused on the exquisite womanflesh squeezing about him. Dumpling was tight, velvety, so hot. He eased back and forth, tasting her, teasing her, spreading her wetness. Her moans further stoked his passions, and even though she was slick now, her virgin flesh gripped him with a pressure and friction that almost shattered his control. He pulled back and penetrated deep, beginning to move in earnest.

The sounds of Dumpling's hoarse cries reached his ears, urging him on. He plunged again and again, heightening the torment, driving them both to ecstasy. At last he fell on her, kissing her as she clung to him and quietly sobbed in pleasure and release.

"You all right, sugar?" Billy asked afterward. He and Dumpling had undressed and lay naked beneath the sheets.

Stretching like a plump, contented cat, Dumpling grinned back. "I'm fine."

He moved aside the sheet and glanced down. "Ain't that blood on the sheet?"

She eyed him dreamily. "Yeah, Billy, ain't no doubt a'tall that you're my first."

"Ah, honey." Brimming with pride, he leaned over and kissed her breast. "Sure you're all right?"

She chuckled. "Reckon I'm as sore as a greenhorn

after a bronco ride—but I ain't never felt better."

Billy cuddled Dumpling close and ran his tongue over her cheek. "Ready for another ride, angel?"

"Just pitch me into the saddle, cowboy."

He chuckled, then turned more thoughtful. "Honey, what did you tell your daddy about us?"

"About what?"

"You know, about yesterday and . . . the women."

She wrinkled her nose at him. "Oh, I just told him we had a spat, that I was mad at you."

"Whew," Billy breathed, intensely relieved. "At least maybe now I have a chance of patching things up with your family."

Dumpling kissed his chin. "Sure, you do."

He smiled. "We should get married, honey."

She brightened. "You mean it?"

" 'Course." Indignantly, he added, "You don't think I'd just take your innocence and not marry you?"

"Well, hot damn, sugar!" Eagerly she kissed him.

Billy kissed her back, then a frown wrinkled his handsome brow. "But what will you tell your daddy when he comes home and finds two busted doors and half the ceiling blowed away?"

Dumpling's face screwed up mischievously. "Why, I'll just tell him you came by, we had a fight, and then you ravished me."

"Dumpling Hicks!"

She giggled. "Maybe we shouldn't get hitched quite so quick, eh, Billy?"

Reaching beneath the covers, he roved his hand over her ample, bare bottom, squeezing until she squirmed in pleasure. "Woman, you're asking for it now."

"I know," Dumpling purred, holding out her arms. "Please, darlin', give it to me."

With a groan of pleasure, Billy hauled Dumpling close and fully complied.

Chapter Twenty-eight

Over the next few days, Jessica saw little of Cole, but she often wondered what he was thinking. It disappointed her that he didn't believe she was from the future—though she couldn't blame him. Mostly she wondered how he really felt about her. He had offered to marry her, but he hadn't said he loved her, and she wondered if he even trusted her fully.

Despite it all, she missed him terribly.

She tried to keep her mind off him by staying busy with her various activities—teaching the children in town, tutoring the boys at home, writing in her journal, and finishing up the history of Mariposa for the Founders' Day celebration in a few more days. Ma was also very busy with her quilting circle, preparing for the bazaar. She even invited the other ladies to the house one afternoon.

By Wednesday, Jessica was ready to take matters into her own hands with Cole, to make another attempt to get him to see things her way. She dressed in riding clothes, then sought him out, finding him in the bunkhouse sitting at a table reading the *Colorado Springs Daily Chronicle*.

She chuckled at the look of intense concentration on his handsome face.

He glanced up with a scowl, studying her in the doorway, his features softening as he took in her flannel shirt and form-hugging denim trousers.

"Well, hi, sugar."

"I never would have pictured this," she drawled back. "You, reading the newspaper."

"You think I'm some kind of ignorant hick?"

"No, I'd say you're a pretty clever, wily sort. Where'd you get the paper?"

"Oh, Gideon Mayhew subscribes by mail, and he gave it to me at church."

"So what's the news from the Springs?"

"Well, the El Paso Club is giving a social for the ladies, a group of Ute Indians has been spotted setting up winter camp west of the city, and Mrs. Motts' Household Hints advises canning one's tomatoes early this year. I'll have to tell Ma."

Jessica laughed.

Folding the paper, Cole stood. "There's also a rumor that old Elijah Miser may run for U.S. Senator in the next election."

"You're kidding."

"Nope." Cole joined Jessica at the door. "I don't know why we're shocked. Sidewinders like him always end up on top."

"We'll just have to see that he doesn't."

"We haven't managed to deter him so far."

"Maybe you haven't tried the right method."

He raised an eyebrow. "Are you hinting I should shoot the skunk and the rest of his consortium? Believe me, I've considered it."

"No, that's not what I meant."

"Then what?"

She sighed. "Let me give it some thought. There must be a better, more legal way to stop him."

"All right." Abruptly he grinned and pulled her close. "In the meantime, what can I do for you, Miss Jessie?"

"Well, you've been keeping your distance," she chided.

He turned solemn. "Have you missed me?"

"Yes."

"Enough to stop lying to me and get married?" he added softly.

She ground her teeth. "Cole, I haven't been lying."

He waved a hand in frustration. "Do you really expect me to believe that haywire tale about your being from the future?"

"Is that why you've been standoffish, because of what I told you?"

"Well, those stories of yours do give a man pause. Not to mention the fact that you're willing to go to bed with me, but not to become my wife."

Jessica bit her lip. "Can you blame me when you don't believe me?"

"Can you blame *me* for wondering if you've been smoking peyote and chewing on locoweed?"

She groaned. "Cole, I want you to do something for me."

He nestled her closer. "Sure, sugar."

She squirmed. "Not that. I want us to go for a ride."

He arched against her provocatively. "Me, too. Lord, honey, I sure have missed you."

"Cole, stop it," she scolded. "I want you to take me to the gorge where you kidnapped me."

"Wherever you want to do it is fine with me."

She shoved at his chest. "We have some talking to do."

"Before or afterward, it makes no never-mind to me."

"Damn it, Cole Reklaw!"

But after the rascal stole a leisurely kiss, Cole dutifully grabbed his hat and left with her.

Half an hour later they were both perched on horseback, overlooking the deep, dramatic gorge where they'd first met. A shiver slipped down Jessica's spine as she stared at the narrow dirt road, at a scene that was at once familiar but also jarring, a landscape that, in her mind, would always somehow hover between two worlds.

"Reklaw Gorge," Jessica murmured.

Cole chuckled. "You mean 'Haunted Gorge.' "

She turned to him in awe. "That's right, it's called 'Haunted Gorge' now."

"It's an old Cheyenne burial ground," Cole explained. "Strange things have been known to happen here."

She shivered. "Woody Lynch mentioned the ghosts."

"Woody Lynch?"

"He was our travel guide that day back in the present, before everything changed. He said the gorge was haunted by outlaws, not Indians. Your gang, in fact."

Cole fell broodingly silent.

"Tell me about that day, Cole. I mean, you and the boys don't normally rob stages, do you?"

"Yes, that was odd," he admitted. "We'd gotten wind of a gold shipment leaving the mines, but when we got there, we found nothing."

"So your spy didn't exactly get you the lowdown, eh?"

He ignored that, though a slight grin gave him away. "Anyhow, the wagon never came. We were on our way back to the farm when Billy spotted the stage and said, 'Hey, let's rob it!' The boys were feeling restless and frustrated, and it seemed a pretty good idea at the time."

Jessica felt awed by the account. "I guess in a way, then, it was destiny—you and me finding each other. You robbing the stage, when you hadn't intended to. Me being on it."

He appeared intrigued by the prospect. "Yeah—destiny. I like that, sugar."

She eyed him beseechingly. "Cole, will you at least try to listen to me again?"

"I'll try," he agreed reluctantly.

"The day you kidnapped me . . . " She paused, drawing a shuddering breath. "I started out in the present, in the year 1999."

Cole rolled his eyes. "Here we go again."

"Hush and listen. I was a history professor at Pawnee College in Greeley, and we were on a summer field trip, doing research on the Old West."

"You mean, studying about now?" he asked in perplexity.

"Right. On the last leg of our journey, we stayed at a dude ranch owned by Woody Lynch, a cousin of our chair, Professor Lummety. Two other male colleagues were along. We had an excursion—a ride in an antique stagecoach, complete with costumes. It was the very stagecoach that used to belong to Lila Lullaby, and now belongs to Buck Lynch. We were supposed to ride out and have a picnic at Mariposa—which in the future will be a ghost town."

Cole shook his head. "Damn, sugar, but you have a vivid imagination."

"It's all true, Cole," she retorted vehemently. "Anyway, the ride was quite bumpy, and soon after we came to this gorge, I hit my head on the roof of the stagecoach, then pricked—well, my derriere—on an old cameo buried beneath the seats."

Cole snapped his fingers. "Lila's old cameo—the one you gave back to her?"

"Right. Then everything became hazy; reality flickered in and out. The next thing I knew, the men I was sitting with all changed into their nineteenth-century counterparts. Professor Lummety became his own ancestor, Sheriff Lummety; Professor Billingsly became—I don't know, a clone of Buffalo Bill, and Stan Wilkins became some tobacco-chewing hick named Slim."

"Uh-huh," Cole agreed cynically.

"Then the five of you came roaring up, robbed the stage, and kidnapped me. The rest, as they say, is history."

He eyed her askance. "That it?"

"Of course not! There's the whole matter of my life in the future—a world I doubt you can even comprehend—not to mention the question of how in *hell* I came to be here with you."

"Search me, sugar."

"Damn it, Cole, you're not helping!"

" 'Cause you're still not making any sense!"

"How would you feel if you were a mere bit of flotsam in the cosmic plan, tossed about at the whim of the Fates?"

He gestured at the gorge. "What do you expect me to say, Jessie? It's obvious you feel you don't belong here with me."

"That's not what I said."

He eyed her sadly. "Are you wishing that stage would come along again and take you away?"

"You believe me?" she gasped.

Expression troubled, Cole replied, "I believe you think you belong somewhere else."

Jessica stared at the gorge for a long moment, then wistfully replied, "Maybe in a strange sense I do wish that stage would come along again. In a funny way, it would be like coming full circle. It might convince me that this is real, even persuade me I'm not crazy. Maybe I need to connect with my other world one last time—perhaps to say goodbye."

"Maybe it's me you really want to say goodbye to," he said, almost bitterly.

Jessica regarded him with her heart in her eyes, and spoke with the force of her torn feelings. "Cole, that's not true. But maybe, just maybe, I may not have any choice in this at all. And that's what scares me the most."

When they arrived home, it was to find the boys once again mounting up out in the yard. Since all four were heavily armed, there was no doubt as to their intent. Jessica's heart sank.

"Jessie! Cole!" Billy called. "We been looking for you

everywhere. Rattle your hocks and let's ride. There's a new shipment coming out from the mines this afternoon."

"Is there?" Cole questioned as he and Jessie halted their horses. "Then I guess we've arrived back in the nick of time."

"You coming with us, Jessie?" Wes asked.

She shot him a baleful look. "I'd have thought you boys would have learned your lesson by now. And what about the Pinkerton agents that may be out tracking you?"

"Ah, we ain't scared," bragged Gabe. "Don't argue with us, Jessie. You coming or not?"

"Yeah, if we hurry, we'll be back in time for prayer meeting tonight," Billy put in eagerly.

"Prayer meeting!" Jessica repeated in disbelief. "It amazes me how you scoundrels can separate the morality of churchgoing from the *immorality* of your lawless ways!"

All the brothers appeared perplexed. "Do you know what she's talking about?" Luke asked Cole.

"Nope," he replied.

Jessica struggled to hold on to her patience. "I'm saying, how can you rob the gold shipment this afternoon, then have the unmitigated gall to show up at church tonight?"

"Why, a'course we gotta attend church," put in Billy self-righteously. "Miss Dumpling and me kissed and made up, and I promised her I'd be there tonight. We don't show, and she'll think . . . Hell, she'll think I'm a dad-blamed *sinner*."

While Billy's brothers guffawed, Jessica waved her hands in defeat. "I give up."

"Guess that means you're going," Billy declared. "Cole, better fetch extry shootin' irons, just in case them Pinky boys shows their cowardly faces. Then let's ride!"

* * *

Jessica couldn't believe it. Here she was again, perched on her knees behind a boulder, on the ridge overlooking the mine road, waiting for the boys—who were hidden in the trees with their mounts—to do their dirty work in the hollow below. She was so tense she couldn't even take notes in her journal, which she'd brought along as usual.

She caught a shaky breath, watching the heavily laden dray move into view. Curiously, there was only a driver and one guard—which was really odd, since Cole had told her the guard had been increased recently. Why would the mine owners backslide now?

Unless this was a trap. The very thought took her breath away. She had scolded the boys about this very possibility—that the Pinkertons could be lying in wait for them—even as they'd ridden here, but the boys had only scoffed at her concerns. Living in isolation as they did, they seemed to have little conception of how most outlaws ended up. As for herself, she'd seen too many reruns of *Butch Cassidy and the Sundance Kid* to expect a happy ending. At least Cole had displayed a modicum of caution, telling her that, if there was trouble, she should make a dash straight to the homebound trail and not wait for them.

As the dray lumbered closer, she anxiously watched the boys storm out from the woods, firing away and overtaking the wagon. But no sooner had they caught up with it than four more riders burst out from the other side of the road, firing at the Reklaws!

Jessica cried out in dismay. Oh, heavens, these must be the Pinkertons, and the Reklaws had waltzed straight into their trap!

Jessica looked on in horror as burst after burst of gunfire blasted out, and smoke filled the hollow. She squealed as she observed Wesley flinch, then slump over in his saddle. Good God, he'd been hit! What could she do? She had a pistol in the pocket of her overalls, but it would be ineffective at this distance.

Reacting out of instinct, Jessica ran over to her horse,

grabbed her rifle, then scrambled back. She flipped the lever and took aim, just over the head of one of the Pinkertons. Wincing, she squeezed off a round, only to gasp as she watched the man's hat fly off. Heavens, she hadn't intended to get that close.

Nonetheless, she managed to stay calm and squeezed off several more rounds, distracting the Pinkertons and causing them to fire in *her* direction. She screamed as a bullet bit into the rock just inches from her cheek.

Luckily, the boys used her brief distraction to their advantage, beating a hasty retreat. Jessica fired a few more rounds behind the gang to discourage the Pinkertons from following them. Then she mounted her horse and rode hard for the homeward trail.

She caught up with the men in an old river bed. The group paused together, the horses whinnying, snorting, and stamping the ground. Jessica winced as she caught sight of Wesley—he was still in the saddle but obviously woozy, his face white, shirt half soaked with blood.

"Damn fools—all of you!" she exclaimed furiously. "Wesley, are you all right?"

He nodded weakly. "Flesh wound, Jessie. I'll make it."

She turned anxiously to Cole to see that his expression was taut with worry. "Cole, we must stop and—"

"Not yet," he cut in harshly. "Jessie, why in hell didn't you follow orders and leave when you were supposed to?"

"Well, it's damn fortunate for all of your butts that I stayed."

His mouth twisted in frustration. "Let's ride. We need to get a safe distance away from here."

"But Wes is bleeding, he could—"

"I'm all right, Jessie," Wesley reiterated hoarsely. "And we'll all die if those Pinkertons catch up with us."

Unable to refute his argument, Jessica galloped off with the men.

Gabe grinned at her. "Though Cole's too proud to say it, I'm not. Thanks for saving our bacon, Jessie."

313

She harrumphed. "God, I can't believe I did that. I shot the hat off one of those Pinkerton agents. It could have been his head!"

"Well, you had to—they were shooting at us," pointed out Luke.

"You were breaking the law!" Jessica sighed heavily. "We all were."

"Well, you needn't worry about us getting in trouble again any time soon," Cole told her. "We'll have to lay low for a spell, now that we know the Pinkertons are involved."

"Now that you've been *forced* to lay low."

"Yeah," he agreed.

"Well, I might have known it wouldn't have been due to some moral epiphany on your parts," she added crossly.

"Don't she say the most peculiar things?" Billy asked Cole.

"Yeah," he agreed.

They rode hard for another mile. As they rounded a bend, Jessica saw Wes slump to one side and almost fall off his horse. Watching Cole grab his brother and yank him upright, she mouthed a thank-you to the Almighty.

Then she turned her beseeching gaze on Cole. "*Please*, can't we stop before Wes falls and breaks his neck—or bleeds to death?"

He glanced behind them. "Yeah, guess it'll be safe to stop for a spell and dress his wound. I see no signs we're being followed."

As everyone pulled up next to a break of aspen, Billy added, "Yeah—as long as we ain't late for prayer meeting tonight."

That evening, the entire family attended prayer meeting, even Wesley, whose shoulder wound proved to be little more than a nuisance once it was cleaned and dressed. After several hours of rest and a bowl of Ma's hearty stew, he seemed almost his old self again. Jessica

314

nonetheless argued that he should stay home; Cole had insisted this would cause suspicion in town.

He proved to be right. At the ice cream social outside after the service, Jessica was happy to see the boys flirting with their sweethearts—Billy and Dumpling in particular seemed barely able to keep their hands off each other, and she even spied them kissing in the shadows. She enjoyed sitting at the long table with Cole and a group of the churchfolk while all of them ate blueberry ice cream.

Then a tense moment ensued when Joshua Hicks asked, "Did you boys hear about the attempted robbery on the mine road today?"

"Yeah," put in Gideon Mayhew. "Hear tell the Pinkertons dry-gulched the Reklaw Gang and even wounded one of 'em badly. But they got away."

"More's the pity," put in Thaddeous Jeter. "Old Miser and his cronies deserve much worse than they got."

Amid chuckles, Henry Holler glanced at Cole and grinned. "You know, there's five of you Lively boys . . . almost makes a body wonder."

Alarmed, Jessica glanced at Cole. Although he smiled back at Henry, she could see the strain in his face.

"Yeah, but if they were the Reklaws," put in Joshua Hicks, "there would only be four of 'em tonight."

As everyone laughed, Thaddeous Jeter remarked, "If they was the Reklaws, I'd shake their hands to a man."

"Hear, hear!" agreed Mayhew, raising his punch cup.

Jessica watched Cole smile and toast with the others, but knew he was feeling as troubled as she was.

In the middle of the night, Jessica jerked awake to see the dark form of a man climbing in her window! Panicking, she spotted her overalls folded over the foot of the bed. She grabbed them, pulled out her pistol, and cocked it.

"Stop right there or I'll shoot you!"

She heard Cole's low whistle. "Easy, honey, it's just me. Kinda jumpy tonight, aren't you?"

"Cole." Intense relief swept her.

"Don't worry, I'm not armed."

She set down her pistol. A moment later, he joined her on the bed, hugging her close and kissing her. Delighted to be in his arms again, especially after the scary episode today, Jessica eagerly kissed him back. Then she felt something hard probing her thigh and reached down to touch it. She was rewarded by his grunt of pleasure.

"You're not armed, eh?" she teased.

He chuckled and began raising her nightgown. "I realized I never did thank you personally for today."

"Cole, we could have all been killed."

Ignoring her admonition, he went on huskily, "I need to teach you to mind a sight better, too. Maybe this will accomplish both." He eased her gown up over her knees.

"Cole!"

He kissed her knee. "Just relax, honey."

Her voice trembled. "I'm trying. But it still shakes me up to realize how close I came to shooting a man."

"Today or just now?"

"Both," she admitted. Now he was hiking her gown up over her hips, his boldness wildly erotic. "Cole, *what* are you doing?"

"Guess." He spread her thighs, leaned over, and buried his lips between them.

In a mere split second, Jessica's entire body became an aching, writhing mass of desire. She arched wildly, but Cole pushed her down, holding her near the source of her torment—his hot lips and wet tongue. His tongue flicked in exquisite little circles that left her gasping and pounding her fist. His rough hands slid up her smooth belly, hiking her gown high, his strong fingers grasping and kneading her bare breasts. Jessica panted and tossed her head. Just when she was certain she had lost her mind, his tongue entered her, sending her spiraling into a climax so wrenching, the aftermath left her weak. Then he surged upward to claim her lips in a voracious kiss.

"That please you, honey?" he murmured.

"God, yes." Still panting, she reached down to stroke him through his trousers.

He grunted. "Jessie, I think we're living a bit too dangerously,"

"I know." She began unbuttoning his fly.

He moaned, rolled her beneath him, and spread her thighs. "I mean the people in town—I think they're catching on."

She shuddered. "You could quit."

"Never." And he demonstrated, kissing her again even as his manhood claimed her deeply.

"Oh, Cole, Cole, I can't stand it." Jessica ripped at the buttons on his shirt, wrapped her arms around him, and crushed her breasts against his naked chest.

"Ah, darling, that feels so good," he rasped, pumping into her. Lifting her hips, Cole eased deeper still until she whimpered and kissed him wildly.

"Lord, I want you so much I could die of it," she whispered.

Abruptly Cole rolled over, bringing her on top of him. "Then take me, love."

Jessica did so eagerly, lowering herself onto him, gasping at the heat and strength of him inside her. She tossed back her head and rode him. He smiled, thrusting high as she pressed down. Moans shook her and she melted inside, consumed by glorious sensations. Cole stretched upward, bracing himself on his forearms, licking her breasts, gently biting the nipples, all the while pounding into her lustily, heightening the pressure of their joining. She sobbed and quickened her pace, pleasuring them both in her desire to be one with him.

With a groan he sat up and brought her down on his sex, thrusting until they both cried out, clutching each other close, exploding in bright splinters of ecstasy.

Chapter Twenty-nine

On Saturday afternoon, Jessica stood with Cole at Mariposa's Founders' Day celebration, which was held in the yard of the church. In keeping with the cool late September day, Jessica was dressed in a green serge suit with a long, pleated skirt, and a small feathered hat, while Cole wore a black wool jacket, gray trousers, and a black hat. Standing at the edge of the crowd, they had a good view of all the festivities.

Around them, colorful booths had been constructed, and humanity of all ages milled about—old gentlemen with canes, young families with small children, widows and couples of all ages. The sounds of laughter and gay conversation, the scents of perfume, pomade, and any number of succulent foods filled the air. The townsfolk happily browsed from booth to booth, purchasing everything from pies, pastries, and sandwiches to quilts, handmade toys, and other craft items.

At several oilcloth-draped tables, a number of attendees had paused to eat and talk happily, while out in the

Bushwhacked Bride

yard, a few couples danced to the music of two fiddlers. Jessica was happy to see Gabe dancing with Beatrice, and Billy with Dumpling, while Wes and Luke ate lunch with their sweethearts.

"Don't the boys look happy?" she asked Cole.

"Everyone does," replied Cole. "Just look at Ma, selling those quilts with the other ladies."

Jessica smiled at the sight of Ma ensconced in black silk, standing inside the quilting booth, pointing out the attributes of a gorgeous patchwork quilt to a young matron. "Joining the church has been so good for her. She's mentioned wanting to invite her quilting guild out to the farm again."

Cole frowned.

"Something troubling you?"

He squeezed Jessica's hand. "I guess I feel rather like we're living in a house of cards, waiting for it to collapse."

"It won't if you men stay on the straight and narrow path."

He eyed her askance. "Even if we do live lawfully, will the Pinkerton boys give up on us? Will Elijah Miser be satisfied before we're all swinging from a hangman's tree?"

"Cole, what bleak thoughts!" Jessica exclaimed. "Why, this is a day of hope, of renewal. Just think, the town of Mariposa has made it for five years—as you'll be learning when I read the town's history later this afternoon."

He nodded. "I'm really proud of you for that, sugar." Looking around, he sighed. "Only, I worry about whether the town will make it another five. Mariposa exists only because of the mine. Once it collapses, I fear the town will, as well."

Jessica bit her lip. "Are you sure a major cave-in is in the offing?"

"Oh, yeah," he replied grimly. "Like I told you after I toured the mines, Miser has riddled that mountain with more tunnels than an anthill, and before long the whole

319

business will give way—and take with it the lives of many of the men in town, I fear."

Jessica glanced at the various families milling about them—the Hickses, the Hollers, the Mayhews. She felt a chill at the thought of the men of these families dying such gruesome deaths. "Cole, we have to do something."

"But what?" He forced a smile. "Hey, I don't mean to spoil the day for you, sugar. Come on, let's get something to eat."

Though she remained troubled, Jessica bravely nodded. "I don't think I can resist the smell of Wilma Hicks's peach cobbler much longer."

They made their rounds, purchasing food and tea from the booths, then sat down next to the Hicks and Holler couples.

Joshua addressed Cole first. "Hey, you folks read the latest *Denver Post?*"

"Nope," Cole replied. "Something in it of interest to us?"

"Yeah. Seems Elijah Miser just announced he's running for U.S. senator in the next election."

"The nerve of that man!" declared Wilma Hicks. "After what he's done to this town!"

"He'll probably get elected," complained Henry Holler. "Hell, that man gets everything he wants."

"Well, someone needs to play a little hardball with that scoundrel," put in Jessica.

"Hardball?" asked Joshua, appearing perplexed.

"I think she means someone needs to set him in his place," suggested Millie Holler.

"Well, we all agree on that," added her husband, prompting everyone to laugh. "But what can we do?"

Cole pointed at his head, then rolled his eyes meaningfully toward Jessica. "Miss Jessie here is thinking on that."

As Jessica stuck out her tongue at Cole, the men laughed and Henry said, "Oh, Lordy, a woman scheming. Miser's *really* in a pickle now."

More mirth followed. As it died down, Joshua Hicks jerked a thumb toward a couple walking off together. "Hey, Clay, your baby brother sure is spending a lot of time around my Dumpling these days. I've been meaning to ask if Bobby's intentions are honorable."

"Certainly," Cole replied, prompting additional chuckles.

Joshua frowned. "You know, while Wilma and me were at church last week, someone busted two locks out at the house and fired buckshot through the ceiling."

"Oh, how terrible!" put in Jessica. "I hope no one was injured."

"Nope—Dumpling claims she was out in the hen house when it happened," Joshua replied dubiously.

"Was anything taken?" asked Millie.

"Not that we know of." Joshua glanced meaningfully at Cole. "I don't suppose your brother knows anything about this?"

"Oh, definitely not."

Joshua appeared unconvinced.

"All four of your brothers seem to have found sweethearts in the church," added Wilma, a mischievous twinkle in her eyes. "I wonder who will be the first to make an announcement."

Glancing off at Billy and Dumpling holding hands beneath a tree, Jessica was pretty sure she knew who would be first.

Billy was gazing ardently into Dumpling's eyes. "Sugar, you shore look purty in that new yeller calico dress," he crooned.

"Thanks, honey." Dumpling stroked the sleeve of Billy's brown wool jacket and smiled demurely. "You sure look fetching in that suit."

"Thanks, sugar. Don't you reckon it's about time we get hitched?"

She giggled. "Why, Billy, you wicked boy." She paused, feigning a wounded air. " 'Sides, I'm still not completely recovered from seeing you with that floozy."

"Aw, hell, honey." Billy wickedly wiggled his eyebrows. "You mean I didn't convince you last Sunday?"

"Well, I might could use a mite *more* convincing."

Though he struggled against a grin, Billy shook a finger at her. "Woman, you're a vixen. First you resisted, then you saw how sweet it could be . . . now you're greedy."

"Yep," Dumpling admitted unabashedly, licking her lush lips. "I'm plenty greedy."

He groaned. "So when do I speak with your pa?"

Dumpling appeared uncertain. "Are you really sure about this, Billy? I mean, what about your brothers? Do you really want me, fat and all?"

Billy squeezed Dumpling's hand and stared at her soulfully. "The devil with them rascals, my brothers. What they think don't matter. It's just you and me from now on. You've made me a man, Dumpling. I love you just the way you are."

Dumpling melted. "Oh, Bobby. I love you, too."

"So when do I ask your pa?" he repeated impatiently.

Dumpling glanced in the direction of the tables. "Well, I don't rightly know. I reckon Pa's still put out on account of the busted doors and the buckshot in the ceiling. And he suspects I may know more than I'm letting on. How 'bout we wait just a few more days?"

"Now you're talking," he eagerly agreed. "You know, if we was alone, I'd love to kiss you right now . . . and a lot more."

Dumpling squirmed in pleasure. "A *lot* more?"

He swallowed hard. "Guess we'll have to find a way, eh, sugar?"

Dumpling snuggled closer. "Yep, we'll find a way . . . "

The rest of Founders' Day was a rousing success. Late that afternoon, inside the crowded church, Jessica read a summary of her history of the town to the enthralled crowd; her finale was hailed with a standing ovation. She then presented the complete text to a grateful Mayor Polk for the town's archives; she had already made a separate copy in her own journal. Following a prayer by Reverend Bliss, the gathering was dismissed. Ma and the boys talked about what a great time they'd had all the way home.

After supper, Jessica sought Cole out on the front porch. She found him sitting on the swing, petting Inkspot. "Cole, I have an idea."

He patted the empty space beside him. "Come sit with us."

She did so, smoothing down her skirts, reaching out to pet the kitten, which was now even bigger than Cole's large hand. "I think we should make a trip to Colorado Springs."

He appeared startled. "You and me?"

"Yes."

"Why?"

"To play a little hardball. Give Elijah Miser some bad press."

"Bad press?"

"Aren't we even now entering the age of yellow journalism? What if we can convince one of the local papers to do an exposé on the consortium and conditions at the Mariposa mines? What would that do to Miser's chances to win a senatorial seat?"

Cole whistled. "Woman, you've got a devious mind."

"Wouldn't it work?"

He frowned. "Well, it might. If we could get one of the newspapers to take us seriously."

"Why wouldn't they?"

"Well, I'm an outlaw, and you're just a female."

"Oh!" Outraged, Jessica sprang to her feet. "And you're a typical male!"

"Now why are you riled?"

323

"Because, Cole, you're selling yourself short. Selling *me* short. Everything in this world is image. Your image. Mine. Even Elijah Miner's."

"I don't follow you."

"We'll go to Colorado City in style. That means stopping off to purchase elegant clothes . . . and I guess it's best that we keep up the same ruse we have here, that you're a farmer named Clay Lively and I'm your cousin, the schoolteacher from back East. We'll have to have separate hotel rooms, of course—"

"Aw, shucks." Cole scowled. "How long do you think *that* will last?"

"Oh, hush. Anyway, we'll go to Colorado Springs, register at the best hotel, and start talking to the newspapers in town about the consortium, and conditions at the mines. When we get the press on our side, we'll start playing hardball with Miser himself. With any luck, all we'll need to do is to stir up a bit of heat to make him come around."

Cole shook his head. "You and your haywire notions. Isn't there a good chance Miser will recognize us from the robbery?"

"I doubt it. That's why our disguises will be so important when we go to Colorado Springs. Besides, we both wore masks during the robbery. I don't think Miser and his cronies even realized I was a woman—and it's not as if we're taking along the entire gang this time."

"I still say you've lost your mind."

She balled her hands on her hips. "Will you escort me to Colorado City?"

Looking her over, he grinned wickedly. "There and to heaven, sugar."

"That's not what I meant."

He caught her hand and pulled her back down beside him. "No, but it's what you want."

Cole leaned over and ardently kissed her, and Jessica found she couldn't agree more. . . .

Chapter Thirty

Jessica and Cole trotted their tired horses down the main street of the small metropolis of Colorado City. Both wore trail clothes; both were exhausted and dirty following a day-long ride.

Although the town itself was flat, in the distance the sharp rise of the Rocky Mountains served as a dramatic backdrop. Jessica gazed at bustling rail yards to the south of them, at long rows of awning-shaded structures flanking them on either side, along with tethered horses and a collection of various conveyances lined up out in the street. She watched two brawling drunkards, locked in combat, come bursting out of a grog shop to land with a crash on the boardwalk and send a housewife scurrying off with her children. She could hear strident piano music and raucous laughter spilling forth from both sides of the street. Although she spotted a few respectable businesses, it was easy to see how this small community had earned the label "Sin City." Indeed, Jessica had already spotted more than one woman of ill repute strutting along in tawdry costume.

"I've never in my life seen so many saloons and dancing parlors," she commented to Cole.

"Twenty-two of 'em," he replied.

She eyed him askance. "That's right, this is your stomping ground."

He grinned, signaling for them to halt before the awning of a large general store. "If you want to buy us those fancy duds to wear in the Springs, Tappan's here should do. And Moffett's Boarding House down at Twenty-fifth is respectable enough for the night. I'll let us a room."

"You'll let us *rooms*," she corrected. "This close to the Springs, we can't afford to take any chances."

Although Cole appeared wryly amused, he replied, "Yes, ma'am."

He dismounted and assisted Jessica down, tethering their horses at the hitching post, then taking out his wallet and handing her several bills. "While you're shopping, I'll walk the horses down to Moffett's and see they're stabled in the carriage house. But first, if you don't mind, I think I'll wet my whistle at Schmickel's Saloon. Maybe I'll hear some more scuttlebutt about Miser or the Pinkertons."

"Good idea. Just behave yourself."

"Always," he drawled.

She rolled her eyes. "I'll meet you at the boardinghouse afterward."

He dimpled. "Buy yourself something pretty, too. We may just go out for an elegant dinner before we leave the Springs."

"I'll be sure to."

They parted company on the boardwalk, and Jessica strolled inside the store, which reminded her strongly of Allgood's in Mariposa, except this establishment was much larger and better stocked. Noting with pleasure that there was a soda fountain, she bought herself a sarsaparilla, although she caught a curious glance from the male clerk due to her masculine attire. After slaking her thirst, she began perusing the ready-made garments on a rack. For herself, she bought three dresses: for daytime wear, an elegant green serge coatdress and a floor-length tailored blue suit, both with matching hats; for the promised evening out, a lovely off-the-shoulder gown of rose-colored silk. For Cole, she selected a handsome black frock coat, a satin brocade vest, two sets of trousers, one fawn and one black in color, two pleated linen shirts, and two black cravats. Completing his ensemble with an ebony walking stick and dress black western hat, she mused that they would indeed go to Colorado Springs in style.

She paid for her purchases and left the store with an armful of boxes. Proceeding down the boardwalk, she passed another saloon, glancing inside to see a scruffy drunkard pawing the sequined "line gal" in his lap. Then in the next block, she was appalled to find herself passing "Lynch's" stable! She glanced inside to view the very stagecoach she'd taken across time, and nearby, Buck Lynch himself was bent over shoeing a horse!

The scene gave her a chill. Good Lord! She mustn't allow Buck to see her! For how could she explain what had happened to her and where she'd been? Juggling her packages and tugging down the brim of her cowboy hat, she sped on.

She had just made good her getaway, and was in the middle of the next block, when she all but collided with a familiar figure emerging from the hardware store. The sight of this second recognizable face staggered her anew.

"Professor Lummety!"

The pot-bellied, mustachioed gentleman, wearing a silver star and ten-gallon hat, squinted back at Jessica. "Begging your pardon, ma'am, but I'm Sheriff Lummety, lawman here."

Jessica felt the color draining from her face. "Oh, that's right. Forgive me. *Sheriff* Lummety."

He snapped his fingers, recognition lighting his features. "Well, I'll be deuced. Ain't you the schoolmarm, the one that was riding on the stage the day we got bush-whacked by the Reklaw Gang?"

"Er—yes," Jessica acknowledged.

He eyed her trail clothes in perplexity. "I hardly recognized you in that getup, ma'am. What happened to you? How did you escape the gang?"

"They—um—released me when they discovered I had no money."

"They did?" Lowering his voice, he demanded, "Did them blackguards molest you?"

"No, not at all," she hastily reassured him.

"Well, thank heaven. Are you teaching at Mariposa now?"

"Er—yes. And liking it very much."

He heaved a great sigh. "I'm so relieved to know you're safe and sound. I been worried about you ever since the robbery. I telegraphed the U.S. Marshal the second we got back to Old Town. I been meaning to head west again and track them varmints, but my lumbago's been killing me—and things have been pretty lively around here."

Hearing a crashing sound emanating from the saloon across the street, Jessica shuddered. "I can imagine."

"So what brings you to Colorado City?"

"Oh, I'm here for some shopping."

He appeared taken aback. "Not the most respectable place for a lady to be out and about." Leaning closer and cupping a hand around his mouth, he confided, "I'd recommend the Springs."

"Indeed. I'm heading there tomorrow."

"You here alone?"

"Er—no, I have an armed escort."

"Who might that—"

Jessica cut in, "Sheriff, can you tell me something?"

"Sure, if I can."

She flashed him an encouraging smile. "I'm a little

328

confused about the day I was kidnapped. Can you tell me when and where I got on the stage?"

Curiously, he blanched, appearing bemused. "You know, that's funny, ma'am. My memory ain't what it used to be. I can't recollect your getting on the stage a'tall, though it would have been here, I reckon. I do recollect you were going to Mariposa to teach. But it's funny, ma'am, I can't recall just how I knew that." He gestured toward the block behind her. "You might ask Buck Lynch—his livery is yonder."

"Thanks," she replied stiffly. "Is Mr. Lynch still running his stage line?"

"Not since the robbery. But I've been after him to start up again. My cousin out at Mariposa keeps writing asking me to come for a visit—and I'm not spry enough to ride all that distance on horseback. Still, I would love to see Wilma and her family—indeed, that's where I was headed the day we was bushwhacked."

"Of course. As a matter of fact, I've met Mrs. Hicks and her family at church."

He beamed. "You have?"

"Very nice people."

"How are Joshua and my nieces?"

"All doing great."

"I'm pleased to hear it." Lummety tipped his hat. "Again, ma'am, I'm so relieved to see you. Let me know if there's anything I can do for you while you're in town."

"Sure. Thank you so much."

He nodded at the boxes she held. "Need help with them packages?"

"Oh, no thanks. Nice visiting with you, Sheriff." She rearranged the boxes and offered her hand.

He shook her hand. "You too, ma'am. Take care, now. And tell Wilma hey for me."

"Sure will."

Numbly, Jessica walked the remaining three blocks to the boardinghouse. Seeing Buck Lynch, conversing with

Sheriff Lummety, had left her awash in unreality and foreboding.

She still didn't fully understand why or how she had crossed time, and speaking with Lummety just now hadn't helped at all. There was something mystical, downright spooky, about the entire situation. Lummety knew she'd been the teacher bound for Mariposa, but he couldn't remember *how* he knew this, or even when she'd joined the stage. And although he'd alerted the U.S. Marshal about the robbery and kidnapping, his physical infirmities had prevented him from pursuing the Reklaw Gang. It was as if there were some divine purpose to her journey here, as if some cosmic puppet master was pulling strings to allow her to spend time with Cole and his brothers!

Yet the joke might well be on her. Running across Lynch and Lummety seemed a bad omen. All her instincts warned her that time could be running out—time for Cole and his brothers, perhaps time for herself. This scared her to death. Would Cole and his brothers be captured, and face the hangman's tree? Would she be hurled back across time again, losing Cole forever?

All these daunting possibilities made her terrified for Cole and his brothers, for herself, and she couldn't wait to reach the shelter of his strong arms again. When she burst inside the small lobby of the boardinghouse, Cole was waiting for her on the horsehair settee. He stood as she approached.

"Sugar, I've got us two nice adjoining rooms on the second floor." He paused, eyeing her pale face. "What's wrong?"

"Let's go upstairs."

"Sure."

He took her packages and they trooped upstairs, entering a large pleasant room with a wood floor, cozy throw rugs, and a four-poster bed.

Cole deposited the packages on the dressing table, then turned to her. "What is it, sugar?"

"Oh, Cole." She fell into his arms.

He groaned, removing her hat and kissing her hair. "Easy, darlin'. You're trembling and you look like you've see a ghost."

Her expression deeply troubled, she replied, "I have. I just ran into Sheriff Lummety."

Cole whistled. "Did he recognize you?"

"Yes."

"Damn."

"Don't worry, I convinced him I managed to escape the gang." She shuddered. "But, Cole, he's planning to come out to Mariposa soon. To visit the Hickses. Wilma's his cousin, you see. He may come as soon as Buck Lynch starts up his stage line again. I saw Buck, too—though he didn't see me."

Cole appeared even more concerned. "Damn . . . If Lummety should come to Mariposa, see me and the boys together . . . "

"I know." Her anxious gaze met his. "Cole, you were right. We *have* been living in a house of cards. And it's going to collapse on us at any moment."

Chapter Thirty-one

Sitting beside Cole in their handsome folding-top buggy, Jessica was filled with awe as they crossed the bridge over Monument Creek and entered the streets of Colorado Springs. Back in Colorado City, she'd insisted they leave their horses at Margery's Stable on the outskirts of town, and hire out the conveyance and team of matched grays, in order to enter the city in style. The fall day was cool, and in keeping with their spiffy image, Jessica was attired in her new serge traveling dress and jaunty hat; Cole wore his new black frock coat, fawn-colored trousers, and black western hat.

Jessica glanced about her eagerly while scribbling notes in her journal. Set amid rolling hills, Colorado Springs lay sprawled beneath the eastern face of the Rockies, with spectacular snow-capped Pike's Peak serving as a backdrop. Although the city was only of medium size, surely no more than five thousand people, it was the largest metropolis Jessica had seen since she'd journeyed back in time. She marveled at the sights they passed—the quaint street lamps, the peddlers with their vegetable, pastry, and cream cheese carts, the ice and milk wagons, the shoppers and businessmen in their elegant Victorian clothing, marching down boardwalks past clapboard storefronts, dormered hotels, mining offices, and liveries. And everywhere she looked were shade trees—ranging from paper birch to elm, cottonwood, poplar, pine, and spruce.

"I've never seen so many trees," Jessica remarked.

"I read once that one of the founders, Major McAllister, planted five thousand of them back in '73."

"Gracious."

As they turned north onto Nevada Avenue, Jessica was amazed at all the convalescent homes and rooming houses lining the street, with invalids crowding the verandas and yards in their chaise lounges, huddling beneath quilts and clutching books. "My heavens," she remarked to Cole. "I knew Colorado Springs was once a mecca for the sick, but I never quite imagined this."

"It's the clean air and high altitude," he replied. "Both known to improve the lot of those with consumption and other lung ailments. Lots of miners end up here. Wish this place had been around back when my stepdaddy took sick."

She touched his hand and smiled. "I'm sorry, Cole."

"Well, we can be happy the facilities are here now." He gestured at a massive edifice to the east of them. "Though the new St. Francis Hospital is already full to capacity, I hear."

"There's a lot of need here," she remarked.

"Sure is. Much of it caused by Miser and his cohorts."

Guiding the team around a corner and heading west on Pike's Peak Avenue, Cole pointed ahead to a massive gray stone structure. "That's the Antlers Hotel, built by General Palmer, one of the town's founders."

Jessica studied the large Tudor masterpiece with its towers, cupolas, and dormers. "It's magnificent. May we stay there?"

333

"Sure, sugar, if that's what you want."

"Don't forget you must register as Clay Lively, not Cole Reklaw. And we'll need separate rooms again."

"Aw, shucks."

She wrinkled her nose at him. "Although there might be some shenanigans after-hours."

"Like there were last night?" he teased.

As they pulled up to the hotel, a valet in red uniform and cap rushed forward. "May I see to your buggy and team, sir?"

"Sure." Cole handed the man a coin.

"I'll have a man bring in your luggage, sir."

Cole alighted and helped Jessica down. A smiling doorman held open the front door, and they entered the massive lobby with its richly patterned Brussels carpet, its high ceilings and brass and glass chandeliers, its handsome walnut furnishings. Not far from the front desk, two smartly attired gentlemen were smoking cigars and playing cards; as Jessica passed, both men popped to their feet, offered clipped bows, and murmured "Madam" with definite British inflection. Jessica nodded back, amused by the men's continental style suits, their well-waxed, curling mustaches and slicked-back hair parted down the middle.

Behind her, Cole whispered, "Lots of English fellas in this town. Reckon that's why they call it 'Little London.' "

"Ah," she murmured.

They paused before the massive desk, also fashioned of finest carved walnut, with an amazing brass sculpture of a big-horned sheep perched at one end.

"May I help you, sir?" inquired the clerk, a short, thin man in a black suit.

"Yes. Two rooms," pronounced Cole. "One for me, and one for the lady—er, my cousin."

"Yes, sir. Our rooms run two dollars a day, but that's including meals. And would you like views of Pike's Peak? It's two bits extra."

Cole winked at Jessica. "Sure, why not?"

"All our rooms are equipped with gas light," the clerk continued, "and there are two—er—bathing facilities on each floor. Do you wish to have telephones in your rooms? That's another ten cents."

"Hot damn!" declared Cole. "Telephones, eh? You folks really are highfalutin'."

"Yes, General Palmer had us add them to some of the rooms, for our most particular guests."

"We'd love to have telephones," Jessica told the man, mainly because she wanted to see one of the quaint devices herself.

Cole registered them, and the desk clerk handed him two keys. "I've got you on the second floor, and your cousin next door. I assume that will suffice, sir?"

"Oh, yes."

"You can take the elevator up, sir."

"Elevator, eh?" Cole repeated. To Jessica he bragged, "Don't worry, I know all about those newfangled conveyances. I rode in one out at the mines."

"My, I'm so impressed," Jessica replied drolly.

They strolled down the opulent carpet to the ornate wrought-iron elevator cage. A bellhop stepped forward. "May I take you up, sir?"

"Sure. Only take care not to scare the lady, will you? She's never been in one of these contraptions before."

The clerk said, "Of course, sir."

Cole patted Jessica's hand. "Don't worry, honey. I'll get you through it. It'll even be fun."

She rolled her eyes.

The clerk opened a folding gate and bid them enter the small cage. Stepping inside after them, he asked, "Which floor, sir?"

"Two."

The man shut both doors and the car lurched upward.

"Hey, take it easy," Cole scolded.

"Yes, sir."

Cole squeezed Jessica's arm. "Don't fret, honey. We're just moving."

Jessica burst out laughing, and Cole shot her a perplexed look.

When the door opened on the next floor, Cole stuck his head outside and glanced about warily. He turned back to Jessica and offered his arm. "It's safe," he assured her.

"You're so funny," she declared, stepping out.

Cole followed, muttering a thank you to the man.

Cole unlocked Jessica's door and followed her inside, whistling at the opulent expanse of rose-colored, brocaded wallpaper, a pink, cut-glass chandelier dripping with prisms, the mahogany four-poster bed and dressing table, and a tufted red velvet Duncan Phyfe settee.

"You happy, sugar?"

Jessica stared in awe at green silk brocade draperies, and roller shades painted with rosy-cheeked cherubs. "I'm overwhelmed. It's like a bordello."

"Bordello?" he scoffed.

"Well, it's very Victorian."

"Woman, I'll never understand you and your loco way of talking."

Before she could respond, there was a knock at the door. Jessica threw Cole a warning look, and he ducked through a side door into his adjoining room. She admitted the bellhop with her luggage. She tipped the man, then opened the French doors and stepped out onto the balcony with its charming wicker chairs. She gazed at the spectacular view of Pike's Peak, its snowy pinnacle agleam in a misty shaft of sunlight. Directly below her on the railroad tracks, a magnificent steam engine of the Denver and Rio Grande sat huffing smoke into the blue heavens as passengers from the adjacent station house boarded the old-style Pullman cars. Jessica could only shake her head at this scene as charming as a Currier and Ives painting.

Cole stepped out to join her. "What a view!"

336

A brisk breeze stirred; Jessica rubbed her arms. "Yes, it's fabulous. Did the bellhop drop off your luggage?"

Cole draped an arm about her shoulders. "Yeah. We shouldn't be disturbed again. Come on back in, honey. You're shivering."

After Cole shut the doors behind them, his gaze came to rest on the antique black telephone sitting on a tea table. "Hot damn, guess that's the telephone. Never seen one before, though I heard you can use it to talk to folks who are far away."

"Try it," suggested Jessica.

Cole strode over to the phone and picked up the receiver, holding it in his hand and staring at it in perplexity. Jessica joined him, and he scowled as both could hear the faint sound of a woman's voice.

He examined the receiver from various angles, his frown deepening. "Hey, there's a woman trapped in there somewhere."

Jessica laughed. "No, silly, her voice is being transmitted through the phone wires. Just put the receiver up to your ear." Taking his hand, she demonstrated, lifting the receiver and positioning it against his ear and mouth. "There. Now listen."

Cole listened intently, then lowered the receiver and whispered, "She's talking again. What am I supposed to do?"

"Listen to what she's saying, and talk back."

He lifted the receiver again. At last, with a perplexed frown, he said, "No, lady, I don't have a number, but I do have a name. You want to hear it?" There was a brief pause, then he added, "Well, you don't have to be nasty about it."

Jessica convulsed with laughter.

Cole lowered the receiver and glowered. "What are you laughing about? I heard a click and now the lady isn't there anymore."

"She hung up on you."

"She *what*?"

Jessica took the receiver from Cole's hand and placed it in its cradle. "She wanted to know the number of the party you wanted to speak with."

"Their *number*? That makes no sense. Why should I give her a number for some other person, when everybody already has a name?"

"Cole, you're so funny. If this has got you mystified, I'll never be able to explain twentieth-century technology to you."

"Huh?"

"In my time, we don't even have to speak with operators to make calls. We just punch numbers on telephones and we can contact any person in the entire world."

"Yeah?" He eyed her askance.

"In my time, we have elevators, but they don't need operators either. We run them ourselves. We get inside them, punch some numbers, and rise dozens of stories in only seconds."

Cole slowly shook his head. "So, you claim you come from a time of numbers. I come from a time of names. I reckon I like my time better."

Her expression turned wistful. "You know, Cole, you may be smarter than I thought. But you still don't believe me about being from another time, do you?"

He slowly shook his head.

She clutched his hands and spoke passionately. "Cole, I wish you would open up your mind just a little."

"Open my mind to something that makes no sense?"

"But it *does* make sense," she argued. "Even now, here, as we stand, the seeds of the twentieth century, of modern technology, are being planted."

"How so?"

"Well, the telegraph has been in existence for decades. Edison has already invented the light bulb. Unless my history fails me, working models of airplanes have already been flown, and even now the first prototypes of automobiles using the Daimler internal combustion engine are in the works. Surely you're familiar with such developments?"

He shrugged. "I read an occasional newspaper."

"Why is it so difficult for you to believe that these inventions will be further developed and enhanced? One day we'll have jet airplanes soaring across the skies, carrying people across countries and continents. We'll have automobiles taking people about their daily tasks, and rockets flying astronauts to the moon. Where now, people's voices can travel far distances, soon their images will be flashed across the airways, as well, though the magic of television. We'll be entertained by motion pictures, gorgeous images dancing across huge screens to the accompaniment of incredibly authentic sound. Fantastic machines called computers will provide information, and link the world together. And soon, visionaries such as H. G. Wells will write about this marvelous world to come."

Cole whistled. "You have quite an imagination, sugar."

"Cole, it's all true."

"If it's true, it sounds like a plumb haywire world to me."

She smiled. "It is a very complicated world, and this world is simpler, more genteel in some ways. Still, there are some marvelous discoveries coming in the future—like miracle drugs and vaccines that can wipe out common illnesses that kill scores of people in these times."

He hauled her close. "Hush now. I've heard enough. I don't like the world you describe—a world of machines and numbers. I like my world of people—and names. Like your name. Like *Jessie*. I like you saying *my* name when we're alone."

"*Cole,*" she whispered.

He smiled, reaching out to touch the tip of her nose with his index finger. "But you know, I think Miss Jessie has been pulling Mr. Cole's leg."

"I haven't," she insisted.

He nodded toward the four-poster bed with its blue velvet counterpane. "And she's about to get her comeuppance."

Jessica grinned and curled her arms around Cole's neck. "Now, *that* she's counting on."

"Then maybe Miss Jessie is smart enough to explain somethin' to me," he went on teasingly.

"Yes?"

"How come I had to rent two beds, when we'll only be using one?"

Jessica laughed. "Well, we could try your bed for variety."

Cole grinned. "Now you're talking."

It was early afternoon by the time Cole and Jessica, well sated and freshly groomed, emerged from her room. Downstairs at the desk, they inquired about newspapers in town, and the clerk told them of several, including the *Little London Times*, the *Colorado Springs Daily Chronicle*, and the *Republic*. Since the *Times* and the *Chronicle* weren't far from the hotel, they decided to walk to both offices.

They stopped first at the tiny *Times* office on Pikes Peak Avenue, only to find the front door locked. Even as they were turning away, a voice with a cultured British accent inquired, "May I help you, madam, sir?"

Jessica turned to see a tall, slender, elegantly dressed gentleman approaching them. "Yes—do you work here at the *Times*?"

"Indeed, I do. I'm the editor, William Sackett, just returning from luncheon."

Jessica offered her hand. "I'm Jessica Garrett and this is my cousin, Mr. Clay Lively."

Sackett shook Jessica's hand, then Cole's. "What can I do for you?"

Cole answered, "We were hoping you might spare a few minutes for us, sir."

"For what purpose?"

Jessica and Cole glanced at each other; then she replied, "To discuss Elijah Miser."

The man's face lit up. "Ah, Elijah. Funny you should mention him, as he's one of my favorite people. Indeed, I just had a delightful lunch with him and several other friends at the El Paso Club. If you're here to give a testimonial to Elijah, I'm ready to record it."

Half-panicked at this pronouncement, Jessica glanced at Cole, and he spoke to Sackett. "Actually, sir, that won't be necessary. We're sorry to have wasted your time."

And he pulled Jessica away with him, leaving Sackett to stare after them in puzzlement.

"Don't you think you were a little abrupt?" Jessica asked.

Cole sighed. "No sense wasting our time if he's Miser's best friend. If we'd told him more, he might have warned Miser."

"I suppose you're right," Jessica agreed wearily. "I hope we'll have better luck next time."

Their next stop was at the *Colorado Springs Daily Chronicle* office, obviously a much more substantial enterprise, ensconced in a two-story white frame building on Platte Avenue. As they stepped inside the front office, Jessica marveled at the quaint setup—the old-fashioned printing press thrumming away, the clerks scurrying about with papers.

A harried-looking man looked up at Jessica and Cole from the front desk. "Yes?"

Jessica answered, "We'd like to speak with your editor."

"Mr. Battle. At the back."

They wended their way through the clutter, pausing before the desk of a rotund, balding man in a striped brown suit; he was peering through his thick spectacles at a typewritten article.

"Are you Mr. Battle?" Jessica asked.

Startled, the man struggled to his feet. "Yes, ma'am."

341

Eugenia Riley

Jessica offered her hand. "I'm Jessica Garrett and this is my cousin, Mr. Lively. We're visiting from Mariposa."

"I see." Battle shook hands with Jessica, then Cole. "What may I do for you folks?"

Jessica flashed her most ingratiating smile. "Do you have a few moments to chat with us?"

The man hesitated, then reluctantly nodded. "Yes, but only a few. Please, have a seat and state your business."

After all three were seated, Jessica offered her most winning smile. "First, I have a question for you."

"Very well."

"What is your opinion of Elijah Miser?"

The man's gaze narrowed suspiciously. "Why do you ask?"

Cole answered, "Let's just say we've had dealings with Miser and we don't cotton to him. What about you, sir?"

Battle frowned for a long moment. "Though I'll deny this if you ever try to quote me, I think the man is a scoundrel. I've lost patience with him due to his attempts to influence the *Chronicle*'s editorial policy. Mostly, I try to steer clear of him and his cutthroat associates on the consortium board."

Jessica and Cole exchanged a relieved look.

"At any rate, folks, I've a deadline here. Please tell me why you're here."

"Very well." Leaning toward him, Jessica confided, "I thought the *Chronicle* might be interested in conditions out at the mines Miser and his cronies own near Mariposa."

"You mean the Aspen Gulch Mines?"

"Yes," Jessica replied. "Miser's been victimizing the citizens of Mariposa for far too long, through deplorable conditions at the mines. And surely, given your feelings about the man, you'll want to write an exposé on him."

Battle whistled. "Wait a minute, miss. You're correct that there is no love lost between Miser and me, but he's also a respected citizen of this town. Moreover, Colorado Springs was built on mining. If I published such unsub-

342

stantiated allegations as yours, I'd be tarred and feathered and ridden out of town on a rail."

"The allegations aren't unsubstantiated," Jessica argued. She gestured at Cole. "My cousin has lived in the area much longer than I have. Mr. Lively, would you explain to Mr. Battle what we mean?"

Cole gave a brief history of the mines, including the various cave-ins over the years and the alarming conditions now. He described his recent visit to the eastern branch. "That hillside is ready for a major collapse," he concluded.

Battle tapped a pencil and scowled. "Perhaps what you tell me is true. But you still haven't explained why I should publish something about this."

"How about so a bully will be set in his place?" Jessica demanded. "And so you won't have the deaths of dozens of miners on your conscience?"

Battle groaned. "Miss, please."

"And you must know Miser is planning to run for U.S. senator," Jessica continued irately. "As a citizen of this state, do you really think he should be representing us?"

Though his expression was troubled, Battle slowly shook his head. "I see your point, and I want to help you. I'm just not sure I can."

Jessica surged to her feet. "Very, well, then. Mr. Lively and I will visit every newspaper in this town until someone does help us."

Battle sighed. "Pardon me, miss, but you'll be wasting your time. Miser has Will Sackett of the *Times* in his back pocket, and I doubt the *Republic* will give you the time of day, either. For that matter, don't count on *anyone* in the Springs daring to cross Miser."

Jessica's chin shot up. "Really? Then I'll go to the *Rocky Mountain News* or *The Denver Post*, and get one of them to write an exposé—beginning with the fact that your cowardly publication tried to bury the truth."

That barb met its mark. Red-faced, Battle surged to his

Eugenia Riley

feet. "Young woman, this is blackmail. You have no right whatsoever to try to intimidate me. Though I'm sympathetic to your cause, I'm in no position to help. Threats will get you nowhere."

Jessica faced him down. "Oh, really? I predict my threats will get me into print."

Battle glared at her, and when she didn't back down, he waved a hand wearily. "Please, miss, sit back down."

Jessica sat down and grinned. Battle followed suit, rolling his eyes at Cole. "Is your cousin always so obstinate?"

"Oh, yes," he confirmed proudly.

Jessica continued earnestly. "Mr. Battle, I'm offering you a scoop. The information is going to be published, one way or another. Why shouldn't you be the first to print the truth?"

Appearing to waver, Battle scratched his jaw. "What about a compromise to get this started? Say, a brief mention in tomorrow's edition that the mines may be unsafe, and that the *Chronicle* will be doing further investigation."

"I'm not sure that would meet my expectations—"

Battle clenched a fist on his desk top. "Miss, you may have your expectations, but I have standards for this paper. I cannot possibly publish anything more substantial without first sending a reporter out to the mines to see conditions for himself."

Jessica hesitated.

"He's right, Jessie," Cole put in.

Sighing, she nodded to Battle. "Very well. But I'll count on seeing at least my basic accusation in tomorrow's paper."

"You will. And may I publish your name as the one responsible for it?"

"Of course."

Battle grinned. "And what should I do when Miser comes storming down here wanting your head—and mine?"

Jessica proudly rose. "Why, you may tell him to call me. Room 226, the Antlers."

"Yes, ma'am," agreed Battle, standing to shake her hand.

Seconds later as they swept out the front door, Jessica noted Cole regarding her with wry amusement. "What's with you?"

Cole carefully took Jessica's arm and linked it through his. "Remind me never to cross you, woman."

Chapter Thirty-two

"You look too gorgeous for words, sugar," Cole said.

"You look pretty spiffy yourself," Jessica replied.

That evening, they sat in the elegant dining room of the Antlers, their table awash in soft gaslight as they ate succulent grilled rainbow trout and drank the finest French wine. Jessica wore her rose-colored gown with its puffed sleeves and low neckline, Cole his black frock coat and a fresh shirt. He was clean-shaven and had never looked more handsome. Around them, other elegantly attired guests ate and talked quietly while obsequious waiters roved about, serving foods and refilling wineglasses.

"I love your hair," Cole continued thoughtfully, staring at her glistening curls, "all piled up fancy-like on top of your head. Makes a fella ache to tumble it down over your shoulders."

His eyes were so ardent, his voice so husky, that Jessica felt her pulse quickening. There was no doubt at all about what would follow dinner. She flashed him a grin. "You're in a romantic mood tonight."

He chuckled, his gaze settling on her daring decolletage. "Sugar, what do you expect, with you all gussied up like that?"

"So it's just my appearance that excites you?"

"Not just," he replied, a teasing light gleaming in his eyes. "Hot damn, I was proud of you today."

"You mean with Mr. Battle?"

"Yes, ma'am. Who woulda thought a delicate-looking female like you could be such a pistol?"

"And I shall continue being a pistol until we get what we want. The power of the press can be awesome, Cole."

He shook his head. "I've just never known a female with notions as outlandish as yours."

"Maybe that's because I'm not from here."

He groaned.

"Am I opening up your mind just a little?"

He reached across the table, clutching her hand. "Maybe I'm unwilling to accept the notion that you might belong somewhere else—or that I might lose you."

She smiled at him tenderly, touched that he had confided in her. "There is so much I don't understand—so I can't blame you for being baffled by it all."

He squeezed her hand. "You know what I wish for at moments like this?"

"What?"

"That we could be married."

Much as Jessica felt thrilled, she was also torn. "Then what? Will you give up your life of crime?"

"Lawlessness and family life don't exactly mix, do they?" His expression turned wistful. "You know, today as we were passing those convalescent homes, I kept thinking about my second pa, Joseph Reklaw."

She nodded. "Your ma told me he died of miner's lung not long after Billy was born."

"Yes, but he was around till I was almost ten, and he was a good pa. Used to take me and the younger boys hunting and fishing. Always lent an ear when we needed one. I miss those days, Jessie. Maybe that's why I keep thinking about us getting hitched and having young ones of our own."

"Those are lovely thoughts, Cole."

He met her gaze solemnly. "And if we do have children, I want to be around for them. I don't want them losing their pa when they're young, like I did."

"Then you'll just have to change, won't you?"

He smiled. "You miss your own family, don't you?"

"Oh, yes. More than you can know."

"Then we want and need the same things, sugar, and there's not much time to waste." His foot nudged hers under the table. "Doin' what we're doin', there could always be a young 'un. In fact, we might want to get hitched before we leave the Springs."

Jessica felt color flooding her face. "Let's not get too far ahead of ourselves, Cole."

" 'Sides, the gang is sure to be found out before long. In fact, I think several menfolks at the church are already wise to us, and are only keeping their silence because they admire what the gang has done for the miners."

She nodded. "I agree. So what would you do?"

"We have quite a grubstake saved up. We could all move out west—Wyoming Territory, maybe. Buy a big ranch." He winked. "Get married, all of us, and have lots of babies."

"That's a lovely plan, Cole. But what if *I* move on in the meantime?"

He shook his head. "Jessie, I still can't even believe you come from another time. How can you expect me to believe you might return there?"

"Will you not believe me unless I disappear?" she demanded.

"You won't disappear. I won't let you."

"I wish I could share your confidence. But after seeing Buck Lynch and Sheriff Lummety yesterday, I'm not so sure."

"You know, you oughta be glad I'm willing to marry a

woman who's plumb haywire," he teased. "Hot as a tempest and lovelier than spring, but crazier than a barking squirrel, anyhow."

Jessica laughed despite herself. "Perhaps the apt expression is 'crazy like a fox'."

He lifted his wineglass. "I'll drink to that." After they toasted, he cleared his throat. "So what will you have us do tomorrow?"

"First, we'll see if Battle keeps his word and publishes the article."

"Then what?"

She grinned. "Start playing some more hardball. We can see the town and go shopping in the meantime."

Cole didn't respond for a moment, turning to watch several musicians with stringed instruments ascend the dais and sit down. As the lovely strains of a Strauss waltz began, he grinned and said, "For now, you can waltz with me."

"Why, I'd be honored," she said.

He stood and offered her his hand; then they strolled to the dance floor together. He led her over the floor to the buoyant tune, waltzing expertly.

"Where did you learn to dance like this?" she asked.

He chuckled. "You'll kill me if I tell you."

"I'll kill you if you don't."

"Me and the boys learned in Old Town," he confessed. "At the dancing parlors."

"Did Lila teach you?" she asked.

"She did." He sighed. "Hope that doesn't make you mad."

She wrinkled her nose at him. "It makes me want to take you upstairs and rip your clothes off."

Cole laughed as he spun her into a turn. "Now, that can be arranged."

Indeed, when they went upstairs to her room, they began kissing each other the instant they were inside the door. His mouth pressing eagerly into hers, Cole pulled at the pins in Jessica's hair, stepping back to watch her curls fall down upon her shoulders.

He caught a shaky breath. "Oh, honey, do you look a beautiful sight, with that tumbled hair and your mouth wet from my kisses. I'm gonna eat you up alive tonight."

"I'm counting on it," she said breathlessly.

He tore off his jacket, threw it across the bed. "Turn around."

She complied, and felt his impatient fingers working the buttons on her gown. Soon he lifted the rustling gown up over her shoulders, folding it over the footboard of the bed.

His eyes devoured her in her petticoats and camisole. His finger traced the lacy edge of her bodice, raising gooseflesh. "How I love that frilly stuff."

She gasped.

"Am I making you hot?"

"Oh, yes. Now you." She reached for the studs on his shirt.

But he backed away, grinning wickedly. "Not yet. I have a better idea."

As she watched, puzzled, he went to the armoire and retrieved both their dressing gowns. He draped hers across her shoulders. "Stay right there."

"Cole, what are you doing?"

He didn't respond, but went to the door, opened it, and poked his head outside. Turning, he grabbed a couple of towels from a nearby stand. "Come on, the coast is clear."

She gasped. "Cole, what on earth is on your devious mind now? I can't go out into the hallway like this!"

"Sure you can."

With these words, Cole grabbed Jessica's hand and pulled her, laughing and protesting, out into the hallway. Quickly they raced down to the end of the corridor; then he pulled her inside the bathroom, shut and locked the door. He turned around and grinned triumphantly. "Now I've got you."

Jessica gazed about at the room, quite large by modern standards, with its old-fashioned toilet with pull chain, washbasin with painted china bowl, and huge claw-foot tub. "Cole! You can't be serious!"

Chuckling, he went to the tub, put in the cork stopper, and turned on both hot and cold water. "Ever since I first saw you bathing on our back porch, I've wanted to make love to you in a bathtub. Now I'm gonna."

"No!" she protested.

"Yes," he rejoined wickedly.

"But—this is a public bathroom—someone could interrupt—"

"Not with the door locked." He leaned indolently against a cabinet. "Now take everything off. I want to watch."

"Cole!"

He straightened and pulled her close. "Don't fight me, Jessie. At home we aren't free to play like this."

She eyed him askance. "I just think we need more privacy."

He caught her hand and pressed his fingers to his swollen manhood. "Honey, we have *everything* we need."

She gulped.

He leaned over, pushed aside her hair, and nibbled at her ear, tickling it with his tongue. She moaned.

Softly he whispered, "Please let me have everything my way tonight."

She pulled back, cheeks hot. "Everything?"

He solemnly touched the tip of her nose. "Everything."

She chewed her lower lip. "And do I get everything my way next time?"

"Sure you do."

"Very well," she agreed primly.

Grinning at her demure response, he backed away. "Now strip."

Jessica complied, slowly removing her camisole, her

351

petticoats, then finally her bloomers, while Cole stood eating her up with his eyes. At last she stood naked, chest heaving as she absorbed his passionate stare.

"What now?" she managed.

He moved closer, reaching out to touch a taut nipple, as steam from the bath rose between them. She closed her eyes and shivered, transported by his touch.

"You're so beautiful," he whispered. "So tight. Already you're aroused for me."

"Oh, yes."

He leaned over and turned off the faucets. "Get in the tub."

Trembling, she complied. The warm water enveloping her body only enhanced the passion coursing through her.

Cole stood at the foot of the tub, staring down at her naked body. "When I first saw you like this, you were all closed up like a tight little rosebud. Now I want you open to me."

"I am, Cole."

His expression turned devilish. "Spread your legs so I can see everything."

She gasped, equally mortified and fascinated at the prospect of his having such an unrestricted view of her charms.

"Am I making you blush, Jessie?"

"God, yes."

"That's what I want."

"Cole—"

"Now do it. Remember, *everything* my way."

Burning to her very core, Jessica spread her thighs wide, heat shooting up her face as Cole drank her in.

"Oh, sugar—you're so damn lovely." Cole sank to his knees beside her and rolled up his sleeve. He dipped a hand into the water, touching the valley between her thighs, moving his fingers back and forth, touching, teasing, raising moans from her. He leaned over and caught her lips in a leisurely, drugging kiss. Then he pushed two fingers inside her—

Jessica sobbed, her tight tissues throbbing at the unexpected, unyielding pressure, then giving way to a hot flood of pleasure.

"You like that, eh?"

She nodded, shivered, and bit her hand.

"Scoot a little closer."

She froze.

"Don't just go wide-eyed on me. Do it."

She slid downward, and his finger invaded more deeply. Shudders of ecstasy shook her.

"What pleasures you the most?" he asked. "What's your hottest spot, sugar?" He pressed even deeper, until she squirmed, then pushed upward.

Cole soon had his answer as she cried out. Kissing her all the while, he stroked the spot relentlessly. She panted and moved against his hand. But just as she was about to climax, there came a knock at the door.

Jessica panicked and tried to push Cole's hand away. He refused to budge, shooting her a warning glance and whispering fiercely, "No!"

"But there's someone outside!" she whispered.

Cole only grinned, even as an annoyed male voice out in the hallway inquired, "Is someone in there?"

"Yeah!" Cole yelled back irritably. "It's occupied. Get lost." He turned back to Jessica. "Now come for me."

Though his words excited her wildly, she was equally horrified. "Have you lost your mind? There's a *man* outside!"

"There's a man in here, and he's gonna have his way with you," Cole retorted stubbornly. "Now start moving, woman."

About to die from mingled mortification and passion, Jessica realized it was futile to argue further with her determined lover. She moved tentatively against Cole's fingers. With a groan, he leaned over and took her mouth with a French kiss while boldly twisting his fingers. She lost all control, whimpering, moving frenziedly, succumbing to an ecstasy she'd never known before.

Seconds later, he pulled back, smiling into her dazed, breathless face. "How 'bout that?"

"Wonderful," she gasped. "But please, let's go."

"Nope," he replied proudly. "My turn now."

"Cole!"

If he had ever doubted he would linger to take his own pleasure, the scandalized look on Jessie's face convinced Cole he would stay. How he loved making her blush and squirm. Watching her take her pleasure had touched him deeply. He stood and quickly stripped off his clothing. Excitement stormed through him anew as he caught her eyeing him, her gaze riveted on his swollen shaft. "You want it, sugar?"

"Oh, yes."

He stepped closer to the tub. "Then prove it."

Her sexy, glistening flesh had never looked more enchanting as she rose to her knees. When her face moved close to his manhood, when he could feel her warm breath on his throbbing flesh, he thought he might explode then and there. Then her hot, delicate tongue contacted the sensitive tip of the shaft, and the pleasure all but staggered him. At once her arms came up around him and her slick fingers dug into his butt, nestling him closer.

"My God," he groaned.

"Your turn to be tortured, cowboy," she whispered back.

So the lady had a few tricks in store for him, too. It was, indeed, torture. Cole thought he might die as Jessica teased him, drawing her tongue over him in tormenting circles. He breathed hard, his manhood now so engorged it hurt. Then her hot mouth closed over him and she sucked him in.

Cole clenched his eyes shut and struggled to hold on to what remained of his control. Her mouth was sweet, her tongue downright sinful. She drew him in deeper—

That did it. In a flash Cole was beside her in the tub, drawing her astride him, then thrusting powerfully. She was burning inside, tight and slick. She cried out softly and he clutched her close. "My Lord, sugar, am I hurting you?"

"In the best possible way," she sobbed back.

Cole's control was beyond him now, and he plundered her slender body, losing himself in decadent bliss. She was so eager, welcoming his deep thrusts, kissing him all over, whimpering softly, and his heart was bursting at her sweet, trusting surrender. Their coupling was fierce, near-violent, hot, wet, splashy. Within seconds they exploded together, shuddering and clinging to one another.

At last they pulled apart to stare at each other in awe, their bodies still tightly locked.

Cole gently stroked her cheek. "Sugar, are you all right?"

Her smile lit his soul. "I'm wonderful."

"Oh, Jessie." Bursting with emotion, he leaned over and tenderly kissed her. "I love you, sugar."

Tears spilled from her eyes. "I love you, too, Cole."

"Oh, honey." Deeply touched by her words, he looked down at her face, then brushed a tear from her cheek. "What's this? Don't cry."

"They're tears of joy."

Cole snuggled her close again, his arms trembling at the feel of her firm, slick breasts against his chest. "I know what you mean, sugar. I'm about ready to bust out crying myself."

She nestled her head under his chin and sighed happily.

They held each other for a long, languid moment; then he glanced about and spotted the floor. "Damn, sugar, look at all that water. Did we make a mess!"

"Do you suppose the gentleman is still waiting outside?"

"Naw—but we'd best clear out, anyway."

They quickly dried each other off, emptied out the bath, donned their dressing gowns, mopped up the floor as best they could, and grabbed their things. But when they stepped outside, both did a double take; Jessica was appalled to note that they had drawn a crowd! A small contingent of guests stood in line waiting for the bath—and all were glowering at them in fierce disapproval. The contingent included an elderly gentleman in brocaded dressing gown, an old woman with a pince-nez, and a young train engineer still in his uniform.

Jessica blushed to the roots of her hair.

Cole merely grinned. "Sorry to keeping you waiting, folks, but the lady had some difficulty with her bath—you know, getting the stopper out."

Ignoring outraged comments and Jessica's horrified look, Cole grabbed her hand and pulled her away with him, laughing all the while.

Later, lying with Cole in the darkness, Jessica whispered, "Do you really mean what you said, Cole? Do you really love me?"

"God, yes, sugar." He kissed her brow. "In fact, when we get back, I'm only going to give you a few more days to adjust. Then we're getting hitched—even if I have to drag you to the altar."

Thrilled but also taken aback, she asked, "Does that mean you're willing to give up your outlaw ways?"

"Yep. I'm willing to do whatever it takes."

Rapt with new hope, she asked, "And you'll share with me—everything?"

"Yes. But you have to share with me, too."

Quietly, she asked, "Will you try to believe me, Cole?"

He sighed in the darkness. "I'll try, honey. But I won't ever let you go."

Tears burned Jessica's eyes again. "Please don't ever let me, go, Cole. Please don't—"

Jessica couldn't say the rest, didn't need to. Cole was kissing her again.

Chapter Thirty-three

The next morning, Cole brought the *Chronicle* in to Jessica with her breakfast tray. Setting the tray on her lap, he winked. "Well, you won, darlin'. Look at page three."

Jessica squealed with joy and tore open the paper. She found the small article and quickly read it:

Are the Aspen Gulch Mines Safe?
E. J. Battle, Editor

Miss Jessica Garrett, a visitor from Mariposa, has complained to the *Chronicle* regarding what she calls "deplorable" conditions at the Aspen Gulch Mines, owned by the Springs's own Elijah Miser and his Aspen Gulch Consortium. Miss Garrett claims that the entire eastern operation of the mine is on the verge of a major collapse, yet the consortium continues drilling.

Is Miss Garrett an alarmist, or are conditions at the mines truly as dangerous as she claims? The *Chronicle* intends to dispatch a reporter to the Mariposa area forthwith to investigate this troubling matter.

Finishing the article, Jessica clapped her hands. "Yes!"

"You're pleased?" Cole asked.

"Well, it could have been a little stronger, though I can understand Battle's taking a cautious approach at this stage. Still, it should be enough to wake up Miser."

"And how," Cole agreed. "Want to stick around till he comes storming over here—or telephones?"

"Of course not. I want to go out and have some fun."

"But what if he calls?"

"Let him sweat it. The hotel can take a message."

"Hardball, eh?" he teased.

"Yep. Hardball."

He reached out, toying with one of her curls. "I might just want to play a little *hardball* myself."

She smirked. "You already have."

They had great fun about town. They shopped and rode a horse-drawn trolley; at noontime, they had the blue plate special at a local drugstore.

Afterward, they retrieved the horses and carriage from the hotel stable and took a drive. As they ambled down a shady street lined with lovely birches and huge Victorian mansions, Cole pointed ahead at a massive stone house with wraparound verandas on both stories and towers at the ends. The handsome front door sported leaded-glass panels; a uniformed maid was sweeping the gallery, while out in the yard, a man was clipping the impeccable hedges.

"That's where Miser lives," he stated.

"Oh!" Jessica gasped. "Talk about conspicuous consumption! That's a house built on the misery of others."

"You said it, darlin'."

She sighed. "Let's go back to the hotel. Seeing that house just spoiled my day."

When they walked back inside the lobby of the Antlers, it was to face a flustered desk clerk. "Miss Garrett, thank God you've returned."

"Something wrong?" she asked.

"Heavens, yes. First, Mr. Battle came charging down here this morning, ranting that Mr. Elijah Miser has threatened to ruin him and it's all your fault." Lowering his voice to a conspiratorial whisper, the man added, "Then this gentleman"—he jerked a thumb toward a man who sat reading a newspaper about twenty feet away—"has been waiting for you all afternoon. And no one could find you."

Jessica glanced toward the familiar-looking stranger. "Who is he?"

"Miser's secretary," came the grim response.

"Ah, I must speak with him, then," she asserted.

"Good luck, miss."

She and Cole crossed the lobby and paused before the man, who was small and fair, with impeccable clothing and a well-waxed mustache. Jessica remembered him from the stage robbery, and was relieved when she spotted no recognition in his pale blue eyes as he glanced up at her and Cole.

Twirling her parasol, Jessica said, "Good afternoon, sir, I understand you've been waiting for us. I'm Jessica Garrett and this is my cousin, Mr. Lively. What can we do for you?"

Setting aside his paper, the man rose and gave them a cool stare. "I'm Calvin Stickles, miss, secretary to Mr. Elijah Miser. Mr. Miser would like to meet with you at once."

Jessica winked at Cole. "Of course."

Stickles escorted them outside to his handsome surrey, then drove them several blocks to a large brownstone building. Inside the posh edifice, they took an elevator to the third floor.

Stickles led them down the hallway to an imposing

Eugenia Riley

door with a frosted panel that read "Aspen Gulch Consortium." Opening the door, Stickles escorted them through the outer cubicle and into a spacious inner office.

Jessica at once recognized the thin, sharp-featured man seated behind the mahogany desk as Elijah Miser. She found him thoroughly unpleasant with hawkish features, shifty eyes hidden beneath bushy brows, and coarse gray-brown hair. To his left on a leather settee reposed a huge, pot-bellied, pug-nosed gentleman she also vaguely remembered.

Stickles addressed Miser. "Mr. Miser, may I introduce Miss Garrett and her cousin, Mr. Lively, both from Mariposa. Folks, this is Mr. Miser and his associate, Mr. Willard Peavy."

Miser stood, flashing his guests a nasty smile, then offered Jessica his hand. "Well, well, so you're the young woman who has maligned me."

Jessica ignored Miser's hand. "I wasn't aware that telling the truth was 'maligning.' "

Appearing taken aback, Miser dropped his hand to his side. "Ah, a young woman of spirit." He scowled at Cole. "You look familiar, sir. Have we met?"

Cole didn't even blink. "Not to my knowledge."

"Mr. Lively is a revered citizen of Mariposa," Jessica put in. "Very active in the church. You may have seen him there?"

Miser ignored her comment. "Sit down, both of you."

Seating herself in a chair next to Cole's, Jessica said sweetly, "What may we do for you, Mr. Miser?"

She noted with pleasure that his eyes flashed angrily. "What may you do? You may ask that contemptible coward, E. J. Battle, to print an immediate retraction of your lies in today's edition."

"Oh, I think not," Jessica responded demurely, smoothing her skirts.

Miser appeared stunned. "Your gall astounds me, young lady. Do you have any idea who I am?"

"I'm well aware of who you are."

"Are you? Then what are you planning to do when I sue you and that turncoat Battle for libel?"

Now Cole surged forward in his chair, shaking a fist. "Don't you go threatening the lady."

Jessica touched his arm. "It's all right, Mr. Lively." She turned to Miser. "I'm afraid, sir, that you have no case. As I understand it, the truth is always a defense against libel."

"How dare you!" he blustered.

"Yes, I dare. Furthermore, what do you intend to do when the *Chronicle* sends a reporter out to the mines to confirm my charges?"

"I'll let no yellow reporter into my mines."

"Then maybe he'll just interview the miners. How well would your sterling reputation hold up then?"

Miser pounded a fist, a muscle twitching in his cheek. "Battle wouldn't dare. Not after I got through with him this morning."

"Not everyone can be bullied by your threats, sir," Jessica went on coolly. "If Battle won't pursue this, I'll contact the *Rocky Mountain News*, or *The Denver Post*. I'll continue until your brand of cruel exploitation is completely exposed. That should do marvels for your senatorial campaign."

He glared. "Damn it, young woman, you don't know who you're dealing with! I'll see you crucified for this."

"Just try it," warned Cole.

All at once, the portly man stood. "A moment, Elijah."

"What is it?" Miser barked.

Peavy moved closer, offering Jessica a conciliatory smile. "Miss, may I ask you something?"

"Of course."

"Why are you doing this?"

She raised her chin. "Perhaps because I don't want to see dozens of miners—good men with families who depend on them—murdered in your deathtrap operation out at Aspen Gulch."

361

That accusation brought Miser out of his chair. "Murdered? Young woman, I'll have you know—"

But Peavy silenced Miser with a raised hand and a warning look. "A moment, Elijah."

His face a study in supreme frustration, Miser sat back down. Jessica could barely contain her glee.

Patiently, Peavy continued, "Miss, we're only businessmen. The mines bring us revenue, and also put food on the tables of the people of Mariposa. Is that so terrible?"

"It will be when most of those miners perish because you've over-tunneled the mines," Cole put in grimly.

Peavy shook his head. "What would you have us do, sir?"

"Close the mines," Jessica and Cole said in unison.

"What?" yelled Miser. "You're mad, both of you."

"No, you're mad not to do precisely what we're suggesting," Jessica retorted stoutly. "Besides, think of the good press."

Miser appeared mystified. "Good press?"

Jessica assumed her schoolteacher mien. "Yes, sir, there's good press and there's bad press. First, I'll tell you about the bad. It goes something like this: You're busy running for senator, and twenty miners die in Mariposa because the mountain collapses on them. Very bad press."

He glowered. "And the good?"

"You close the mines now, give all the miners a generous stipend that will feed their families until they can reestablish themselves in farming or other ventures."

Miser waved a hand. "Now I know you're out of your mind."

"Wait a minute, Elijah," put in Peavy. "Don't we have Aspen Gulch pretty much tapped out?"

"So what if we do?"

"Wouldn't it be better to close it down now rather than risk a major cave-in during your senatorial campaign?"

Miser rapped his fingertips on his desk.

"Not to mention, we've been plagued with all those

362

robberies out at Mariposa, and the Pinkertons haven't been able to catch the Reklaws."

At the mention of the gang, Jessica stole a glance at Cole and was pleased to note he didn't even blink.

Miser waved Peavy off. "I'll give it some thought."

"You may have until the end of the week," Jessica informed him. "Or I swear, you will rue the consequences."

Again Miser popped out of his chair. "Young woman, how dare you threaten me! I'm warning you—"

Jessica, too, rose. "No, I'm warning *you*, sir. Either we see an announcement in Friday's paper that you're planning to close the mines and pension the miners, or I promise you that within a fortnight, there will be a major exposé published here or in Denver detailing how you've exploited the downtrodden out in Mariposa."

"Young woman, that's blackmail!"

This time Cole answered proudly for Jessica. "No, sir, it's hardball."

Miser's expression was utterly perplexed as Jessica and Cole triumphantly turned and walked out of his office.

Chapter Thirty-four

"Who would have believed Miser would cave in?" Jessica said.

"After seeing you in action, who would doubt it?" Cole dryly replied. "I think the article in the *Republic* did the trick. Battle warned us that the *Republic*'s editor would never run a piece—but you convinced him."

"Yeah—although Miser was too proud to admit defeat to our faces."

Five days later, Cole and Jessica were on horseback, warmly dressed for the brisk fall weather, and riding close to home. They were navigating the narrow red dirt road snaking through the mountain passes east of Mariposa. Jessica took deep breaths of the crisp, evergreen-scented air and enjoyed her view of late-blooming wildflowers, stands of aspen turning colors, and above them, snow-capped peaks soaring into the hazy heavens.

Elijah Miser hadn't given up without a fight. But after Jessica had arranged for an article two days ago in the *Republic*—an in-depth piece that had accused Miser of abu-

sive conditions at the mines—Miser's associate Mr.
Peavy had called on Jessica and Cole, relaying the news
that Miser had agreed to their terms: He'd close the mines
and pension the miners if they would agree to leave town
and never darken the door of another Colorado Springs
newspaper.

"Do you suppose the news has reached Mariposa yet?"
she asked Cole.

"That Miser is closing the mines? I doubt it. I expect
the tidings will come from us first."

Jessica tapped the pocket of her shirt. "And I've got a
copy of Miser's announcement in yesterday's *Little London Times* to prove it."

Cole frowned. "Jessie, everyone in town may not be
thrilled. Some folks may even say we've gone meddling."

"Why?"

"Because mining has been this town's livelihood.
Sure, Miser is offering each miner a stipend to save face.
But folks in these parts will essentially have to start
over."

"It's better than letting all the men be killed."

"True—but I may have a better solution." He pointed
ahead at a fork in the road, at a narrow, twisting trail
heading north. "Let's turn off here."

"But that isn't the way home."

"I know. There's something I want to show you."

"You like being mysterious, eh?"

"Yep."

Though perplexed, Jessica followed Cole's lead as he
guided his horse up an obviously abandoned trail clogged
with roots and undergrowth. They ascended a hillside
dotted with yucca and piñon pine, finally pausing in a
clearing before an opening in the rock that was covered
with boards. A pitiful gray shack was collapsing on itself
off to one side, amid weeds and rubble.

"What's this, an abandoned mine?" Jessica asked.

Dismounting, Cole chuckled and approached her

horse. "I wouldn't call it a mine, darlin'," he said, offering his hand.

Accepting his assistance, she slid to her feet. "What would you call it?"

"A failed example of coyoting by a fool."

"Coyoting? What's that?"

"Come along and you'll see."

Cole moved aside some boards and he and Jessica crawled inside the dank, dark expanse. Wrinkling her nose at the unpleasant musty smell, she shivered as he lit a hurricane lantern, then gazed about at a small dirt room cluttered with boards, axes, and other debris. The room tunneled off into the mountain and ended in an obvious cave-in—a huge pile of broken rock.

"This excavation was started by a coyoter," Cole explained. "Coyoters are mavericks who dig mines on their own. Since they seldom bother with safety measures such as supporting timbers, most of 'em end up buried alive."

Jessica looked at the pile and grimaced. "You mean whoever started this mine—"

"Has likely returned to dust in that heap of debris yonder."

She shuddered. "Why did you bring me here?"

"For this." He strode to another corner of the small room and began moving aside rubble, revealing a medium-sized black box.

"A safe!" she cried. "So this is your cache, your hideout."

"Yep."

"It's not very big."

Cole flipped the dial and opened the safe. "Come have a look."

Jessica strode to his side and hunkered down, gazing at a number of gold bars and piles of currency. She whistled. "Wow. An impressive stash, but hardly the accumulation I'd expect from years and years of robberies. Where's the rest, Cole?"

He chuckled. "Here I am trusting you with the location of my hoard, and you're greedy for more, woman."

"Not greedy. It just doesn't make sense that this is all you'd have."

He shut the safe and stood, offering her a hand up. "It's not all, but it's enough."

"I agree. But what happened to the rest? Did you give it to your spy out at the mines?"

He grinned sheepishly. "What spy?"

"Come on, Cole, 'fess up. You have a spy, or you'd never have known when those shipments were coming through."

"All right, then, I'll confess. We do have a spy, an old friend of my real pa's, though I took a blood oath never to divulge his name. And, yes, we've compensated him well. But that isn't where the rest of our fortune is."

"Then where?"

"Remember when Billy and me went away for several days on business?"

"Yes. I thought you were off chasing women."

"Well, we weren't. Every couple of months, we take our plunder off to some small mining town, convert it to cash, and deposit the money in the local bank. That way, we have our wealth safeguarded in several banks in the state."

"Very smart of you."

He gestured toward the safe. "What we have here is our getaway money, the grubstake we'll use if we have to leave Colorado in a hurry."

"And the rest?"

"That's what I wanted to tell you about. The last time Billy and I were gone, I made some arrangements. I set up a trust for the miners of Mariposa and their families."

"You did?"

He took her hand and smiled at her tenderly. "I'm serious about what I've been telling you, sugar. You've gone and reformed me. I think all of us need to move on and make a fresh start, just like we discussed. And after we're gone—well, the rest of our fortune will go to the citizens

367

of Mariposa. It's only fitting that the miners get it. They dug it out of the ground, after all."

Deeply touched by his disclosures, Jessica flung herself into his arms. "Oh, Cole, I'm so proud of you! And I love you so much."

He clutched her close. "I love you, too, sugar. And as soon as the boys persuade their sweethearts, we'll all get hitched, then move on. Deal?"

"Deal!"

When they arrived at the farm, Jessica and Cole were bemused to note an unfamiliar buckboard parked in the yard. "Looks like someone's come calling," Cole muttered. "Wonder who."

"At least it doesn't look like a lawman," she remarked.

"Yeah."

They dismounted and walked inside to view an amazing scene in the parlor. Billy and Dumpling, appearing supremely happy, were seated on the settee together, with Dumpling's mother and father on either side of them. Ma was seated in the rocker, Gabe and Luke in the wing chairs. Wes squatted on the hearth.

Equally astounding, everyone was eating apple pie and drinking coffee.

Ma spotted Cole and Jessica first. Her weathered face split into a wide grin. "Well, speak of the devil. Welcome home, you two."

"Howdy, folks," Cole said with a perplexed frown. "Miss Wilma, Joshua, Miss Dumpling." He raised an eyebrow at his mother. "What's going on here?"

"Well, Bobby and Dumpling just made an announcement."

Before Cole or Jessica could comment, Dumpling burst out, "Bobby and me is engaged. He asked my pa and Pa said yes!"

"Yeah, we're gonna get hitched!" added an exuberant Billy.

"Well, this is wonderful news," said Cole, grinning.

"Indeed," added Jessica. "Congratulations to you both."

As the betrothed couple beamed, Ma glowered at Gabe. "Well, don't just set there. Offer the lady your chair."

"Yes, ma'am." Gabe shot to his feet. "Miss Jessie."

"Thanks." She sat down.

Ma struggled to her feet. "I'll go fetch Jessie and Clay some pie and coffee so's they can help us celebrate."

After Ma lumbered out of the room, Cole grinned at Dumpling and Billy. "When did you two decide this?"

"A few days after you left," said Billy.

"Well, it's great news."

Joshua was eyeing Cole and Jessica curiously. "If you don't mind my asking, Clay, where have you two been?"

With a wave of his hand, Cole deferred to Jessica.

"Mr. Lively and I went to Colorado Springs," she explained.

Both Wilma and Joshua appeared shocked. "Without a chaperon?" Wilma asked.

Joshua winked at Jessica. "Now, you two ain't kissing cousins, are you?"

As the boys chuckled, Jessica felt herself blushing. "Actually, the trip was business. We decided to play a little hardball with the Aspen Gulch Consortium."

"You did? What do you mean?" asked Joshua.

Jessica glanced questioningly at Cole, and he said to Joshua, "Guess we may as well tell you, since the news will be out soon enough. Jessie here persuaded Elijah Miser to close the mines."

"She did?" Joshua appeared quite taken aback. "But what about the town?"

"There's not much future for the town once the mine collapses," Cole said. "You know it's on the verge, Joshua."

"And Mr. Miser will be paying each miner a stipend

369

for two years," Jessica went on. "Enough to get you by till you can get started at something else—farming or ranching, perhaps."

At this bit of news, Joshua appeared somewhat less crest-fallen. "Well, then there could be cause for celebration. Aside from Dumpling and Bobby's good tidings, that is." He grinned at Cole. "And after the mischief you two have been up to, I'm betting Miss Garrett's people may show up with shotguns to make you two do the right thing."

While Jessica was wishing she did have "people" here to share her joy, the boys laughed and Cole winked at her. "I'm more than willing," he said.

"Wonderful!" declared Wilma, clapping her hands.

"And there may be even more good news," put in Gabe.

"Oh?" Wilma questioned.

Luke spoke up. "Yeah, the rest of us boys ain't gonna let Bobby out-trump us and beat us to the altar. Ain't that right, Co— er, Clay?"

"Yep," agreed Cole proudly, his gaze fixed tenderly on Jessica. "Looks like there will be a *lot* of weddings in these parts before long."

After the Hicks family had left, and Ma had gone into the kitchen to prepare supper, Gabe, Wes, and Luke continued to tease Billy. Gabe drawled, "Hey, Wesley, Luke, looks like we got us some sparkin' to catch up on or brother Billy may show us up good."

With a derisive laugh, Luke added, "Aw, I think Billy needs a head start on the rest of us—considering it may take one of them newfangled steam wagons to push Miss Dumpling up the aisle."

Muttering a curse, Billy shot to his feet. "I warned you rascals not to insult my Dumpling!"

"Boys, hold it," put in Cole wearily. "Jessie and I are tired, so quit your bickering. And aren't you forgetting something?"

Blank looks greeted his question.

Jessica filled the gap. "You're outlaws, all of you. How do you propose to marry women from these parts?"

"Easy, we'll ask their pappies just like Billy did," asserted Gabe.

"And we been talking about this among ourselves," added Wes. "We figure it's about time we give up our life of crime—now that we're all gonna be respectable married men."

Jessica was amazed. "That's wonderful."

"But good intentions alone may not be enough," added Cole.

"Why not?" Billy asked. "Didn't you two just tell us Miser is closing the mines? So what's left to rob?"

Cole replied, "The problem is, we're all still wanted men with bounties on our heads. Even if we quit robbing, lawmen or Pinkerton agents will still be hunting us."

"And do you boys remember Sheriff Lummety?" Jessica asked.

Luke snapped his fingers. "Wasn't he on the stage the day we kidnapped you, Jessie?"

"Indeed he was. And I ran into him in Colorado City." As the younger boys went wild-eyed, she hastily added, "Don't worry, I convinced him I escaped you. But he told me he plans to visit Mariposa as soon as Woody Lynch starts up his stage line again."

"So?" asked Luke.

"So, what if he comes out here and recognizes all of you?"

"We had masks on," argued Billy.

"Yes, but if he were to find out there are five brothers in these parts, all about the same sizes and ages of the men who robbed the stage . . . " Ominously, Jessica finished, "Well, it wouldn't take a rocket scientist to put two and two together."

Billy scratched his head. "What's a rocket scientist?"

Cole answered for her. "What Jessie means is . . . Well, she and I have discussed this, and we've decided it may

371

be best for us all to pull up stakes and move on." He turned to Billy. "You know, like we discussed, little brother."

Although Billy nodded, he appeared skeptical. "Yeah, but maybe we ain't all ready yet."

"And where would you have us go?" demanded Wes.

"Far away," pronounced Cole. "Perhaps to Wyoming Territory."

Mutters of alarm poured forth from the boys. "Wyoming? With our sweethearts here?" protested Gabe.

"They might come with you if you persuade them to marry you," suggested Jessica.

The boys exchanged dubious glances. "And leave their families behind?" asked Luke. "That would be asking a lot."

"Yes, it would be," put in Jessica, "but every day we remain here, the five of you are living on borrowed time."

Gabe looked unconcerned. "Aw, Jessie, you worry too much. Everything will be fine."

Jessica glanced at Cole's worried face and realized they both knew otherwise.

Chapter Thirty-five

During the next week Jessica remained gripped by a sense of foreboding, although no catastrophes occurred. She and Cole did hear from Joshua Hicks, who told them that Elijah Miser had sent his secretary, Calvin Stickles, out to the Aspen Gulch Mines. Stickles had announced that the mines would close within a month, and had given the miners details of their pensions, which were modest but adequate. Of course, Jessica was aware that Cole had made additional, far more generous provisions for the men and their families, but the miners would not learn of these arrangements until the Reklaw family was far gone from Colorado.

The family did plan to move on in the near future, just as soon as the rest of the boys could convince their sweethearts to marry them and leave the state. Already the engagements themselves were firming up: Cole and Jessica were certainly willing; Billy and Dumpling were discussing wedding dates; Luke soon announced that Minerva had accepted his proposal; and within days, Wes declared that Maybelle was willing, too. Although Gabe still hadn't quite convinced Beatrice, more and more it looked as if a quintuple wedding was in the offing.

As the days passed and no harm befell the brothers, Jessica began to relax more and let go of some of her fears that they might be arrested. In fact, she felt downright happy the following Sunday morning when they all sat in church together before the service. On one side of the aisle sat Ma, Jessica, and Cole, with Billy in the pew behind them, waiting for Dumpling; across from them sat the other three boys with their sweethearts. As the pianist played "Lead, Kindly Light," Jessica reflected on how far the Reklaw family had come—from lawlessness to respectability—and she was filled with pride for them.

Then Jessica's bubble burst as she watched the Hicks family troop down the aisle—first Dumpling and Peaches, then Joshua and Wilma—with none other than Sheriff Jedediah Lummety hobbling along behind them! Even as Jessica's heart lurched at the sight, Dumpling rushed ahead, face aglow as she joined Billy in his pew. Then as the parents and Lummety passed, Wilma and Joshua smiled and waved at Cole and Jessica. But the sheriff all but stopped in his tracks, staring hard at Jessica, at Cole, at Billy with Dumpling, then across the aisle at the rest of the brothers. At last, frowning in perplexity, he trudged on, sitting down with Joshua and Wilma at the front of the church.

Noting Cole's grim expression, Jessica whispered in his ear. "Did you see that?"

"Yep."

"Should we leave?"

"Nope. That'd only make things worse. Just be calm and everything will be fine." He turned away to speak with Billy.

Jessica wished she could share Cole's confidence, but also realized he was right. For all of them to flee now would be disastrous.

She felt Ma nudging her and turned. "Yes?"

Her expression worried, Ma whispered, "Who's the newcomer with the Hickses?"

Jessica lifted an eyebrow and slowly replied, "The sheriff from Colorado City. And Cole says we should all stay put."

Although Ma blanched, she revealed no other sign of agitation, calmly nodding to Jessica.

Then Jessica spied Luke desperately trying to catch her eye from across the aisle. Turning toward him, she watched him nod curtly toward Lummety, then mouth the words *What do we do?* Jessica solemnly shook her head and pressed a finger to her lips. Although Luke waved a hand in exasperation, he remained in his pew and turned to pass on her message to his brothers.

Reverend Bliss climbed the pulpit and announced an opening hymn. Standing with Cole, Jessica caught sight of Lummety turning to stare suspiciously at her again. She flashed him a brilliant smile, and he lowered his gaze to his hymnal.

Jessica felt ready to jump out of her skin throughout the service, but managed to maintain a calm facade. The minute church was over, Billy whispered urgently to Cole, "Shouldn't we leave?"

"No," he answered adamantly. "We'll take our time." He turned toward his brothers across the aisle—all of whom were expectantly watching him and appeared ready to bolt—and soberly shook his head.

Thus the entire crew spilled slowly out into the churchyard with the others. But the Reklaw brothers gathered in a tight circle with their women beneath a large oak tree.

Jessica felt sickened as she watched Joshua and Wilma stroll up with Lummety. But she smiled and extended her hand to Lummety. "Well, Sheriff. How nice to see you again. So Buck Lynch finally brought you out here?"

Lummety shook her hand. "He did, indeed."

Jessica glanced about. "I don't see his stagecoach."

"He brought me here to Mariposa yesterday and headed back to Colorado City just before church this morning. He'll be passing back through in a week or so to carry me home."

"I see."

The sheriff jerked his thumb toward Joshua. "I was just asking my brother-in-law here to introduce me to the family my niece Dumpling is marrying into."

Dumpling spoke up brightly, breaking the tension. "Why, Uncle Jed, I'd be happy to do the honors." Wrapping her arm around a tense Billy's waist, she announced, "This here's my fiancé, Bobby Lively, and his brothers, Clay, Walt, Gill, and Lyle. The two ladies is Bobby's ma, and his cousin from back East, Miss Jessie Garrett."

Lummety glanced sharply at Jessica. "You're related to these people?"

She raised her chin. "Yes, indeed."

Lummety studied the five brothers with a scowl. "So, five men in the same family. Rather reminds me of a group of outlaws I know of—also five brothers in the same family. The initials of their Christian names are even the same. Kind of peculiar, don't you think?"

As Joshua and Wilma exchanged glances of alarm, Billy stepped aggressively toward Lummety. "Just what are you implying, Sheriff?"

His harsh words brought a gasp from the women as more churchfolk pressed forward to observe the confrontation. Cole stepped between the two men. "Easy, brother. The sheriff here didn't mean anything by his words. Did you, Sheriff?"

Ignoring Cole, Lummety turned to the crowd that had now gathered. "Folks, I'd like to tell you a story. Couple months back, I attempted to come out here to visit my kin, in the company of Miss Jessica Garrett here. That's when the Reklaw Gang robbed the stage we was on, and kidnapped Miss Garrett. Now, when I finally make it out here, I find this young lady in the company of five men who appear very much like the outlaws who robbed the stage and bushwhacked her."

Mumblings of fear poured forth from the crowd. Appearing very concerned, Joshua Hicks glanced from Cole and the others back to Jedediah. "How can you be so sure of that, Jed?"

"Yes, there must be a mistake," put in Reverend Bliss.

"Did you see their faces during the robbery, Sheriff?" added Henry Holler.

"No, they wore masks, but any fool could tell they're the same men. They all have similar names, plus they're all the right sizes. One is big, three are tall and skinny, and"—Lummety's gaze came to rest with contempt on Billy—"one's a runt."

"How dare you!" declared Billy.

"Yeah, Uncle Jed, I won't hear you insulting my sweetheart!" put in a fuming Dumpling.

"Look, Sheriff," reasoned Cole, "you're jumping to the wrong conclusion. This is all just coincidence."

"Coincidence, my butt." Lummety hauled out his Colt pistol, raising gasps from the crowd, and leveled it on Cole. "I'm placing the five of you under arrest for robbery and other crimes. You can explain the rest to the judge, boys."

As the Reklaw men stood grim and white-faced, Dumpling turned desperately to her father. "Pa, do something! Don't let him take my Bobby away!"

Expression torn, Joshua pleaded, "Jed, don't you think you're being a bit hasty—"

"Hell, no," Jed cut in, shifting his pistol to Billy just as he was reaching inside his coat. "Now hold it right there, son. You boys got any shootin' irons, I want 'em hitting the ground right now."

Billy dropped his hand. "And what if I say no?"

"Then I'm dropping you where you stand."

"No!" screamed Dumpling, thrusting her body in front of Billy's.

Amid more shocked sounds from the congregation, Billy tried to shove her aside. "Woman, get out of the way before you get your fool self killed. I don't need you protecting me."

Jessica glanced frantically at Cole. "*Do something.*"

But even as he was stepping forward, a new shudder rippled over the group as Joshua Hicks tried to grab Lummety's pistol. Shrieks rose from the women as the two men began wildly struggling over the weapon; then the pistol discharged into the air, scattering the group like panicked sheep.

A second later Joshua seized control of the pistol and pointed it at Lummety. "Back off, Jed!" he yelled, red-faced.

Jed trembled in fury. "Joshua, I'll have you know you're interfering with a lawman in the performance of his—"

"I said back off! You always were a sanctimonious blowhard, and I'm about ready to shoot some of that hot air out of you."

Even as Lummety trembled in fear, a panicked Wilma beseeched Joshua. "You ain't gonna shoot my cousin, Josh!"

"I will if he don't mind his manners," Joshua replied obdurately. "Hands up, Jed."

Glaring, Lummety complied. "I'll see you in jail for this, Joshua."

Now Wilma shook a fist at Lummety. "You ain't locking up my husband, Jed, or I swear I'll wring your fool neck myself."

Lummety gulped, and the crowd thrummed with tension.

Joshua raised his free hand. "Now hush, everyone." As the congregation quieted, he turned to Cole. "Well, Mr. Lively—or Mr. Reklaw, or whoever you are—I 'spect you'd best gather your kin and get out of town. I'll keep Jed here locked up till tomorrow to give you folks a head start."

"You won't," declared Lummety.

"Shut up!" ordered Joshua.

Lummety grimaced and clamped shut his mouth.

Cole stepped toward Joshua. "Then you believe we're the Reklaw Gang?"

Joshua laughed. "Several of us men have had our suspicions for some time now. But we kept our hunches to ourselves 'cause we liked what the gang was doing for the miners."

Henry Holler added, "But, folks, the cat is out of the bag now. You really do need to hightail it."

Cole glanced at the grim-faced Jessica and his equally sober mother. "I suppose you're right."

"What about our women?" Billy asked.

Joshua glanced sternly at Billy. "Son, you can't take my daughter with you."

Henry Holler stepped forward, speaking to the other three boys. "Nor can you men take my girls."

As wails rose from the girls, Luke demanded, "Why not?"

"How can you even ask that?" Henry retorted. "That's no life for decent young women, on the run from the law with a gang of outlaws."

"But I want to go with Bobby!" protested Dumpling.

As she spoke, the three Holler sisters consulted tensely among themselves, then Beatrice declared, "And us three want to leave with our men, too."

"Well, you can't!" declared Henry.

"And you can't leave, either," Joshua told Dumpling. Amid a chorus of female sobs, he added to Cole, "Go on, now. Leave."

Cole's expression had turned bitter as he glanced from Joshua to Henry. "Don't you men think my brothers are good enough for your daughters?"

Joshua cocked the pistol. "Neighbor, don't push it. Get out of here now, all of you, before I change my mind and give Jed back his pistol."

Even as he spoke, Mr. Holler grabbed a rifle from his buckboard and pointed it toward the men. "I'm backing up Joshua. Get going."

His features livid, Cole turned to his brothers. "Come on, boys. We're not welcome here."

"But our women!" protested Billy.

"Leave them behind."

These words brought lamentations from the girls and violent protests from the boys as Dumpling Hicks and the Holler sisters clung to their men.

"Cole, we ain't leaving without them," Billy said adamantly.

Cole drew himself up with dignity, facing down his youngest brother. "What are you going to do, Billy? Shoot the girls' fathers, their mothers, maybe even the good folks of this town? 'Cause that's what it's gonna take for them to leave with you."

Billy wavered, his expression miserably torn, as Dumpling clung to him, sobbing.

"Listen to your brother, son," Joshua warned. "He's speaking the truth. And let my daughter go."

Billy hesitated another long, agonizing moment. Sensing his indecision, Dumpling gazed up at him, her expression one of stark anguish. With tears now burning in his own eyes, Billy reached out and brushed a tear from his sweetheart's flushed cheek. "Honey, you gotta go with your daddy."

"No, let me stay!" Dumpling pleaded. "I don't believe you're an outlaw, Bobby Lively. Not for a minute. And even if you are, I don't care."

In a steelier voice, he repeated, "Go with your daddy, honey."

"No, Bobby, don't make me," she implored.

He gently pushed her away. "Go!" he ordered hoarsely, in a voice that made her flinch. He turned to his brothers. "The women stay."

Luke, Wes, and Gabe stood stoic-faced with their

women. Not waiting for more argument, several men from the church rushed forward to pull Beatrice, Maybelle, and Minerva away from them.

Only the sounds of female wailing could be heard in the background as the five Reklaw men turned and proudly escorted Ma and Jessica to the buckboard.

Chapter Thirty-six

They drove away, Jessica wedged between Ma and Cole, the boys in the back. She glanced at the younger Reklaws; their faces were grim. Turning around, she noted that Cole's features were clenched with fury, while Ma was wiping away tears.

"That's it, then, boys," Ma announced hoarsely to the group. "We'll pull up stakes and move further west. We've saved us up a good grubstake for this very day— didn't we, boys?"

No one answered.

Jessica turned to Cole. "Don't you have anything to say?"

His dark gaze, burning with pride and outrage, met hers. "What can I say, Jessie? Didn't I warn you this would happen? I told you if we got too cozy with the town, sooner or later we'd be exposed. Now look what you've done to my brothers. You've broken their hearts. It would have been better never to have taken them to Mariposa."

Again noting the boys' glum faces, Jessica responded,

382

"Cole, how can you say that? Think of all your brothers have gained. They've grown from coarse criminals to decent young men."

"Yeah, but it's a world they were never meant to live in," Cole replied bitterly. "To heck with that town, I say."

Jessica was horrified. "How can you condemn the town, when you know there are good men there who must have known about the gang for ages but kept your secret? And when everyone defended you today? If not for Joshua Hicks, you'd all be in jail."

Harshly, he replied, "Defending us was one thing—accepting us, another. It was fine to humor us, to let us act as champions for the downtrodden miners, until it was all brought home. Sure, the miners helped us escape, but when push came to shove, my brothers weren't good enough for those men's daughters."

At last understanding Cole's wounded pride and anger, Jessica implored, "Cole, put yourself in the fathers' shoes. If it were your daughter, would you want her to marry a known criminal? To live on the run, just as Mr. Holler feared?"

Jessica's pleas fell on deaf ears. His expression grim, Cole worked the reins and said not another word to her.

When they arrived back at the farm, the boys jumped out of the buckboard, then huddled together. Approaching the house with Ma, Jessica was appalled to watch the four make a beeline toward the barn. "Where are you men going?" she called out.

Billy whirled. "We're gonna go rob Buck Lynch's stage."

"What?" Jessica cried.

"He's the one that got us in trouble with our women, by bringing old Lummety out here," asserted Gabe. "He's got it coming."

"Yeah!" added Luke.

"No!" Jessica retorted, rushing toward them. "I thought

you boys promised me you'd give up your life of crime. You can't start backsliding now. You'll lose everything."

"We've already lost everything," put in Gabe. "We've lost our women."

"Yeah, and Buck Lynch is gonna pay," Billy added.

Jessica turned to Cole. "Please, stop them."

He only shrugged. "Aw, let the boys blow off some steam while you females start packing."

"Cole!" Wildly Jessica beseeched Ma. "Eula, please, can't you help?"

But Ma only shook her head. "Cole's right. It's too late, now. Come on, Jessie, let's pack."

In a panic, Jessica whirled back toward the boys. But Ma was right—it *was* too late. The boys had already disappeared inside the barn. She tried to entreat Cole again, but the pride and anger on his face stopped her cold.

"It's all over now," Ma lamented. "All over now."

When Jessica followed Ma into the house, she found the morose woman mumbling these words, dirge-like, as she swung her broom across the kitchen floor.

"Aren't you going to do anything about the boys?"

Ma shrugged her shoulders. "What's to be done now?"

"You could try to stop them from committing another robbery and making things worse."

"What's the point? Cole is right that you never should have taken us into town to that church. You've gone to meddling and made things much worse."

"Do you think having your sons rob the stage will improve matters?"

"Can't see how it makes much difference," Ma muttered.

Jessica flung a hand outward. "So what would you have us all do now?"

"We'll pull up stakes and start over, just like we agreed."

"And your boys will take up their life of crime again?"

"Yeah, they probably will."

Jessica regarded Ma in disbelief. "What has happened

to you? I thought you were determined to reform your boys."

Ma glanced up, her bitter gray eyes meeting Jessica's. "I was till you went and broke all our hearts, till we found out what that town is really like. Them folks think they're all fine and good, but they're narrow-minded hypocrites. Now I'm plumb through fighting. And if you don't want to see Cole and the others in jail, I'd advise you to help me start packing, missy."

Jessica trudged off to her room and made a stab at packing. A few minutes later, she spotted Cole sitting on the front porch swing, and went outside to join him. Even though his expression remained remote, she tried again to reach him. "Cole, please, go after your brothers. If you don't want to do it for me, go inside and look at your mother's face. She's heartbroken."

Cole stood. "And who did that to her, Jessie?"

She stood, balling her hands on her hips. "Well, if I did, it was with the best of intentions. I was trying to better all of your lives. I'm not going to apologize for that, Cole Reklaw!"

He regarded her with suspicion and hurt. "Are you coming with us?"

"I don't know. I don't think I know you anymore."

He stepped closer, passion burning in his gaze. "Jessie, you always knew me. You just wouldn't accept me. At heart, I'm an outlaw. We're all outlaws."

"I refuse to accept that."

He shook his head resignedly. "I thought I could change—that we could all change—but now I know better."

Hurt seared Jessica. "Do you? Well, I'm not leaving with a man I can't respect."

Tightening his jaw, he glanced away. "Look, I need to get going again, go to the hideout and fetch our grubstake."

"That's right, Cole," she replied harshly. "Run."

They were regarding each other angrily when both

tensed at the sounds of hoofbeats. Jessica glanced off to the west to see two buckboards approaching, stirring up dust.

"Looks like trouble," Cole muttered. "I'll fetch my rifle."

She grabbed his arm. "No, Cole, wait. Just look—it's the Hicks and Holler families!"

He gazed ahead, doing a double take. "You're right." He eyed her balefully. "Don't look so happy, sugar. You think they're coming for coffee and apple pie?"

"If not, why are their daughters with them?" She laughed and clapped her hands. "My heavens, Reverend Bliss is there, too!"

Cole strained his neck. "Hot damn—woman, you're right."

Both waited anxiously as the buckboards came to a halt in the yard. The entire Hicks and Holler clans were present, as well as the reverend. And from the beaming expressions on all the girls' faces, Jessica knew this small caravan was bringing good news.

Joshua Hicks hopped out of the first conveyance, and Henry Holler climbed out of the second. As the two men approached the porch, Joshua turned back and said, "Preacher, you wait with the women while we speak with Clay."

Bliss waved from the first buckboard. "Certainly, Joshua."

There was dead silence as the men climbed the steps. "Clay," Joshua said warily.

"Joshua," Cole responded with equal caution. "So where's your brother-in-law, the sheriff?"

Joshua smiled sheepishly. "I think we were all a bit hasty back at the church."

"Yeah, Pa, you sure were!" called Dumpling.

As several of the women tittered, Joshua scowled at his daughter. "Hush now, Dumpling, and let your pa handle this." He turned back to Cole. "Now, Clay—"

"Where's Lummety?" Cole persisted.

Henry answered, "Gideon Mayhew is guarding him for us."

"So you men haven't come to arrest us?" Cole inquired.

"Hell, no. We've come because . . . " Lowering his voice, Joshua confided, "Well, the girls wouldn't give me or Henry any peace unless we all came out here."

"I see. What do you have in mind?"

"First, we want the truth from you," said Henry.

"All right."

"Are you boys the Reklaw Gang?" Joshua demanded.

Cole glanced at Jessica, then defiantly answered, "Yeah, we are. What about it?"

Joshua eyed Cole sternly. "Now, Henry and me have some mighty unhappy girls. They want to run off with your boys, and they swear if we don't let 'em, they'll do it on their own." He sighed. "We know if we don't let 'em go, we'll lose 'em. Maybe not today or tomorrow, but sooner or later we will."

Henry added, "So Joshua and me figured we may as well take charge of things and do this on our own terms."

"What are your terms?" Cole asked.

"First, what are your brothers' intentions?" Joshua countered. "Where are you folks heading? What will you do?"

"We'll go as far as possible, maybe even Wyoming Territory, and buy a big ranch."

"And will you give up your lawless ways?" Henry asked.

Glancing briefly at Jessica's tense face, Cole replied, "I think I can answer for myself and my brothers there. I know I'd be willing to give up lawbreaking—for the love of the right woman." He looked again at Jessica, and when she smiled back tenderly, eyes filled with forgiveness, he broke into a grin.

The fathers consulted among themselves a moment, then Joshua said, "All right, sir, here are our terms. We'll allow our daughters to marry your brothers. But the boys have to take a blood oath that they'll never again break the law. And once you move away, they have to let the girls write their mothers, let them know where you are, so we can all visit."

Cole nodded. "Sounds fair enough."

Jessica cleared her throat. "Cole, aren't you forgetting something?"

"What?" he asked blankly.

"The *boys*," she said pointedly.

"Oh, the boys." For once the masterful Cole went pale.

Joshua was glancing around. "Yeah, where *are* the boys?"

With a cough, Cole recovered. "Actually, they were all pretty upset and went for a ride to blow off some steam. Jessie and me'll go fetch 'em—won't we, darlin'?"

She glowered at him.

Cole turned toward the house and yelled, "Ma!"

Ma emerged on the porch with her broom, regarding the visitors with anger and mistrust. "What are these folks doing here?"

"They've had a change of heart," Cole answered. "Looks like we'll be having us some weddings, after all."

Ma dropped her broom and pressed her hands to her sagging cheeks. "Oh, my stars!"

"Yeah," Cole went on urgently. "I was just explaining to Henry and Joshua how the boys went riding off to— you know—blow off steam—"

"Yeah," she agreed, grimacing.

"And how Jessie and me'll go fetch 'em back to be with their ladies. Maybe you can entertain these folks while we're gone?"

Ma brightened. "Why, sure. Come on in, folks."

Happy pandemonium erupted as the girls and their parents swarmed toward the house.

While Cole saddled their horses, Jessica quickly changed into her riding clothes. Rushing out of her room, she grabbed her journal and pencil from the dresser, stuffing both in the pocket of her overalls. She had a feeling she might see quite an eyeful shortly.

Moments later, as she and Cole galloped away from the farm hell-bent-for-leather, she hurled a glare at him.

"Jessie, please, don't say it," he implored.

"I *am* going to say it! I'm so mad at you for letting those boys go rob the stage, I could just spit nails."

Humbly, he replied, "I know, darlin', and I don't blame you. I acted like a dang fool, and I'm sorry. Looks like I've got some sweet-talking to do."

Hotly she replied, "A *lot* of sweet-talking to do, mister. And, by damn, if you ever again even hint that you may return to your outlaw ways, I'll punch out your running lights."

He nodded. "Yes, ma'am."

"Lord, I just hope we can reach the boys in time."

"The stage will be slow, you can count on that. My bet is the boys will be waiting to overtake it at Haunted Gorge."

"Then let's ride!"

They rode hard for the gorge. They had just reached the crest overlooking the hollow when they saw the familiar stagecoach move into view beneath them. As they halted their horses at the summit, Jessica squinted at the scene below and shuddered. "My God, Cole, this is so eerie, just like the day we met! I'm getting the weirdest feeling—"

Cole gazed at her in puzzlement. "Me, too, sugar. But where do you 'spect the boys are?"

Even as he asked the question, Jessica spotted four masked riders galloping out of the woods on either side of the road. As the four pursued the coach with pistols blazing, she was again swept by *déjà vu*. "There they are! My Lord, Cole, this *is* just like the day you five kidnapped me."

He nodded. "Come on, Jessie. Let's stop the rascals before real harm is done."

They galloped down into the valley, chasing the boys and yelling to get their attention, but they were too far away to be heard. They watched the boys overtake the stage, watched it grind to a halt in a cloud of dust.

They still weren't within shouting distance, so Cole fired two warning shots into the air. Ahead of them, the four riders reigned in and turned their mounts; in that moment the entire tableau of the robbery appeared frozen in time.

At last they reached the boys, halting their own horses. Jessica noted that the passengers were still inside the stage, and the driver was cowering on top.

"Stop!" Cole yelled. "You boys have got to stop."

"Damn it, Cole, what are you doing here?" Billy demanded. "You're spoiling all our fun."

"You boys are about to spoil your futures," Jessica declared.

"Aw, don't give us that again," scoffed Gabe.

"No, it's true," insisted Cole. "All your sweethearts are waiting for you at home."

"What?" cried Wes.

"Their fathers had a change of heart," Jessica explained. "They'll let the girls marry you, if you boys promise to give up your lives of crime."

The boys glanced at each other in amazement.

"And if you boys know what's good for you, you'll hightail it straight home and eat some humble pie," added Cole.

"Cole, are you joshing us?" Billy asked suspiciously.

"Nope, it's the God's truth," Jessica answered.

All at once, Gabe let out a yell of victory. "Then what are we waiting for, boys?"

"Yeah, what are we waiting for?" Billy echoed. He tipped his hat at the driver. "Sorry, pops. Men, let's ride!"

The boys hooted their triumph, wheeled their horses, and went galloping off for home.

"Come on, Jessie, we need to ride, too," said Cole.

"Shouldn't we check on the passengers first?" she asked.

He shrugged. "Suit yourself."

Jessica dismounted, strode over to the coach, and opened the door. As she did so a new wave of unreality staggered her. She did a double take, followed by a triple take, staring flabbergasted at the stage occupants even as they regarded her with equal consternation.

For she was looking not at the expected nineteenth-century citizens, but at her own three colleagues from the present—Walter Lummety, Stan Wilkins, and Harold Billingsly! All were still wearing the same costumes she remembered from before.

No, this must be an illusion, Jessica thought. It must be, or surely she had lost her mind. She closed her eyes, certain the bizarre mirage would vanish. But when she opened them, the scene before her had not shifted one bit.

Walter Lummety, appearing as astounded as Jessica, was the first to find his voice. "Professor Garrett, what on earth has happened to you, and why are you dressed in that ridiculous getup?"

"Professor Lummety," Jessica gasped back. "Is it really you"—her gaze shifted to the other two—"and Stan and Professor Billingsly?"

"Of course it is really us," Walter answered irately. "And I repeat, where have you been? We were all driving along when we hit a huge bump. Then you disappeared! Then we lost our way and . . . Well, I don't know what happened to us after that. Do you know, Harold?"

Billingsly shook his head. "I've no idea—but we do seem to have been traveling around in circles forever."

Even as Walter and Harold continued to debate the matter, Jessica straightened and turned in awe to Cole. "I can't believe this is happening. Cole, I want you to meet my colleagues from the year 1999."

He recoiled. "You're joshing me."

"Nope." She jerked a thumb toward the inside of the stage. "Have a look for yourself."

Cole leaned over and glowered suspiciously at the men. Taking note of Walter, he went wide-eyed, then turned back to Jessica. "But I thought Sheriff Lummety was under guard back in town."

"He is," she assured him.

"Then how in hell can he be in two places at once?"

"He can't," she replied. "This is Professor *Walter* Lummety, Sheriff Lummety's descendant . . . from the future."

Glancing sharply at Lummety, Cole shook his head. "You're pulling my leg."

"Damn it, Cole, I'm not! Look at him *carefully*."

Cole did so, peering at Walter and frowning. "Well, I'll be hanged. This man looks like the sheriff, but he's younger and not as stout." He straightened and regarded Jessica in awe. "Does this mean all that hokum you told me is true? Are you really from the future?"

"Yes, it's true. And I am."

He gestured at the men, then slowly shook his head. "If it's true, then did you wish this to happen?"

Jessica gasped, remembered the last time she and Cole had been here, and the wish she'd made. "You know, perhaps I did."

His face tight with hurt and disappointment, Cole asked, "Then is this your one chance to return to your own world?"

"You know, it might be," she said in awe.

"You would leave me, woman?"

Seeing the vulnerability on Cole's face, Jessica quickly made her decision, shaking her head and gazing at him with love. "No, Cole. At one time, I did want to go back, but not any longer. My world is here—with you." She slipped into his arms.

"Oh, Jessie." Cole clutched her close and kissed her.

In the meantime, the men began to clamor for an explanation. "Professor Garrett, I must insist you tell us what on earth is going on here!" declared Lummety. "Where are we and who were those masked men? And who is this stranger pawing you?"

As Cole released her, Jessica flashed Water a smile, then pulled her journal from her pocket and extended it toward him. "Walter, please take this."

"What is it?"

She pressed the volume into his hands. "Everything that has happened to me is explained inside. Please give this journal to my parents, tell them I love them and I'm fine. Now I think all of you had best continue on your way. I'm staying here."

"W-what?" sputtered Walter. "We've finally found you, and now you propose leaving again?"

"Miss Garrett, this makes no sense whatsoever," protested Billingsly.

Jessica held up a hand. "Please, guys, just read the journal. Then you'll understand."

Ignoring the men's protests, Jessica closed the stage-coach door. She glanced up at the driver, only to laugh as she spotted Woody Lynch for the first time in months. "Hello, Mr. Lynch."

He tipped his hat. "Ma'am. Ain't you comin' back with us?"

"Nope. But don't worry, I'll be remembering you through a certain gentleman I know here who looks a lot like you."

He squinted in confusion. "Who might that be?"

"Never mind," laughed Jessica. "I think it's time for you to head on back to the Broken Buck."

"Yes, ma'am."

"Godspeed."

Buck snapped the reins, and the stage rattled off.

Cole pulled Jessica close again. "Well, I'll be damned, sugar. If I hadn't seen it with my own two eyes—"

"You never would have believed it," she finished for him.

"Reckon we'll ever see those fellows again?"

"No, I think that chapter in my life just came to a close," she happily replied.

"Good." Cole kissed her ardently, and held her close for a long moment. Then he glanced off to the east and whistled. "Damn, sugar, that blamed stagecoach has already disappeared. How in Sam Hill—"

"I'll explain later. For now we have things to do."

He broke into a grin. "Yeah, you're right. We need to rustle our hocks and get back to the house. There's a preacher waiting there to perform a quadruple wedding."

She hugged him tight. "Make that quintuple."

Cole's face lit with joy. "Oh, sugar. Now you're talking."

At home, at sunset, five beaming couples stood on the porch of the Reklaw farmhouse before Reverend Bliss, who stood facing them on the steps as he read from the order of service. Out in the yard, Ma and the girls' parents looked on and wiped tears.

"Dearly beloved, we are gathered here to join these five men and these five women in holy matrimony," Bliss intoned solemnly.

Jessica felt a tear of joy as she gazed at four ecstatic female faces, and at five male faces lit with pride and joy. As Bliss began pronouncing the vows, her gaze lingered lovingly on Cole, her heart bursting with happiness as he winked back tenderly. They'd come through so much together, and now victory was theirs. Everything that had happened to her had happened for a purpose. Even meeting her colleagues from the present for a final time had helped bring her full circle. She'd been granted the grand adventure of experiencing life in a new century, the gift of a bright and happy future there. And the greatest miracle of all was that she knew where she belonged now— in this time, with her beloved Cole.

Wink & A Kiss # THE BEWITCHED VIKING

SANDRA HILL

'Tis enough to drive a sane Viking mad, the things Tykir Thorksson is forced to do—capturing a red-headed virago, putting up with the flock of sheep that follow her everywhere, chasing off her bumbling brothers. But what can a man expect from the sorceress who put a kink in the King of Norway's most precious body part? If that isn't bad enough, he is beginning to realize he isn't at all immune to the enchantment of brash red hair and freckles. But he is not called Tykir the Great for nothing. Perhaps he can reverse the spell and hold her captive, not with his mighty sword, but with a Viking man's greatest magic: a wink and a smile.

___52311-6 $5.99 US/$6.99 CAN

Dorchester Publishing Co., Inc.
P.O. Box 6640
Wayne, PA 19087-8640

Please add $1.75 for shipping and handling for the first book and $.50 for each book thereafter. NY, NYC, and PA residents, please add appropriate sales tax. No cash, stamps, or C.O.D.s. All orders shipped within 6 weeks via postal service book rate. Canadian orders require $2.00 extra postage and must be paid in U.S. dollars through a U.S. banking facility.

Name_____
Address_____
City_____State_____Zip_____
I have enclosed $_____ in payment for the checked book(s).
Payment <u>must</u> accompany all orders. ☐ Please send a free catalog.
     CHECK OUT OUR WEBSITE! www.dorchesterpub.com

Lady of the Night

Cordia Byers

Manacled to a stone wall is not the way Katharina Fergersen planned to spend her vacation. But a wrong turn in the right place and the haunted English castle she is touring is suddenly full of life—and so is the man who is bathing before her. As the frosty winter days melt into hot passionate nights, she realizes that there is more to Kane than just a well-filled pair of breeches. Katharina is determined not to let this man who has touched her soul escape her, even if it means giving up all to remain Sedgewick's lady of the night.

___4404-8 $5.99 US/$6.99 CAN

Dorchester Publishing Co., Inc.
P.O. Box 6640
Wayne, PA 19087-8640

Please add $1.75 for shipping and handling for the first book and $.50 for each book thereafter. NY, NYC, and PA residents, please add appropriate sales tax. No cash, stamps, or C.O.D.s. All orders shipped within 6 weeks via postal service book rate. Canadian orders require $2.00 extra postage and must be paid in U.S. dollars through a U.S. banking facility.

Name_____
Address_____
City_____State_____Zip_____
I have enclosed $_____ in payment for the checked book(s).
Payment <u>must</u> accompany all orders. ❑ Please send a free catalog.
CHECK OUT OUR WEBSITE! www.dorchesterpub.com

THE IMPOSTOR ELAINE FOX

Melisande St. Clair knows who she is and what she wants, and when Flynn Patrick steps out of the water and into her life, she knows that his is the face of which she's dreamt. But when she is forced to travel with the handsome stranger, he claims he is from another time and makes suggestions that are hardly proper for a nineteenth-century lady. Although she believes no one could mistake him for an English gentleman, the Duke of Merestun swears that Flynn is his long-lost son. Suddenly, Flynn seems a prince, and all Melisande's desires lie within reach. But what is the truth? All Melisande knows is that she senses no artifice in his touch—and as she fights to remain aloof to the passion that burns in his fiery kiss, she wonders which of them is truly . . . the impostor.

___4523-0 $5.50 US/$6.50 CAN

Dorchester Publishing Co., Inc.
P.O. Box 6640
Wayne, PA 19087-8640

FRANKLY, MY DEAR... SANDRA HILL

By the Bestselling Author of *The Tarnished Lady*

Selene has three great passions: men, food, and *Gone with the Wind*. But the glamorous model always found herself starving—for both nourishment and affection. Weary of the petty world of high fashion, she heads to New Orleans for one last job before she begins a new life. Then a voodoo spell sends her back to the days of opulent balls and vixenish belles like Scarlet O'Hara.

Charmed by the Old South, Selene can't get her fill of gumbo, crayfish, beignets—or an alarmingly handsome planter. Dark and brooding, James Baptiste does not share Rhett Butler's cavalier spirit, and his bayou plantation is no Tara. But fiddle-dee-dee, Selene doesn't need her mammy to tell her the virile Creole is the only lover she ever gave a damn about. And with God as her witness, she vows never to go hungry or without the man she desires again.

_4042-5 $5.50 US/$6.50 CAN

Dorchester Publishing Co., Inc.
P.O. Box 6640
Wayne, PA 19087-8640

SANDRA HILL

Sweeter Savage Love. When a twist of fate casts Harriet Ginoza back in time to the Old South, the modern psychologist meets the object of her forbidden fantasies. Though she knows the dangerously handsome rogue is everything she should despise, she can't help but feel that within his arms she might attain a sweeter savage love.

___52212-8 $5.99 US/$6.99 CAN

Desperado. When a routine skydive goes awry, Major Helen Prescott and Rafe Santiago parachute straight into the 1850 California Gold Rush. Mistaken for a notorious bandit and his infamously sensuous mistress, they find themselves on the wrong side of the law. In a time and place where rules have no meaning, Helen finds herself all too willing to throw caution to the wind to spend every night in the arms of her very own desperado.

___52182-2 $5.99 US/$6.99 CAN

Dorchester Publishing Co., Inc.
P.O. Box 6640
Wayne, PA 19087-8640

Please add $1.75 for shipping and handling for the first book and $.50 for each book thereafter. NY, NYC, and PA residents, please add appropriate sales tax. No cash, stamps, or C.O.D.s. All orders shipped within 6 weeks via postal service book rate. Canadian orders require $2.00 extra postage and must be paid in U.S. dollars through a U.S. banking facility.

Name_____

Address_____

City_____ State_____ Zip_____

I have enclosed $_____ in payment for the checked book(s).

Payment <u>must</u> accompany all orders. ☐ Please send a free catalog.